to Derorguila
TRADE ROUTE
ABORNOK
Vispir
Pass
FORTS
OHOGAN MOUNTAINS
Kabor
Prok
Goyk
Place of
Learning
LAMARILU
Lamar
Virk
THE DYLEX
ELL
Virkar
Bonorar
Ruwenda
Citadel
Bonor
GREAT CAUSEWAY
Lake Wum
Tass Town
GREEN
MIRE
Tass Falls
TASSALEYO FOREST
FOREST
Great Mutar
N
W
E
S
Let
to Var
Kovuko
©Claudia Carlson

# Lady of the Trillium

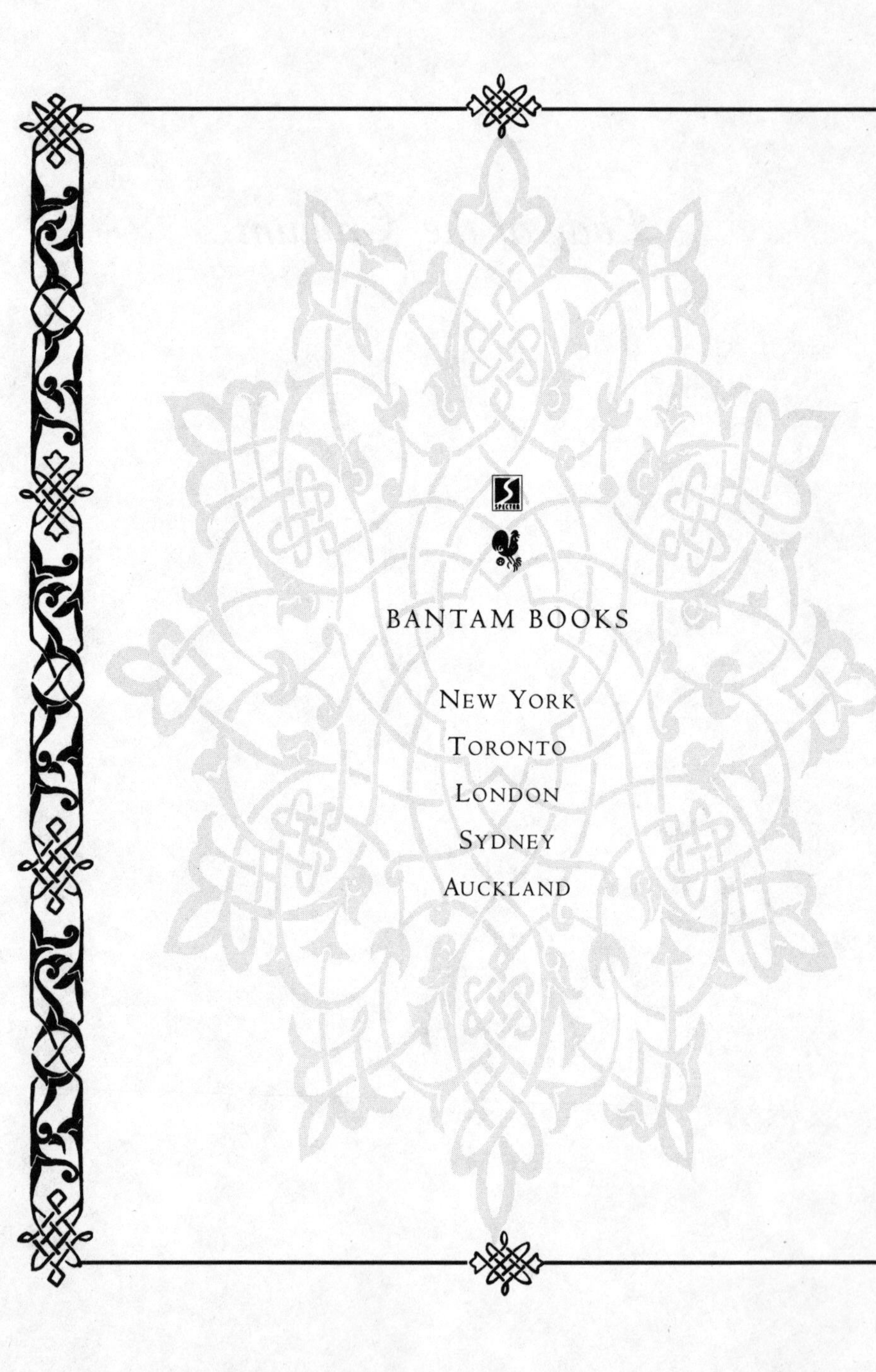

BANTAM BOOKS

NEW YORK

TORONTO

LONDON

SYDNEY

AUCKLAND

Marion Zimmer Bradley

# Lady of the Trillium

ISBN 0-553-09299-5

*Published simultaneously in the United States and Canada*

---

*Bantam Books are published by Bantam Books, a division of Bantam Doubleday Dell Publishing Group, Inc. Its trademark, consisting of the words "Bantam Books" and the portrayal of a rooster, is Registered in U.S. Patent and Trademark Office and in other countries. Marca Registrada. Bantam Books, 1540 Broadway, New York, New York 10036.*

---

PRINTED IN THE UNITED STATES OF AMERICA

❋ ❋ ❋

*This book is dedicated to all the*
*people at Ice Castle,*
*without whose support and*
*encouragement*
*it would never have been completed.*

## *Acknowledgment*

I have often compared writing a novel to giving birth to a child (although, if one goes by gestation period, *Mists of Avalon* was an elephant), and it is customary to acknowledge and thank the people who helped in the endeavor, the midwives, as it were.

For this particular book, I would like to acknowledge the efforts of my cousin and secretary, Elisabeth Waters, whose contribution to this work went beyond midwifery and into the realm of surrogate motherhood. Thank you, Elisabeth.

# 1

*The stone Tower of Noth stood desolate, surrounded by dying weeds. The little bit of water remaining in the moat was covered with scum, and the smell of death filled the air. The girl ran across the drawbridge, through the courtyard and the garden, into the chamber of the Archimage, only to see the old woman die and her body crumble to dust. As the girl stood there, stunned by the suddenness of it all, the entire Tower turned to dust around her and blew away, and the only thing left was the white cloak of the Archimage. . . .*

Haramis, the White Lady, Archimage of Ruwenda, woke suddenly, feeling very old, especially in contrast to the young girl she had been in her dream. This was not particularly surprising; she was old, *several ordinary lifetimes old by now,* she thought ruefully. As Archimage, soul-bound to the land, her life span had been lengthened long past those of her two sisters. Though born at one birth, their destinies had separated long ago, and now she, the eldest of the triplet princesses, was the only one left.

Kadiya, the second of the sisters, had been the first to leave. After the great battle with the invaders from Labornok and the evil sorcerer Orogastus, she had disappeared into her beloved swamps with her Oddling companion and her talisman, the Three-Lobed Burning Eye, which formed part of the great magical scepter the triplets had used to defeat Orogastus. For a time she and Haramis had communicated occasionally by scrying, but Kadiya had vanished many decades ago. *By now,* Haramis thought, *she must be long dead.*

Anigel, the youngest, had married Prince Antar of Labornok, uniting their two kingdoms, and died peacefully of old age, surrounded by her children and grandchildren. The combined throne passed on through her descendants. Was it her grandchild or great-grandchild who held it now? Haramis couldn't remember; the years slipped by too fast. Maybe it was even a great-great-grandchild.

Haramis, the eldest, had been chosen to replace the Archimage Binah as guardian of the land. Ruwenda had prospered over the years, and Haramis loved the land as if it were her own child. In a way, it was.

But now she was having strange dreams. This was the third night in a row she had relived Binah's death in her dreams and awakened in the morning too tired to get out of bed. Was this a warning that she was to die soon?

Perhaps the time was nearing for a new guardian to take over. If her successor were chosen soon, Haramis might even have time to train her. Haramis would have appreciated some training when she had been chosen, but had been given none. She wanted to do better by her own successor. But who would her successor be?

Binah had simply handed Haramis her cloak and died, and the Tower where she had lived and worked had crumbled to dust along with her body. Haramis, who had been until that moment heiress to the throne, had been trained since childhood to be Queen, not Archimage. She had found the sudden shift in her duties disconcerting, to say the least. This was not the legacy she wished to leave for *her* successor.

Haramis dragged herself out of bed, ignoring aching joints and a general feeling of malaise. If she were still living in the Citadel of Ruwenda, where she had grown up, she would doubtless have felt much worse—the Citadel was a typical stone castle, impossible to heat. But the Tower where Haramis had lived since becoming Archimage was warm inside, even though the Tower was located near the Labornok/Ruwenda border at the top of Mount Brom and the season was winter. Orogastus had held the Tower before her, and he had furnished it with every luxury he could track down and steal or purchase. He had specialized in devices of the Vanished Ones. While a good many of these were dangerous weapons, some of the devices were quite practical and made daily life much more comfortable.

Orogastus, unfortunately for him, had never quite grasped the distinction between the leftover technology of the Vanished Ones and true magic. He had depended so heavily on the former that Haramis and her sisters had been able to destroy him with the latter.

To Haramis the difference between magic and ancient technology was so obvious, though difficult to articulate, that she still could not understand how Orogastus could have been so stupid, especially since he had possessed some magical abilities of his own.

Haramis still winced when she recalled the glamour he had briefly cast over her—for a few weeks she had even fancied herself in love with him. *But that seems to have worked against him,* she remembered. *He missed several opportunities to harm me, even after I made it clear I did not love him. It was as if he were convinced that he loved me and could not harm me, and I would necessarily love him in return and help him in his plans.*

She crossed to an ornately carved wooden armoire and took a silver bowl out of one of its drawers. Placing it on a table in the center of the room, she filled it half-full with clear water from a pitcher at her bedside, and bent over it.

Water-scrying was practiced by several of the Oddling races who lived in the swamps surrounding the Citadel. The Oddlings were not humans; they were aboriginal descendants of the original inhabitants of the land. Some of the Oddling races were fairly human in appearance, while others looked like the stuff of nightmares, but generally they lived at peace with the humans.

The Nyssomu were among the more human-looking Oddlings, and several of them had served at the Ruwendan court when Haramis was a child. Her best friend, Uzun, a Nyssomu and the Court Musician, had possessed quite a bit of magical ability in addition to his musical talents, and it was he who had taught Haramis to water-scry. It was a notoriously unreliable method of divination, and only slightly better as a method of communication, but Haramis discovered that when combined with her powers as Archimage, it was quite accurate. It was easier and more reliable, however, if done on an empty stomach.

Now she cleared her mind as much as she could, although she found it impossible completely to banish her recent dream, and looked into and through the water.

Almost at once she seemed to be flying through the air, as if on the back of one of the great lammergeiers that carried her at need, approaching a tower. She recognized it as the main tower of the Citadel, a comparatively recent addition built by humans (within the last five hundreds), as opposed to the main building, which was another survival from the time of the Vanished Ones.

She landed lightly on the roof of the Tower and allowed her spirit body to sink through the trapdoor into the uppermost chamber. Now, in her vision, the room was empty. The last time Haramis had been there in reality this room had been filled with Labornoki soldiers trying to capture her and Uzun, and only the timely arrival of two lammergeiers to carry them away from the top of the Tower had enabled them to depart alive. Memories of that long-ago day returned as Haramis continued to backtrack her former escape route.

The next floor down had been a dormitory for some of Citadel's soldiers. To the best of Haramis's recollection, the crazy idea of making the soldiers sleep seventeen flights of stairs up from anything else had been her grandfather's. Her father had been much more a scholar than a warrior and hadn't bothered to change the arrangement.

But obviously someone had been sensible enough to scrap this custom before it became hallowed by tradition. Although the room still contained half a dozen cots and their associated clothing boxes, there were only two people in the former barracks, and they were children, a boy and girl who both seemed to be about twelve years old. They sat facing each other on the floor, in the center of a pool of sunlight coming through an open window.

"I think it works by light," the boy was saying. He was slender, with dark thick hair in need of cutting. It fell across his face as he bent over the object they were studying, and he shoved it back absently. It fell back as soon as he removed his hand, but he ignored it.

"It can't be *just* that," the girl objected. She had bright red hair, done in sloppy braids that fell to her waist. Haramis hadn't seen hair like that on anyone since her sister Kadiya, and from the look of her, this girl took just about as much care of her appearance as Kadiya had. Both children were dressed in clothing that was obviously handed down from older siblings, and neither seemed to feel any need to take any thought to keeping it clean. The wooden floor appeared not to have been swept in months, if not years, but the dust was disarranged in patterns that suggested that these children, or someone else, were in the habit of sprawling on the floor, heedless of dust and splinters. And the girl was even thinner than the boy. *Doesn't anyone feed these children?* Haramis wondered.

"It doesn't work in the dark." The boy was still arguing his point.

"Oh, I agree that it needs light in order to work, but if it were just light that activated it, all of the tunes except the bottom one would play at once."

Haramis's vision-self crossed the room to see what the girl was holding. She recognized it at once; it had been one of her favorite toys when she was a child. It was a music box, surviving from the time of the Vanished Ones, a cube that played a different tune depending on which side one set it upon.

"Look, Fiolon," the girl pointed out, holding the cube so that one edge touched the floor between them. "If it were just light, it should be playing at least one tune now—it's getting direct sunlight." She shifted it to lie flat, and a tune started. "See? It has to have one face flat on the floor or"—she lifted it straight up and the music continued unchanging—"parallel to the floor."

"Horizontal, you mean," the boy said.

"It's the same thing, if the floor is flat. Now look." She turned the box to one side, moving it slowly and carefully. "The tune stops when you tilt it more than two finger widths, and when the new side is horizontal there's a pause before the music starts again. And during that pause," she finished triumphantly, "I can feel something shifting in the cube. The music doesn't start again until whatever it is reaches the bottom." She shook the cube next to her ear. "There's some kind of liquid in here. I'd love to open this up and see what's inside and how it works."

Fiolon reached out and grabbed the toy from her hand. "Don't you dare, Mikayla! This is the only one we've got, and I like it. If you break it, I won't marry you when we grow up."

"I'd put it back together," Mikayla protested.

"You don't know that you could put it back together," Fiolon pointed out with quiet practicality. "You don't know what the liquid is—it's too heavy to be water—and you'd certainly spill at least some if you opened this. And we don't have anything else that lets us know what the music of the Vanished Ones was like."

Mikayla laughed. "You just don't want to risk destroying *any* source of music. I think your father must have been a musician."

Fiolon shrugged. "We'll never know."

Mikayla took the cube back and hefted it in one hand. "I think you're right about the liquid. This does feel too heavy to be water, and the whatever-it-is inside moves too slowly for it to be floating in water." She sighed. "I wish we could find more of these."

"Me, too," Fiolon agreed. "Maybe then we'd get some more tunes."

"And if we found a duplicate, I could take it apart and find out what's inside."

"Why do you always want to know how things work?"

Mikayla shrugged. "I just do. Why do you always want to write a song about everything?"

Fiolon matched her shrug. "I just do."

They looked at each other and burst out laughing.

Haramis started to chuckle, and found herself back in her Tower looking at the bowl of water. Her breath had disturbed the surface, breaking the vision.

*Well,* she thought, *they certainly seem intelligent enough, but I have difficulty seeing her as Archimage. I'll have to find out more about her—and about him. From his remark about marriage, it sounds as though they might be betrothed, but it's certainly odd that he doesn't seem to know who his father is. And while their clothes are clearly handed down, they were good clothes originally, and the children don't speak like servants.*

Haramis dressed quickly and went to eat breakfast. She had letters to write and messages to send.

Information about the land was as accessible to Haramis as her heartbeat. Information about people was much more difficult to obtain. It took several weeks for Ayah, a Nyssomu servant at the palace, to receive the Archimage's message, get leave to visit her sister, and get far enough away from the Citadel so that a lammergeier could fetch her without being seen. Nobody in the royal family knew that Ayah's sister worked for the Archimage, and Haramis wanted to keep things that way.

But finally a lammergeier arrived at the Tower with a well-wrapped-up Nyssomu on its back. Haramis went out to meet the bird and carried the little woman indoors herself. The main drawback to living where she did was that her Nyssomu servants could not safely go outside. Even after almost two hundreds, Haramis still recalled vividly the day her friend and companion Uzun had nearly frozen to death while they were searching for her Talisman. She had lost an entire day's travel backtracking to a lower altitude and thawing Uzun out, before sending him back to the lowlands and continuing alone. The Vispi were the only Oddlings that could survive in the mountains, and even they preferred to live in isolated small valleys warmed by hot springs.

So Haramis carried a well-wrapped bundle into the Tower and turned her guest over to Enya, her visitor's sister, to be taken to her room and given some refreshment after her journey. What Haramis wanted to know had waited this long; it could wait a few more hours.

When the three of them were gathered in Haramis's study, sipping from mugs of hot ladu-juice, Haramis asked Ayah about the children she had seen in her vision.

"Princess Mikayla and Lord Fiolon?" the Oddling asked in surprise. She obviously wondered what interest Haramis had in the two children, but Haramis chose not to explain—at least not at the moment. She merely waited until the woman continued.

"Mika—Princess Mikayla—is the sixth of the King's seven children. The King concentrates on the education of his heir; the Queen fusses over her 'baby'—who is now ten years old, and the other four are close together in age and tend to band together." The Oddling woman shook her head. "So nobody cares much what Mika does, and Fiolon's parents are dead—or at least his mother is. If they didn't have each other, she would be a very lonely child, and so, I suspect, would he."

Haramis considered that. "I always had Uzun for my best friend," she said, smiling fondly at a polished wood harp with a bone inlay at the top of its post that stood next to her chair. She ran a hand along its back as if stroking a household pet. "But still, I can't imagine what childhood would have been like without my sisters. They were always there—whether I wanted them to be or not." She pulled her thoughts back to the present. "So how does Fiolon fit in? Exactly who is he?"

Ayah continued her report. "Lord Fiolon of Var. His mother was the youngest sister of the King of Var—our Queen is the middle child. Fiolon's mother died when he was born, but it was over six years before our Queen persuaded the King to allow her to foster her late sister's child."

"And Fiolon's father?" Haramis had been wondering about that point ever since she had heard the children's conversation.

Ayah shrugged. "Nobody knows. His mother wasn't married."

Haramis raised her eyebrows. "The sister of the King of Var had a baby and nobody has any idea who fathered it? Given the lack of privacy in any palace I've ever seen, that seems incredible. Surely somebody must at least suspect who her lover was."

"Gossip has it that she died claiming that one of the Lords of the Air fathered her child."

Haramis raised her eyebrows. "I had never heard that the Lords of the Air took corporeal form—let alone fathered children."

Ayah sighed. "She was dying, Lady, and probably delirious. But I agree—it is odd that nobody knows who fathered him. Very odd."

Haramis shrugged. "I doubt that it matters. Every large family has surplus children. Are he and Mikayla betrothed?"

Ayah shook her head. "There's some talk of it—Mikayla falls into your 'surplus' category as well, as much as any princess can—but there's no formal contract. I think it might well be a good thing; they're very fond of each other."

"That's a pity," Haramis said. "Since Mikayla is to be the next Archimage, she'll have to give him up."

Ayah's jaw dropped. "Mika? The Archimage?" She hesitated a long moment before continuing. "White Lady, I really don't think she'll like that."

"It doesn't matter whether she likes it or not," Haramis said calmly. "One does not volunteer for this life. It is her destiny, as it was mine."

# 2

*Haramis felt she could delay no longer. She did not* want to think of her successor left as she herself had been—suddenly plunged into being the Archimage of Ruwenda without a clue as to what that might entail. And so she must, cruel and premature as it might seem to her (and obviously to Ayah), begin to educate Mikayla for the office she would hold one day.

Ayah remained for several days at the Tower, with Enya to keep her company, while Haramis made her preparations for the journey to fetch her successor. She could, of course, simply have summoned a few of the great lammergeiers to carry her to the Citadel and bring her and Mikayla back to the Tower. But she wanted Mikayla to see in detail the land she would be bound to, and so, on the day she sent Ayah off by lammergeier, she mounted one fronial and loaded supplies and camping gear on a second and set out for the Citadel to the south where her sister Anigel had lived and died.

The first few days of travel were in the mountains. It was very cold, even though the weather was mild for winter and no new snow fell. (Haramis felt that she was suffering quite enough traveling through the snow that was already there without permitting additional snow to fall.) Despite a well-lined sleep sack, she ached in every joint when she woke in the mornings. But by the end of the fifth day she was out of the snow and watching the sun sink red and swollen over the marshes to her west.

Most of the way now she traveled by long-unused secret paths through the marshes of Ruwenda. Once she had known every step of these paths as well as the shelves of her own library. From the aching of her muscles, if nothing else, it was evident to her that she had indeed dwelt for far too long in retirement within the walls of her own comfortable Tower. It was true that while all was well with the land there was no need for her to leave the Tower, but still, she thought, she should get out more. How many years had it been since she had seen the land other than in vision trances? Despite her aching body, it was good to be out and about.

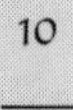

In physical appearance, she had put on the semblance of an ordinary woman, no longer young, although still appearing hale and fit despite her snow-white hair. This was the appearance she had always used when traveling about the land, even when she had still been a young girl. It ensured that she would be treated with a certain amount of respect, but not with the superstitious awe that the recognized presence of the Archimage would evoke. But by the end of each day, she wondered whether this semblance of fitness were not as much a lie as anything that would have indicated her more Arcane powers—or her true age.

She could, she reminded herself again, have justified summoning one of the lammergeiers who served her, and she was frequently tempted, especially late in the afternoons, to emphasize the urgency of her mission in that way.

But it seemed to her that setting all Ruwenda astir by landing in the courtyard of her however-many-times-great-niece's home in such a fashion would give the girl—and possibly even her parents, who ought to know better—an entirely erroneous idea of what the duties and difficulties of being Archimage were, as well as an essentially flawed idea of the proper uses of magical power. There was nothing at all magical about the fronials; Orogastus had kept a stable of them (since he could not summon the lammergeiers, fronials were his only means of transport to and from the Tower), and Haramis had simply continued his breeding program.

Orogastus, always flamboyant, would almost certainly have arrived on this errand by lammergeier if he could have. But that was not Haramis's way.

So she went on, unattended, frequently leading the fronials when low-hanging vegetation made riding impossible, with nothing outwardly magical about her except her white cloak and staff. Her Talisman, the Three-Winged Circle, worn on a chain about her neck, was hidden by her clothing. She wore her stoutest boots, bespelled somewhat against the rain and fog of this season, and against their wearer's being lost on the confusing roads —not that the Archimage should have the slightest need of the last spell, but she had dabbled in spell casting since childhood, and she liked to keep in practice.

This journey was a good time to refresh her own memories of the roads and pathways of Ruwenda, for she had not traveled them afoot for many a year. So, though she could have chosen any kind of entourage she wished, or any kind of real or magical conveyance, she forbore magic for this journey, and traveled on foot and by fronial. But she hoped that in spite of this, her great-great-niece would sense some magical purpose in her journey.

It would be a good start to her training if the girl turned out to have some natural magical ability. From what little Haramis had seen of her, Mikayla seemed more likely to try to analyze exactly what made a spell work rather than work to learn the feel of a spell, but she had been the girl in Haramis's vision of her successor, so obviously it was ordained. She did not think it possible that Fiolon, being both male and from Var, could possibly be her intended successor.

Her leisurely journey through the swamps took another four days and nights, during which time Haramis renewed her acquaintance with more of the land of Ruwenda—mostly in the form of mud—than she really cared to. She had dwelt so long among the snowy mountains that she had forgotten just what mud was like. Snow could be brushed off, and any little bit that might be left would evaporate soon after she got indoors again. Mud stuck to her, dried on her skin, and itched. It was a relief when her path joined the Great Causeway and she exchanged the muddy trails for a paved road.

Now that the road was easier, and she no longer needed to watch every step she took, she was free to look around her. Although winter was always rainy in the vicinity of the Citadel, today was one of the rare days of sun and mild temperatures, treasured as a break in the dreariness of the season. Birds chirped in the trees that lined the Causeway. When she reached the meadow that covered Citadel Knoll, she saw that even in midwinter, the black trillium flowers were blooming everywhere. She chuckled aloud. When she had been a child, the Black Trillium had been a rare and magical thing, so rare that there was only one plant in existence, in the care of the Archimage. But after Haramis and her sisters defeated Orogastus, the flowers had sprung up magically all over the knoll. Now they were as common as weeds—and probably, thought Haramis with wry amusement, as little regarded.

It was late morning when she arrived at the Citadel, where she was greeted by the King with surprise so great it amounted to stupefaction.

"Lady Archimage, you honor us greatly," the King said, looking somewhat nervous. "How may we serve you?"

The Queen, on the other hand, seemed to regard Haramis's arrival thus unheralded and unattended as no more than the eccentricity of an old woman, and made allowances for it. "You must be exhausted, Lady!" The housekeeper came hurrying up in response to the Queen's glance in her direction. "Let the servants take your things to the guest chamber and care for your beasts, while you rest from your journey."

Ten days of coping with the winter weather and the whims of two slightly crotchety fronials (they didn't mind the mountains much, but they *hated* the swamps) had left Haramis short not only of breath but of temper.

"You can skip all the ceremony," she said shortly. "My business is not with either of you, but with Mikayla."

"Mikayla?" The King looked blank.

"Your daughter Mikayla," Haramis said through gritted teeth. She had never suffered fools gladly, and she had spent so much of her time alone for so many years that she was badly out of practice in court manners. Furthermore, as Archimage, she didn't have to care what people thought of her. "Sixth of your seven children. You do remember her, don't you?"

The King managed a nervous chuckle. "Yes, of course I remember her. But she's just a little girl. What do you want with her?"

Fortunately for what remained of Haramis's temper, the Queen was of a more practical frame of mind. Briefly Haramis was reminded of her own parents, the scholarly and extremely absentminded King Krain and the capable and gentle Queen Kalanthe. The Queen sent the housekeeper to be sure that the guest chamber was made ready and the fire lit in it immediately, that servants brought in Haramis's baggage, and that the two fronials were cared for. She dispatched Ayah, who, to Haramis's complete lack of surprise, had been hovering behind the housekeeper, with orders to find the Princess Mikayla and bring her to the small parlor immediately. She then led Haramis to the parlor, seated her in the most comfortable chair, and sent for refreshments. "Dinner will be served soon," she explained, "but perhaps a bit of dried fruit and cheese would be acceptable?"

Haramis sat straight in the chair, being careful not to let her weariness show. Outside, in the bright sun, she had felt well, but indoors it was gloomy and damp, in spite of the fire. She looked at the King, who had trailed after them and was now standing uncertainly near the doorway. She could tell that he would rather have had time to prepare Mikayla for a meeting with her elderly kinswoman. From what little she had seen of Mikayla, she suspected that the Queen felt the same, but she hid it better than her husband. Or perhaps, Haramis thought, the King really *was* trying to call Mikayla to mind. If he thought she was a little girl, he obviously hadn't paid much attention to her lately. Haramis had the feeling that today was going to be quite a shock to him.

The food arrived, and Haramis ate politely, restraining her impatience. Ayah would find Mikayla as quickly as anyone could, and it would be unwise to show too much impatience.

But when Ayah returned, she was alone.

"Where is my daughter?" the Queen demanded.

Ayah looked unhappy. "Not in the Citadel, Your Majesty. I'm very much afraid that she's gone off with Lord Fiolon on one of their exploring trips again."

The Queen sank into a chair and pinched the bridge of her nose as if a sudden headache had struck her. Unwelcome as this news undoubtedly was to her, Haramis had the distinct impression that it was not a complete surprise. Indeed, the Queen's only audible comment was a soft, "Why today?"

The King, however, did not seem to understand a situation about which even Haramis could make a good guess. Of course, Haramis's sister Kadiya had been in the habit of disappearing into the swamps for weeks on end, accompanied only by the Nyssomu hunter Jagun, her favorite companion, so Haramis had some familiarity with this sort of behavior. Princess Kadiya had spent enough time among the Nyssomu to earn the mire-name "Farseer" and to be inducted as an honorary member of the Nyssomu tribe.

"Exploring trips?" he blustered. "Explain yourself, woman! Are you saying that my daughter is running around the swamps alone?"

"No, Majesty," Ayah said hastily, "I'm sure she's not alone. She and Lord Fiolon have many friends in the Nyssomu village just west of the Knoll, so I'm sure they went with a guide, at the very least."

The King seemed about to explode; men, Haramis thought, always asked about nonessentials. But Haramis chose that moment to take a hand.

"Where would they have gone?" she asked calmly.

"I heard them talking last month about some ancient ruins up the River Golobar," Ayah said, "but they were agreeing that the river level wasn't high enough to take a boat up that far. Of course," she added diffidently, "it has rained quite a bit since then."

Haramis knew the ruins in question, although she had never been there in person. They lay where the Blackmire met the Greenmire, up the River Golobar almost halfway between its source and the point where it flowed into the Lower Mutar River, about a day's journey west of the Citadel. Allow a day to get to the Golobar, and probably at least a week, under ideal conditions to get to the ruins, assuming, of course . . .

"The Skritek!" Haramis said suddenly. "She does know that there is a large concentration of Skritek in that area, does she not?"

"What?" the King roared, almost drowning out the Queen's gasp of horror.

"Don't you know *anything* about your realm?" Haramis snapped at him. "It's certainly clear that you know next to nothing about your family."

"Don't worry, Mama; the Skritek won't hurt Mika," a child's voice said reassuringly from the doorway. "She talks to them and they leave her alone."

Haramis was inclined to doubt the truth of that statement.

Certainly *she* could turn away ravening Skritek with a command, but *she* was the Archimage.

The Skritek, commonly called Drowners, were known for their habit of concealing themselves underwater to lie in wait for their prey, which included all other Oddlings (such as the Nyssomu) and large animals, then drag it down to be drowned before they ate it. Their hunting habits out of the water were even worse; on land they hunted in packs. Haramis had even seen them attack humans; in fact, a pack of Skritek had wiped out part of King Voltrik's army. Since King Voltrik of Labornok had invaded Ruwenda, killed her parents, and was trying to kill her and her sisters, Haramis had managed to restrain her tears at the time.

And those were the adults. In some ways, the younger ones were even worse. Skritek laid eggs and abandoned them. Skritek were the only Oddlings to have a true larval stage, which fended for itself as best it could—which was fairly well—until it spun a cocoon, changed, and emerged as a small, ravenous adult. Haramis had the uneasy feeling that one of the groves of dead trees that the Skriteks used for their metamorphosis was along the children's proposed route. She resolved to check on this as soon as she had a chance.

But right now, the Queen was proudly introducing her "baby" —the ten-year-old Prince Egon. He bowed properly over Haramis's hand, to her well-concealed amusement. This one was a little charmer, all right. He had masses of gold curly hair and big innocent-looking blue eyes—in fact he looked quite a lot like Anigel. *Must be a throwback,* Haramis thought. *I hope he's got brains, although with those looks he probably could survive without them.*

"So your sister talks to Skritek, does she?" Haramis asked. "What does she say to them?"

"She says they are forbidden to wage war against humans."

Haramis was surprised. This was true, and enforcing this prohibition was one of the Archimage's duties. But how would Mikayla know of this—and under what circumstances had she been discussing it with any of the Skritek? She did not think the Skritek took the prohibition very seriously. But if Mikayla thought otherwise—

Obviously, it was important for Haramis to make Mikayla's acquaintance as soon as possible.

# 3

The river had been just deep enough for the flat-bottomed boats used by the Nyssomu to reach the ruins. Mikayla, Fiolon, and their Nyssomu guides Quasi and Traneo had spent several days swapping places back and forth in the boats, taking turns poling them through the shallows and rowing upstream when the water was deep enough. It was hard work, but they kept at it, from sunrise to sunset each day.

When it was too dark to see where they were going, they pulled the boats ashore, ate a carefully rationed portion of the dried meat they had brought along for the journey, and slept in one of the boats, with the other one inverted and tied securely on top of the first. This meant that they didn't have to stand watch at night. The Skritek, the only predator large enough to rip apart the boats, wouldn't bother humans without provocation, and as long as Quasi and Traneo slept between Mikayla and Fiolon, their scent would not be noticeable to a passing Skritek. In fact, by the time they reached Skritek territory, they all smelled more of the swamp than of anything else.

They had spent almost two days traveling through Skritek territory, when traces of the ruins they were searching for appeared at the edge of the river.

Fiolon pointed excitedly. "Look, there was a village here once. Maybe in these ruins we can find more music boxes—or something equally interesting."

"I don't believe there could be anything else nearly as interesting," Mikayla teased. "Not to you, anyhow."

"Princess," ventured one of their Oddling guides, the little Nyssomu named Quasi, "you don't want to go into these ruins. The ones farther upriver are more interesting."

Mikayla regarded him suspiciously. "You want us to travel farther upriver through Skritek territory and run a greater risk of encountering them? What's wrong with these ruins?"

"They look fine to me," Fiolon protested, "and I want to find out more about the Vanished Ones."

"And I really want to find some more of those music boxes," Mikayla added, "and see how they work."

Traneo, seemingly frightened by something, ventured to say, "The King would be very angry if anything happened you, my lord; he charged me straightly to make certain that no harm befell either you or the Princess."



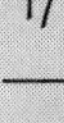

"That's nonsense," Fiolon said. "The King doesn't care what I do. I don't think the King even knows we're here."

Mikayla was so appalled by the air of utter conviction with which Fiolon spoke, and the probable truth behind it, that for a moment she could find nothing to say. Then she turned back to Quasi and said, "But you still haven't said why these ruins might be dangerous."

"Well," Quasi said nervously, rolling his eyes, "they're still alive."

"Alive?" Fiolon said. "The ruins? Are you telling us that the buildings were—and still are—alive? I've never heard that even the Vanished Ones could make buildings live."

"If anyone goes into them," Quasi said in quavering tones, "voices come out of the ground and speak in an unknown language."

"Suppose there are still some devices of the Vanished Ones working in there!" Mikayla said excitedly. "We've got to go in!"

"Not now!" Traneo said urgently. "It's almost nightfall. Please, Princess, don't do anything hasty. Sleep on it—do not enter until morning—if enter you must."

"All right, then, let's find a safe place to make camp," Mikayla said. "And—I don't know about you, but I'm getting hungry. Aren't you?"

Fiolon said, with quiet literalness, "I've been hungry for the best part of three days. You were the one who insisted we should ration our supplies."

"I still think it's a good idea," Mikayla said, "because if we run out of food we will have to go home. And I don't want to do that —not yet anyway."

"So what do you think we ought to do?" demanded Fiolon.

"I think we should let Quasi and Traneo find a proper campsite."

Fiolon turned inquiringly to Quasi, who said quickly, "We do not have much time before dark, my lord; but I will do my best."

They continued upriver for a bit, then Traneo signaled to send the boats to shore on a little promontory, covered with round smooth stones. "We can try this, Lord Fiolon. At least here, no Skriteks could hide in the long grass."

"They certainly couldn't," Mikayla agreed. "There's not enough grass here to hide anything larger than a meadow-funt." She jumped out of the boat to search for dried grass to use as kindling for a fire. But the second she set foot on the ground she froze.

"Mika?" Fiolon, still in the boat, looked inquiringly at her. "What's wrong?"

"Something," Mikayla said, "but I don't know exactly what it is. Something feels wrong, something in the ground."

Traneo had already climbed from the boat and was prowling about, deciding exactly where to set up camp. Mikayla followed him, moving slowly and trying to pinpoint the source of her uneasiness.

She came to the patch of smooth stones and tripped over one. To her astonishment it did not feel hard to her feet but somehow soft and leathery. While she stood looking at it, it began to rock slowly back and forth. Surely she had not kicked it that hard, had she? While she still stood startled, looking at it, it split with an odd tearing sound, and from the widening crack, an ugly green snout appeared, topped by two black and bulging circles.

Mikayla had never before seen a Skritek in the larval stage, but she needed no one to tell her that she saw one now. Its ugly mouth opened to reveal two rows of appallingly long and sharp teeth, although it lacked the tusks of an adult, and was only a seventh of the size of a Skritek fully grown.

She was entirely unprepared for the quickness with which the ugly thing moved. Although it was not more than a foot high, it seemed almost to grow larger as she looked at it. It crawled with appalling haste in their direction, seized Traneo between its claws, and started dragging him toward the water. To her horror it began to devour the Nyssomu without even killing him first. Traneo shrieked.

Mikayla did not believe the creature could see yet—a leathery white film still covered part of the bulging eyes—but even while she stood, half-frozen in shock, it finished biting the Oddling's head off. Traneo's scream was cut off in midhowl, and only a splash showed where the Nyssomu had been dragged under by the horrid Skritek hatchling.

Mikayla jumped backward, tripped over a rock, and measured her length in the sand. Terror surged through her; she had faced death before while hunting, but never in such an ugly form. She tried to scramble hastily to her feet, but another of the eggs wriggled under her foot, throwing her to the ground before another emerging Skritek larva. She had landed flat on her back and the breath had been knocked out of her, so for the moment she lay helpless in the sand. The small Skritek had actually opened its mouth when a stone came flying from behind her and struck the Skritek on its extended snout. It staggered back and fell sideways.

Sobbing with relief, Mikayla scrambled to her feet, and fell against Fiolon, who with more roughness than gallantry dragged her into a boat and pulled away from the shore. In midstream, Mikayla recovered a little of her self-possession. She was still crying for Traneo—nobody should have died like that, literally being eaten alive—but at least she was no longer hysterical, and she was able to release her grip on Fiolon's arm, which made it much easier for him to control the boat.

"I take it that—that thing was a Skritek, and those round things like stones were Skritek eggs," Fiolon said.

Quasi, in the boat behind them, holding on to their stern, grimly assured them that this was indeed the case. Mikayla shuddered and looked at the shore.

"I can cope with the adult Skritek, but not with those things! I like them even less now I have seen them at such close range," she remarked. "That's definitely as close as I ever care to get to one. If that was your stone, Fiolon, thanks; I think you saved my life. What should we do now?"

Fiolon said in a shaky voice, "I think we should go back to the ruins. I'd rather have strange voices than hatching Skritek."

"I agree," Mikayla said. "Look at those eggs!" Onshore, other eggs were rocking and splitting asunder; as each emerging hatchling lurched toward the rest one of its new-hatched fellows fell upon it, gnashing the dreadful teeth, and tore it to bits. Soon the entire shore was a mass of tearing, clawing, and rending hatchlings, strewn and smeared with their ugly greenish-black blood. The remaining party in the stream turned away their eyes in disgust as the boats slipped rapidly downriver.

For a few moments all was silent in the boats; Fiolon stood in the bow, steering between the darkening shores, while Quasi still held the boats together. Mikayla, still shivering a bit, moved to help Quasi. She had, of course, seen the famous Drowners before, but with the few she had met, she had always been able to make herself understood. Creatures she could not communicate and reason with were quite another story!

Mikayla and Fiolon both woke up with the dawn, ready to go explore the ruins. Quasi wasn't enthusiastic at all, but since his choices were to stay behind alone or accompany the children, he went with them, grumbling all the way.

They picked their way carefully along the overgrown path to the ruins, watching carefully for any stonelike eggs, but finding none.

"I guess their nesting site was upstream, and not here," Fiolon commented idly.

"We hope," Quasi said darkly.

"I don't feel any danger here," Mikayla remarked. "Quasi, you said that folk coming in here heard voices—but are there any stories of any of the Folk being harmed here?"

"Most people, Princess, have sense enough to run when they hear strange voices," Quasi said tartly.

"In other words," Mikayla translated, "no. Nobody has ever been harmed here."

"That we know of." Quasi did not sound happy.

"We'll just keep an eye out for skeletons, then," Mikayla said, feeling much more cheerful in spite of the Oddling's dire warnings.

"Look!" Fiolon said, so suddenly that for a moment Mikayla

thought he had indeed found a skeleton. "That building ahead—it looks intact!" Both children rushed forward, Quasi scurrying unhappily after them.

The building was indeed intact, and as they crossed the threshold the voices Quasi had mentioned started.

"They don't sound threatening," Mikayla remarked, stopping to listen.

Fiolon was listening intently. "I think that they're saying the same thing in different languages—some sort of welcome or announcement, perhaps. Listen to the cadences; do you hear how similar they are?"

Mikayla listened until the voices fell silent, but shook her head. "I'm afraid I haven't your ear, Fiolon, but I'm sure you're right. Come, Master Musician, let's see if we can find you another music box." She hooked a hand around his elbow and dragged him farther into the building.

The building was stone, made up of large rooms, with large latticework windows that had let in lots of daylight. Even now, with vines twining through the lattices, it was still light enough that they did not need torches.

"I wonder if this was a school," Mikayla said as they passed through a room full of benches and tables.

"Maybe it was a theater." Fiolon had preceded her into the next room. "Look how the benches are on risers around the stage."

"Yes," Mikayla said, "this does look like a picture of a theater I saw in a book at home. But couldn't a school have its own theater?"

"It would have to be a very rich school," Fiolon pointed out.

"Maybe, compared to us, the Vanished Ones were rich," Mikayla said. "Even some of what must have been small trinkets to them are beyond price for us." She poked her head into a smaller room behind the stage. "I think this is some kind of storeroom, but it's dark. Do you have a torch?"

Quasi reluctantly produced a torch and tinderbox, while grumbling that perhaps some things weren't meant to see the light.

Mikayla ignored the grumbling, but thanked him as she took the torch from his hand. Together she and Fiolon entered the room and gasped in astonishment. The room was full of racks and shelves and cupboards. Fiolon went back into the theater room to get a second torch from Quasi while Mikayla began to examine the shelves. The first one was full of face masks, stylized, but definitely human faces in shape and color. They had holes for eyes so that the wearer could look through them, and a smaller hole as part of the mouth, obviously to breathe and speak through. Next to the shelf was a rack of costumes, but when Mikayla tried to take one off its peg, it fell to pieces in her hand. She gulped in dismay. "What did I do?"

Fiolon lit his torch from hers and fingered through the fragments on the floor. They crumbled still further at his touch. "You didn't do anything, Mika," he reassured her. "This is some kind of silk, and silk rots as it ages. Anything that touches it would make it fall apart."

"Oh, good," Mikayla said. "I'd hate to think I was wantonly destroying valuable history."

Fio shrugged. "You can't touch this stuff without destroying it. I'm going to check the cupboards. If there are music boxes in this room, they'd have to be in one of them."

"Or we'd be hearing them now," Mikayla agreed. "I'll take a quick look at the rest of the racks, and then I'll start on the other end of the cupboards and we can meet in the middle."

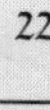



Fiolon grunted in acknowledgment, already opening cupboards in a methodical fashion. Mikayla passed the rest of the costumes, being careful not to brush against them, and then came to a rack full of silver spheres about the diameter of her thumbnail. Each sphere had a loop set on the top of it, and they hung from different-colored ribbons, made of some sort of material Mikayla had never seen before. Judging from the length of the ribbon, they were intended to be some sort of pendant, and they seemed to come in paired sets. Mikayla touched one gently with a fingertip and it chimed softly as it swung back and forth.

Soft as the sound was, it caught Fiolon's attention. "What have you got there?" he asked, joining her.

"I don't know," Mikayla said, "but they're pretty, aren't they?"

Fiolon was already testing for pitch up and down the line. "The different colors are different tones," he said absently.

"I like this one." Mikayla picked up one of the pair with green ribbons and put it around her neck. "Here," she said, dropping its mate over Fiolon's head, "at least we've found something musical." She ran a finger over the ribbon around her neck. "And whatever this ribbon is made of, it's a lot stronger than silk." She moved to the far end of the cupboards. "I'll start on my share of the cupboards now."

Fiolon shook the chiming ball next to each ear, then tucked it into the front of his tunic, before returning to the cupboards. After he explored a few more, there was a cacophony of sound as he opened one. "Look, Mika!" he shouted.

Mika laughed. "I don't have to look, I can hear. They certainly sound strange all playing at once, don't they? How many are there?"

"Seven," Fiolon replied, stuffing several into his belt pouch. Mikayla joined him and put the remainder into her own pouch. Silence fell as they were removed from the light.

"Can we go now?" Quasi's voice came from outside. "Please?"

Mikayla and Fiolon exchanged long-suffering glances. "Well," Fiolon admitted, "I guess we can. I'm not sure, Mika, but I think we've even got a duplicate here."

"And we don't know how many of those wretched larval Skritek survived and if they're likely to come downriver," Mikayla admitted. "We can always come back when it's not their hatching season."

"Good," Quasi said in heartfelt tones. "Let's get out of here—I'd like to get home in one piece!"

Mikayla tucked her little sphere down the front of her tunic so it wouldn't catch on things on the path back to the boats, and they put out the torches and returned to the river.

Quasi surveyed the boats sadly. "We'd better leave one here," he said. "We can all fit in one, and we'll get home much more swiftly if we're not trying to manage two boats among the three of us." The children agreed, and they quickly transferred their remaining supplies to one boat. They pulled the other one high up on the shore and turned it upside down.

"We can retrieve it next time we come here," Mikayla said.

Quasi snorted, and pushed them off from the shore.

The river carried them quickly downstream, and soon they were approaching the point where the Golobar emptied into the Lower Mutar River. Mikayla squinted, trying to get a better look at the water ahead. "The current looks much faster than it was when we came up it," she remarked intently.

Quasi looked up and gasped. "Stay low in the boat and hold on tightly," he ordered, but as the children moved quickly to obey him, the boat entered the Lower Mutar River and was flipped over like a child's toy boat in a strong breeze.

# 4

*Fortunately the boat had been almost to the opposite* bank of the Lower Mutar when it capsized, and the current carried its three occupants in that direction. Fiolon found his footing fairly quickly, grabbed Quasi, and shoved him up onto the bank.

Mikayla, however, had come up under one of their blankets, which was floating on the surface. Her first attempt to breathe got her a mouthful of blanket, so she quickly spat it out, ducked back under the water, and punched upward with both fists as she stood up. This left her standing in a pocket of air defined by her hands and her head. Walking carefully backward and keeping her hands up in front of her, she kept the airspace intact until she came out from under the blanket to find Fiolon staring at her.

"That looked really strange," he said. "For a moment there I was afraid you were going to drown."

"No," Mikayla said, "but it felt as if I were going to inhale that blanket." Together they dragged the blanket out of the water and spread it over a branch to dry, knowing they'd need it when night came.

"Look at the bright side," Mikayla said, wringing water out of her dripping braids. "At least we're out of Skritek territory."

"And not all that far from home," Fiolon added. "Quasi, can you bespeak your village?" Some of the Oddlings could speak mind to mind over short distances, and Quasi was quite talented at it.

But Quasi was staring dumbstruck at the sky. The children followed his gaze and saw two enormous birds descending toward them.

They were at least three times as large as any bird Mikayla had ever seen in her life, but as they came closer she realized that they were even bigger than she had thought at first. They had white bodies which were almost the size of a fronial's and wings banded black and white, but their necks and heads had no feathers on them and were about the same color as Mikayla's skin. Their eyes were black and had a look of intelligence Mikayla had never seen in a bird before. Their beaks were dark brown and had a hole in each side near the top of the beak.

Within seconds the birds had dropped from the sky to land beside the bedraggled wanderers. There was a strange woman sitting on the back of one of the birds. Both children stared in astonishment. "I didn't know that birds could carry people," Mikayla said to Fiolon.

Fiolon didn't answer her; he just sat and stared.

The lady, however, seemed impatient. "Mikayla," she said, reaching down to grab the girl by the arm, "sit here in front of me." She half hauled the girl into position. "Fiolon," she added, pointing to the second bird, "climb aboard." Fiolon moved slowly to do as he was told, staring dubiously at the great bird and dragging Quasi with him. The Oddling hesitated until the lady nodded to him, then took his seat at the very back of the bird's neck.

The lady spoke to the lammergeiers and they flew. Mikayla would have thought she was dreaming, but the pain in her arm where the lady had wrenched it when she hauled her onto the bird, and the extremely unpleasant sensation of wet clothing freezing on her body as they flew, convinced her that she was awake and, at least for the minute, alive.

Within an hour they were at the Tower—the same distance that Haramis had traversed so laboriously on her fronials.

Mikayla noticed when the bird they were riding began to lose altitude and the air grew slightly thicker and warmer, although "warmer" was certainly a relative term. She raised her head slightly from where she had pressed her face into the bird's feathers to protect it from the stinging wind and looked over the bird's shoulder. The bird's path slanted down toward a white Tower, set into a ledge in the mountain. Given the snow surrounding it, it might have been invisible had it not been liberally decorated with black trim around all the windows and black crenellations around the upper level. There was a balcony large enough for the lammergeiers to land on, and that appeared to be their destination.

The birds landed, furling their wings, and Mikayla, freed from the lady's grip, slid to the pavement. By now her clothing had frozen; it crackled as she moved. She turned to see if Fiolon was all right.

Fiolon was also on the pavement, holding Quasi's unconscious body, completely ignoring the birds that were taking flight around them. "Quasi!" he said urgently, shaking the little Oddling. "Wake up!"

The lady walked stiffly over to them and reached down awkwardly to touch Quasi's forehead briefly. "He can't hear you," she said briskly. "Bring him, and follow me." She turned and walked through a doorway into the Tower without even looking back.

Mikayla helped Fiolon lift Quasi's body. She was dismayed by how cold and unresponsive it was as she and Fiolon, both stiff with cold and hampered by frozen clothing, struggled to maneuver it through the doorway. Quasi didn't even flinch when they inadvertently banged him into the door frame.

When they got inside, they found the lady standing at the end of the hall, staring down the stairs. There was the sound of several sets of light footsteps rushing up toward her, followed by the arrival of five servants: three Nyssomu and two Vispi. Mikayla had never seen a Vispi before, but she recognized them at once from descriptions in the books she and Fiolon had read.

The Vispi were more human looking than the Nyssomu, taller, with narrower faces, and what looked to Mikayla like normal noses and mouths with small even teeth. Like the Nyssomu, they had larger eyes than humans did, but green instead of gold. They had silver-white hair and pointed ears, three fingers on each hand and fingernails that were virtually claws.

"Welcome back, Lady Haramis," the Nyssomu woman said respectfully.

"Thank you," Haramis said briefly. She indicated Quasi's limp form and pointed to the two Nyssomu men. "You and you, take this and thaw him out. You," she said to the Vispi woman, indicating Mikayla, "take the girl and get her cleaned up and dressed." To the Vispi man, she added, "You take the boy." As they were relieved of Quasi's body and towed off up another staircase, Mikayla heard Haramis add, "Draw me a bath, Enya, and make sure the fire is lit in my study. We'll eat there when the children are dressed."

As she soaked her chilled body in a warm tub, it occurred to Haramis—and not, she thought, before time—to wonder what Mikayla's parents would think of the abrupt disappearance of their young charges. She cast out her thoughts to one of the nearby lammergeiers, asking it to carry one of her servants to take a message to the King and Queen. When the lammergeier agreed, she told Enya to choose a servant for the journey and be sure that he was dressed warmly enough for travel by lammergeier. Enya nodded and left the room.

"I'm getting too old to go flying about like this," she grumbled to herself as she soaked in the tub, waiting for her chilled limbs to warm and become more responsive to her commands. Why, she wondered, had she brought them all here, instead of just returning to the Citadel? None of them had been dressed to fly in this climate, and that Oddling could have been permanently frozen. Haramis knew better than to bring an unprotected Nyssomu up into these heights—even more than two hundred years later, she remembered the day she had allowed Uzun to attempt to go into the mountains with her when she was searching for her Talisman. She touched her fingers to the Three-Winged Circle, which still hung by its golden chain between her breasts. On that occasion she had lost two days travel taking Uzun downhill and thawing him out. She should have remembered that before she let a Nyssomu mount a lammergeier. He would have been safer in the swamp. And she didn't need either him or the boy here. The only one she did need here was Mikayla. *Am I getting senile?* she wondered.

She frowned, considering the question. She had discovered in her long career as Archimage that sometimes she did things that seemed strange to her at the time, but there would turn out to be a good reason for her actions, even though the reason was unknown to her when she acted. She felt that this was one of those times, but what could the reason be? The only thing that came to mind was that Mikayla's parents might have refused to let her take their daughter, but from what she had seen of them, that did not seem likely. And if they had tried to stop her, she would have taken the girl anyway, and there is nothing they could have done about it.

She shrugged, got out of the tub, and dressed in her warmest clothes, even though her rooms were not at all chilly. Then she went to see her guests.

Her servants had found them various garments, although nothing that really fit either child properly. Soon the children were seated dry and warm, albeit rather oddly garbed in a random assortment of ill-fitting clothing, before a fire in Haramis's study, with one of her housekeeper's good meals before them. Enya was very much pleased by this for, as she had often complained to Haramis, the Archimage did not eat enough to keep a bird alive; and Enya, who liked cooking, found the healthy appetites of the children a most welcome challenge to her considerable talents.

Quasi had been thawed out enough to join them, but he was still rather sluggish and ate little. Both children seemed concerned about him and asked him repeatedly how he was feeling until Haramis finally lost her patience and told them to be quiet and eat.

But when at last the empty dishes had been magically banished to the kitchen again, the Archimage glared at her young guests and at Quasi, who sat with folded hands, silently respectful beside them.

"Tiresome little beasts," she remarked crossly, "I wonder if any of you three will prove to be worth the trouble to which you have put both me and my lammergeiers."

Quasi, who had revived considerably during the meal, probably due to the fact that he was sitting next to the fire, said rather pertly, "Begging your pardon, Lady—and it was very good of you to come after us and I'm sure we're all most grateful—but we didn't none of us ask to be whisked away here. And what the King and the Queen will be thinking when no one can't find any trace of the princess and the young master, I'm sure I don't know."

"That's right," piped up Mikayla, "Mama and Papa will be

most terribly worried when they don't hear any word of us from anywhere."

"Don't you dare to be impertinent," the Archimage growled. "I have sent a message to the King and the Queen, and they will know soon enough that you are both safe with me. And from what I've seen of your parents—and heard of your behavior," she added cuttingly, "it will be several days before they even *begin* to worry about you." Mikayla bit her lip and dropped her eyes to her lap.

Secretly Haramis thought that if Mikayla's parents and Fiolon's guardians had a few days of worry about the children, it would only serve them right for taking such poor care of their charges, and for the way in which this had resulted in her, Haramis, having her Tower turned upside down by these unexpected guests.

"But you must understand," Mikayla said earnestly, "that we really didn't *need* rescuing at all. After all, madam"—she was not at all sure who the Archimage might be, but if only because of her abundance of white hair, she was sure that the elder lady was somehow entitled to respect—"we did escape from the Skriteks, and we managed to get to shore safely, and we weren't far from Quasi's village. So we really were getting along quite well, and if you rescued us you must have done it because you had some reason of your own, or some use for us, hadn't you? So it really isn't our fault that we're here, is it?"

Fiolon said, shocked, "Oh, Mika, you shouldn't sound so ungrateful. I'm sure that whoever the Lady is, she'll have had excellent reasons for what she did."

Until that very moment it had not occurred to the Archimage that neither of the young people had the faintest idea of who she was. She raised her head and said irritably, "Do you not know who I am?"

"We don't have the faintest idea, Lady," Fiolon said politely. "I suppose by your birds you must at least be a mighty sorceress. I have heard of only one woman who could command the lammergeiers, and I believed that she died many years ago. You could not possibly be the old Archimage of Ruwenda?" He hesitated. "Or could you?"

Haramis realized that she should have been prepared for this—if she had really thought about it, she would have known that none of them had ever set eyes on her before. And from what she had seen of the King's attitude toward them, she would wager that their education had been neglected as well.

"I am not the old Archimage, no," she declared. "Her name was Binah, and she died many years ago, before any of you young people were born. I am the new Archimage—it would hardly be right to say the young Archimage now—and my name is Haramis."

Fiolon gasped, obviously the name meant something to him, but Mikayla still looked blank. Haramis frowned at her. "I am also your kinswoman. Don't imagine that I am proud of the relationship," she added cuttingly. "I'm not."

Mikayla rose to her feet and curtsied. She had beautiful manners when she chose to use them, Haramis realized, presumably having been schooled extensively in court etiquette by the Queen. But it would appear that she seldom chose to use them.

"Is it permitted to ask why we have been brought here, my Lady Archimage?"

Haramis sighed; she had lost almost all her enthusiasm for choosing this impertinent young girl as her successor. But after all, what choice did she have? It wasn't really her choice to make, just her job to train the girl. At least, Mikayla was Anigel's great-grandchild—or was that great-great-grandchild?—and must have some of her ancestress's talents. She would simply have to make the best of it.

She summoned all her self-control and said, "Like all creatures, I am mortal. I must train my successor before I die. Would it please you, Mikayla, to become Archimage when, as all things must, I pass on to whatever is the next stage of existence?"

Mikayla stared at her, her mouth hanging open. Haramis hoped that her expression was merely astonishment, but it bore a definite resemblance to horror. It was several minutes before the girl managed to speak.

"The idea had never occurred to me, my lady. What does an Archimage do?"

"Mika!" Fiolon's reproving whisper wasn't quite soft enough. Haramis turned her attention to him.

"Did you have something to say, young man?" she inquired acidly.

Politeness lost out to curiosity rather quickly. "Are you the Archimage Haramis who was one of the triplet princesses?" he asked. "The one who fought the great battle with the evil sorcerer Orogastus and defeated him . . ." His voice trailed off and he looked around excitedly. "This is the Tower that he used to live in, isn't it?" he asked enthusiastically.

Haramis raised her eyebrows. "It is," she replied. "How do you come to know those old stories?"

"I like music," Fiolon said self-consciously. He looked down and traced a half circle in the carpet underfoot with his toe, "and I've memorized every ballad I could find, including all the ones by Master Uzun." The strings of the harp that had been sitting quietly in the corner rippled softly, as if it had heard something that pleased it. Fiolon looked sharply at it; Mikayla didn't seem to hear anything.

"He does more than just 'like music,'" Mikayla said proudly. "He can play any instrument I've ever seen, and he has a beautiful voice. The King has him play at court whenever we have visitors."

Haramis smiled at the boy. "Perhaps you will play for me before you leave, then."

Fiolon bowed as well as he could while seated. "I should be honored, White Lady."

"When are we leaving?" Mikayla asked.

Haramis turned to her, repressing a sigh. *I hope Binah never found me this unpromising,* she thought. "*You* are not leaving, Mikayla," she said. "You are to remain here so that I can train you as my successor."

"But I'm going to marry Fiolon," Mikayla protested, reaching out to him. He took her hand and held it, but he looked grave; obviously he had more of an idea of what was happening than she did. "That's the only good thing about being the youngest princess; my parents already have enough daughters for all the alliances they need, so they said that Fiolon and I could marry. We're going to live on a small estate near the Greenmire, and explore the ruins there, and teach our children about the Vanished Ones. . . ."

Her voice trailed off as Haramis just looked at her. "Our betrothal is to be announced next spring," Mikayla protested. "My parents *promised.* I'm just an extra princess—nobody has any use for me."

"*I* have a use for you," Haramis said firmly. "The land has a use for you." She glared at Fiolon until he released Mikayla's hand, with obvious reluctance.

"Fio?" Mikayla tried to cling to him. He patted her on the back and let her go.

She looked at him, then at Haramis. "Am I not to be given any choice?"

"No," said Haramis bluntly. "It is far too important to be left to the whim of a child."

Mikayla looked at her for a long minute, and Haramis could almost see the wheels of thought going round in the young girl's head.

She said, "If I am not to be given a choice, then I suppose it does not matter what I think about it." She curtsied to the Archimage more politely than Haramis had expected and said, "I am here to do your will, Lady Haramis."

But Haramis felt that she was catching a bit of the edges of Mikayla's thoughts, and the girl's body language was most expressive. Mikayla might do Haramis's will, but it would be a long time before this was also Mikayla's will. A very long time indeed.

*Maybe I* should *have waited until I was at the point of death and dropped the job on her then,* Haramis thought wearily. *Training this one is not going to be easy.*

# 5

*It was silent in the Archimage's study, with no sound* except the snapping of the fire.

Fiolon got up and walked to a beautifully inlaid harp every bit as tall as he, with silver strings and a frame of satiny reddish wood with white bone inlay at the top of its pillar. "What a beautiful harp, Lady Haramis," he said. "May I play upon it? I am sure its tone is as beautiful as any harp I have ever heard."

Haramis said in surprise, "Can you play the harp, young Fiolon?"

"Yes, I can, though I am really not expert. I have had lessons on many instruments; but I think of all of them, the harp is my favorite. It is almost impossible to make any sound upon a harp that is not beautiful."

"I think you are right," said Haramis, and rose to her feet. "But this is no ordinary harp; nor does one play upon it, as with any ordinary instrument. This is Uzun, my wisest of Oddling counselors."

"That's Master Uzun?" Fiolon asked in excited surprise. "I thought he must have died long ago."

"When at last he came to the end of his natural life," Haramis explained, "it was my first act of great magic which conjured him into this harp so that I might always have the benefit of his wise counsel. I will introduce you to him; and if he is willing he may speak or even sing to you."

Mikayla muttered, "I never heard such nonsense in my life. How can a harp be a counselor, whatever he was in life?"

"I don't know," Fiolon said softly. "But at least so far, I am willing to believe anything the Lady says; do be careful, Mika."

Haramis shot Mikayla a sharp glance but she said nothing. As she approached the harp she said, "Good evening, Uzun."

"Good evening, Lady Haramis." The voice was strong and plangent, with a sweet singing tone, and did indeed seem to come forth from the sounding board of the tall harp that sat motionless on the carpet. Haramis glanced at Mikayla out of the corner of her eye. The girl appeared not quite ready to believe the evidence of her own ears. She was obviously telling herself that it must be some kind of clever trickery.

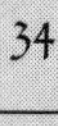

"And who are the young people?" asked the voice. "I do not think I have met them before."

Haramis said, "Master Uzun, I would like to introduce two of my young kinsfolk: Princess Mikayla of Ruwenda and Lord Fiolon of Var, the son of the late sister of the King."

"I am very glad to meet your kinsfolk, my lady," Uzun replied, his voice rippling up and down his strings. "It is right that you should have someone to help you in the bearing of so many and such heavy burdens. Is it she whom you have chosen to take over your burdens when you are no longer able to do so?"

"How well you know me, Uzun," Haramis said fondly.

She looked at Mikayla, and she felt she could hear the thoughts running through the girl's immature, undisciplined mind. The harp didn't have eyes—at least not so far as she could tell, so how could it see them? Certainly there was something very strange going on here, and obviously Mikayla was still trying to reason out what it was and how it worked.

Haramis said sharply, "Now do you believe me, you foolish girl?"

Mikayla looked dubiously at her. "My lady, are you really asking me to believe that you turned a person—a *dead* person—into a harp?"

"Good, you are so far honest at least," Haramis said briskly. "If you doubt me, always say so honestly, and I will try to explain; better to express honest doubt than to pretend agreement. Better always to tell the truth, even if the truth will make me angry." *And speaking of anger . . .* "You are angry with me now, are you not, Mikayla?"

Mikayla glared at her. She said, "Yes, I am." She turned and glared at Fiolon, too. "Don't look at me like that, Fiolon; she asked me. And considering that she has essentially kidnapped both of us, announced her intention of keeping me here against my will, and then told me she can turn a person into a harp without so much as a by your leave, I don't think you can realistically expect me not to be annoyed with her—at the very least."

Fiolon looked up and gulped. He said, "But, Mika, do you really think it's a good idea to get angry at someone who can turn you into something else? I mean, even if you are angry, you don't have to lie about it, just keep your mouth shut."

Uzun's voice sang through the harp. "Princess Mikayla, you are being unfair to our Lady Haramis. She certainly did not turn me into a harp without my consent, and she worked very hard to do it."

Mikayla walked over to Uzun's side, reached up, and touched a tentative finger to the bone inlay on the harp. "How did she do it?" she asked. "Was this bone part of your body? Did she kill you to work the spell, or did you die naturally and she just chopped up your body? And obviously you can hear, but can you see? Can you move by your own will?"

"Your thirst for morbid detail can wait until you have had enough training to understand what you are talking about," the harp replied. "And, for future reference, I prefer not to be touched without my consent." Uzun's rich voice sounded annoyed as it vibrated into silence, and Haramis smiled.

Fiolon asked, "Where did he go? Tell him to come back—I mean, ask him, please."

Haramis looked grave. "Even I do not give orders to Uzun, my boy. I am afraid that between you, you children have really managed to offend him, and it may be a considerable time before he speaks to either of you again—or to me, because I allowed you such rudeness as to question him."

Mikayla rolled her eyes. "Why would he blame you for our behavior? You met us only today; it's not as if you had anything to do with our upbringing or training. What could he possibly think you could do about the way we act?"

But Fiolon said, "You should be polite to him, Mikayla—I told you about him, remember? He was the court musician to King Krain, and an amateur magician as well, and he accompanied the Princess Haramis on the first part of her Quest."

Mikayla looked at him and shook her head. "Honestly, Fio, do you remember everything from every song you've ever heard?"

Fiolon thought about it for a moment. "Yes, I think I do," he replied.

Mikayla sighed. "Well, try to remember that I don't. A lot of your favorite songs are nearly two hundreds old, and they all sound alike to me. And who was King Krain?"

"He was my father," Haramis replied, "and he was murdered horribly when the Labornoki army invaded—I'll spare you the gruesome details. It's time for you to go to bed now, and you don't need nightmares." She yanked abruptly at the bellpull and then sat in a silence none of the others dared to break until Enya appeared. Then she ordered Enya to see that the children and Quasi were put to bed, and she stalked from the room without even waiting for Enya's acknowledgment of her orders.

Behind her retreating form, Fiolon whispered to Mikayla, "I don't think you should have mentioned her father. In fact, if I were you, I wouldn't mention her family at all."

A little while later the children were put to bed in the Archimage's guest room, in two narrow beds side by side. Haramis went to her room and set up her scrying basin. "Let's see what these two do when left alone together," she muttered to herself.

At first there was nothing interesting to see. Mikayla, who had after all had a long and tiring day, was quickly asleep. Fiolon, however, seemed restless and unable to fall asleep. He kept turning over and over in bed, and sitting up at intervals, before lying down and trying to go to sleep again without success.

Haramis suspected that he was remembering the scene before the fire with Uzun, and that he wished to go downstairs again and make his peace with Master Uzun before he slept. The boy obviously had sense enough to realize that the one thing Mikayla did not need was to make an enemy of Master Uzun.

*And he is right,* Haramis thought, *Mikayla should take care to be on good terms with Uzun; even in his present form, he is the only one of my counselors still living. Except for a few Oddling servants, most of them Vispi, there isn't anyone else living in the Tower besides me and Uzun.*

When Fiolon got out of bed and started downstairs, Haramis made no move to stop him. She sat quietly and watched, prepared to derive what amusement she could from the coming confrontation. Uzun had always been uncommonly stubborn; it would be interesting to watch how Fiolon coped with him.

The study was empty except for the flickering of the coals of the fire on the great harp, whose wood glowed reddish bronze in the firelight. Fiolon knelt on the hearth rug before the harp and whispered, "Master Uzun, I beg you to forgive my cousin Mika; she really doesn't mean any harm. It's just the way she is; she never believes anything unless she can see it and measure it. She's the sort of person who likes to take things apart to see how they work; she's not good at taking things on faith or believing in magic she can't reason out rules for."

Master Uzun obstinately kept silence. Haramis waited and watched. Then it obviously occurred to Fiolon—whether it was his own thought or whether it somehow came to him from the silent magician before him—that if Master Uzun was to forgive Mikayla, the girl must come herself and beg his pardon for her thoughtless words. He rose to his feet and headed for the stairs. Haramis continued to follow his path in the scrying bowl.

Fiolon lost no time. He stole quietly upstairs to the guest room where Mika was sleeping. No more was visible of his cousin than one red curl above the pillow. Fiolon tweaked it and Mikayla surfaced and opened her eyes.

"Fio? Why aren't you asleep? It isn't morning yet, is it? It's still dark! What's the matter?"

"Mikayla, you must come down to the study at once and beg Master Uzun's pardon."

"Are you out of your mind, Fio? It's the middle of the night! He'll probably be asleep—assuming he sleeps." She frowned at him. "And your voice sounds funny. Are you getting sick? We all got badly chilled on the journey here, and you probably worse than I. At least I was between Haramis and the bird, so I was sheltered somewhat, but you must have taken the brunt of the winds." She reached out a hand to touch his forehead and gasped. "Fiolon, you're burning with fever. Get back into bed right now!"

Fiolon scowled at her and said, "Not until you apologize to Master Uzun."

Mikayla sighed. "Oh, very well. Anything to make you stop acting like an idiot. You're sick, Fiolon; you should be in bed." She got out of bed, stopping only to slip a pair of warm slippers on her bare feet, and followed him down the stairs.

The red coals of the fire had burned down to a sullen glow. Fiolon made up the fire and fanned it to a small flame, while Mikayla knelt before the gleaming harp.

"Master Uzun," she said with contrition, and rising, she dropped a deep court curtsy.

"I entreat you to forgive me, Master Uzun," she murmured ceremoniously. "If the Lady Archimage does indeed choose me as her successor, I shall want friends here. I most humbly beg your pardon, and I assure you that I meant no offense, nor did I mean to doubt you." She was silent for a while. "Please do forgive me, sir," she whispered again after a few moments.

There was silence in the room. Then with a long sound like a sigh, Uzun's strings sighed a ripple of music and he breathed, "Indeed I do forgive you most heartily, little mistress—Princess Mikayla. We shall be friends, I hope, from this moment. And you, too, young Master Fiolon. It was courteous of you to wish to amend this misunderstanding." What he did not say—but Haramis, watching from her room, understood it, nevertheless, as clearly as if Uzun had spoken aloud—was that he would like to further his acquaintance with Fiolon. But Uzun would guess that Fiolon would not be remaining here much longer.

"You must not think of yourself as a prisoner here, Princess," Uzun said, almost as if he were picking up Mikayla's thoughts. "It is a great honor to be chosen as Archimage, and I am certain that you will do the job well when the time comes. And you will have the benefit of proper training—a luxury the Lady Haramis did not have."

"Why did she choose *me*?" Mikayla asked. "I'm really not the magical type." Beside her, Fiolon gave a feeble snort of laughter. Obviously he agreed with her assessment of her character.

"The Archimage doesn't choose her successor," Uzun explained. "Actually, I believe the land itself makes the choice. But when the time comes, the Archimage knows, so that she can pass on the office."

"How was the Lady Haramis chosen?" Fiolon asked curiously. "Your ballads never quite said."

"Alas for my weakness." Uzun sighed. "I wasn't with her then.

I had to leave her when she journeyed into the mountains here in search of her Talisman."

"You would have frozen to death if you had tried to follow her," Mikayla pointed out gently. Haramis was glad to see that the child appeared to have at least a little appreciation of other people's feelings. "Quasi got frozen today and had to be thawed out; remember how sluggish he was at supper?"

"Quasi?" the harp asked. "Was that a Nyssomu with you? Nobody introduced him to me."

Mikayla stared intently at the harp for several long seconds. "You are blind," she said with certainty. "And you can't move, can you? You're a person trapped in a harp who can hear and talk, but that's all. How could she have done this to you?"

"She wanted to keep me alive," Uzun said quietly.

"You taught her magic when she was a child," Fiolon said, hastily changing the subject. "That's in one of the Chronicles. Is that why she was chosen, because she already knew magic?"

"It can't be," Mikayla objected before Uzun could answer. Haramis suppressed a sigh. Obviously in Mikayla's case good manners were intermittent in the extreme. "Because then I wouldn't have been chosen. I don't know much magic, Fio—you're the one who can do magic."

Fiolon blushed so deeply it was visible even in the flickering firelight. "Just little tricks, nothing like Master Uzun or the Lady Archimage. But all three of the triplets could work magic, Mika, so I'll bet you can learn. You've never tried to work any major spells, so you have no way of knowing if you have any magical ability or not." He thought for a moment and added, "I'm pretty sure you do have some sort of magical ability—remember, you said that something was wrong just before the Skritek started hatching."

"I know I have no interest in magic," Mikayla muttered. "It's a pity she didn't chose *you.*"

Uzun said softly, "I know this undoubtedly comes as quite a shock to you, child, but it will turn out for the best. You will see."

Mikayla sighed. "All I ever wanted to do was marry Fiolon and explore the Mazy Mire."

"Then you have more in common with the Lady Haramis than you realize," Uzun said. "She was betrothed to Prince Fiomaki of Var. Fifty days before the wedding day, King Voltrik's army attacked Ruwenda. And she was heiress to the throne. Believe me, Princess Haramis had a lot of plans that didn't include being

Archimage." A sound like a chuckle rippled along the strings. "And I didn't have to be there to be sure that she must have given the Archimage Binah quite an argument about it."

*I certainly tried,* Haramis thought, *but when she died so suddenly, it did rather cut short the discussion.*

"You must return to your beds now, young people," Uzun said. "I wish you a very good night and pleasant dreams." His tone left no room for doubt in either of their minds that they had been dismissed, as if from the presence of a courtier. Both children bowed to him and went upstairs to bed. As soon as they had fallen asleep, Haramis emptied the scrying bowl and made her way somewhat stiffly to her own bed—sitting in one position over the bowl had not been kind to her body. As she fell asleep she thought that Uzun was likely to be very helpful in training Mikayla. The Lords of the Air knew that she was going to need all the help she could get!

# 6

*It was Haramis's firm intent that Fiolon depart for his* home the next day. She wanted to waste no time in separating him from Mikayla. The girl would learn what Haramis wished to teach her more quickly without the distraction of her childhood playmate's presence. It was time for Mikayla to grow up and take on an adult's responsibilities.

Unfortunately, Mikayla had been correct the night before when she said that Fiolon was sick. By the time the children woke —rather late in the morning—he was having trouble breathing and complained feebly that his chest hurt. When Haramis came to check on him herself, Mikayla glared at her.

"He has lung fever, Lady," she snapped, "which is only to be expected after the time he spent yesterday flying through cold air in soaking-wet clothes. Did you even *notice* that his clothes were frozen on his body by the time we got here?"

Actually, Haramis had been sufficiently cold and miserable herself by then that she hadn't noticed, but it did not seem a good idea to admit that. "Don't make such a fuss, girl," she said. "I'm sorry he's ill, but my housekeeper will take good care of him and he'll recover soon." *He had better,* she thought, *I want him out of here as soon as may be.* "As for you"—she frowned sternly at Mikayla—"his illness is no excuse for you to be still in your night-clothes at this hour of day. Get dressed at once, and then come to my study." She swept out of the room, ignoring the stamp of slippered feet behind her.

It was a full half hour by the time Mikayla turned up in the study as ordered. By then, the breakfast Haramis had ordered for the child was cold. Haramis herself had eaten hours earlier. "You have a choice, Mikayla," she told the girl. "You can be on time for meals or you can eat them cold. Today, you have chosen cold breakfast. Eat it quickly; we have a lot to do."

Mikayla shoved cold porridge into her mouth and said, "What?"

"Don't talk with your mouth full," Haramis said automatically. "You need to learn about magic, starting, no doubt, at the very beginning. You do at least know how to read, I trust."

Mikayla nodded and continued to eat porridge. She didn't seem to notice the taste or the temperature, or even to be truly aware of the fact that she was eating it. Haramis frowned. Obviously this was not someone who could be motivated through food. What did this girl value, other than Fiolon? How could Haramis reach her?

Mikayla finished the last bite and dropped her spoon in the empty bowl with a clatter. Haramis sent the dish back to the kitchen with a wave of her hand—and Mikayla didn't even look impressed. Of course, she had seen Haramis transport away the dirty dishes the night before, so she knew it was possible, but if she were going to simply take magic for granted . . . Well, maybe that would be a help in her training—at least she wouldn't spend hours marveling over every little thing. But surely *some* sense of the wonder of it all was desirable.

Haramis took Mikayla to the library, where she started with a simple explanation of basic magic and how it worked.

"It is clear that you know very little of magecraft, Mikayla. Let this, then, be your first lesson in that art. A mage must never do anything without need, no matter how simple. I sent Quasi home this morning by lammergeier because he would have frozen to death otherwise. I called the lammergeiers to you two at first, only because when I rescued you from the river there was grave danger. You had lost your boat, and you had not yet learned much about communication with the Skritek-kind. So I was forced to rescue you from that danger into which folly had led you before you were schooled to extricate yourselves. Do you understand?"

"No," Mikayla said. "I don't understand. In the first place, we weren't in any particular danger. The nearest Skritek were a half day's journey away—by boat, going downriver!"

"Meeting up with the Skritek is not a risk a sensible person takes with her own life, nor a risk a responsible person takes with the lives of her companions."

Mikayla shuddered involuntarily, remembering Traneo's fate. But she remembered a few other things as well. "We weren't far from Quasi's village. When you dragged us out of there and brought us here, Quasi nearly froze to death and Fiolon got lung fever. But other than *that,* my Lady Archimage, is it wrong to use the lammergeiers?"

"It is not wrong," said the Archimage, carefully ignoring the girl's sarcasm. "It is only unwise and unnecessary. Who knows when some grave danger to us, or to the land, may arise, and the lammergeiers be overwearied when I most need them? A day will come, I trust, when you will know what is and what is not necessary—and you will not find that knowledge written in any book, nor stored in any of the devices of the Vanished Ones. If you do not find that knowledge imprinted within your own heart, Mikayla, then, when you most need it, you will be without it. This is the only thing I can teach you, and if we are fortunate, that will be enough. Everything else, spells and such things, you could learn from some Oddling herb-wife. That is what Orogastus never knew—though there are some who would not care to hear me say so."

Mikayla had fastened on something else the Archimage had said. "You said that we had not yet learned much of how to communicate with the Skritek-kind. Will you then teach me the language of the hatchling Skriteks?"

The Archimage nodded. "It is more accurate to say you will learn to communicate with them within your heart. That knowledge may not be in words; I do not know if they truly have such a thing as one could call language; but you will be able to understand them."

"To understand a hatchling Skritek? I think I would rather learn to kill them!" Mikayla was still seeing in her mind's eye how Traneo had been devoured by that Skritek hatchling.

"That is a very cruel and shortsighted point of view. In the purpose of life there may be some reason even for the Skriteks; though I confess I do not yet know it." She noted Mikayla's surprised glance with inner amusement. "Oh, yes, there are many things even I do not know." She could tell this was a new idea to Mikayla, that there was anything the old sorceress did not know.

"You feel about the Skritek thus, because you personally can put them to no use, is it not so?" Haramis continued the lesson.

"I cannot imagine what good the Skriteks are to anyone."

"Is that the Skriteks' fault, or is it the failure of your imagination?" the Archimage asked. "If nothing else, their eggs are some use as food for the Oddlings."

Mikayla found herself wondering why the Oddlings did not keep some kind of domestic fowl instead; but it was true that there was no place in the Mire to house and run yard fowl of any kind. She thought that the advantage of not coping with Skriteks would at least allow the Oddlings to seek out some other food. But she did not want to sound quarrelsome, and so she held her peace.

Haramis lectured on for the rest of the morning. Then she selected a book on scrying and handed it to Mikayla. "After lunch, start reading this. And remember that I shall be questioning you on it later, so be sure to pay attention to what you are reading. Always remember, there is nothing in the world more important than learning. You never know when some seemingly insignificant thing will turn out to be vital. It's usually not the big things that kill or save you, it's the little details. So learn carefully and well."

Mikayla nodded, but she looked bored and rebellious. *Oh, well,* Haramis thought, *I don't care how she feels about me, just as long as she learns. But I don't understand her. I would have given everything I ever owned for the education I'm giving her—why can't she see its value?*

Mikayla disappeared after lunch while Haramis was in her study talking to Uzun. Haramis had assumed that she was in the library until she went to find her for dinner. But the library was empty, as was the bedroom she had told Enya to assign to the girl—had anyone told her that this was now her room? Haramis rolled her eyes and went down the hall toward Fiolon's room, willing to bet that she would find the girl there.

Sure enough, she heard Mikayla's voice as she approached the room. She stopped just outside the door to hear what the girl was saying. It took her only a few seconds to realize that Mikayla was not carrying on a conversation; she was reading aloud from the book on scrying. Haramis poked her head around the door. Fiolon was asleep, but Mikayla sat on a wooden stool at the side of his bed. With her left hand she held one of his hands, and she was balancing the book on her lap with her other hand and reading it aloud to him.

"I don't think he's getting much out of this," Haramis remarked, "and it's time for dinner."

Mikayla, sticking a finger in the book to mark where she was, twisted in place to look at Haramis. "If you mean that he's not absorbing every word I read," she said coldly, "no doubt you are correct. He was delirious before he fell asleep. But the sound of my voice does seem to calm him. Besides," she added before Haramis could protest her choice of reading location, "when I read aloud to him, I remember more of what I'm reading than I would if I were reading to myself."

Haramis decided it wasn't worth arguing about. She was tired and hungry and not used to having children about. "Come and eat dinner," she said, "and after dinner, I expect you to go to your own room."

"I have another room?" Mikayla asked.

"Yes," Haramis said firmly, "you do. I'll have Enya show you where it is after dinner."

Mikayla looked around the room that Enya showed her to. It was still on the same floor as the one Fiolon was in, which Mikayla was glad of. She didn't intend to be separated from Fiolon if she could possibly avoid it. One wall of the room was stone, obviously the outer wall of the Tower. It had two small glazed windows, through which nothing could be seen in the dark, but the rest of the wall was covered with tapestries.

The room was surprisingly warm for an outer room in a stone building, even though the remaining walls were covered with wood paneling and there was a fireplace surrounded by colored tiles. Mikayla investigated and found a small grille in the wall next to the bed, at about the level of her knees. Warm air flowed out through the grille, and that, combined with the heat from the fire, explained the room's unusual warmth. Mikayla pictured in her mind the other rooms she had seen and was pretty certain that she had seen grilles like this one in all of them. That explained why the Tower was warm enough for Haramis to keep Nyssomu servants in this climate, and it was probably also the reason why the Vispi here wore such filmy draperies instead of normal clothing.

The bed was grander than anything Mikayla had ever slept in. Its canopy was carved of gonda wood and hung with brocade, and the mattress was at the level of her shoulders. It had soft sheets and a large down comforter as well as three down pillows. Mikayla decided that she was in no danger of catching cold here, but she wasn't at all sure she wouldn't suffocate.

Someone had laid out a nightgown for her on a bench by the bed, next to the wardrobe. Dropping the book on scrying, which had not proved quite as dull as she had feared, on a table that was placed, along with a pair of red leather chairs, next to the fire, she put on the nightgown, climbed the three steps of the miniature wooden staircase set next to the bed, and wriggled her way under the covers. It *was* a bit suffocating, but Mikayla fell asleep too quickly to care.

In the next few days she learned many interesting things, even though she missed her home. After she had finished the book on scrying, Haramis taught her to scry into the Greenmire, which was the southern section of the Mazy Mire. Since this was on the other side of the country from the Tower on Mount Brom, it did at least establish that Mikayla could learn to see the entire land.

Haramis made her scry it in detail, right down to the tiny stinging insects, which made Mikayla glad to be in the Tower watching them, instead of in the swamp being stung by them.

"I suppose you can think of no reason for their existence, either?" Haramis asked Mikayla, with the air of a challenge.

Mikayla, looking at the ugly little things, said morosely that she personally could think of no special reason for their existence; but that, knowing something of the way Haramis's mind worked, she was quite sure there must be one, even if she herself did not yet know it. In any case she supposed the fish in the Mire enjoyed catching them, and they were some good, even if only for fish food.

"Good," said the Archimage, "you are beginning to understand some things about this land." Mikayla could not imagine what good that knowledge would be to her, but she supposed someday the Archimage would tell her—at least if it was anything she ought to know. And if not, she supposed there was no reason to burden her mind with it.

She spent every afternoon in Fiolon's room, reading whatever book she had been assigned aloud to him and telling him about her lessons. She noticed, however, that Haramis seemed determined that she and Fiolon not be alone together; after that first day, even when he was still sick and raving, there was always a servant there with them. As the weeks went by, Fiolon's fever broke and his mind cleared. Mikayla found it a considerable relief when he could carry on intelligible conversations again. But still, one of the servants was always with them, so Mikayla felt certain that Haramis's concern was not for Fiolon's health.

In fact, Haramis had a very lively concern for Fiolon's health; she was most eager to see him healthy enough to leave. But he had been very ill, and while his mind was healing rapidly, his body was not. He remained thin and pale, and it required the efforts of both Mikayla and a servant to move him from bed to chair.

At the beginning of summer, fearing that Fiolon might have some disease in addition to the lung fever, Haramis went so far as to send a lammergeier for a Vispi healer from the village of Movis on Mount Rotolo.

Mount Rotolo was the westernmost of the three mountain peaks of which Mount Brom, where the Tower was, was the eastern one. The middle peak, Mount Gidris, was sacred; no one lived there. Haramis herself had been there only once, on her Quest to fetch her Talisman. It had been in an ice cave on the southern flank, and the cave had collapsed around her when she removed the Talisman. Her lammergeier had pulled her out in the nick of time and Haramis hadn't been back to Mount Gidris since. She didn't intend to return there, either.

The healer examined Fiolon carefully, talked to him alone for a long time, spoke briefly and reassuringly to Mikayla, and told Haramis to have patience. "He'll be with you for some months yet, I feel," she told Haramis, "but he will recover fully in time. I am certain of that."

So Haramis continued to teach Mikayla in the mornings, refrained from asking how she spent the afternoons, and made certain that there was always a servant in Fiolon's room when Mikayla was not with Haramis. At least the girl was making progress. As the months went by she mastered scrying, as well as the simple teleportation Haramis used to clear the table or fetch a book from the library, although she made Mikayla fetch books in person so that she would learn where each book belonged and would be able to reshelve them properly. "Remember always that a book misshelved is knowledge lost." Mikayla sighed, nodded, and memorized the proper location of each book on the library shelves.

She also learned communication with the lammergeiers, although Haramis would not allow her to ride them. She now had clothing suitable to wear indoors, but nothing heavy enough to be worn outside ever found its way into her wardrobe. Mikayla intended to do something about that someday, but she was also learning when and how to resist Haramis and how much she could get away with. As long as she was allowed to see Fiolon every day, she tried not to upset Haramis too much.

It wasn't her fault that Haramis walked in one afternoon to find her and Fiolon playing teleport catch. Teleport catch was a game they had developed; it was played with a small—and preferably unbreakable—object. Today they were using a ladu fruit. The point of the game was to teleport the object to a place somewhere within arm's reach of the other person, who then had to catch it by hand without letting it hit the floor or the bed and then teleport it back. Since the object could be materialized anywhere in the half circle in front and to both sides of you, spotting the object in time to catch it was tricky—unless, of course, you cheated a bit and used telepathy to tell where the other person was sending it, which didn't work if the other person was using shields against telepathy. . . .

They had worked out several variations of the rules and the game had become quite competitive. Today they were both shielding their minds, which took a fair amount of concentration. Haramis watched from the doorway for quite a while before they noticed she was there. She had plenty of time to observe that while Mikayla was quite competent, Fiolon was much better than that.

The next day, Haramis had the healer back, and Fiolon started intensive physical therapy. He was walking within a week, however reluctantly, and two weeks later Haramis decreed that he was well enough to return home to the Citadel. She completely ignored Mikayla's protest that Fiolon was too ill—or had been too ill—to be sent home in the depths of winter. "Not that the climate here is any different in the summer," she added.

"We'll start studying weather and land sense next," Haramis informed her. "I assure you that you will soon learn to notice the difference in seasons—even here."

# 7

*The Archimage ordered riding clothes and camping gear* assembled for Fiolon. Since the Tower was not stocked with much in the way of human clothing, it was fortunate that he was small enough to wear Vispi clothing when necessary. As soon as the servants had packed supplies for him and dressed him in warm clothing, she led him and Mikayla down the long flights of stairs which finally opened onto a great plaza at the front of the Tower. Mikayla hadn't noticed this plaza before; they had landed on the top of the other side of the building when they arrived and she hadn't been outdoors since. With Fiolon for company, she hadn't been getting too stir-crazy, but she was afraid that this was about to change. She had spent a large part of her life outdoors before coming here, and she had been accustomed to coming and going as she wished for several years before being shut up in the Tower. Fiolon's imminent departure was making Mikayla feel very anxious; she felt even more like a prisoner than she had before when both of them were there.

Haramis had neglected to provide her with any clothing heavy enough to be worn outside, and Mikayla suspected that the omission was deliberate. At the moment she was wrapped in one of Haramis's cloaks, which was too long for her but would keep her from freezing while she said good-bye to Fiolon.

But Mikayla's feet, in the slippers she wore, were getting very cold and wet. The plaza was ankle-deep in snow.

There was a great chasm on the far side of the plaza, with no apparent way across it. Mikayla expected to see the Archimage summon the lammergeiers. Instead a large door to their left opened, and a Vispi led a pair of fronials down a ramp that led upward beyond the door. Mikayla gaped at them. "How do they get across there?" she asked pointing to the chasm. "Magic?"

The Archimage looked cross. "Not a bit of it," she answered. "When Orogastus built this Tower, he equipped it with every bit of the technology of the Vanished Ones that he could beg, buy, or steal. Of course," she added with disdain, "*he* thought it was sorcery. I think even after so many years, he never knew the difference. But you, Mikayla, at least, should learn what that difference is. It is not right to command the lammergeiers when nonmagical methods will work. This will be one of your most important lessons; when it is right to use sorcery, and when it is not."

"And I'm really going to learn it from someone who uses sorcery to clear the breakfast table," Mikayla muttered rebelliously.

Haramis ignored her. With practice, it was getting easier—and the Lords of the Air knew she was getting plenty of practice.

The fronials were a fine matched pair, and Fiolon watched with amazement as they stood quietly while his baggage was put on one of them by the Vispi groom.

He looked over the edge of the great chasm, with a river flowing at the bottom. "This would be very fine, Lady, if either the fronials—or I—or my baggage—could fly," he said politely. "Are you going to teach me to fly? Or can these fly already?"

"No, of course not," said Haramis. "Although Orogastus probably thought that *this* was sorcery." She pulled from the depths of her robe a small silver pipe and blew on it. It emitted a high, thin tone, and as the children watched in amazement a narrow steel causeway extruded from the edge of the chasm and quickly grew into a bridge.

Mikayla gasped. She thought there might be something very interesting in learning about this new technology—at least as interesting as the music boxes she and Fiolon had scrupulously divided between them. She had kept three, two of which were duplicates of ones they had found, and the rest he had carefully packed along with the clothing and food the Archimage had provided him. As long as she was stuck here with the Archimage, she might as well learn as much as she could. And preferably learn things that interested *her,* not just what Lady Haramis thought a proper young Archimage-in-training ought to know.

Unfortunately, Haramis seemed to have no interest in technology, and she definitely had no feel for it. *She can complain all she wants about my lack of feeling for magic,* Mikayla thought, *but at least I can feel technology. All she can do is use it—if she can figure out somehow how it works—or if Orogastus told her how it worked before she killed him.*

Ignoring the Archimage's disapproving glare and the snow soaking her house slippers, Mikayla slogged across the plaza to where Fiolon was preparing to mount the lead fronial. "You will be careful, won't you?" she said. "I don't know why she's sending you off on a fronial in the middle of winter—" She didn't finish the sentence.

Fiolon put an arm around her shoulders and gave her a reassuring hug. "I'll be careful, Mika. I've camped out in the winter before—we did this a few years ago, remember?"

"Yes, but you weren't alone then. I was with you, and we took two of the guardsmen along—it was the only way my parents would let us go; they said it was too dangerous otherwise." Mikayla bit her lip. "I don't think Haramis would mourn overmuch if you met with a fatal accident." She looked straight into his eyes. "But I warn you, Fio, if you go and get yourself killed, I'll never speak to you again!"

They both chuckled at the silliness of that threat. "I won't get killed," Fiolon said. "I promise." He looked at Haramis and sighed. "She's glaring at us again, and I really do need to leave before it gets dark."

"Yes," Mikayla agreed, "I know you do."

"Then maybe you would consider letting go of my jacket," Fiolon said.

Mikayla looked down at her hands. She was clinging to the sleeves of Fiolon's short jacket so tightly that her knuckles were white. She forced her stiff fingers to release their grip, then defiantly leaned forward and kissed Fiolon on the cheek. "Take care," she said fiercely. "And fare well."

"Be well, Mika," Fiolon said, patting her shoulder and turning to mount the fronial. He looked down at her. "Try to be good."

"Do you really think Haramis is going to give me any chance to be otherwise?" Mikayla tried to smile. She didn't want Fiolon's last memory of her to be of a tear-streaked face.

She held the smile by pure effort of will until Fiolon had his back to her and was halfway across the bridge. By then Haramis had crossed the plaza to join her. She put a hand on Mikayla's shoulder, but Mikayla angrily shrugged it off.

As they stood watching Fiolon ride out of sight across the causeway and down the slopes, with the second fronial behind him on a leading rope, Mikayla asked again, "Why should you have sent him on this long journey alone by bad roads and passes and through heavy snow, when you can command the lammergeiers and by tonight he could have been safe in his own bed?"

Haramis sighed. "How many times do I have to tell you, Mikayla, that it is not wise to use the lammergeiers if it is not absolutely necessary?"

Mikayla shrugged. Fiolon was out of sight by now, and the girl returned to the Tower and started to trudge up the stairs, head bowed and eyes cast down to the step in front of her. Haramis followed slowly, with an occasional pause to catch her breath, but Mikayla maintained a steady automatic pace all the way up to the living quarters in the middle of the Tower. And she didn't speak to Haramis for the rest of the day.

That evening after supper, Haramis gave her a small fabric-covered box. When Mikayla opened the latch, she found that it contained two silver spheres. When she picked one up, it made the same sort of chiming noise as the small spheres she and Fiolon had found in the ruins, except that this one was louder and lower-pitched, probably because its diameter was approximately twice that of the one she still wore about her neck.

She hadn't shown it to Haramis, and since she kept it tucked under her clothes, its chiming was muted, so she didn't think Haramis knew about it. Mikayla had the firm intention of keeping it, as a reminder of Fiolon and how happy they had been that day in the ruins. Haramis often spoke of her approaching death, leaving Mikayla to hope that she might be free within a few years. Haramis couldn't separate Mikayla and Fiolon if she were dead.

If Haramis knew of the small sphere pendant, she made no mention of it, merely telling Mikayla to pick up the second sphere. It chimed at a slightly lower pitch, even though the spheres were outwardly identical.

"Why do they chime at different pitches, Lady?" Mikayla asked.

"Do they?" Haramis asked in surprise. "I never paid that much attention to the sound. What I want you to do with them is this—" She took both spheres into one hand and rotated them silently about each other first in one direction and then in the other. "You try it."

She handed the spheres back to Mikayla. Side by side, they were the same width as Mikayla's palm, and when she tried to rotate them, they clinked against each other and made clanging noises as they moved. She tried to rotate them the other way, and promptly dropped one, which rolled off her lap and onto the floor with a loud clang. Mikayla winced at the sound and hastily crawled under the table to retrieve the sphere.

When she resurfaced, Haramis was looking at her with an expression of long suffering. "Take them to your room and practice with them before you go to bed each night and when you wake up each morning. At least if you drop them on your bed, they won't make so much noise." She stood up, obviously preparing to retire for the night. "You need to practice with these until you can rotate them in either direction, in either hand, silently."

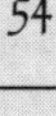

This prospect seemed so unlikely to Mikayla that she didn't even think to ask why she should learn to do this until after Haramis had already left the room. Sighing, she put the spheres back into their box and went up the stairs to the bedroom Haramis had assigned her. She undressed and put on her nightgown, thinking that she might as well go to bed, since there was nothing else for her to do here anyway.

She had thought that she was lonely as a child, before Fiolon had come to live at the Citadel, but then she had had her family, even if they did ignore her much of the time. And the servants at the Citadel had been friendly. Here only Enya, the housekeeper, spoke to her at all; if she passed any of the other servants in the hallways they pretended that she was invisible—or perhaps that they were. Uzun was willing to talk to her now, and she sat with him sometimes when Haramis was busy elsewhere in the evenings. But Uzun, being a harp, couldn't move at all. And Mikayla, by means of careful questioning interspersed with more general conversation, had discovered that he was indeed blind. Apparently he had fallen into his final illness quite suddenly, and

Haramis had changed him into a harp because it was the first spell she could find that would ensure his continued consciousness. Mikayla had heard of blind harpers, and of course harps didn't have eyes, but most harps weren't sentient. Uzun had excellent hearing, even better than Mikayla's, which was quite good, and used that to compensate for his lack of sight and mobility. But still he knew only what happened within his hearing, in the Archimage's study and the hallway just outside it. Mikayla often wondered just how much he minded it. She was certain that it bothered him to some degree; she could sense a sort of sadness emanating from him even when his "voice" was most cheerful, and when he played songs just for himself, they tended to be melancholy.

Sitting cross-legged on her bed, she took out the spheres again. She shook each one next to her ear, listening to the difference in tone and wondering how this was achieved. She wished that Fiolon was there to ask about them—or even to show them to. *He would love these,* she thought wistfully. *I wish he were here now. I wonder how he's doing on his journey home.*

She held the spheres along the palm of her right hand and pulled the little sphere on the green ribbon free from her nightgown. She amused herself by striking it gently against the two larger spheres and listening to the sounds it made. She noticed that, for some reason, when she touched it to the top of the two larger spheres, it was reflected three times in each sphere, and when she held it beside them and looked down at the arrangement, there was a triangle between them, outlined in reflected spheres. At first she could see the palm of her hand through the triangle—after all, that *was* what was there—but after she stared at them for a minute her vision blurred, and as it cleared she could see Fiolon, curled up in a sleep sack next to a small fire. She was so startled that she dropped the spheres on her bed, and when she tried again, she couldn't get the vision back. But she fell asleep that night with a smile on her face, thinking that perhaps the spheres might have uses Haramis didn't suspect.

Mikayla awakened shortly after dawn the next morning, and promptly picked up the spheres again. She was curious to see if she could summon up again the vision of Fiolon she had seen the night before. She rolled the spheres in her hand, a trick she found was getting easier—at least in the direction she was moving them—until she felt in her consciousness the faint beginnings of a trance state. The spheres in her hand grew warmer, almost so warm as to be uncomfortable. She touched the sphere that hung around her neck to the other two and looked at their conjunction.

Sure enough, there was Fiolon, asleep in a sleep sack spread on the ground near the pair of tethered fronials. *What a lay-abed,* Mikayla thought in amusement. *I wonder if I can wake him up.* She gently shook the arrangement of spheres in her hands, causing them to chime softly.

In her vision, Fiolon opened his eyes and sat up suddenly, reaching for his breast. Was his sphere chiming as well? Mikayla wished that she could hear as well as see what was happening around him.

Well, perhaps she could. At least she could try. She felt herself reach out somehow, with her mind, and something seemed to stretch inside her head. Now she could hear the soft snorting noises of the fronials, and the rustle of tree branches, and even Fiolon's breathing, which was somewhat ragged, as if he had been wakened suddenly from a dream.

"Fiolon?" she said softly, not sure whether she spoke aloud or not. "Can you hear me?"

Fiolon twisted his head to look all about him. "Mika? Where are you?"

*This is wonderful!* Mikayla thought. *Maybe the Archimage can't separate us after all.*

"I'm still stuck in this wretched Tower, Fio—where you left me!" she added accusingly. "But I think I've discovered something interesting. Look at the sphere around your neck."

Fiolon looked all around him again, then shrugged and pulled the sphere out from under his tunic. It chimed as he moved it, and the small sphere in Mikayla's hand chimed as well, even though she was holding it perfectly still. The larger spheres touching it chimed in resonance with it. Fiolon held his sphere in front of his face, and his face appeared in Mikayla's small sphere, overlaying the scene of his surroundings. "I can see your face in this, Mika!" he said in surprise. "What is this, some sort of magic? Did the Archimage teach you this?"

"No, she didn't," Mikayla snapped. "I do still have a brain, Fio; I didn't drop it in the river when she dragged us onto the lammergeiers. As for these being magic," she added, thinking it over, "I think she'd be very cross to hear you call this magic. Remember where we found these—they're probably some sort of device the Vanished Ones used to communicate with each other. Maybe they used them in the theater so that they could prompt an actor who forgot his lines."

"You may be right," said Fiolon. "There were lots of different ones, but the two we took were a matched set. Maybe they are linked to each other. But if they were just made for use in the theater, how can we talk over this much distance?"

"I have a theory about that," Mikayla explained. "Haramis gave me a box with two spheres of the same general type, but larger in size—I wish you were here to see them; they're exactly the same size, but their pitches are different, and when I asked Haramis why, she didn't seem to know or care—I don't think she ever even noticed. Do you suppose she can't hear differences in pitch?"

"I've heard that there are some people like that," Fiolon said. "I think they call it tone-deaf. But she would hardly have made Master Uzun into a harp if she were tone-deaf—or if she weren't particularly fond of music. And the old songs all say that she was very musical."

"Maybe the ability to hear pitch degrades when one gets old," Mikayla said. "She's very old, isn't she?"



"A bit over two hundreds," Fiolon said. "She was about to be married when the last Great Threefold Conjunction occurred, and the next one is due in about four years from now. So she's probably between two hundred ten and two hundred fifteen."

"But people don't live to be that old!" Mikayla protested. "Are you sure?"

"She's not exactly an ordinary person," Fiolon said. "She's the Archimage. And I'm very sure that if she's the Haramis who was one of the triplet princesses who defeated the evil sorcerer Orogastus, then she's over two hundreds old."

"I don't think I'd *want* to live that long," Mikayla said, shuddering. The spheres in her grasps chimed softly.

"Why did she give the spheres to you?" Fiolon asked curiously.

"She told me to practice rolling them around in my hand, but I haven't a clue as to why."

"I'll bet it's to make your fingers more supple and give you more control," Fiolon said. "You've seen the magical gestures the Oddlings make—like the one against the evil eye. She's probably going to be teaching you magic that requires you to use your hands and fingers very precisely."

That made sense to Mikayla. "You may be right; it certainly

seems reasonable. The Lady Archimage doesn't deign to explain anything to me or give reasons for anything she tells me to do." She sighed. "It's a pity she didn't choose you instead; you already use your hands more precisely than I'll ever be able to do. I can't even play a small lap harp."

"But she chose you, Mikayla, and she has to have known what she was doing. After all, she is the Archimage."

Mikayla shrugged. "She certainly does seem to do as she pleases. Look what she did to poor Uzun. But I'm glad that I can talk to you, even if we can't be together." She chewed on her lower lip. "I really miss you. Why did she have to separate us? I bet I'd learn what she wants me to much faster if you were learning it with me."

Fiolon looked grave. "Does she know you're doing this? Talking to me through the spheres?"

Mikayla shrugged. "I have no idea. It depends on just how omniscient she is, I guess. On the off chance that she doesn't, I don't think I'll tell her just yet, so I'd better get up and dressed before somebody comes looking for me. I'll talk to you again later, all right? I'm supposed to practice with these spheres when I wake up and just before I go to bed, so it'll probably be one of those times."

"If you're sure that the Archimage won't object . . ." Fiolon said uncertainly.

"I'm sure that if she does object, she'll let me know," Mikayla said. "Please, Fiolon; I need all the help I can get. I'd never have reasoned out why she wanted me to practice with the spheres—you can really help me, if you will."

"Of course I will, Mika. As long as I can."

Mikayla did make some effort to learn what Haramis wished to teach her, but she found it very difficult. When she was feeling charitable, she told herself that Haramis had never taught anyone before, in addition to having had no formal training herself, so it made sense that the "lessons" she gave were haphazard and not well organized. Mikayla coped by discussing everything with Fiolon, who seemed to have a much better intuitive understanding of magic and related subjects than she did, and if neither of them could work something out, she waited until Haramis had retired for the night and crept down to the study to ask Master Uzun. He almost always had the answer or could tell her where in the library to look it up. She became quite fond of the Oddling/harp and often went down to see him at night just to talk, even when she didn't have any specific questions. She was lonely, and she suspected that Uzun was much more lonely than she would ever be. Uzun told her a lot about what Haramis had been like as a child, although that information wasn't of much use now.

"Surely she must have changed a great deal after she became Archimage," Mikayla said one night as she sat by the study hearth near Uzun. "The girl you describe isn't much like the old woman I have to deal with."

"For a while," Uzun said thoughtfully, "she did change. She was softer, less sure of herself, less certain that her way was the right way to do everything. But, as time passed, and everyone she used to know died off, she started to change back."

"And then some." Mikayla sighed. "By now, she's convinced that her way is the *only* way to do things. Her rules are the only ones that matter—and her rules aren't even consistent." She rested her chin on her drawn-up knees and stared into the fire. "She says that we shouldn't use technology, like the devices of the Vanished Ones, and that magic should be used only for important necessary purposes—and then she uses magic to send the dirty dishes back to the kitchen. But let her catch me and Fiolon using exactly the same magic to play catch and sharpen our skills, and she pitches a fit and sends him away, by fronial, through the snow, in the middle of winter. I don't think she even cared if he caught lung fever again, just as long as he didn't do it here and inconvenience her."

There was the descending glissando of harp strings that was Uzun's equivalent of a sigh. "I know it's hard for you, Princess," he said, "but try to be patient with her. Fiolon did reach the Citadel safely, you know that."

"Yes, thanks to the Lords of the Air," Mikayla said. "But I miss him so much! If Haramis didn't have to be parted from you, why did Fiolon have to leave?"

"I think you had better go to bed now," Uzun said. "It's very late, and you do need *some* sleep."

"In other words, you're not going to tell me." Mikayla got to her feet. She didn't bother looking for a candle; by now she knew every inch of hallway between her room and the study and could cover the distance silently in pitch blackness. "Good night, Uzun."

"Good night, Princess."

• • •

But Mikayla's attempts to have patience with Haramis were somewhat less than successful. One particularly frustrating lesson a few days later was simply more than she could cope with. She hadn't had enough sleep the night before, and what sleep she had managed to get had been disturbed by nightmares. She had a headache, lunch had tasted funny, and she suspected that she was coming down with a cold. She felt generally wretched, and her lesson reflected it. She dropped her spheres at least five times before Haramis gave a long-suffering sigh and told her to put them away, and then she managed to knock over the scrying bowl. At the time it had contained only water, not the water-and-ink mixture they sometimes used, but Haramis had looked pained and made a fuss over mopping up the water.

Haramis had a knack of making it clear, without having to use words, that she considered Mikayla badly raised, stupid, lazy, unmotivated, and totally unworthy to be Archimage. While this attitude did hurt, Mikayla could have tolerated it if it had meant that Haramis was willing to give up and send her home. But Haramis wasn't. She started, for at least the fiftieth time, her standard lecture on how lucky Mikayla was to be getting this training instead of being thrust into the job unprepared as she, Haramis, had been, and why couldn't Mikayla put a little effort into her lessons, and why was she being such a sulky, ungrateful brat. . . .

Mikayla could have given the entire speech herself from memory. She was doing her best, even if it wasn't very good today, and she was so angry that she wanted to throw every portable object in the room at Haramis. Since this, however, would probably have resulted in at least a modified magical duel, which was a bit more than Mikayla wanted to try today, she used words instead.

"Before you came and kidnapped me," she screamed at the Archimage, "I had a life, and a family—even if they didn't pay much attention to me. I had a friend, and you brought me here and sent him away. You never asked if I wanted to be Archimage—you told me I was going to do it, you dragged me off to this horrid waste, and started making me learn all these stupid lessons regardless of whether I wanted to learn them or not!

"Before you kidnapped me, I was free. I could go out if I wanted to, I could study what I wanted to. I don't know how you ever expect me to get any land sense here; I'm about as cut off from any contact with the land as I could possibly be. You won't even let me go outdoors, much less into the Mire or the Dylex or any region in this land where anything grows!

"Maybe at home nobody cared much about me, but at least they weren't bothering me. They weren't hovering over me every minute of the day saying 'you must do this' and 'an Archimage mustn't do that.' Before I came here I was Mikayla; now I'm just 'Haramis in training.' I want my life back! I want my self back! I hate it here! I wish I were dead!

"Every time I find some device of the Vanished Ones that's actually interesting or fun to play with, and something I could learn something from, you take it away and tell me that it's just a distraction from the study of pure magic which is the proper pursuit of the Archimage—which is incredibly hypocritical, considering that you've lived for centuries in a Tower that Orogastus put together with all the technology of the Vanished Ones he could amass! But the Archimage isn't supposed to use anything practical; the Archimage has to be one with the land. Well, I don't *want* to be one with the land! I want to be one with myself! I want my self back! *I don't want to grow up to be like you!*"

By the end of this outburst Haramis was staring at her, with her mouth actually hanging open, apparently at a loss for words. Mikayla fled to her room and locked herself in before Haramis could decide on a course of action. She stayed locked in her room for the rest of the day, and no one called her for dinner.

When she went down to breakfast the next morning, Haramis acted as if nothing at all had happened. She simply announced the lesson plans for the day as if she had never heard Mikayla speak a word against the idea of becoming Archimage. Mikayla had a sudden vision of years of this, of sitting across from Haramis at mealtimes, of listening to Haramis lecture endlessly on. . . . Mikayla felt doomed. She wished that she could just curl up somewhere and die. But she was young and healthy. And besides, she didn't really want to be dead—she just didn't want to live this way.

# 8

*Haramis looked at Mikayla, who sat across the breakfast* table from her, listlessly stirring her cooked grains, and suppressed a sigh. It had been almost a year since Fiolon had left, and Mikayla was definitely still showing magical talent, although her powers had not increased as Haramis had hoped they would once Fiolon was out of the way and Mikayla wasn't wasting her time and energy with him. Haramis was uneasy. She had expected Mikayla to improve when Fiolon was gone, but the child had promptly developed a major case of the sulks. By now, it seemed to have sunk into her basic personality. Was this sullen girl really intended to be the next Archimage?

It wasn't that she was rude anymore, Haramis reflected. Her behavior in that respect had improved markedly since Fiolon's departure. She was quiet, speaking only when spoken to; she was obedient, doing exactly as she was told. But the second she finished any appointed task, she slumped into the nearest chair or onto the nearest bench and stared at her lap. She appeared to have no real interest in magic, despite her undoubted aptitude for it, and worse yet, she seemed to have lost all interest in anything else in life. Of course Haramis knew that she herself wasn't interested in anything much outside of magic, but surely she wasn't so depressing about it. Uzun was more alive than Mikayla seemed at the moment. And he ate almost as much.

"Mikayla." The girl raised a blank face from her bowl to meet Haramis's eyes. Haramis tried to think of something to say to rouse her. Unfortunately nothing came to her. "Did you practice with the spheres this morning?"

"Yes, Lady." The tone was flat, and there was no change in the expression—or lack thereof—on the child's face.

"How are you doing with them?"

"Very well, Lady."

*This conversation is going nowhere fast,* Haramis reflected grimly. *I was young once, surely I* ought *to be able to communicate with her.* "You'll have to show me later how you're coming along with them," she said, trying to sound pleasant and encouraging.

"As you wish, Lady."



Haramis gave up. "Eat your breakfast, child," she ordered. She strongly suspected that without a direct command, Mikayla would sit there, stirring the stuff and staring at it for the rest of the morning. She made a mental note to ask Enya to find out what foods Mikayla liked and serve them; she didn't want the girl to lose more weight than she already had.

*What is there here that might interest her?* Haramis thought back to her first vision of Mikayla, playing with Fiolon and the music boxes, wanting to take one apart to see how it worked. *If she likes the music boxes,* Haramis reflected, *she'd probably be interested in other devices of the Vanished Ones. And goodness knows Orogastus left enough of them lying about here. I shoved them all into the storeroom on the lowest level when I came here, but some of them probably still work. I'd have to look at them first, however, because some of them are probably lethal.* For Haramis, who was not at all fond of technology and hated rules that had to be reasoned with the head, instead of felt in soul and heart, this was an onerous chore.

*She'd probably love Orogastus's "magic mirror" as well,* Haramis thought grimly, *but I want to wait until her scrying is more reliable before I show that to her. I don't want her to think that Vanished Ones' devices can be an acceptable substitute for our own abilities.*

• • •

Leaving Mikayla to finish her breakfast, Haramis went to her study. She sat in her chair and leaned Uzun against her shoulder, as if he were in truth the harp he was in seeming. She stroked her cheek against his satiny wood—a liberty that Uzun tolerated, realizing that something was seriously troubling his oldest friend.

"Honestly, Uzun, I don't know what I'm going to do with that girl."

"She does just what you tell her to," Uzun pointed out.

"True." Haramis sighed. "It's the way she does it. If it weren't impossible, I'd think that I had gotten the wrong child, but she was definitely the one in my vision."

"Are you sure that you're supposed to be training her?" Uzun asked. "The Archimage Binah didn't train you, and you've done a fine job."

"You trained me, Uzun," Haramis pointed out. "I didn't come to the job head-blind. Mikayla had no magical training whatsoever before she came here."

"She obviously has magical ability," Uzun said consolingly. "And she's learned a lot over the past two years. She used to come here in the evenings and tell me what she was learning, and she and Fiolon came to visit me every night from the time he could walk until he left."

"They did?" Haramis said in surprise.

"I guess they must have waited until you went to bed and wouldn't see them," Uzun remarked. "I did wonder why they were up and about so late."

"She does have talent, but she doesn't seem to want to use it," Haramis protested. "I was never like that—I was following you around demanding that you teach me before I could walk properly!"

She slumped back into her chair, releasing Uzun suddenly and unexpectedly. He rocked a bit as he settled back onto his base. The harp let out a sound midway between a twang of strings and what would have been a gasp in a human. "Haramis?" Uzun said in inquiry, and then more urgently: "Haramis! What's wrong?"

Haramis was unable to reply. She felt very strange. The entire left side of her body had a pins-and-needles sensation, as if she had slept on it wrong, and when she tried to move, she found that she couldn't. Even half her face seemed frozen in place. She felt very confused, as if something were seriously amiss, but she didn't know what. Was there some disaster with the land that she had failed to notice? *Am I dying?* she wondered. *I can't be dying yet; Mikayla's not trained!*

It seemed forever that she lay slumped in the chair while Uzun vibrated agitatedly next to her, but in truth it couldn't have been more than the third part of an hour. Then whatever it was—some sort of spell?—wore off and she could move again. But why would anyone cast a spell against her? She had no enemies.

She found she didn't want to think about this now. So she tried to calm Uzun and make light of the incident. "I'm sure it was nothing, Uzun; I probably slept at an odd angle last night, that's all." *But it does remind me of the work yet to be done.* She pulled herself out of her chair, trying to hide the effort it took. "I'm going to find Mikayla. I think it's time I taught her weather magic; it's an important part of the Archimage's work."

"I think it's a bit soon for that, Lady." Uzun's protest was formal, and Haramis ignored it.

"I'll be the judge of that, old friend." She smiled at him, momentarily forgetting that he could not see her, partly to take away the sting of her words and partly to hide how frightened she suddenly felt. *I may not have as much time as I thought.*

"You always were stubborn." Uzun's voice rippled through a soft glissando along the strings. "Do as you wish; you will anyway."

Haramis found Mikayla in her bedchamber, sitting cross-legged on her unmade bed with her back to the door, hunched over something in her hands.

"What are you doing?" she inquired.

Mikayla jumped, and two silver spheres fell onto the bed. Haramis walked over and picked them up. She thought that she saw Mikayla shove something into the neck of her tunic, but she wasn't sure, and anyway she had more important matters on her mind.

She handed the spheres, which were unusually warm—no doubt from the warmth of Mikayla's hands, to her and said, "Put these away and come to the workroom. It's time for the next phase of your training."

She turned on her heel and walked out of the room, ignoring the groan of inarticulate protest behind her.

Mikayla dragged herself into the workroom just as Haramis was about to lose all patience and send Enya to fetch the girl. But she knew that scolding the child would only set her back up, so she forced herself to smile at her instead.

"Come join me here at this table, child. Do you recognize it?"

Mikayla slouched over to the side of the table and looked down at it. It was a variation of the traditional sand-table used for military battle planning, but instead of an expanse of blank sand and a collection of military counters, it used several different colors of sand, a few rocks, quite a bit of finely crushed white stone, and water. And, remarkably enough, it broke through Mikayla's indifference. For the first time in ages, Haramis saw a flash of interest in her face and intelligence in her eyes.

"It's the Kingdom," Mikayla said promptly. "Here's the Greenmire"—she pointed to the green sand—"and here's the junction of the Golobar and the Lower Mutar rivers, where you" —she hesitated—"found me and Fiolon."

Haramis wondered if the word Mikayla had censored was "kidnapped" and noted that she had not mentioned their Oddling companion at all, despite the fact that he had been with them at the time.

"Here's the Blackmire," Mikayla continued, "and the Goldenmire, and the Citadel is on this rock here. And we're here." She pointed unerringly to the heap of crushed white stone that represented Mount Brom. "And Fiolon's here," she added defiantly, indicating the Citadel Rock.

Haramis chose to ignore that last remark. "You are correct, Mikayla; this table is a model of the land. But it is not a toy or merely a map. It has a use. Can you guess what that is?"

Mikayla started to roll her eyes, then quickly lowered them. "No, Lady," she replied, sinking back into her stupid-and-submissive act. Haramis wanted to shake her.

"Stay here and study it, then, until you can think of a use for it," she said tartly. "I shall see you at luncheon." She turned on her heel and stalked out of the room.

Five minutes later she was pacing the study, venting her exasperation to Uzun. "That child is going to drive me insane!" she complained, explaining what had transpired in the workroom.

Uzun's strings rippled uneasily. "Maybe she already has. Are you saying that you left her alone and unsupervised and told her to play with the sand-table?"

"Of course not," Haramis replied impatiently. "I told her to study it, not to touch it."

"Did you forbid her to touch it?" Uzun asked anxiously.

"No, I didn't. She'd probably mess it up just to spite me, the little wretch. Why are you so worried, Uzun?"

"Because that table is one of the most powerful magical objects in this Tower," Uzun said bluntly, "and despite the names you call her, the Princess Mikayla has a good mind and considerable natural magical ability."

"Which she refuses to use," Haramis pointed out.

"That could change at any time," Uzun warned. "I believe that you are seriously underestimating her. And it doesn't take much intelligence to discern that the table can be used for weather magic, especially if the bowls of water and the powdered rock you use for rain and snow are sitting next to it."

"They're in the rack at the end of the table, where they belong," Haramis informed him. "Where else should they be? Without the activating spell they're just flakes of rock and drops of water."

"New spells can be created to do the same job the old ones did," Uzun said sternly. "Magic is a matter of focus and intent, and Mikayla does have both."

"You worry too much, old friend." Haramis smiled fondly, moving to his side to stroke the smooth wood of his frame.

"Indeed?" Uzun said in a soft ripple, sounding almost amused. "Did you intend for it to be raining here today?"

Haramis whirled and dashed to the study window. Uzun was right; a thin stream of rain was falling precisely into the center of the courtyard, and the snow was melting in a circle around where the rain fell. She heard the harp chuckling behind her as she cursed under her breath and ran for the workroom, where she arrived with a stitch in her side and difficulty breathing.

"Stop that!" she gasped.

Mikayla looked up from the table, where she was carefully dripping water off of her little fingertip onto the image of Mount Brom. "I believe that I've figured out what this table is used for, Lady," she said calmly. "It appears to work quite well for weather witching."

Haramis felt a sharp stabbing pain in her head and forced herself not to clutch at it. Bad enough to be gasping for breath without displaying further signs of weakness. "I told you to study the table, not to touch it or play with it!" she snapped. "I told you it was not a toy."

Mikayla looked bewildered. "But if it were dangerous, Lady, surely you would not have left me alone with it. And how was I supposed to study it without touching it? One learns about things by experimentation, by forming a theory, testing the theory, and creating a new theory if the first one doesn't work, until one has a model that accurately represents reality—or at least the portions of it that one needs to deal with. And you need a bigger sand-table," she added. "This one doesn't have room for Labornok or Var, and surely Labornok at least is your responsibility; the kingdoms have been united for almost two hundreds now."

Haramis's head felt as though it were about to split open, and she did not feel up to debating with Mikayla or anyone else her alleged responsibility to the inhabitants of a country that had attacked her home, violently murdered her parents and everyone else they could get their hands on, and tried to do the same to her. Even if the events in question had occurred a long time ago, in Haramis's memory they were as clear as if they had happened last week. *I must be getting old,* she thought, *if I can remember long-ago events more clearly than recent ones.* Aloud she said simply, "Go and wash for dinner, Mikayla. I shall see you at the table."

As she left the room to find some willow-bark tea for her headache, she heard Mikayla's voice behind her.

"But it's only lunchtime."

After lunch, Haramis gave Mikayla an old Chronicle on the history of Ruwenda to read, hoping that this would at least keep the girl out of trouble for the rest of the day. She felt much too tired to deal with her.

Haramis went to her room, feeling a need to be by herself for a while, although she was trying hard not to think of the strange episode of that morning. She lay down on her bed, planning to rest just for an hour or two, but her weariness overcame her and she didn't stir until Enya came to see why she hadn't come down for dinner.

"Dinner?" Haramis sat up and pushed her hair out of her face. "Is it dinnertime already?" She looked out her windows and was surprised to see that it was dark. "I must have fallen asleep."

"You certainly did, Lady," Enya replied. "I already fed Princess Mikayla, and she's sitting talking with Master Uzun, so you don't need to worry about her. Why don't you just stay here in your room and let me bring you a tray? You look as though you could use the rest."

"Thank you, Enya," Haramis said. "I am a bit tired and a tray in my room sounds like a good idea."

As soon as Enya left, Haramis dragged herself out of bed and went to look in her mirror. Enya was correct. Obviously she had overtired herself, for the glamour that she usually maintained automatically, the spell that made people see what she wished them to see when they looked at her, was gone. The face that stared back at her was her true face, pale and gaunt and old. "I'd better stay in my room until I get my strength back," she muttered to herself. "Uzun can't see me, and Enya knows what I am. But it's a bit soon to have to explain this to Mikayla."

Haramis had forgotten that Mikayla had seen her earlier in the day. In fact, Mikayla had been staring at Haramis all through lunch, and Haramis hadn't even noticed. And now Mikayla was having a long talk with Uzun.

"Is the Lady Haramis ill, Uzun?" she asked him. "She didn't look well at lunch, and she didn't come down for dinner at all. Enya says she's just tired, but she looked a lot worse than tired today."

"What do you mean by 'worse than tired'?" Uzun asked.

Mikayla sighed. "I wish you could see," she said. "Usually she looks sort of ageless—I mean her hair is white, but she doesn't really look old."

Uzun sighed, a faint ripple of harp strings. "She used to have black hair when she was a girl, but when she became Archimage she changed the color to white, and she was only about two decades old then, not old enough for white hair to be natural. She made herself look older then, too—as if she were four decades old or so—and then she kept that appearance for as long as I could still see her. I don't know if her appearance changed after I became a harp. . . ."

"It didn't," Mikayla said. "She looked like that every time I saw her—until today. Today her hair was a sort of grayish yellow and she looked really old. And her face was thin and sort of sunken. Was she using a spell to change her appearance all those years?"

"A very minor one," Uzun said. "Properly it's called a glamour, not a spell."

"Oh, I know that one!" Mikayla said. "I used a variation of it when I was very small. That's the spell you use to keep people from noticing you when you don't want them to see what you're doing, like when you want to go play outdoors and don't want to get stopped on your way out of the castle. Or if you're in a room and someone you don't want to see you comes in—you just sit very still and think 'I am not here' and they don't see you."

"Sounds like the same basic principle," Uzun agreed.

"Are you saying I could have used it to make it appear that I was neatly dressed when my clothes were streaked with mud and my braids were coming apart?" Mikayla asked. "I should have learned that version, too; it would have saved me a lot of scoldings."

Uzun chuckled. "A glamour can be used for that, yes. But I suspect that in your case, Princess, the scoldings were more of a minor nuisance than a serious problem, so you never bothered to learn to use a glamour in that way."

Mikayla giggled. "You're right. It always seemed so stupid to me, the idea that I should look clean and beautiful at all times. If you go out in the swamps, you get muddy, and that's all there is to it. And nobody *really* cared what I looked like unless it was some sort of special occasion, and then I let the maids dress me properly and stayed clean and neat until it was over."

She frowned, considering how this would apply to Haramis. "So if the Lady Haramis has been maintaining a glamour to keep her appearance the same for decades and decades, and now all of a sudden the glamour is gone, either she's suddenly stopped caring, or—or she's sick and has no energy to maintain it?"

"I'm afraid you are right," Uzun said. "She had some sort of seizure while she was sitting with me this morning—for a while she couldn't talk or move. She said it was nothing, and then I pointed out to her that it was raining and she left rather abruptly."

"She told me to figure out what the table was used for," Mikayla said with mock innocence, "as if it weren't perfectly obvious as soon as I looked at it. But it's strange," she continued, "it's not just something that you can use as a tool to make weather—although you can certainly do that quite easily with it. When I touch it, it's as if I can feel the land through it, even though it's just a small model of the true land."

" 'Feel the land'?" Uzun said encouragingly. "What do you mean by that?"

"Don't you know?" Mikayla asked in surprise. "The land is alive, Uzun, and all of it fits together; anytime one thing changes, everything around it does as well."

"And you can sense that," Uzun said. "How long have you been able to feel the land?"

Mikayla shrugged. "All my life, I guess. As long as I can remember, anyway—it was always there in the background. It just got a lot stronger when I touched the table, that's all. Does Haramis use the table to tell her what's happening in the land? Is that why she stays here all the time, instead of traveling about the land?"

"Perhaps it is," Uzun replied. "She's never said."

"But this morning she didn't notice it was raining until you told her?" Mikayla asked. "That doesn't sound good."

"She was somewhat distracted," Uzun said, adding smugly, "and I do have excellent hearing. Don't worry about it, child; she'll probably be fine in the morning."

# 

*With Haramis spending the evening in bed, Mikayla* took advantage of the opportunity. She went to her room, picked up the box with the spheres that Haramis still had her practicing with, and went to the workroom.

While she hadn't been able to contact Fiolon every night and morning, over the past year she had done it often enough so that it was quite easy to do by now. It was even getting fairly easy to rotate the spheres in each hand the way Haramis wanted her to—Mikayla had been practicing that, too. But tonight she twirled them only long enough to build up enough power to establish the link.

"Fio," she whispered excitedly when she saw his face, "I've got something terrific to show you. Are you someplace alone?"

Fio nodded. "I'm in our old playroom," he said. "Nobody is going to bother me here." He frowned for a moment. "In fact, without you here, everyone is just ignoring me. It's pretty lonely."

"I'm sorry," Mikayla said sincerely. "I miss you, too. I wish you were here and I could share this with you firsthand, instead of through the spheres."

"Share what?" Fiolon craned his neck, looking curious.

"Look." Mikayla held the spheres over the table, moving them around so that he'd get a good view.

"It's Ruwenda!" Fiolon said at once. "And it's better than any map I've ever seen. If I get ink and parchment, can you hold the spheres long enough for me to copy it?"

"That shouldn't be a problem," Mikayla replied. "Haramis and the servants have gone to bed, and Uzun isn't exactly ambulatory. We've got the rest of the night if we need it. Get what you need, and contact me with your sphere when you're ready."

"Can I reach you with just mine?" Fiolon asked. "We've never tried that."

"We won't know until we do," Mikayla pointed out. "If I don't hear from you in a candlemark, I'll bespeak you again. But I'm sure you can do it; you're a much better natural magician than I am."

Fiolon smiled, breaking the contact without further comment. Mikayla sat by the window, manipulating the spheres and looking down into the courtyard. She frowned when she noticed what her earlier rain had done. The snow had melted over a large expanse of the courtyard, but it had still been wet when darkness fell and the temperature dropped. Now the courtyard was a sheet of ice, glistening in the moonlight. "I'd better do something about that," she said to herself, "or we'll have folk sliding all over the place and breaking bones come morning." She sighed. "I really shouldn't have made it rain in the first place; it was awfully petty to meddle with the weather just to annoy Haramis."

She went back to the sand-table and studied the bowls at the end of it. She pressed a fist idly into the crushed white rock. It made a sound as it moved under her knuckles, the sound of footsteps in snow. *Of course!* she realized. *The water is rain and this is snow! I should have figured that out this morning; after all it* is *what the mountains are made of.*

She felt a warmth inside her head and heard Fiolon's voice. "Mikayla, can you hear me?"

"Yes, I can," she answered, bringing the sphere up to her face so she could see him. "Here, I'll hold the sphere so you can see the table, and you can draw it while I work."

"Work?" Fio asked.

"Weather witching," she explained briefly, ignoring Fiolon's "Oh, of course."

She grinned. "Haramis left me here alone this morning with orders to figure out what the table was used for. Obviously she thought it would take me all day—if I *ever* figured it out. She came back here in a big hurry when I made it start raining in the courtyard!"

"Are you sure it wasn't coincidence?" Fiolon asked, falling into their common argument/counterargument pattern. "Doesn't it usually rain there in the spring?"

"Haramis certainly seemed sure enough when she was yelling at me. It's the first time I've ever seen her out of breath. Serves her right, though; she shouldn't treat me like an idiot."

Fiolon opened his mouth, then closed it. Mikayla figured that he had decided not to give her his opinion of her intelligence. "Besides," she added, "it never rains here, even in the summer—it always snows."

"So what is this work that you are doing now?"

"Minor repairs. When I made it rain this morning, it melted a lot of the snow, and now the courtyard is a sheet of ice."



"So are you going to melt the ice?"

"It's after dark here, Fiolon, and the temperature has dropped. Melting the ice would be working against nature."

"You're right," Fiolon said, still sketching busily. "I should have thought of that. And if you make it hot enough to melt ice in the middle of the night, you'll probably cause flooding someplace."

"Or avalanches," Mikayla agreed. "No, I think the best thing to do now is to simply put a thick layer of snow over the ice. That way everyone will be wading through snow and the snow should help keep them from slipping. Then, if it gets a bit warmer naturally in a day or two, I can get Haramis to show me how to melt the ice enough to dry the courtyard." She looked at the various bowls placed around the table. "Besides, I'm not sure what one uses to produce heat in a location—"

"A torch?" Fiolon suggested.

"Maybe. But I'm pretty sure that this crushed marble stuff is for making snow—and if it isn't, I'll find out quickly."

"Try it, then," Fiolon said, "but do be careful. Is it all right if I watch? I want to see how it works."

"Certainly." Mikayla picked up a small handful of the granules of white stone and spilled them carefully from her hand onto the

Tower on the table, concentrating on snow. She visualized snow falling softly onto the Tower and its surroundings, gently covering the ice in the courtyard, frosting the roof and the balconies. She seemed to float in midair just outside the Tower watching the snow drift around her. It was a very strange feeling, one she had never experienced before. As she concentrated further she felt as if she were growing smaller, shrinking to snowflake size, becoming just another crystal falling slowly through the night, picking up moisture and converting it to lacy patterns of snowflake. . . .

The pale light of dawn woke her. She was lying on the floor, next to the table, and every muscle in her body was stiff and sore. *Why am I sleeping on the floor when I have a perfectly good bed?* she wondered. Then her memories of last night returned, and she jumped to her feet, wincing as her body protested. She hurried to the window and looked out.

"I did it!" she exclaimed in delight. The courtyard was covered with snow, and looking at the railing of the nearest balcony showed her that it was almost exactly the depth she had planned. She wondered if it had been the proper depth when she fell asleep and the spell had stopped then or if it had continued while she slept until it reached the desired amount. Maybe Haramis would tell her, if Haramis was in a good mood this morning. And Haramis would probably be in a much better mood if Mikayla was found in her room practicing with the spheres when it was time for breakfast.

Mikayla tiptoed all the way to her room, changed into her night robe, got into bed and thrashed around to give it a properly slept-in look, and reached for the box containing the spheres. But as she reached out her arm she suddenly became aware of how tired she was. "It won't hurt to sleep for a little bit longer," she said to herself. "It's still early. And cold." She let her arm drop to her side, snuggled under the covers, and fell asleep again almost instantly.

When she woke again the sun was streaming through her window —she had forgotten to close the curtains. "Oh, no," she said, scrambling out of bed and into the clothing nearest to hand. "I'm late for breakfast!" Pausing only long enough to run a comb through her hair, she ran for the dining room, slowing down to a walk as she approached it. Her mother had told her that a princess never *ran,* and she had said it often enough that Mikayla had developed the habit of entering a room at a ladylike pace, regardless of what her speed had been as she came down the hall.

Breakfast was laid out on the sideboard, but there was only one plate. *Haramis must have eaten earlier,* Mikayla thought. *I only hope she's not too angry at me for oversleeping.* Mikayla made a hasty breakfast of cold toast and ladu-fruit cider that had been hot but was now room temperature. Then she went looking for Haramis.

She tried the study first, but when she poked her head through the door, Uzun sat there alone in his place at the side of the room. "Who's there?" the harp strings sang softly.

"It's Mikayla," she replied. "Good morning, Uzun." She had grown very fond of the Oddling/harp, especially since Fiolon had left. Before that, Uzun had seemed more Fiolon's friend than hers, as if he simply tolerated Mikayla because Fiolon liked her. But after Fiolon's departure, Mikayla had continued to spend time with Uzun, who was much more sympathetic and easier to talk to than Haramis.

Mikayla thought it rather cruel of Haramis to have stuck Uzun in his present form. It must certainly be a trial for him to be blind. Even if he *had* agreed to this transformation, it still seemed to Mikayla that it was selfish of Haramis to keep him bound like this.

"Good morning, Princess Mikayla," Uzun said politely. "Did you sleep well?"

In her mind Mikayla could still hear her mother's frequent admonition: "That's a greeting, daughter, not a question." She hadn't realized until she came here just how much of her mother's instruction she had absorbed. Back when she had been living at the Citadel, she—and everyone who knew her—would have sworn that her mother's words affected Mikayla no more than rain did a waterbird.

Now she found herself replying automatically. "Yes, thank you, Uzun. And you?" She caught herself. "I'm sorry, I don't know whether you sleep or not. But if you do, I hope that you slept well."

"I'm not sure whether I sleep or not, either, Princess," the harp replied. "If you ever come in and have to wake me up, then we'll both know. But I'm fairly sure I don't dream."

"Do you miss it?" Mikayla asked curiously.

"Yes." The reply was as bleak as a harp could sound.

Mikayla bit her lip. *I wish I weren't always hurting his feelings,* she thought. *I wish I were more like my sisters. I wish I were home with my mother.* Aloud she said only "I'm sorry." After all, there wasn't much more she could say, and Mikayla had no doubt of her ability to make a bad situation worse if she kept talking. Time to change the subject.

"Do you know where the Lady is this morning, Uzun?"

"No." The harp sighed. "She didn't come in to say good morning today."

"That's odd," Mikayla said. "It looks as though she ate breakfast."

"Ring the bell, child," Uzun said briskly. "Ask Enya what has happened."

Enya arrived a few minutes later. Uzun was demanding to know Haramis's whereabouts before the housekeeper was even though the doorway.

*He may be blind, but at least he has excellent hearing,* Mikayla thought. *I think he heard her coming at least half a minute before I did.*

"She's gone," Enya explained. "One minute she was sitting there eating breakfast and staring into space—you know the way she does, Princess—and the next minute she just left her food, went and got her cloak, and flew off on one of those great birds of hers."

"Where did she go?" Uzun asked. "Didn't she say?"

"Well, Master Uzun," Enya replied uneasily, "it's not my place to question her comings and goings, and I really shouldn't say. . . ."

The harp strings jangled angrily, and Enya twisted her apron nervously between her hands. "She flew south, maybe toward the Citadel. I don't know for sure."

Mikayla gasped in horror, filled with sudden foreboding. "Fiolon!" she said, running full tilt from the room. She didn't stop until she was in her bedchamber with the door bolted. She grabbed for the box and spilled the spheres into her hand. They almost seemed to twirl of their own accord, and the power came almost instantly as she touched the sphere she wore to them. This time hearing, not sight, was the first sense she picked up. No doubt Fiolon's sphere was tucked safely inside his shirt, but the argument going on around him was clearly audible.

. . .

"You must be mistaken, my lady Archimage," the Queen was saying with cold certainty. "My daughter may be a bit of a hoyden, but she is not immoral. Nor is my sister's son."

"She *is* mistaken," Fiolon said angrily. "I never touched Mikayla that way. We were going to be betrothed last year and then married. I certainly had no reason to wish to dishonor my future wife."

"She is not your future wife!" Haramis snapped angrily.

"During the period of time you are referring to, my lady," Fiolon replied, "I can assure you that we considered her as such. I love Mikayla, I shall always love Mikayla, regardless of what you do to her, and I would never have done anything to harm her."

"This is ludicrous," the King protested feebly. "Look at him—they're little more than children. And," he added with more firmness, "for most of the past two years Mikayla has been living with you. They couldn't have lain together unless you were lax about chaperoning them."

"What?" Mikayla gasped aloud.

Apparently Fiolon could hear her, but fortunately his urgent "Hush!" was covered by the adults' voices.

*But I'm not old enough to lie with anyone,* Mikayla thought. *I remember when my older sisters reached marriageable age, and I'm not that mature yet—which is odd; they were about my age when it happened to them. Is Haramis doing something to keep me a child? No, she couldn't be; if she were, she'd realize that what she's saying about me and Fiolon is nonsense. Maybe it's a side effect of studying magic. . . .*

"And if they were *not* physically intimate," Haramis snapped, "just how do you explain the fact that they're bonded together like this?"

"What do you mean by bonded?" the Queen asked.

"Linked, connected, permanently in contact with each other," Haramis said impatiently. "Why do you think you have snow all over the Citadel Knoll?"

"Oh, no!" Mikayla whispered.

"What does the snow have to do with this?" The King sounded totally confused.

"Ask the boy," Haramis said coldly.

"It was an accident," Fiolon said quietly. "I didn't mean to make it snow here. I was watching Mikayla, who was making it snow at the Lady's Tower, and we both fell asleep, and somehow the weather spell got duplicated here."

"What do you mean 'Mikayla was making it snow'?" Haramis asked sharply. "She doesn't know how to make it snow!"

"Lady," Fiolon said politely, "if you look at the table, it's really pretty obvious how to make it snow. She was doing it because the rain she made earlier in the day had left the courtyard still wet at dark, and it froze solid. She didn't want the servants falling down and getting hurt when they started work in the morning."

"Wouldn't melting the ice have been simpler?" the King asked. "And how does putting a layer of snow over it help?"

"It would take a lot of energy to melt ice in the mountains at night," Fiolon explained. "It's cold and dark, so you can't use the sun to help—and the moons aren't strong enough. And if you did produce enough energy to melt ice in a cold stone courtyard near the top of a mountain, you'd have melted enough of the surrounding snow to produce at least an avalanche, if not flooding, farther downhill. As for putting snow on top of ice, when you're stepping into snow, it helps hold your legs where you put them; and if you do fall, you fall on something softer than ice."

"Hmm," Haramis said thoughtfully. "And did Mikayla work all of this out for herself? Or did you help her?"

"We talked about it, deciding what would be best to do," Fiolon said. "We're used to working as a team. But most of it was Mikayla; she's generally the one who comes up with the original ideas. My part is usually to make sure she doesn't charge headlong into something without thinking it through. And we knew how snow over ice works from all the camping we did in the mountains three years ago."

"I didn't realize you'd ever seen snow before," Haramis remarked idly. She sounded much calmer now.

Fiolon, however, was suddenly feeling anything but calm. "Are you saying, Lady," he said through clenched teeth, "that when you handed me two fronials and a sack of supplies and sent me back here, on a journey that runs through snowy mountains for at least four days, you thought I knew nothing about snow?"

"I didn't really think of it one way or the other," Haramis said. "Why?"

"Lords Above!" Fiolon exclaimed angrily. "You really don't have any regard for life or people—or anything except your own convenience! If I didn't know how to make camp in snow, I would have died—didn't that ever occur to you? Or is that what you wanted—to be sure that Mikayla and I were separated! I warn you, Lady; if you kill me, I'll come back and haunt you, and I'll be right by Mikayla's side as long as she lives—and afterward!"

Haramis's voice was long-suffering as she addressed the King and Queen. "I realize that everyone considered these two children surplus, but it would have been convenient if *someone* could have spent a little time civilizing them. I have never encountered such poor manners before in my life."

"Don't blame *them,*" Fiolon snapped. "They did teach us manners. But being treated as things instead of people tends to bring out the worst in us; and you, Lady, definitely treat people as things. Look what you did to Uzun!"

"Uzun is not the subject of this discussion; you and Mikayla are." Mikayla could hear Haramis's footsteps and guessed that the Lady was pacing over to the window. She reached out with her mind and added sight to the link with Fiolon. He was watching Haramis, who was glaring out the window at the snow. The glamour, Mikayla noted, was back; Haramis looked the same as she always had. But now Mikayla knew it was an illusion.

After several minutes of staring out the window, Haramis turned her attention back to Fiolon. "I've taken care of your little snowstorm," she informed him. "It will all melt within a few hours. As for your bond with Mikayla"—she looked around the room, then walked over to a display of swords on the wall and took one down—"I'm going to sever it. I suggest that you cooperate."

"What happens if we don't?" Fiolon asked. Mikayla could feel a great deal of determination that the bond be kept intact. She wasn't sure how much was hers and how much his, but a lot of it was in his voice.

Haramis's lips thinned in annoyance. "I'll break the bond anyway, I'll keep breaking it if you try to reestablish it, and I'll have you sent back to Var, assigned to the Royal Navy, and sent as far out to sea as possible. Nobody can maintain a bond that far away, especially across running water." She swept the sword in an arc through the air, with the sharp edge pointing down, several feet in front of Fiolon's body. Fiolon and Mikayla cried out together in pain, and the bond broke.

# 10

*The next thing Mikayla knew, she was lying on her side* on top of her bed, curled up in a ball and holding her stomach, which felt as if someone had set fire to the front of her tunic. Her head burned, too, from the center of her forehead up across the top of her head. She heard a whimpering sound, and after a few minutes she realized that she was the one making it. She bit her lip and forced herself to be silent, but the pain continued. She tried to straighten out, but that hurt even worse, so she lay curled up on her side and waited for it to go away. It was still there when she lost consciousness again.

Mikayla woke again when someone started pounding on her door. *Go away,* she thought. *I don't want to be awake.* She tried to ignore the noise and go back to sleep.

"Princess Mikayla." Enya's voice was full of concern. "Are you all right?"

"I'm fine," Mikayla called, although her voice came out as rather a croak.

"It's time for lunch. Don't you want any?"

The thought of food was truly repugnant at the moment—in fact Mikayla didn't think she'd ever want to eat again in her life. "Thank you, Enya, but I'm really not hungry. Tell the Lady that I'm busy studying and don't want to stop for lunch."

"She's not back yet," Enya replied. "Do you know where she is?"

"Probably still at the Citadel," Mikayla replied, trying to figure out times involved. It had been midmorning when she had been watching Haramis, and now Enya said it was lunchtime. . . .

*So I've only been unconscious for a couple of hours—on and off.* Aloud she said, "If she's not back by dinnertime, don't bother to cook anything—I'll raid the kitchen when I take a break." She hoped her voice sounded as if she were absorbed in her studies, rather than in pain.

Apparently Enya didn't notice anything wrong, for she simply said, "As you wish, Princess. Oh, and Master Uzun would like to see you at your convenience."

"Thank you, Enya. I'll go see him presently." *When I can manage advanced functions like standing up and walking.* She heard the housekeeper's footsteps move away, and then fell asleep again.

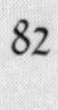

When she next woke, it was dark outside and the only light in her room came from the embers of the fire, which had died down to almost nothing. It was cold in the room, despite the warm air coming from the grille by the bed. Mikayla was cold, too; she hadn't even had the energy to pull a blanket over her earlier.

Cautiously she straightened her body. It was stiff from long hours in one tense position, but the worst of the pain was gone. Now she simply had a stomachache and an empty feeling inside. "I'm going to get up," she told herself, as if saying it aloud would make it happen, "and I'm going to go to the library and find the description of that spell Haramis used on us. And I'm going to find out how to reverse it." She moved slowly over to the edge of the bed, then slid over the side of the mattress to a standing position on the floor, still holding on to the bed. After a moment, when she was reasonably sure that her legs would support her, she picked up the candle from her table, lit it with a word of command, and headed toward the door.

She still felt weak and dizzy, so it took her a few minutes to get the door unbolted, but she finally managed it. Then she headed for the library.

As she passed the study there was a commanding ripple of the harp's strings. "Mikayla!"

*Oh, that's right, Uzun wanted to see me.* She poked her head into the study, which was also dark, except for the fire. The fire in the study was always kept burning so that the temperature would stay the same for Uzun. Harps, whether sentient or not, did not react well to changes in temperature. Uzun had explained this to Mikayla in great and highly technical detail during one of their late-night talks.

"Come in and sit down, child—or fall down, whichever is easier," Uzun said sympathetically. "And tell me what in the name of the Lords of the Air is going on around here! Haramis hasn't returned; you're a wreck—what happened?"

Mikayla set her candle down carefully on the table and dropped her body a good deal less carefully into the chair next to it. In fact, she missed the chair and wound up on the floor in front of it. She leaned back against the seat of the chair and closed her eyes. It was too much work to move anymore.

"I'm not sure exactly what happened myself, Uzun," she said, "but, Lords, how I hurt!"

"I know about the rain yesterday," Uzun prompted her. "Did you do the snow last night as well?"

"Yes," Mikayla said dully. "I didn't want the servants to slip on the ice and get hurt. Nobody did, did they?"

"Not to my knowledge," Uzun said. "Go on."

"When I was making it snow, I was linked to Fiolon." Mikayla started to cry. "He was sketching the sand-table, because it's better than any of the maps we have. Even if I'm stuck here, he still ought to be allowed to go exploring, don't you think?"

"I don't see why not," Uzun replied, "as long as he doesn't go into the Mazy Mire alone or do something equally dangerous."

"He doesn't do dangerous things," Mikayla said, sniffling. "I'm the reckless one, I'm the one who does stupid things—he's the one who gets us out of trouble when I get us into it."

"A valuable quality in a friend," Uzun said gravely.

"Yes." Mikayla started crying again, this time mostly from anger. "But Haramis doesn't see it that way. Do you believe that she actually went to my parents and accused Fiolon and me of immoral behavior!"

"Why ever would she think that?"

"Just because it snowed at the Citadel when I made it snow here. She said that Fiolon and I were bonded, and she was going to break the bond, and then she took a sword off the wall, and . . ." Mikayla paused. "I'm not sure exactly what she did next; it hurt and I fainted. And I don't know what she did to Fiolon and I'm worried about him."

"The spell you're describing is fairly simple," Uzun said. "You swing a sword through the space between the two people, which snaps the bond temporarily, then you visualize a flame burning the cord or cords that bound them together."

"That would certainly explain the way I feel," Mikayla said. "I hurt from the top of my head down to my stomach."

"But nothing below the waist hurts?" Uzun asked.

"No. Why should it?" Mikayla asked in bewilderment. "What does hurt is more than enough."

"The cords attach to different points on your body depending on the type of bond you have," Uzun explained. "If you and Fiolon had been married, for example, the pain would go down as far as your legs. Since it stops at the waist, obviously Haramis is mistaken."

"Fiolon told her that before she started swinging that sword around," Mikayla said. "But would she listen? No. She *never* listens!"

"It's not her strongest skill," Uzun agreed. "But I'm worried about her."

"Because she's not back already?"

"Partly that," Uzun admitted, "but she doesn't always account to me for her comings and goings. No, I feel that there is something wrong with her. She had some sort of seizure yesterday morning before your lesson, and then she flew off to the Citadel when she probably should have rested for at least a few days."

"And it's not as if she needed to do anything about the snow at the Citadel," Mikayla pointed out. "Even in the middle of winter, it would have all melted by midafternoon, and it's late spring now."

"She does have a bit of a temper," Uzun admitted, "and she's used to doing things her own way." He sighed. "Princess, do you feel well enough to try to scry for her and see if she's all right?"

"I don't know," Mikayla said slowly. "I guess I can try. But I really do feel sick—sort of empty and hollow inside."

"Please try," Uzun pleaded, "for my sake, if not for hers. If I could still scry, I'd do it myself."

"For your sake, Uzun, I'll try it." Mikayla pulled the small sphere out of the front of her tunic. *I don't have the energy to go find a proper scrying bowl, and if I can scry at all, I can do it with this.* "I still think it was rotten of her to make you blind."

For the first time, Uzun didn't argue with her or automatically leap to Haramis's defense. He just sat there quietly while Mikayla stared into the sphere, focusing beyond the reflected firelight.

She was standing in the playroom in the Citadel's old tower, staring out the window toward Mount Brom. It was dark, except for a candle on the floor behind her, and the sound of rain pouring down outside the window explained why there was nothing much to see outside. And there was only one person who was likely to be in the playroom.

"Fiolon?" she whispered.

"Mikayla?" Fiolon's voice whispered back. "Are you all right?"

Suddenly she was fine. Her head didn't hurt, her stomach didn't hurt, and the empty feeling inside was gone—except for the fact that now she was hungry and very much aware of the fact that she hadn't eaten anything since breakfast.

"Yes, I'm all right now," she said. "How about you?"

"It just stopped hurting," he replied. "Does this mean that we've reestablished our bond?"

"I think so," she said, turning to the harp. "Uzun, all of a sudden Fiolon and I don't hurt anymore. Does this mean that our bond is back?"

"Yes, it does," Uzun answered.

"Hey! I can hear him!" Fiolon exclaimed.

"Good," Uzun said. "Listen carefully, then. You established the bond in the first place by spending a lot of time together, didn't you?"

"Just about every waking moment for seven years," Fiolon confirmed.

"And even when Haramis tried to separate you, you both tried to stay together: you thought about each other often, and you tried to far-speak each other—and succeeded, am I not right?"

"You're right," Mikayla admitted.

"So it would take a lot of effort to break such a bond. Even were it not a strong one, even if you did not both possess much magic—"

"We do?" Mikayla gasped. "I mean, I know Fiolon has talent in that direction, but me?"

"Yes, both of you. But even if you did not, the bond would be hard to break because it has been in existence for so many years.

If both of you wished to break it, and you both worked at it, you could probably get rid of most of it within a month or two, although it would still probably reactivate in emergencies. If only one of you wished to break it, it would take at least a season or two of hard work—more if the other person was fighting your attempts."

"Does this mean that Haramis can't break it?" Mikayla asked hopefully.

"Against both your wills?" Uzun said dryly. "I very much doubt it."

"She certainly can't do anything about it at the moment," Fiolon said. "I'll bet she can't even tell that it's back."

"What happened to her?" Uzun asked anxiously. "I knew something had gone badly wrong!"

"I'm sorry, Uzun," Fiolon said. "I know you're fond of her—and the healers do think she'll recover in time," he added hastily. "But she had some type of brainstorm this morning. I missed part of it; I was writhing on the floor in pain at the time, but she collapsed, and she can't move the left side of her body at all, and she can't summon the lammergeiers—she wanted to send you a message, Uzun—and it's hard to understand when she tries to talk because only half her mouth moves." He paused, then added, "I can call the lammergeiers, but I was afraid that would only upset her more, and she's already really upset with me."

"Who's taking care of her?" Uzun asked anxiously.

"Ayah, mostly, and some healers from the Greenmire. They're giving her swamp-worm venom to thin her blood and keep it from blocking off more of her brain. They seem to think that a lot of the damage can be reversed, that she'll be able to move her left side and walk again and so forth."

"What about her magical abilities?" Mikayla asked.

Fiolon shrugged. "At the moment she doesn't seem to have any. And nobody knows whether they'll come back. Uzun, does that mean that Mikayla is the Archimage *now*?"

"Oh, no!" Mikayla exclaimed. "I'm not nearly ready to be Archimage!"

Uzun considered the question. "Probably not," he said finally. "If the power had passed to Mikayla, she'd know it. We'll just have to wait and see what happens."

"What do you mean 'if the power had passed to Mikayla'?" Fiolon asked. "Would Mikayla automatically become Archimage if Haramis died?"

"Yes," Uzun replied, "assuming, of course, that Haramis is right in thinking that Mikayla is her proper successor. If she's wrong, the power would pass to whomever it was supposed to go to."

"You mean somebody else could wind up as Archimage and we wouldn't even know it?" Mikayla asked.

"In theory it is possible, but it is highly unlikely," Uzun said firmly. "I'm pretty sure that you *are* meant to succeed her, Mikayla."

"Uzun? What happens to you if Haramis dies?" Mikayla asked. "I mean, if she made you into a harp by a spell and extended your life beyond its normal span by her will and her actions, do you die when she does?" Mikayla, feeling very insecure all of the sudden, crawled over to Uzun and put an arm around his forepillar. "Do you know anything about the spell she used on you?"

"It's in a book in the library," Uzun said. "You can look it up tomorrow. Right now, young lady, you can eat something and get a good night's sleep. You're no good to yourself or anyone else in the shape you're in. And as for you, Lord Fiolon," he added, "have you eaten anything today?"

"Not since breakfast," Fiolon said. "First I was in too much pain, and then everyone was fussing over the Lady Haramis, and I just wanted to be alone, so I came here—"

"Where is 'here'?" Uzun broke in.

"Here?" Fiolon echoed him. "Oh, that's right, you can't see. I'm sorry. Here is the old guard barracks at the top of the Tower. You and Princess Haramis went through here when you were escaping from the invaders; I'm in the room two floors down from where the lammergeiers carried you away."

"Yes, I remember the place," Uzun said. "It's not used for the guards anymore?"

"No, it's empty, except for a few old pieces of furniture. Mikayla and I have used it as a playroom for years."

"I see," Uzun said. "I'll bet no one is in any hurry to look for you there when you're missing."

"No, since it's up seventeen flights of stairs, it's not a popular destination for the servants. And usually no one misses us, as long as we turn up on time for meals."

"Very well," Uzun said. "What I want you to do is this. Eat something and sleep; you need your strength as much as Mikayla does. Then, in the morning, go to Haramis and tell her that you dreamed of me, and that in the dream I told you that I knew of Haramis's illness and that I would care for and teach Mikayla until Haramis returns home."

"All right," Fiolon agreed. "That should work out well. She'll probably assume that it was a sending from you, and if she thinks it was you using your powers, she probably won't ask if Mikayla and I have reestablished the bond."

"But if she thinks about it at all," Mikayla protested, "she'll realize that we must have. Uzun, you said yourself that she couldn't break it without our cooperation."

Uzun sighed, a faint ripple along the strings. "She is quite capable of assuming that you'll cooperate just because she told you to. And if she's suffering from a brainstorm, she may *not* think about it at all. In fact, she may not be thinking of anything at all."

# 11

*Haramis wakened. Sunlight was streaming into her* room and across her, which was odd, because there wasn't a window there. But now there was. *No, that's right, the sun always came in like that, I remember playing with the dust motes when I was a little girl.* Her body felt strange, as if she had slept on it wrong; her left arm and leg were asleep and wouldn't wake up. In fact, she couldn't seem to move them. With some difficulty, because a lot of her muscles didn't seem to want to work, she turned her head away from the sun and saw a boy sitting at the right side of the bed. *I should know him,* she thought, but at the moment she couldn't quite place him.

"Where is my mother?" she asked. "Where's Immu? Where are my sisters?" She barely noticed that her words came out slurred.

The boy seemed to have no trouble understanding what she was saying, but he turned pale and gulped. "Do you know where you are, Lady?"

"The proper form of address is 'Princess,' not 'Lady'—do you not know whom you are addressing?"

"Uh . . ." The boy hesitated for a moment, then blurted out, "Who do you think you are?"

"I *know* I am Princess Haramis of Ruwenda, Heiress to the Throne," she snapped. "Who are you, and what are you doing here if you don't know even that?" She cast her eyes around the room. Why was she alone with this ignorant boy? "Who changed the hangings in my room? And where is everyone? Where's Uzun?"

"Uzun is at the Tower," the boy said hastily. "He came to me in a dream last night and told me that he knew of your illness and that I was to tell you that he would care for and teach the Princess Mikayla until you were well enough to do it yourself again."

"Who is Mikayla, and who are you?"

"Mikayla is—well, Mikayla is a distant kinswoman of yours. You were teaching her magic before you became ill. I am Lord Fiolon of Var."

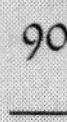



"Are you related to my betrothed, then?" Haramis asked. "Did you come here with him?"

"Prince Fiomaki?" The boy still looked uneasy. "He and I are distant kin, but he isn't here now."

"When will he arrive? Our betrothal is to be celebrated soon."

"I don't know," Fiolon said. "But I shouldn't stay here talking and tire you; I was just supposed to deliver the message from Master Uzun. Why don't you try to rest, Lady—I mean, Princess. I'll tell the housekeeper you're awake."

Haramis made a face, which felt strange. "Immu will probably insist on dosing me with one of her horrible potions. How long have I been ill? And what is wrong with me?"

The boy left without answering; in fact he almost fled from the room.

Haramis sighed. Something very strange was going on. But she was very, very tired—much too tired to worry about it. She went back to sleep, which would have surprised her if she had been capable of being surprised.

Mikayla was dawdling over breakfast, which she was eating in the study so she could keep Uzun company. She still felt rather listless, but she reminded herself that the events of yesterday and last night would have tired anyone. Even though the horrible pain of having her bond with Fiolon severed had gone when the bond came back, her body still remembered it.

She felt the sphere against her chest grow warm at the same time that Uzun said sharply, "What is that noise?"

Mikayla fished the sphere out of the front of her tunic. It shook violently, making as close to a jangling sound as something that small could make. "Fiolon must be trying to reach me," she explained. "We found these small spheres in some ruins we were exploring in the Blackmire—they're about the size of my thumbnail," she added, remembering that Uzun couldn't see. "Haramis ought to have given you eyes, at the very least," she complained, angry on Uzun's behalf. The harp was silent.

Mikayla sighed and continued her description. "The ones Fiolon and I took were a matched pair, and they seem to be some sort of device that the Vanished Ones used to communicate over distances, although I think that Fiolon and I are using them over more distance than they were originally designed for."

The sphere shook even more, swinging back and forth on its ribbon, even though Mikayla wasn't moving it. "I'd better see what Fiolon wants; he seems upset." She looked into the sphere, and Fiolon's face looked back at her.

"There you are, Mika," he said. "It certainly took you long enough to answer!"

"I was eating breakfast," Mikayla said calmly. "What's wrong?"

"Is Uzun there with you?"

"I'm right here," Uzun replied. "Is it Haramis? Is she worse?"

"Well, she doesn't seem to remember me or Mika, which *might* be considered an improvement," Fiolon replied, "but when I told her I was from Var, she asked if I had accompanied her betrothed, and where was he, and where were her mother, and her sisters, and Immu—Immu was the housekeeper when Haramis was a young girl, wasn't she? The same Immu who went with Princess Anigel on her Quest?"

"Yes," Uzun said. "Are you saying that Haramis thinks she's still a young girl?"

"She certainly seems to think so," Fiolon said nervously. "She asked who changed the hangings in her room, so I guess when they put her to bed they put her in the room she had as a girl. I suppose that would contribute to her thinking that. And when I called her 'Lady' she told me that she should be addressed as 'Princess' and that she was heiress to the throne of Ruwenda."

He sighed. "I gave her your message, Master Uzun, and then I got out of there before I had to explain to her that most of the people she was asking for have been dead for almost two hundreds."

"Oh, my," Mikayla said. "How extraordinary. She doesn't know she's the Archimage?" She thought for a minute. *Maybe this lets me out of here. Maybe I don't have to—* "If she doesn't remember me, do I still have to study to be Archimage?"

"Yes, you do," Uzun and Fiolon said together.

"Well, if she's forgotten about me, maybe she'll pick someone else," Mikayla said hopefully.

"Don't count on it," Fiolon said. "At the minute she barely knows her own name."

"And today is the day you were planning to find the spell she used to turn me into a harp," Uzun reminded her.

"Yes, that's right," Mikayla said. *Even if Haramis has forgotten about me, I'm not leaving Uzun all alone. He doesn't deserve that.* "I remember now; we talked about that last night." She teleported the dirty dishes back to the kitchen. "Is there anything you want me to do, Fiolon?"

"While you're in the library, see if there's anything on brainstorms and memory loss," Fiolon said.

"I'll look," Mikayla promised, "but medicine doesn't seem to be one of Haramis's interests. But as long as she's going to be gone for a while, I'll poke around the Tower and see what I can find—I'm sure there's a lot of stuff here that she never got around to showing me."

"I'll check what's left of the library here," Fiolon said. "That should keep both of us out of trouble for today at least."

"Fio," Mikayla said slowly, "she's really sick, right?"

"Yes, but don't worry, Mika; the healers say she'll recover pretty completely over time."

"How much time?"

"I think you can count on several months at least," Fiolon said. "The healers aren't exactly saying, but that's the feeling I get."

"Several months," Mikayla repeated, being careful to keep her face grave. Inside she felt like singing. Months! Time without Haramis hanging over her, spying on her, glaring at her across the table at meals, wanting her to be something she wasn't and didn't wish to be. . . . "Well, if she reaches a point where she remembers my existence, greet her for me."

"And give her my love," Uzun said swiftly.

"I will," Fiolon promised. "And at least she remembers you, Master Uzun. That's a good sign, isn't it?" He sighed. "I'm off to stir up the dust in the library. If you hear coughing coming from your sphere, Mika, ignore it."

Mikayla giggled. "I shall. Good luck with your search. I'll let you know if I find anything."

"Do that," Fiolon replied. "Good luck to you also." His face shrank away as he moved the sphere away from it, then he put his sphere away and Mikayla's reflected nothing but her surroundings.

Mikayla stood up. "I'm going to the library, Uzun, but I'll be back at lunchtime. I'll have Enya serve all my meals in here as long as it's just the two of us—unless you would prefer more time alone?"

"Definitely not!" Uzun said emphatically. "I've spent more than enough time alone for one lifetime."

"I'm sure you have," Mikayla said. *I still don't understand how Haramis could do this to someone she claims to love. Talk about selfish behavior.* "I'll make finding the spell she used on you my first priority."



It took her several days, but finally she had a book she thought might be it. She brought it to the table with her, but waited until Enya had left the room before she opened it. Lunch was unusually skimpy, just bread and cheese, with sliced ladu fruit for dessert; evidently the household staff was demoralized by the news of Haramis's illness. Mikayla had let Uzun tell Enya about it, figuring that he could probably make it sound better than she could, but Uzun had an attack of his occasional pessimism. . . .

*If the food doesn't improve in a few more days,* Mikayla thought, *I'll go down to the kitchen and talk to the cook myself. In the meantime a diet of bread and cheese isn't going to hurt me.*

"Uzun," she said, walking around the harp to examine him closely, "did the bone at the top of the forepillar come from the top of your skull?"

"I think so, Princess," the harp replied, "but I wasn't conscious for that part of it."

"Do you mind if I tip you toward me a bit so I can take a better look?" Mikayla asked. "You're about the same height I am, so I can't see it without tilting you or standing on a chair and leaning over you—and the chairs here aren't good to stand on; they're too soft."

"You can tilt me," Uzun said, "but do it carefully. *Don't* drop me!"

"I'll be careful," Mikayla promised. She grasped the harp firmly with one hand on the forepillar and one on the back of the frame and braced the top of the frame against her chest. *At least this way if he falls, he'll land on me.* She studied the fragment of bone carefully, twisting her head to compare it with the drawing in the book on the table next to her. Then she cautiously pushed Uzun back to his normal upright position and held him there until she was sure he was stable. "It looks like the top of a skull, all right; the lines on the bone match the lines in the drawing in the book. And according to this, it also needed somebody's blood —probably Haramis's—to fill a thin channel in the center of the forepillar."

"That sounds right," Uzun said. "I remember that part. I was dying, and Haramis was standing over the craftsman who was building the harp, telling him to hurry. And when he was done, it still had a hole in the top of the forepillar. I remember watching Haramis cut her arm and hold it so that her blood ran into the hole . . . in fact, that's the last thing I remember. The harp didn't even have strings then."

"She probably strung it while she was waiting for the bugs to eat the flesh off of your bones," Mikayla said, munching on a slice of ladu fruit.

"Bugs?" Uzun sounded scandalized.

"Yes, apparently they do a much faster and neater job than having a human or Oddling try to remove the flesh without damaging the bone. You just bury the body in a tub of soil with the right mix of bugs, and in a few days, you have a nice clean skeleton."

"Haramis always was efficient," Uzun said faintly. "And if you're still eating lunch as you discuss this, I suppose you share her lack of squeamishness about such matters."

"Well, it's not as if you were conscious at the time," Mikayla pointed out. "Or even alive."

"Thank the Lords of the Air!" Uzun said fervently.

Mikayla frowned down at the book. "All right, now I know how she turned you into a harp. By the way, how long ago was this? As I recall, she said it was her first act of great magic."

Uzun thought about it for several minutes. "She had been Archimage for about two decades then, so I wouldn't say it was her first great spell. But I believe that it was the first time she used her power for personal gain," he said slowly. "Princess, if you can't make me a new body, can you set me free from this one when Haramis dies?"

"Easily," Mikayla said. "To free you to move on to the next phase of existence, whatever it may be, all I have to do is take the bone fragment from the harp, grind it to powder, and cast it to the winds. And," she added fiercely, "I'm not Haramis. I'll release you anytime you ask me to, no matter *how* much I'll miss your company!"

To her surprise, she burst into tears then, and she couldn't stop crying. "I'm sorry, Uzun," she sobbed, "I don't know what's wrong with me."

"I suspect you're more worried about the Lady Haramis than you are admitting to yourself," Uzun said gently.

"But I don't even like her," Mikayla sobbed, "and she *hates* me! She's always criticizing me. Nothing I ever do is good enough—and when I do something better than she expected me to she's furious. She took me from my home and family, she's kept me here for over two years now—I can't even go outside because I don't have any clothing but lightweight indoor tunics and a couple of night robes! She sent away my best friend; she tried to break the bond between us, and she hurt us both—and do you know what the worst of it is? She expects me to be grateful to her! I can't understand that at all! Why would *anyone* be grateful for what she's done to me?"

Uzun sighed. "She's giving you what she thinks she would have wanted at your age; that's why she expects you to be grateful."

Mikayla sat in silence for a time, thinking that over. "You know, Uzun, you are exactly right. She's even said so, now that I think of it: things like how she would have killed for the opportunities she's giving me—and she probably would have, too. She must be the most cold-blooded person I've ever met." She took the last slice of ladu fruit and stuffed it into her mouth. "Does she think that you should be grateful that she turned you into a harp, too?"

"I think she feels just a little guilty about that now, especially since you and Fiolon came here and made your opinion of it obvious. I think she regrets making me blind."

Mikayla snorted. "I'll bet she regrets a lot more making you immobile and unable to travel. Of course, she remembers you, but from Fiolon's description, it sounds as though she's forgotten you're a harp. Any guesses as to how long it will be before she demands your presence in her sickroom?"

Uzun sighed. "If she doesn't remember that I'm a harp, I imagine she'll be asking for me the next time she wakes up."

"And if she does remember that you're a harp," Mikayla added, "she'll probably start trying to figure out how to package you for shipment to the Citadel."

Uzun came as close to shuddering as was possible for a harp. "Riding on the back of a lammergeier was terrifying enough when I had hands to hold on with. And I don't think my frame would survive the changes in temperature and humidity."

"Nobody will send you anywhere if I have anything to say about it," Mikayla promised. *But do I have anything to say about anything?* "Uzun, who's in charge with Haramis away and ill?"

"I don't know," Uzun said. "The question has never come up before."

"It might be to our benefit to convince the servants that I'm in charge at present," Mikayla said. "Subject to your advice, of course, since you're continuing my magical training." *And maybe I can order some warm clothing so I can go outside occasionally.*

"That sounds reasonable," Uzun said. "After all, Haramis did designate you as her successor."

"Good," Mikayla said decisively. "I'll just act as though I'm in charge, you'll back me up, and with any luck no one will question it. Once everyone is in the habit of obeying me, it will take a direct order from Haramis herself to do anything to you that you don't want done.

"As for transforming you," she continued, as something suddenly occurred to her, "you said that Haramis had been the Archimage for two decades when she turned you into a harp."

"Yes," Uzun said. "Is that important?"

"Was Haramis always as enthusiastic about books as she is now?"

"Yes, from the day she learned to read, she was always studying. She had read every book in the Citadel library at least once by the time she was fourteen."

*And I've only read about a quarter of them,* Mikayla thought. *No wonder Haramis seems to think I'm lazy and stupid. But I do have other interests, which is more than she seems to.*

"And did she live here in this Tower from the time she became Archimage?"

"She moved here just after Anigel was crowned Queen, and

Haramis had been Archimage for about a month then, I think. But she had spent some time here with Orogastus, during her Quest for her Talisman."

"So," Mikayla said, coming to her point, "by the time she turned you into a harp, she would have read every book in the library here, wouldn't she?"

After a few seconds of stunned silence, there was a ripple along Uzun's strings that was the most despairing sound Mikayla had ever heard in her life. It sent chills down her backbone. "Yessss," the harp whispered. "She had read them all. So there is no other spell."

"Not necessarily," Mikayla said with all the reassurance she could project. "But it's probably not in the library. I'm going to start exploring the rest of the Tower this afternoon. There are a lot of things that Haramis isn't interested in, and that's doubtless where the answers we seek are to be found."

Uzun sighed. "It's true enough that if it's not a book or a musical instrument, Haramis is likely to ignore it. But, Mikayla, be *very* careful when you start poking around. Orogastus collected many things, and some of them are deadly."

# 12

*Mikayla decided to start her explorations at the top of* the Tower and work down. She suspected that the bottom might be where the most interesting things were, but it wasn't impossible that there was something at the top, and she wanted to be sure she didn't miss anything. From what she had seen in all the time she had spent here, Haramis never went much above or below the middle of the Tower.

The upper floors of the Tower were filled with all sorts of junk, dusty boxes full of old clothing (Mikayla spent one entire afternoon playing dress-up in clothing much too big for her, even as she told herself that she was wasting time and was too old for such games anyway), and barrels of old dishes. There was a chest containing some strange garments of silver, complete with gloves and a pair of strange silver masks. They were obviously a set, one for a man and one for a woman, but they felt strange to the touch and gave Mikayla a sort of crawly feeling down her spine. She packed them back carefully without even thinking of trying them on. *Did these belong to Orogastus?* she wondered. *I'll bet they did, but who was the woman's costume made for? Did Haramis ever wear it?*

After several weeks of exploring everything in the main Tower except Haramis's bedchamber—Mikayla knew that Haramis would be very annoyed with her if she went poking about there without permission—Mikayla was finally ready to explore the lowest level. She had high hopes that she would find something useful there. So far, she hadn't found any devices of the Vanished Ones, and Uzun had told her that Orogastus *had* collected them and brought them there. Since she hadn't found his collection yet, it must be somewhere on the lowest level—or maybe below it. She didn't know what was down there, but she wanted to find out.

Mikayla followed the winding stone stairway down from the living area, past the kitchens, and continued down. She was surprised to discover that it went even farther down than the stables, which she had thought were on the bottom level of the Tower. But the stairs branched there, with one branch leading straight down to the plaza and the other curling below the ramp that led from the stables to the plaza.

Under the stables was a large storeroom, fully the circumference of the Tower. Mikayla spoke the command that provided light in the rest of the Tower, and a single lamp, suspended from the ceiling, sputtered to life. It flickered dreadfully; obviously its wick was in need of trimming.

By the faint illumination provided by the old lamp, Mikayla could see the contents of the room. It was crowded with crates and barrels, placed haphazardly, but still leaving room to walk around them all. They were all labeled, in large letters visible even in the dim light, but none of the labels was in any language Mikayla could read.

*These don't look like household food stores,* Mikayla thought, looking around with a sigh. *I'm probably going to have to open every single container in here to determine what's inside.*

The floor was made of a strange silvery-black material, which Mikayla was sure she had seen before. She knew as she looked at it that there was something she should know about it, something important, but she couldn't remember what at the moment. *It will come to me,* she thought.

She continued to the back of the room. *Best to start at the far end and work my way back—Lords of the Air, what's that?*

"That" was a tunnel at the very back of the room, leading away from the Tower. Judging from its direction and the fact that it was carved out of solid rock, the tunnel went straight into the mountain. There were lamps hanging from spikes driven into the wall at regular intervals, but they weren't lit.

Mikayla whispered the word that lit the lamps upstairs. To her delight, it worked here as well. The lamps flared to light, starting with the ones nearest her and extending down the tunnel, as if the flame were being passed from lamp to lamp. All of Uzun's warnings vanished from Mikayla's mind as she hurried into the tunnel, heedless of the cold rock under her slippers and the fact that her breath was making a fog in the cold humid air.

The tunnel ended at a large door, almost twice Mikayla's height, and covered with frost. Mikayla, too excited to worry about such mundane matters as frostbite, grasped the large ring that served as a door handle and tried to pull the door open. It moved reluctantly, and the hinges shrieked as if she were causing them serious injury, but Mikayla scarcely noticed. She went through the door as soon as she had tugged it wide enough for her body to fit through it.

She found herself in a large vaulted chamber of rough stone, with patches of black ice scattered irregularly around its walls. The floor here was paved with plain black stone tiles, and the same black stone had been used to make cupboards set into the walls as well as what appeared to be doors to other rooms. She tried one of the doors. Pushing against it had no effect; it felt like leaning against a wall. There was nothing on it to pull at it with, just a slight groove at one side of the panel. She suddenly realized that it was supposed to slide, rather than be pushed or pulled, and hooked her fingertips into the groove. It opened with surprising ease.

The room behind this door was shallow, only about six paces deep, and it was very cold. *I definitely need to get some warmer clothes,* Mikayla thought, tucking her hands into her armpits and stamping her feet. She knew she wouldn't be able to stay here much longer without risking serious injury, but this was the most interesting thing she had ever seen. *Does Haramis know about this?* she wondered.

Most of the wall she was looking at was covered with frost, but in the center of it there was a dark gray area that was relatively clear. Mikayla could see herself dimly reflected in the dark shining surface.

"What is it?" she gasped, almost in awe.

As she stood and stared the mirror brightened, ever so slightly, and a voice came from it, in such a faint whisper that Mikayla thought she was imagining it.

"Request, please."

*I'm dreaming,* Mikayla thought. *Or I've been spending too much time with a talking harp. Mirrors don't talk.*

*Of course, neither do most harps. Maybe this is some sort of strange scrying device. I wish Uzun were here. Of course, if he were, he'd . . . he'd want to see Haramis.*

"I want to see Haramis," she said aloud.

"View Princess Haramis of Ruwenda?" the voice whispered.

Mikayla shivered. The voice was definitely not human. "Yes," she said as firmly as possible.

"Scanning." A picture appeared in the mirror, as if Haramis were just on the other side of the mirror. The colors were dim, but the details were clear, and Mikayla recognized the guest room in the Citadel where Haramis lay sleeping. Ayah sat by the side of the bed, keeping watch over the old woman. Mikayla noticed that the glamour Haramis always used in the presence of other people was absent, but at least her breathing sounded strong and regular.

The picture vanished suddenly, and the faintest of whispers said, "Backup power exhausted. Recharge of solar cells necessary for further operation."

*It's not the only thing that needs the sun,* Mikayla realized suddenly. *I'm freezing here!*

She forced herself to slide the door to the mirror room closed, then hastily went back through the cavern and leaned her shoulder on the door from the outside to close it, not wanting to touch it with her bare skin, but afraid that the devices might be harmed if the doors were left open.

The lights in the tunnel were burning low. *It's a miracle that they work at all,* Mikayla thought as she hurried up the tunnel as fast as she could move. *I'll bet the servants never come down here. I'll have to ask Uzun about this place; maybe he knows something. But first I need a hot bath, and before I come back here I need warm clothes, and boots, and mittens!*

By the time she had thawed herself out—using the tub in Haramis's bathing room to do so—it was past time for dinner. She dressed in two of her indoor tunics, which left her feeling only slightly chilled, and went to talk to Uzun, pausing only long enough to stop by the kitchen and collect a tray of food and a pitcher of hot ladu-juice to take to the study with her.

"Uzun," she asked, after she had eaten her food and drunk half the pitcher of ladu-juice and was feeling much more human, "have you ever heard of a cave in the mountain, under this Tower?"

"Yes," Uzun said slowly. "Haramis told me that Orogastus worshiped the Dark Powers in caves of black ice there, and that he had a magic mirror that would let him see anyone in the Kingdom, just by saying their name. He used it to show her sisters to her."

"Is what the mirror shows true, then?" Mikayla asked.

"As far as I know," Uzun said. "Do I gather you found it? I thought it had stopped working long ago. What did you see?"

"Haramis sleeping in a room at the Citadel, with Ayah—she's one of the servants—sitting by her bed."

"I know Ayah," Uzun said. "She's Enya's sister."

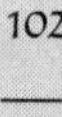



"Really?" Mikayla was startled, then thoughtful. *Perhaps the Archimage isn't as all-knowing as she would have us believe, but simply has spies planted around the Kingdom.*

"How did Haramis look?" Uzun asked anxiously.

"She didn't have her glamour," Mikayla said, "so she looked old and tired, but her breathing was strong and regular and she seemed to be sleeping peacefully. They seem to be taking good care of her at the Citadel," she added reassuringly. "By the way, did she say that Orogastus's mirror *was* magic or that he *said* it was?"

"She said that he called it a magic mirror."

"That would explain it. It's not magic at all, Uzun; it's one of the old devices of the Vanished Ones. And it doesn't work very well; it showed me what I asked to see briefly and then said that it needed more power." She frowned, trying to remember the words. "It said something about recharge of solar cells."

"What's a solar cell?" Uzun asked.

"'Solar' means having to do with the sun. . . ." Mikayla's voice trailed off as she realized why the silvery-black floor had looked familiar to her. She scrambled to her feet. "I'll be right back," she told Uzun, before running for her room and the music boxes she had hidden there.

She returned a few minutes later with one, and set it down between the candles on the table, transporting her dinner dishes back to the kitchen to get them out of the way. The box began to play softly in the candlelight.

"That's Haramis's old music box," Uzun said. "It was her favorite toy when she was a child. I didn't know she'd kept it. It must be getting old, though, the music used to be louder."

"She didn't keep it," Mikayla said. "At least I would think that the one Fiolon and I found in the playroom at the Citadel was hers. It's still there, too. This is one of the ones we found in the ruins near the Golobar River—right before Haramis found us."

"*One* of the ones?" Uzun said in a voice as close to excited as Mikayla had ever heard from him. "You found others? Did any of them play different tunes?"

Mikayla laughed. "You're as bad as Fiolon. We found six or seven, I think. He took most of them home with him when Haramis sent him away, but I have two more in my room. Would you like to hear them?" *A silly question, I'm sure.*

"Of course I would," Uzun said, "but later. This is important to you for some reason besides its music—you were talking about solar cells right before you suddenly ran off to get it."



"Yes," Mikayla said. "You just remarked on how soft the music is. Listen carefully." She lit four more candles around the box, and the music grew louder.

"It's louder," Uzun said, "but still not as loud as it should be."

"When you heard it before, was the sun shining on it?" Mikayla asked.

"Yes," Uzun said promptly. "Haramis kept it on a table near the window when she was playing it. If she put it away in darkness, it became silent."

"Exactly!" Mikayla said with satisfaction. "It gets its power from light—preferably sunlight, because it's the brightest and, presumably, provides the most power." She extinguished the extra candles, and the music soon grew soft again. "Do you remember what the box looked like, Uzun?" she asked.

"Only vaguely, I fear," Uzun replied.

"On each side," Mikayla said, "there is a small piece, worked into the overall design, of a silvery-black material. Listen to what happens when I cover them." She carefully put a fingertip over each of the pieces, and the music died away into silence. "The rest of the box is still getting light," she told Uzun; "all I've covered is the silver-black stuff. I think these must be solar cells, small ones—a music box doesn't take much energy. But Orogastus's so-called magic mirror must need a lot. He built this Tower, didn't he?"

"Yes, so the stories say," Uzun said. "And it certainly wasn't here in my father's time."

"The floor of the room under the stables is made of what looks like the same material as these 'solar cells.' And it's the same level as the courtyard—do you know what the courtyard looks like when it's not covered with snow?"

"No," Uzun said. "I've never seen it when it wasn't."

"I did," Mikayla said, "the night of the day I made it rain, before I made it snow to cover the ice. With the ice all over it, I couldn't be sure, but I think the courtyard might be a solar cell. In fact, I think the entire Tower is built on top of what was supposed to be the power supply for the devices in the ice caves. That would be just the sort of thing Orogastus would do, thinking the devices were *magic.*" The word twisted sarcastically in her mouth as she thought of what Haramis had said about Orogastus and true magic. "It never would have occurred to him to look for a physical power source, and I'll bet he wouldn't have recognized one if he walked across it—literally."

"I think you are very probably right," Uzun said. "Can you prove it? And can you make this mirror work so that you can watch over Haramis?"

Mikayla frowned. "We could put torches in the storage room under the stables, but much of the floor is covered, and torches may not be bright enough. . . . I think I may need to use weather magic. Uzun, you told Fiolon to tell Haramis that you would teach me—I assume that means you *can* teach me?"

"Of course I can teach you, Princess," Uzun replied, sounding somewhat offended.

"Can you teach me weather magic? In your present form?" Mikayla asked. "I don't doubt for a moment that you can *do* magic—or could do it—but you're going to have to tell me everything and rely on my eyes and my ability to describe results. Those aren't exactly ideal teaching conditions."

"We'll manage," Uzun said briskly. "We have no other choice. What is it you want to learn first?"

"Well," Mikayla said, trying to think of all the necessary steps, "first I'd better make sure—first thing in the morning—that my theory about the plaza being a solar cell is correct. I'll sweep a bit of it clear—at the edge of the chasm so we can just pitch the snow down there. I should be able to get a few of the Vispi to help, don't you think? They can handle the cold.

"Which reminds me," she continued, "I'm going to have to raid Haramis's wardrobe for tomorrow; I don't own anything I can wear to go outside. And I'll have to get the servants to make me some warm clothing. I'll ask Enya at breakfast time, but I may need you to back me up. I suspect that Haramis may have ordered that I not have warm clothing so that I wouldn't be able to escape from here."

"Surely not!" Uzun gasped. "Haramis wouldn't do that."

"Then it must be coincidence that all I have are lightweight indoor tunics and slippers fit only for indoor use—the pair I was wearing the day Fiolon left were ruined when I went outside in them, and I could go outside only because Haramis let me wear one of her cloaks. And I need warm clothing even if I'm *not* going outside—you can't imagine how cold the ice caves are!"

"Then we'll get you warm clothing," Uzun said. "I had forgotten how cold it is here, outside of this room and the other rooms at mid-Tower. It's been so long since I've moved from this spot. . . ."

*Oh, bother,* Mikayla thought in dismay, *now I've upset him again.* She hastily went back to the original subject. "If the plaza is a solar cell, I'll shove as much snow into the chasm as possible, then use rain to clear the rest. The plaza slopes a little bit toward the chasm, so that ought to work. Do you know anything about the geography around here? Is putting rain and snow into the chasm going to harm anything?"

"To the best of my recollection," Uzun said, "no. But remember that what I know of this area is derived from scrying and watching Haramis use the sand-table. It's too cold for a Nyssomu to be outside—if Haramis needs to send one of us to the lowlands with a message, she seals him in a special version of a sleep sack and straps him onto a lammergeier. The lammergeier flies to a village in the lowlands, near the end of the Great Causeway, where the villagers unpack the messenger, and he continues on foot or by fronial from there."

"How does he breathe?" Mikayla asked curiously. "The sack must be pretty close to airtight if it keeps a Nyssomu anywhere near his normal temperature."

"It gets pretty stuffy," Uzun admitted, "but, as the lammergeier flies, the village isn't far away, so we're in no danger of suffocating."

"Wouldn't it be simpler just to send one of the Vispi?" Mikayla asked.

Uzun actually laughed at that. "The Vispi refuse to leave the mountains. They are adamant on that subject."

"Why?" Mikayla asked.

"I'm not sure," Uzun said. "Perhaps part of the reason is to preserve their legendary status as the 'Eyes in the Whirlwind' whose true form no one ever sees."

"Come morning," Mikayla said decisively, "they can whirl some snow from the plaza into the chasm." She ticked off the steps in her mind: find out if there really is a solar cell there, uncover it if there is, let the sun charge the cell. . . . "I've got it, Uzun. The next weather magic I need to learn is how to keep the skies clear. Can you teach me that?"

"Easily," Uzun assured her.

"Thank you," Mikayla said. "I've got a busy day tomorrow, so I'm going to bed now. Good night, Uzun."

"Good night, Mikayla," the harp replied, its strings absentmindedly starting to play a lullaby. Mikayla went down the hall, smiling as the music drifted after her.

# 13

*Mikayla came down to the study early the next morning,* just as the sun rose, carrying the spheres Haramis had given her. "I thought of something after I went to bed last night, Uzun," she said. "I may not need to have the servants here make me warm clothes. I can have Fiolon bring me some from home. Even if my own don't fit anymore, there are always the hand-downs from my older siblings—the housekeeper has several chests full of them."

"The Lady won't like it," Uzun warned.

"Won't like what?"

"Having Fiolon here."

"Then she should have stayed here and stayed healthy enough to be in a position to object," Mikayla snapped. "She can't very well train me to be the next Archimage when she doesn't even remember my existence!"

"Maybe she does by now," Uzun said hopefully.

"That's why I brought the spheres with me," Mikayla said. "We can bespeak Fiolon and see how she's doing."

"Very well." Uzun sighed. "It's not as if I could stop you anyway."

"You make it sound as though I'm proposing to practice black magic! What does Haramis have against Fiolon anyway?" Mikayla had wondered about this for a long time, ever since she had realized that Haramis disliked Fiolon.

"He's male."

"And?" *That's hardly a reason, and surely she has some reason for disliking him, though I can't imagine what it could be. He's always been better behaved than I am, and he was polite and respectful to her, which is more than I was.*

"I think that's all, really," the harp admitted. "The only male human sorcerer she ever met or heard of was Orogastus, which was not much of a recommendation."

"It was also almost two hundreds ago!" Mikayla protested. "That's an awfully long time to distrust an entire sex based on the actions of one person!"

"Haramis is a woman of strong opinions," Uzun said mildly.

"Strong, unchanging opinions," Mikayla agreed grimly. "If you weren't being so polite, you'd call her unreasonably stubborn." She sighed. "Let's see if Fiolon can tell us how she's doing."

Getting in touch with Fiolon was a bit more difficult than usual, since Mikayla had to wake him up in the process. But finally his sleepy face appeared in her sphere and he grumbled, "What do you want?"

"Good morning to you, too," Mikayla replied. "First, Uzun would like to know how Haramis is doing."

"The healers seem encouraged," Fiolon said, "but I was in there yesterday—very briefly—and she called me a Labornoki spy. She seems to be up to the point in her life where the invasion was taking place. She keeps asking where Uzun is, and why he isn't in attendance on her, so she obviously doesn't remember that she turned him into a harp."

"Oh, I wish I could attend on her!" Uzun said passionately. "Do you suppose that if we packaged me very carefully . . ."

"No, I'm afraid not," Mikayla said. "You wouldn't fit in one of the sleep sacks she uses to transport Nyssomu, and you're the wrong shape to strap onto a lammergeier's back. And Haramis would be very upset indeed if you were damaged in the attempt. Besides, at this point, it might be quite a shock to her to find out that she had turned you into a harp."

"I suppose you're right." Uzun sighed.

"So, Fiolon," Mikayla continued hopefully, "she doesn't remember either of us and probably won't for quite a while, right?"

"It looks that way."

"Good," Mikayla said with satisfaction. "And nobody else is likely to question your absence if you say you're going exploring."

"What am I exploring?" Fiolon asked cautiously.

"You'll love it," Mikayla promised him. "Orogastus built this place on top of a series of ice caves filled with devices of the Vanished Ones. And then he collected everything of theirs he could find—and it's all in barrels and boxes in the level under the stables. It's an absolute trove of knowledge!"

"Some of which may be *extremely* dangerous," Uzun admonished them.

"If you're planning to poke around and mess with devices Orogastus collected, I'd better come keep an eye on you," Fiolon said with more enthusiasm than Mikayla had heard from him since Haramis sent him away.

"Absolutely you should," she agreed promptly. "Who knows what sort of trouble I might get into without you here to restrain my enthusiasm for strange and new things?"



"Shall I bring back the fronials the Archimage sent me here on?" Fiolon asked.

"No, leave them there," Mikayla said. "She may need them when she's well enough to come home. I've been talking to the lammergeiers, and none of them can bespeak her since she took ill."

Uzun gave a gasp of dismay, and Mikayla hastily added, "Of course, that may change as she gets better. Right now she presumably doesn't remember that she's *supposed* to be able to speak to them, and that may be the only problem.

"Anyway," she continued her instructions to Fiolon, "pack all the warm clothing you can get your hands on, for you and for me. Go into the clothing chests if you have to—I think I've grown a bit taller since I've been here. But what fits you will probably still fit me. Be sure to bring warm mittens and boots; it's very cold in the ice caves, and we'll probably have to spend quite a bit of time there. Then tell the servants something plausible to explain your absence—don't tell them you're coming here, not after that stupid scene Haramis made right before she took ill—and go east on the Great Causeway until it crosses the river. Then go north half a league on the west bank of the river, and a lammergeier will meet you there. Have you got all that?"

"Yes," Fiolon said promptly, his sleepiness completely gone. "I should be there about midday or shortly thereafter."

"Wonderful," Mikayla said. "I'll have Enya make up a room for you, but I may be a bit vague about how long you'll be staying."

"That's probably a good idea," Fiolon agreed, "since we don't know how long I will stay."

Mikayla bundled up in the warmest clothes she could find in Haramis's room. When Enya protested against her borrowing Haramis's clothing without permission, Mikayla took the opportunity to tell her that she was expecting Fiolon later that day with her own clothing and to ask Enya to prepare a room for him. "As for the Lady Haramis, they are caring for her at the Citadel and are hopeful about her recovery, but I'm afraid that at present she's in no condition to give permission for anything. Until she recovers, I shall be continuing my studies under Master Uzun's direction."

Enya might not have been happy about it, but there wasn't much she could do. At Mikayla's request, she assigned one of the Vispi to help Mikayla dig snow off the plaza. Enya didn't like it, but Mikayla didn't care.

It was great to be outdoors. Mikayla felt more alive and more real than she had since she had first come to the Tower. Being shut up indoors with Haramis made her feel like a shadow or a ghost, but now, outside in the sunlight, she felt wonderful, perhaps even slightly larger than life, connected to the rest of the world, instead of cut off from it. And Fiolon would be with her again today. Mikayla was happier than she ever remembered being in her entire life. Even the grumbling of the Vispi whom Enya had assigned to help her couldn't dampen her spirits.

It took the two of them the rest of the morning to clear snow completely off a small area of the plaza next to the chasm, but by midday, Mikayla was able to return indoors, soak in Haramis's tub until her body thawed out, then order a very large lunch to be served in the study, where she gave Uzun the good news.

"It's a solar cell, all right," she said, "thank the Lords of the Air. If the solar cell hadn't extended across the plaza, we'd probably have had to tear down the building to recharge the cell." She grinned. "Haramis *really* wouldn't have liked that."

"So what will you do now?" Uzun asked.

"I've asked the Vispi to shove as much of the snow on the plaza into the chasm as possible; that will mean that I'll have less of it to melt when I make it rain, which I plan to do tomorrow. This afternoon, you can explain to me how to keep the temperature high enough so that the rain doesn't turn to snow, and how to keep the skies clear once I've got the plaza free of snow. It's a good thing that the plaza is on the south side of the Tower—at least it will get what sun there is. But it will probably still take several days to recharge the power. Once I've got the mirror working reliably, I can use it to check on Haramis. And it's possible that it—or maybe something else stored down there—will give me the clue I need to learn how to make you a new body."

"New body?" came a voice from the door. "Is there something wrong with the harp?"

"Fiolon!" Mikayla leapt to her feet and ran to hug her friend. It felt wonderful; she hadn't realized how starved she had been for human contact, and how much she had missed Fiolon. He had grown more than she had while they had been apart; when she had seen him last they had been the same height, but now he was half a head taller than she was. But he still felt the same, solid and reassuring, her best friend, her other half. Their psychic bond was a good thing, but being with him in person was much better.

"I'm so glad to see you!" She dragged him to a seat at the table, sat down across from him, and looked him over. His hair was longer than he had worn it before and was windblown from the journey, but to Mikayla he looked beautiful, especially when he looked up and smiled at her. She felt warm all over. "Are you hungry?" she asked. "I ordered enough lunch for both of us."

"Good," Fiolon said, reaching for a plate. "I'm starved. But I brought everything you asked for. And I brought all the music boxes, too—it occurred to me that Master Uzun may not have heard all the tunes on the ones we found in the ruins."

"That was very thoughtful of you, Lord Fiolon," Uzun said, in tones as close to enthusiastic as Mikayla had ever heard from him. "I shall look forward to hearing them."

Fiolon paused to gulp down a large bite of food, then turned to Uzun. "Is something wrong with your harp?" he asked anxiously.

"No, not at all," Uzun said. "It's just that with Mikayla here and Haramis gone, I'm finding being a harp to be rather confining."

Fiolon nodded. "There is a difference between loving music

and *being* music," he agreed, "and keeping track of what Mikayla is up to is not something you can do if you're stuck in one place. I'll do what I can to help."

"You can start by studying weather magic with the princess," Uzun said tartly. "We don't need any more accidental snowstorms."

The three of them spent the rest of the afternoon in technical discussions of weather and how to control it, and Uzun ordered them to bed directly after supper. "You have a busy day ahead of you tomorrow, and you'll need all your strength."

Neither Mikayla nor Fiolon was disposed to argue with that statement; they went to their rooms immediately. They'd both had one busy day already.

The next morning, they ate breakfast early and went over the process with Uzun one more time before going to the workroom. With two of them to power the spells, making it rain wasn't difficult at all. Once they had the basic spell set, they moved to the window to watch it work.

At first it was just soft rain, almost a heavy mist, but as the storm gathered itself together the rain grew heavier. In the workroom, which lacked the warm air grilles of the living quarters, it was cold and damp.

"This is really depressing weather," Fiolon remarked.

"But it *is* clearing that plaza," Mikayla pointed out.

"How can you tell?"

Mikayla smiled at Fiolon's grumpy tone. She had always been the optimist of the pair. Still, he did have a point. Between the rain and the wind and the snow higher up on the mountain, there was a great cloud of dim fog all around the Tower, and visibility was limited. Mikayla admitted, but only to herself, that she had not anticipated the fog. It looked like the ghost of a giant Vispi.

"Be thankful Haramis isn't here," she said. "Remember how when she was starting to teach me, she'd pick the most horrible, seemingly useless things and demand that I tell her what they were good for?"

Fiolon nodded. "So what's the fog good for?"

"If you watch the way it drifts, you can tell which way the wind blows here. Rain and snow are a little too solid and heavy; the fog is light enough and visible enough so that you can see the pattern."

"Hmm." Fiolon studied it for several minutes. "The wind

seems to be coming from the west—from Mount Gidris. That's where Haramis found her Talisman, you know."

"Did she?" Mikayla asked. "No, I didn't know. What's on Mount Gidris?"

"A bunch of ice caves, which tend to be rather unstable. Don't go exploring there, Mika, all right?"

"I'm not planning to—oh, no; I think we've got trouble." Mikayla pointed to the precipitation still falling from the sky.

It was late afternoon, and the rain was beginning to change to hailstones. "Stop it," Fiolon said, dashing back to the table. "Quickly!"

Mikayla was right behind him, and together they pushed the storm down the slope and away from the Tower. When the clouds were gone, the sun shone faintly near the western horizon.

"The courtyard's still wet"—Mikayla sighed—"and it will probably freeze over tonight. I do hope that once the cell is charged, we'll be able to find some way of keeping it free of snow."

"Me, too," Fiolon said. "I'd hate to have to go through this every few days."

"Well, we're done for today at least," Mikayla pointed out. "We'll try to finish up tomorrow. Let's go down to the kitchen; I want to get something hot to drink and to tell the servants to stay out of the plaza. I don't want any of them hurt."

Enya found a couple of small stools for them to sit on and provided hot drinks for them at once; she had a large pot of hot ladu-juice set over the fire. Next to the fire were several very unhappy-looking Vispi.

"What did you do to the weather?" one of them asked in the voice of someone too wretched to care that he was being rude to his social superiors. "It's not supposed to be *wet* here! The damp hurts my lungs." He coughed miserably. The rest of the Vispi just huddled near the fire and looked unhappy.

He was correct, Mikayla realized. When it snowed here, the air stayed dry. In fact, even the *snow* in this region was on the dry side for snow. And the air was very thin at this height.

She remembered Uzun's laughter when she asked why Haramis didn't use the Vispi to carry messages to the lowlands. "That's why you don't leave the mountain, isn't it?" she asked. "You're used to thin, dry air. It's not the heat that bothers you, it's the humidity."

"My grandsire tried to go down the hill once," one of the younger Vispi said. "He didn't go far, and when he came back, he said it was like trying to breath adop soup!"

"He was right," Fiolon agreed. "After you've been up here awhile, you adjust to the air here. Then when you descend, what you're breathing feels much too thick and warm." He shrugged. "I readjusted after a day or so, of course, but I'm not at all sure that a Vispi could. I've never heard of one that did."

"I shan't ask any of you to go down the hill, then," Mikayla said. "As for the rain and the fog, it should be gone in another day or so, or by tomorrow if we're really lucky. Which reminds me, everyone should stay off the plaza—I'm afraid it's going to turn into a sheet of ice again tonight."

The Vispi groaned, and even the Nyssomu, who didn't go outdoors, looked depressed. Enya sighed. "Princess, do you mind if I make up pallets on the floor here for the Vispi and let them sleep by the fire?"

"Not if you don't mind," Mikayla replied. "It's your kitchen. They certainly won't be in my way here; so as long as they're not in yours, I certainly have no objection." She rose to her feet. "Thank you for the hot drinks, Enya. Fiolon and I will get out of your way now. Will an hour from now do for dinner? You don't have to cook something fancy, anything warm will do—even adop soup."

Enya chuckled. "Dinner will be in the study in an hour, Princess. And I think I can do better for you than adop soup."

Drying the plaza was a bit more difficult than Mikayla had anticipated. Even when the sun was high the next day, it was still too cold to melt the ice and dry the solar cell. And high clouds kept drifting overhead from the direction of Mount Gidris, hiding the sun a good part of the time. At one point, it even began to snow briefly, causing both of them to dash to the workroom to stop it.

Finally Mikayla and Fiolon bundled up in warm clothing, took a pair of torches each, and started melting the ice by nonmagical means. Since the plaza sloped gently downhill from the Tower door to the chasm, they started at the door. Once that ice melted, the water was warm enough to help melt the ice farther on. Bit by bit, they worked their way across the plaza. By sunset, about a third of it was clear of ice and dry.

"I think that's all we can do for today," Mikayla said, straightening up with a sigh. Her back hurt from spending so much time stooped over holding a torch near the ground. *Oh, well,* she thought, *at least my feet are warm.* "I think we'll be able to finish this tomorrow."

"If we're lucky," Fiolon groaned. "And if our muscles hold out."

"We may have charged part of it already," Mikayla said cheerfully. "The torches aren't just heat, they're light as well." She looked at Fiolon. "Do you want to see the ice caves now?"

A low moan was his first response. Then he added, "Tomorrow, all right? All I want now is a hot bath and a warm dinner."

"Me, too," Mikayla said. "We can check out the caves at midday tomorrow—we'll be wanting to take a break then anyway."

"I don't doubt that in the slightest." Fiolon sighed. "Mika, are you sure that this is going to work?"

"I'm not absolutely positive," Mikayla admitted, "but I think that the chances are very good. The mirror said that the solar cell needed to be recharged, this plaza certainly looks like the part of the music boxes that has to be exposed to light for the music to play, and we are exposing it to light. So it should work."

"It sounds as though it should work," Fiolon agreed, "and I certainly hope that it does. I would hate to have done all this for nothing."

# 14

Mikayla went to bed immediately after dinner and slept the sleep of total exhaustion. When she woke the next day, she was horrified to find that the sun was already high; she had slept through half the morning. She scrambled out of bed and into her clothing, ignoring the agonized protests of her sore muscles.

She went down the hall and poked her head into the room assigned to Fiolon. He wasn't visible, but the lump in the bed revealed that he had overslept as well.

"Fiolon!" she called.

After a minute, the bedding twitched slightly and there was a reply—if one counted "Mmmph?" as a reply.

"I'm going out to work on the plaza," Mikayla informed him. "You can join me whenever you're ready."

She stopped briefly in the study on the way downstairs to say good morning to Uzun and to tell him where she was going. The harp returned her greeting but made no other comment. She continued on to the kitchen, where she grabbed a hunk of bread and a couple of torches. She lit one of them in the fire, noticing with a small part of her mind that the Vispi who had been huddled there in misery the other night were gone, and hurried down the remaining stairs and outside.

She stopped just outside the door and stared around her in amazement and delight. The sky was a brilliant blue, without a single cloud visible anywhere she looked. The sun was shining brightly over the entire plaza, and the air was warm! Actually, the air still felt cool as she breathed it and where it touched her face, but its temperature was obviously above freezing, for nearly all the ice on the plaza had melted. The section she and Fiolon had gone over the day before was still dry, as was an area quite a bit beyond it. Perhaps a fifth of the plaza, closest to the edge, had water running down it, dripping into the chasm below.

Mikayla ate her bread while she inspected the plaza, then lit the second torch from the first and continued the task of drying the portion of the plaza that was still wet. To her delight, the job went quickly, and she had made significant progress by the time Fiolon joined her. With his help, the job was soon done. By lunchtime, they surveyed a clear, dry plaza/solar cell, which was efficiently soaking up the sun's light. When Mikayla, out of curiosity, took off her mittens and gloves and bent to touch the ground, she nearly burned her hand. She was so excited, however, that she didn't care.

"This should do it, Fiolon," she said. "The mirror should work now. Let's go look at it!"

"Did you eat breakfast?" Fiolon asked.

Mikayla stared at him. "How can you think of food at a time like this?"

Fiolon chuckled. "Because it *is* a time like this, and because I know you, Mika. Once you get into the cave, you're going to want to spend the rest of the day there. So let's eat lunch first, all right?"

"Lunch." Mikayla looked at him in disgust. "The wonders of the Vanished Ones wait for us and you want to go eat lunch."

"The wonders of the Vanished Ones aren't going anywhere," Fiolon pointed out. "They've been here for at least a couple of hundreds, so they can wait for us a little bit longer. Besides," he added with a grin, "your stomach is growling."

Unfortunately, he was correct. Mikayla's stomach obviously didn't share her enthusiasm for research. "Oh, all right"—she sighed with a martyred air—"if you insist."

"I do insist," Fiolon replied, grabbing her arm and towing her toward the kitchen.

After lunch they took a lantern—Fiolon vetoed torches on the grounds that some of the material stored on the lower level might be flammable, explosive, sensitive to heat, or have all of those properties—and went down to the storage level. Fiolon examined the writing on the boxes with interest. "I wish I could read this language," he said.

"Or even puzzle out this alphabet," Mikayla added. "Maybe we can find some way to learn it."

"That *would* be interesting," Fiolon admitted, following her into the tunnel.

Since they had a lantern with them, Mikayla did not bother to light the ones along the tunnel, but simply hurried along until she and Fiolon arrived at the door to the cave. Together they dragged

the door open enough for them to go through and then Mikayla led the way to the room with the "magic mirror."

"Oh!" Fiolon gasped, obviously impressed.



"Request, please," the voice said. The voice was much stronger than it had been a few days before, and Mikayla noticed that there was less frost on the wall around the mirror, giving the

mirror a larger surface area.

"View Princess Haramis of Ruwenda," she said promptly.

"Scanning." The picture appeared in the mirror, as it had before. But the colors were no longer dim, and the details were so clear that it seemed as though one could reach out and touch Haramis, who lay sleeping, with Ayah sitting by the side of the bed, keeping watch over her. Haramis still looked like a sick old woman, but her breathing was strong and regular—and clearly audible through the mirror. Mikayla could even hear the soft creak of the chair when Ayah shifted her position in it.

"By the Flower," Fiolon whispered. "I wonder what else it can do?"

"I wonder," Mikayla murmured.

"Request, please," the voice said again, although the view of Haramis did not change.

"View Quasi," Mikayla said, curious as to how their old friend and guide fared these days.

"Subject not on file," the mirror replied.

*It doesn't know who Quasi is,* Mikayla realized, *but there may be another way to get the same results.* "View Citadel Knoll," she said.

The mirror obligingly displayed a picture of the Citadel and the knoll around it. The viewpoint made it appear that they were hanging in midair above it, looking down.

Mikayla chewed her lip, trying to guess how to word the next request. "View land to the west of the Citadel Knoll," she said, hoping that the mirror would understand her words as she meant them.

"Static view or scan?" it asked.

Since Mikayla wasn't sure what the choices meant, she picked one at random. "Scan."

The picture in the mirror began moving, as though they were flying westward from the Citadel. Mikayla mentally tucked this away as the mirror's meaning for "scan" and watched carefully for Quasi's village. "Stop," she said as soon as it came into sight. She frowned at the picture in the mirror. It didn't look right. The colors were wrong for this time of year.

"I wish we could see this closer," Fiolon muttered beside her.

"Close view on structures?" the mirror asked.

Mikayla and Fiolon looked at each other and shrugged in perfect unison. "Yes," Mikayla replied.

The village in the picture grew larger, as if they were dropping toward it. Now Mikayla could see why the colors were wrong. The vegetation around the village was dying. As the picture in the mirror got closer to the ground, she could see several Nyssomu sitting on a bench outside one of their huts. Quasi was one of them.

"There's Quasi!" Fiolon said excitedly. "I haven't seen him in ages, not since Haramis brought us here." He frowned. "He looks a lot older, doesn't he, Mika? Has it really been that long?"

Mikayla counted on her fingers as the mirror said, "Identify subject Quasi."

"He's the one in the middle," she told it absently, while adding to Fiolon, "No, it's only been two years—or maybe three. I tend to lose track of time here, but it hasn't been that long."

In the picture Quasi's figure was suddenly outlined in bright red. "Subject Quasi?" the voice asked.

"Yes," Mikayla replied. "That's Quasi."

"Subject Quasi marked for future reference."

*Whatever that means,* Mikayla thought. Then the mirror added sound to its picture.

"The rains are out of season," one of the Oddlings was saying.

"And the ground trembles," another one added as he approached the group on the bench. "These are evil omens."

"Why does the Archimage not mend the land?" someone asked. "Quasi, you have met her. Is she not a powerful sorceress? Why does she allow this to happen?"

Quasi looked unhappy. "She's ill," he said. "One of my sisters is a healer—"

"We know that," the first Oddling interrupted him.

"—and she was summoned to the Citadel several weeks ago to treat the Archimage," Quasi continued. "With swamp-worm venom," he finished ominously.

Apparently everyone in the group knew what that implied, judging from the virtually identical looks of dismay. "Will she recover?" one asked.

"My sister thinks so," Quasi replied. He looked around at the dying plants. "Let us pray to the Lords of the Air that she will recover soon. It goes ill with the land when the Archimage grows old and ill."

Mikayla frowned and noticed that Fiolon looked dismayed as well. Now that Quasi mentioned it, she could feel what he was talking about. Dimly she could sense wrongness throughout Ruwenda, as if the land itself were ill. She felt a bit ill herself. The land was out of control; things were going wrong, and she felt that she should be able to fix them, but she didn't know how. Obviously her need for magical training had just become much more urgent than it had been when Haramis was well and controlling everything. Which meant that finding Uzun a body so he could train her properly should be done right away. Could the mirror find help for her?

Mikayla pondered how to word her question. "Scan magicians," she said, a bit tentatively.

"Specify all or by race."

Mikayla thought about that one for a minute. "Human," she finally said.

The mirror displayed a series of pictures of humans working magic, changing from one to another at short intervals. Mikayla recognized one of them as a magician who came to the Citadel from time to time—he had produced some truly spectacular illusions for one of Prince Egon's birthday parties. Suddenly she gasped and said, "Stop!"

"Hold this display and mark for future reference?"

"Yes," Mikayla said, staring in fascination at the screen. A small group of humans stood around a table on which a wooden statue of a woman lay. One of them was anointing the body with some kind of ointment while one stood at the head, swinging a thurible that gave off a thick cloud of incense, and one held something to the mouth. The statue had painted open eyes and looked amazingly lifelike.

A man stood to one side, reading aloud. "Opening of the mouth," he said, obviously beginning a set of instructions. The phrases that followed made no sense to Mikayla, but she continued to watch as they went through the ceremony, dressed the statue in fresh clothing, and lifted it to a standing position. A pile of clothing that had apparently been removed from it earlier lay on the floor next to the table.

Mikayla looked at their surroundings, trying to find some clue as to where they were. A small room with a low ceiling, which was quite crowded with the number of people in it. The room was apparently cut out of solid rock, but there was no ice on the walls. Mikayla suspected that it was probably in the mountains somewhere, but where? "Where are they?" she wondered aloud.

"Locate Temple of Meret?" the voice asked.

"Is this view the Temple of Meret?" Mikayla asked.

"Yes."

"Locate Temple of Meret," Mikayla repeated.

The view changed to a map of the Peninsula. There was a black dot, which Mikayla realized was her own location, and a red dot on the north side of Mount Gidris, near the top of the mountain, but definitely on the Labornoki side of the peak. Some lettering appeared next to both dots, but it was in the same unknown alphabet as the lettering on the boxes outside.

"I do wish I could read that!" Fiolon said in frustration. Mikayla didn't blame him. He had been silent and patient while she had been watching the magic, probably realizing, as she did, that the mirror would consider anything said to be a new request.

Obviously that was how it viewed Fiolon's outburst. "Initiate reading tutorial?" it asked.

Mikayla and Fiolon looked at each other, wide-eyed with surprise. *What is this thing?* Mikayla wondered. *I do hope we can get it to tell us someday. In the meantime . . .* She nodded at Fiolon to indicate that he should answer the mirror.

"Yes," Fiolon said, his voice cracking with a mixture of excitement and nervousness.

"Name of student?"

Fiolon gulped. "Fiolon of Var," he replied.

"Name of second student?"

Mikayla exchanged a glance with Fiolon, shrugged, and said simply, "Mikayla."

The mirror went blank and then showed a character, next to a picture of a small house. "Alef," it said.

"Alef," Fiolon repeated.

The mirror repeated the process with four more characters, and then it showed only a line of five characters without their accompanying pictures. One of them lit up.

Fiolon was silent, and Mikayla wondered what the mirror wanted him to do. But she didn't dare ask, or say anything. After about half a minute, the mirror said, "Alef."

"Oh, I see," Fiolon said. "It's testing me to see if I recognize the letters."

"Alef," the mirror repeated.

"Alef," Fiolon replied.

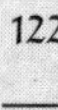

The letter flashed again, and Fiolon said "Alef" without being prompted. Apparently the mirror approved, for it went on to the next letter. Fiolon rattled them off with no further hesitation. The mirror then repeated the exercise again. Fiolon did it perfectly, and the mirror went back to displaying individual characters, new ones this time.

Fiolon and the mirror went through the process four more times, with the final display showing twenty-five characters in five lines of five. Apparently this was the entire alphabet, for after Fiolon had named them all correctly, the mirror said, "Lesson One completed for student Fiolon of Var."

It displayed the alphabet again, and said, "Student Mikayla." Mikayla didn't get the sequence perfectly right the first time, for she hadn't been paying attention quite as closely as Fiolon had, but she got it on the second try, and the mirror said, "Lesson One completed for student Mikayla." Then it added, "Power level low. Hiatus for recharge." The mirror went blank, and Mikayla and Fiolon quietly left the room, closing the door carefully behind them.

As they went back down the tunnel Mikayla was surprised to find that her feet hurt. "How long were we standing there, anyway?" she asked.

"I don't know," Fiolon replied, looking at the lamp he was carrying. "But it was long enough to burn a lot of lamp oil."

They stopped by the kitchen to return the lamp, and Enya said, with obvious relief, "There you are! Where did you two disappear to? You're three hours late for dinner, and Master Uzun has been fretting about you."

"Does this mean you're not going to feed us?" Fiolon asked anxiously. "We didn't mean to be late; we were exploring and lost track of time."

Enya shook her head. "Boys!" She sighed. "No matter what the race, they're all the same. Yes, of course I'll feed you. You two go up to the study and assure Master Uzun that you're alive and well, and I'll bring your dinner up there."

"Thank you, Enya," Mikayla said. "We'll try not to be late for meals again."

Uzun was inclined to be querulous about their having been gone for so long.

"I'm sorry, Uzun," Mikayla said. "But I've got good news. I think we've located some people who can help make you a new body."

"Really?" Uzun said in astonishment. "So soon? Where? And who?"

"There's a place on Mount Gidris called the Temple of Meret," Mikayla said.

"That's right," Fiolon said, frowning, "it *was* on Mount Gidris. I'm not sure you should go there, Mika."

"I know you said it was unstable on this side," Mikayla began.

"Very unstable," Uzun interjected.

"But the Temple is on the other side, and it didn't look at all unstable. That wasn't an ice cave; that was a regular cave, carved out of solid rock. And if it were unstable, they wouldn't be working there."

"It is true," Uzun said slowly, "that Princess Haramis's Talisman was in an ice cave on this side of Mount Gidris. But the cave collapsed when she removed the Talisman, and only her faithful lammergeier Hiluru saved her from dying there, with her work unfinished."

"Since the only way I'm likely to be able to reach the Temple of Meret at all is by lammergeier," Mikayla pointed out, "I can fly out at the first sign that the north side of the peak is unstable."

"That's true," Fiolon said. "But I still have a bad feeling about this."

Mikayla fingered the green ribbon around her neck. "I'll bespeak you every night," she said. "I promise. That way you'll know how I'm doing, and you can tell Master Uzun."

Fiolon looked at her in surprise. "You expect me to stay here without you?" he asked. "What if the Lady Haramis comes back?"

"If she comes back, then you can leave," Mikayla said.

"Since she'll undoubtedly throw me out," Fiolon pointed out, "I'll have to."

"But it doesn't look as though she's coming back anytime soon," Mikayla said, adding, "and you can check every day in the ice mirror. That way you'll have some warning of her return, and you can tell me so that I can get back before she does.

"But the main reason I want you to stay here is so that Master Uzun won't be alone," she continued. "He can't go down to the ice mirror and see how the Lady Haramis is doing; if you aren't here, all he can do is sit here in the study and brood. And that wouldn't be fair to him at all!"

Fiolon nodded. "You're right, Mika. I should have thought of that."

Uzun said formally, "You are welcome to remain here as my guest, Lord Fiolon. I would welcome the opportunity to share my music with you—and I believe you mentioned some music boxes from the ruins of the Vanished Ones?"

Fiolon's face lit up. "I'd be delighted to learn anything you could teach me about music, Master Uzun. And I'll be happy to share the music boxes with you."

"Good," Mikayla said. "That's settled then." She added to Fiolon, "And when you check on Haramis in the mirror, you can continue your reading lessons."

"Reading lessons?" Uzun asked. "Don't you already know how to read?"

"Not the language of the Vanished Ones," Fiolon said. "The mirror seems to have some sort of teaching program, in addition to its ability to let you watch a person or people and to show you where they are. Come to think of it, Mika, I'll probably be able to see you in the mirror. It should know who you are from the language lesson."

"And even if it doesn't," Mikayla pointed out, "it knows where the Temple of Meret is." She tried to figure out how the mirror's ability to locate people might work. If it could view only people it knew . . . "How did the mirror know who I meant the first time I asked to view Haramis?" she wondered aloud.

It was Uzun who answered that. "It had been asked to view her before," he explained. "Orogastus used the mirror to keep track of Haramis and her sisters. She told me about it."

"I wonder how he first identified them to it," Mikayla mused.

The harp was silent.

The next morning Mikayla went down to the mirror with Fiolon. Haramis was awake, but still seemed to be trapped back in her past. She was still asking where Immu and Uzun were, and what was going on, and was the army of Labornok close by, and why wasn't anyone telling her anything.

"She sounds really cross," Mikayla said. "Even though her speech is still rather slurred, you can tell." She sighed. "I know it's selfish of me, but I'm glad she's not here. At least at the Citadel there are a lot of people who can take turns taking care of her."

"That's true," Fiolon said, thinking it over. "There aren't many servants here, and they all seem to have plenty of work just keeping this place running. It would be awkward to have her be sick like that here."

"Very," Mikayla agreed. "I bet everyone would expect me to take care of her—and I'm not a good nurse. Besides, Haramis doesn't even *like* me!"

Fiolon looked back at the screen. "At the moment I'd say she still doesn't remember you. Maybe when she recovers, you'll get the chance to make a new start with her."

"Maybe," Mikayla agreed glumly. "But I don't think it will help. I don't think I could ever be the kind of person she would like."

Fiolon silently patted her on the shoulder, and then had the mirror start Lesson Two of the reading program.

At lunchtime, Mikayla said good-bye to Uzun, surprised at how reluctant she was to leave him. *I guess it's mostly because he's the only one here who has been willing to accept me as I am, without pressuring me to change into a copy of Haramis.* "You and Fiolon take care of each other," she said, trying to keep the tremor out of her voice. "I'll be back as soon as I can with your new body."

"Fare well, Princess," Uzun said. "And be careful."

"I shall," Mikayla said, "but I really don't think that side of the peak is unstable."

"The peak may not be," Fiolon muttered, "but the Lords of the Air alone know about the people."

# 15

*The lammergeier dropped her off on the path, just out* of sight of the Temple, and Mikayla followed the path to the Temple's main entrance. The land felt different on this side of the mountain, almost wild, as if it had no Archimage and never had. *But surely Haramis is Archimage of Labornok as well as Ruwenda,* Mikayla thought.

The Temple was easy to find; it seemed to radiate energy, although it was energy of a type Mikayla had never encountered before. It didn't draw power from either the land or the air, and the energy that she sensed did not seem to act upon the land. It floated in the air, like the fog had at the Tower when she had been working weather magic. Yes, she realized, that was what it reminded her of; it seemed to be some sort of excess, something unheeded, shaken loose from whatever the primary magic being worked was.

Casting a glamour to make herself unremarkable, as Uzun had taught her, she went inside quietly and followed the sound of voices. The outermost portion of the Temple was an enormous room. The ceiling was so high that Mikayla could barely see it, and while the room was full of pillars, fashioned in many different forms, the pillars were far enough apart that a full-grown lammergeier could fly between them with its wings fully extended.

Mikayla examined the pillars she passed on her way through the hall. The ones nearest the entrance were an icy blue white and were shaped like stalactites and stalagmites meeting in the center. The only light in this hall was the daylight spilling in from outside, so it got darker as she went farther into the cave. But there was still enough light to see that the design of the pillars changed as one moved away from the entrance. The ones farther in were many different colors and were in the form of various types of plants—mostly trees, although Mikayla did recognize a few flowers among them. And a good many of them were things she didn't recognize. She wished she were looking at them through the mirror and could ask it to identify them.

The next room in had a higher floor and lower ceiling and was lit by a pair of oil lamps hanging from the ceiling at the front of the room. There was a dais below the lamps, hidden on one side by a curtain; the rest of the room had wooden benches decorated with elaborately carved designs set on both sides of a center aisle. The benches were nearly all filled, but Mikayla found a seat in a back corner. No one seemed to notice her; people were talking to their neighbors and presumably waiting for something to happen.

Then two people in long black robes with golden masks covering their faces entered and took their places on the dais. One of them said something brief that Mikayla didn't catch, and the people in the room all sat down and grew quickly silent.

Then they started chanting, and everyone else joined in. After a few minutes Mikayla found herself singing along with everyone else—even though she had never heard either the words or the tune before in her life. This was not even a style of worship she had ever encountered before. It was as if the chant was in the room, and if you were in the room—even if you were wrapped in a dark cloak, hidden in an unlit corner, out of everyone's sight—you were part of the chant. Or maybe it was part of you.

"Meret, Thou Lady of the Southern Peak, have mercy upon us."

"Meret, Thou who makest the Noku, the River of Life, to rise from the Underworld to give life to the Land, have mercy upon us."

"Meret, Thou who savest us from the venom of the Worm, have mercy upon us."

"Meret, Thou who . . ."

The chanting was simple and repetitious; anyone—however simpleminded, unmusical, or unfamiliar with the entire idiom—could pick it up in a few minutes. Mikayla wondered vaguely if it had been designed that way on purpose.

In any event, it was making Mikayla feel very strange. She felt as though she were falling asleep, but she couldn't be, because she was still singing. Still her eyes kept closing despite her best efforts to keep them open, and her head dropped forward until her chin touched her chest. *This is magic,* she realized suddenly. *It's not a type I'm familiar with, but this is definitely magic.* She concentrated long enough to get a basic personal shield around herself and her thoughts, and then, feeling safe enough for the moment, relaxed back into the chant.

After about half an hour, the chanting stopped, and one of the figures in the golden masks, a man by his voice, began speaking. Some of what he said was familiar to Mikayla; she remembered reading bits of it in several of the books in Haramis's library. But as the man went on speaking she realized that his account differed from the ones she had read. At one point, she found herself opening her mouth and saying aloud, "That's not true!" Fortunately she didn't say it loudly, and her voice was lost in the chorus of folk loudly agreeing with their leader. At least now Mikayla was awake, free of whatever spell the chant held.

He was a convincing speaker, she had to admit that. He seemed completely sincere, and quite possibly was. But the doctrines he was advocating, such as the need for sacrifice, and the efficacy of blood (he was a bit vague about *whose* blood) to wash away the troubles that beset the people, were centuries out-of-date. The one thing of which Mikayla was perfectly sure was that the books she had read about this sort of religion were old, very, very old. And Haramis had told her that blood sacrifice had been stopped in Ruwenda long before even the Archimage Binah was born. So why was anyone advocating it now?

*Well, this is Labornok, not Ruwenda,* Mikayla thought. *But Labornok and Ruwenda were united almost two hundreds ago, when Prince Antar married Princess Anigel. And Prince Antar was the only surviving member of the Labornoki royal family. I think.*

*Granted, as the youngest princess, I never really studied history or government, but surely Labornok is ruled from the Citadel. How has this religion survived here?*

*Still, if this is what it takes to get Uzun a proper body, I guess I should be glad it survived, however it did. And if Haramis used her own blood to put Uzun into the harp, then blood magic can't be totally forbidden or wrong.*

Besides, there was magic in the room; Mikayla could clearly feel the power being raised, and there was no blood being shed here now. She was no stranger to power; even as a child she had used it sometimes for simple things such as mind-speaking to Fiolon, although she had never realized that what she was doing was magic until Haramis started training her.

But the power with which she was familiar was a solitary power, raised by one person, even though that person might be drawing on things outside herself, such as boosting the power by sitting in direct sunlight, for example, and using the sun's warmth. And since Haramis had started her on the cram course in "How to Be an Archimage in Many Difficult Lessons," Mikayla had learned much more about how to use other power sources for magic.

But what she had learned from Haramis was still basically a solitary magic, linked with the land, but not with other people. Here was a group of people being molded into a single source of power—even Mikayla, despite her training and her shields, could feel herself being sucked in. Who controlled this power, and what was being done with it?

The man stopped talking, and the chanting started again. This time, although the congregation was chanting the same words as before, as was the man who had been speaking, the other person at the front of the room—and several other women, judging by their voices—were singing something in counterpoint in a different language. Mikayla couldn't see any other woman there, but there was the curtain on one side of the dais. Perhaps the singers were hidden behind it. The overall effect was exotic and mysterious, *perhaps,* Mikayla thought, *even spooky.*

Despite her unease, the chant took hold of Mikayla again. It soon seemed to her that it had always been with her and would go on forever; she could hardly remember a life that had not been spent in this room, chanting along with everyone else. Mikayla did not notice when she fell asleep.

• • •

"Well, what have we here? A gift from the Goddess?"

Mikayla sat up, blinking, and focused on the young man standing over her. It took her a moment to orient herself, to remember that she was in the Temple of Meret and to realize that she had fallen asleep on the bench where she had been sitting. The man, apparently about three or four years older than she was, still held a broom carelessly in one hand. *He must have been sweeping the room,* Mikayla thought. *I guess my glamour wore off while I was asleep, so he found me when he reached this corner.*

"Looking for someplace warm to sleep?" the young man asked, leering unpleasantly at her. "You can sleep with me, girl—I'll bet we will become good friends." He dropped the broom against the bench, leaned over and pinned Mikayla against the wall, and kissed her. At first, shock held her motionless, but when he tried to force his tongue between her lips, she was overcome by outrage. Making a fist, she slugged him in the stomach as hard as she could. He released her and doubled over, trying to get his breath back.

"How dare you?" she exclaimed, breaking free of him and retreating toward the center of the room so that he couldn't pin her in the corner again. "Have you gone mad? You can't treat me like that!"

"By the Worm, what's the matter with you, girl?" he snarled, getting his breath back and approaching her again, albeit more warily than before. "You're carrying on as if you were a royal virgin!"

"I am!" Mikayla snarled back.

"Of course you are," he snapped sarcastically, "and I'm the Husband of the Goddess Meret!"

"Really?" a dry voice interrupted from the front of the room. "Strange; I thought I held that office." From his voice, Mikayla was pretty sure that this was the man who had led the chanting. He was dressed in a long black robe, but he no longer wore the gold mask over his face.

Mikayla decided that she liked his face. He had gray hair and regular features, and the lines on his face hinted at a sense of humor. "What seems to be the problem, Timon?"

"She"—Timon indicated Mikayla scornfully—"says she's a royal virgin."

The Husband of the Goddess regarded her thoughtfully. Then he made a sudden gesture with his hands, his fingers twisting in a pattern Mikayla could not follow. A blue light surrounded her, and she gasped.

"You have nothing to fear, child," the Husband said, "as long as you tell the truth. Are you a virgin?"

"Yes," Mikayla replied. The blue glow remained steady.

"As you can see, Timon," the Husband said, "she *is* a virgin. And virgins are scarce enough here that we don't want to lose one." He looked sternly at the young man. "So forget whatever you were thinking about her. And leave her alone in the future." Timon glowered, but bowed his head in apparent acquiescence.

The Husband turned to Mikayla. "Come with me, my child."

Mikayla briefly considered bolting for the exit and summoning a lammergeier to carry her away from here, but reminded herself that she was here to get Uzun a new body. *There's no point in running away quite yet,* she told herself. *And I don't think the Husband of the Goddess Meret means me any harm. Actually, he seems nice. Maybe he'll be willing to help me.*

The priest led her through the entrance in the front of the room by which he had entered, down a hallway to the left, and into a room that was apparently the Temple library. Mikayla was still surrounded by the blue glow—it had moved when she did—but she ignored it as she looked around at all the scrolls. *They have a bigger library than the Citadel and the Archimage put together,* she thought in awe. *Surely they will have the answers I need to help Uzun.*

The Husband clapped his hands sharply twice, and a young boy, clad in a short black tunic tied with a cord at the waist, ran into the room.

"Yes, my Father?" he said, apparently expecting to receive orders.

"My respects to the Eldest Daughter of the Goddess Meret, and I should appreciate it greatly if she would join me here as soon as possible."

The boy didn't answer; he simply bowed and ran from the room. Within minutes there was the sound of sandaled footsteps in the stone hall, and a tall woman in a black robe came in.

"What do you wish, my Father?" she asked deferentially. Then she saw Mikayla. "Who is this?"

The Husband sat in an elaborately carved chair and pointed to a bench behind Mikayla. The woman sat down in a simpler chair by one of the reading tables, and Mikayla took that as her cue to be seated on the bench. The Husband smiled at her encouragingly. "I'd like you to answer a few questions for me. You said you were a virgin, is that true?"

"Yes," Mikayla said, trying not to sound bored. She was getting tired of repeating it. *What's so important about being a virgin?* she wondered. *Everyone is one at birth.*

"And you are of royal birth?" The woman's eyes widened, but she remained silent.

"Yes," Mikayla said again.

"Who are your parents?"

Mikayla didn't know why, but she felt a sudden reluctance to give her parents' names. Perhaps it was the memory of something Uzun had said to her in the course of her studies with him. "Names have power," he had told her. "To know a person's name is to have power over that person."

"My father is the King of Ruwenda and Labornok," she said simply, "and my mother is his Queen."

"Is she royal?" the priest asked.

"Princess of Var," Mikayla replied briefly.

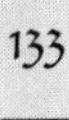

"Your pardon, my Father," the woman said quietly, "but if I may?" He inclined his head, and she turned to Mikayla. "Does this mean that you are a direct descendant of Prince Antar of Labornok?"

"The one who married Princess Anigel?" Since coming to live with the Archimage, Mikayla had learned more about the triplet princesses and their Quest than she had ever wanted to know, despite her general lack of attention when the subject came up. But Fiolon and Uzun spent so much time trading ballads on the subject back and forth that it was impossible for Mikayla to avoid getting the general outlines of the story.

"Yes," the woman replied.

"Then I am," Mikayla said. "He and Anigel were my I-don't-know-how-many-greats-grandparents."

"A princess of the royal family of Labornok," the woman said softly. "I can hardly believe it. Truly Meret favors us."

"Indeed She does," the man murmured. "Do your parents know that you are here?" he added, returning to more practical matters.

"No," Mikayla said. "If they think about me at all, they probably think I'm locked up in the Archimage's Tower." Two sets of eyebrows raised, and two sets of eyes regarded her thoughtfully.

"Locked up?" the man asked. "Why?"

"The Archimage has some crazy idea that I'm supposed to be her successor," Mikayla explained. "She took me when I was twelve, and I haven't seen my family, or left her Tower, since then."

"It sounds perfectly miserable," the woman remarked sympathetically. "Where does the Archimage think you are now? And why did she let you go?"

Mikayla shrugged. "She didn't let me go, and she doesn't know where I am. Last I heard, she didn't remember my existence." At their questioning looks, she continued. "She took ill while visiting the Citadel, with some sort of brainstorm. She doesn't remember a lot of things, especially recent things, and she's had me for only about two years."

The Husband and the Eldest Daughter exchanged glances.

"Two years," he said, almost to himself. Obviously this meant something to him.

"She's been training you as her successor," the Daughter said. It was not a question, but Mikayla nodded anyway.

"That explains quite a lot," the Daughter remarked.



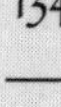

*Have they noticed the strangeness in the land, too?* Mikayla wondered. *Haramis should be Archimage of Labornok as well as Ruwenda; has her illness disturbed the balance here as well? It didn't feel quite that way to me, but I don't know Labornok the way I do Ruwenda.*

"Yes," the Husband agreed, turning back to Mikayla. "Why have you come here, then?"

Mikayla decided not to try to explain the "magic mirror." She had noticed how angry Haramis got when she mentioned devices of the Vanished Ones, and she didn't want these people angry with her. "I have a friend," she explained, "and he needs a new body. And I saw this Temple in a vision, and there were people working on a statue." She frowned, trying to remember exactly what it was she had seen and to figure out how best to describe it. "They were performing some sort of ritual, something about opening the mouth. And I thought perhaps the people here could help me make a new body for my friend."

"What's wrong with the body he has now?" the Husband asked.

"It's a harp."

"A harp?" the Husband sounded incredulous. "Are you sure?"

"Of course I'm sure," Mikayla said. "I've been living in the same Tower with him for years. He's a harp, and he's blind, and he can't move. And that makes him very unhappy since the Archimage took ill, because he can't scry and see her the way I can. And she keeps asking for him—apparently she's forgotten that she turned him into a harp about one hundred and eighty years ago—and he wants to go to her. And he can't."

"He's been a harp for nearly two hundreds?" the Husband asked.

Mikayla nodded.

"How was that done?"

"Somebody made the harp," Mikayla explained, "and the Archimage put some of her blood in a channel in the middle of the pillar, and there's a part of the top of my friend's skull at the top of the pillar. He doesn't remember exactly how it was done, since he was dead for part of it."

"So you have access to a piece of his original body—this skull fragment," the priest said thoughtfully, "and his spirit resides in this harp. Yes, I believe that under the circumstances, we could make a new body for him." He looked at her. "What is your name?"

The blue glow still surrounded her, and Mikayla was fairly sure that it was some sort of truth spell. And if she wanted their help, refusing to answer was probably not a good idea. "Mikayla."

"Princess Mikayla." The Husband bowed his head slightly to her. "I believe that we can give you what you want. Are you prepared to give us something in return?"

"If it is within my power," Mikayla replied cautiously. *What do I have that they could possibly want?*

"We want a month of your time each year for the next seven years," the Husband said. "Each spring, when the river rises and the three moons come together, will you spend a month with us, as a Daughter of the Goddess, living with the other Daughters and taking part in the rituals?"

"Somebody would have to teach me the rituals," Mikayla said. *I can't imagine why one more Daughter for the rituals would be worth much, but if that's all they want, I should be able to manage it. And it will at least be a change from listening to Haramis scold me or Uzun mope about Haramis's illness.*

"We will teach you everything you need to know," the Eldest Daughter said. "But you do realize that you will have to remain a virgin for the next seven years?"

"That's not a problem," Mikayla said. "Haramis wants me to remain a virgin for the rest of my life."

"Haramis is the Archimage?" the Husband asked.

*Ooops!* Mikayla thought. *I didn't mean to give them her name. On the other hand, it's in so many ballads that it's hardly a secret.* She nodded.

"Have you made any vows to her?" the Husband asked. "Or to anyone else?"

"No," Mikayla said, with just a bit of the resentment she felt toward Haramis showing in her voice. "She's always been too busy telling me things to ask me to promise anything."

Both of them smiled at her. "We are asking," the Husband said. "In exchange for a new body for your friend, will you spend a month with us each year for the next seven years?"

"Yes," Mikayla. "I will."

"Very good," the Husband said. "I will speak to He Who Causes to Live about the body for your friend. It will take him seventy days to give birth to the new body; can you remain with us that long?"

Mikayla thought of the image of Haramis as she had last seen her. *It doesn't look as though she'll be recovered enough to miss me before seventy days are up,* she thought. *Seventy days isn't long. And even if she does come back sooner, it's worth it. I don't care if she does get angry with me for leaving the Tower. Uzun is a friend; he's been good to me, and I want to help him.* Aloud she said, "Yes, I can stay here that long."

"Excellent," the Husband said. He turned to the Daughter. "I commit her to your charge, Eldest Daughter."

The woman stood up, and Mikayla hastily followed her example. "Yes, my Father," the woman said, bowing. She turned to Mikayla. "Come with me, Little Sister."

Mikayla bowed briefly to the priest. "Thank you, my Father," she said. He smiled and nodded to her, clearly dismissing her from his presence.

The Eldest Daughter took Mikayla's hand and started towing her rapidly down the hall. "You will be housed with the Daughters of the Goddess," she explained. "We do not use personal names here. I assume that you do know that true names have power; I notice that you did not give the names of your parents. As one of the Daughters of the Goddess, you will address Her Husband as 'Father.' I am addressed as 'Eldest Sister' and the other Daughters are called 'Sister.' Is that clear?"

"Yes, Eldest Sister," Mikayla replied, paying careful attention to what she was being told. She had the definite impression that she was expected to learn these lessons quickly and correctly. And for the first time in over a year, she cared about what she was being taught.

She was here by her own choice, and for her own reasons. She had given her word and accepted theirs, a situation quite different from that at Haramis's Tower. She wasn't sure exactly what they wanted from her or what she was supposed to learn, but for Uzun's sake and to accomplish her goal of getting him a proper body, she was going to try her hardest to be what they wanted her to be. *Besides,* she thought, *they asked me if I were willing to do this; they didn't just tell me to do it and expect me to obey like some mindless puppet.*

They entered an antechamber, then passed through a curtained doorway on the far side of it. On the other side of the curtain was a large chamber cut out of the rock of the mountain and brightly lit with torches set in the wall at frequent intervals. A number of other rooms with brightly colored curtained doorways led off it. "The Daughters live in these apartments," the Eldest Daughter told her. "You are not to go beyond the curtain we just passed without permission, and you must never leave these rooms unless one of the other Daughters is with you. Do you understand?"

"Yes, Eldest Sister."

"Good." The priestess clapped her hands together sharply; the sound echoed through the rooms. Four young women came out of various side rooms to gather in the central chamber. They appeared to range in age from four to six years older than Mikayla, and they looked at her curiously, but they seemed pleasant enough. They were dressed in heavy white, long-sleeved, high-necked robes, tied with white cord at the waist. "We have a new Sister," the Eldest Daughter announced, indicating Mikayla.

"Welcome, Sister," the others murmured in chorus. Mikayla noted that they spoke in unison and on the same pitch.

"I thank you for your welcome, Sisters," she replied. She hoped that she would fit in here. At least they were all smiling at her. Unlike Haramis, none of them seemed to dislike her on sight. Maybe they would even be friends.

"Your room will be the one with the green curtain," the Eldest Daughter informed her. "There is a chest in there with clothing that should fit you. Please put it on, and rejoin us here. You have much to learn."

"Yes, Eldest Sister." Mikayla hurried to do as she was told.

# 16

*Mikayla looked quickly around the room assigned to* her. It was small and had a very low ceiling; she could reach up and put the palms of her hands flat against it without having to straighten her arms completely. Along one wall was a bed, with some sort of fur that Mikayla did not recognize serving as a blanket. Next to the head of the bed was a stand with a pitcher of water, a washbasin, and a rough towel. The clothing chest that the Eldest Daughter had mentioned was at the foot of the bed.

Mikayla changed into a white gown like the one the other Daughters wore. There were several of them in the clothing chest, as well as a couple of gowns in other colors. She was glad to find that the high neckline hid the ribbon of the sphere she wore around her neck and that the fabric was thick enough to muffle any noise it might make.

Unlike the Archimage's Tower, these rooms did not have much in the way of heating, which was doubtless why the clothing was so heavy. But the only shoes in the chest were sandals. Mikayla put them on, remembering that both the Husband of the Goddess and the Eldest Daughter had worn sandals. Perhaps everyone here did, especially if they didn't have to leave the Temple. Mikayla considered what she had seen as she approached the Temple. From the air, it was virtually invisible. Even if one was looking straight at it, which could not be done from above, it appeared to be a natural cave. Perhaps the people living here didn't leave, but in that case, where did they get food and other necessary supplies?

*Stop it,* Mikayla told herself. *This is no time to try to analyze every detail of their society. I'll have plenty to do trying to keep up with the things they want me to learn.*

She returned to the main room. There was a single long bench at the far end of the room, in front of a fireplace. The other Daughters were sitting there waiting for her. One of them, the one sitting on the end, patted the spot next to her, and Mikayla quickly slid into place.

The Eldest Daughter stood and faced them. "Since our new Sister does not know our ways yet, we will start with the dawn chant." She fixed her eyes on Mikayla. "I shall sing a line and you will repeat it." Mikayla nodded.

"Hail to you, O Meret . . ."

"Hail to you, O Meret," Mikayla dutifully repeated. To her relief, all the Daughters were repeating it with her, helping to cover up any mistakes she might make. She had the uneasy feeling that the Eldest Daughter heard all her mistakes anyway, but at least she didn't feel alone and exposed, the way she had when Haramis had been teaching her.

"Lady of Eternity, Queen of Gods . . ."

"Lady of Eternity, Queen of Gods . . ."

"Many-Named, Holy of Form . . ."

"Many-Named, Holy of Form . . ."

"Lady of Secret Rites in Thy Temple . . ."

"Lady of Secret Rites in Thy Temple . . ."

By the time supper was served, a frugal meal of bread, fruit, and water, they had gone through the chants for Dawn, the First Hour after Dawn, the Third Hour, the Hour of the Sun at Zenith, the Ninth Hour, the Hour When the Sun Embraces the Sacred Peak, and the Second Hour of Darkness. Mikayla no longer wondered why all the Daughters spoke in unison; she thought it would be a good deal more remarkable if they did not.

While the Daughters ate, the Eldest Daughter read a long and boring story about a simple farmer whose volumnial was unjustly taken from him by a dishonest steward. When the farmer took his case before the magistrate, the magistrate was so impressed by the farmer's elegantly expressed arguments that he dragged the case out for more than nine sittings of his court so that he could listen to the eloquence of the farmer.

Finally the magistrate decided in the farmer's favor, so that justice was done in the end, but Mikayla noticed that the end was a very long way from the beginning. *My father would have settled this case at the first hearing,* she thought. *Any sensible person would have.*

"Tell me, Youngest Sister, what do we learn from this story?"

For one horrible moment Mikayla thought that the Eldest Daughter was addressing her. Then one of the other Daughters answered, and Mikayla realized that "Youngest Sister" must be some sort of honorary title, for the girl answering was obviously not the youngest of the other Daughters.

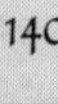

"We learn the value of silence, and of simplicity of speech when speech is necessary," the girl replied. "If the farmer had not been so eloquent, his case would have been settled at its first hearing. The grandeur of his words cost him much."

*About a year of his life at least,* Mikayla thought, *and maybe more, depending on how often the magistrate sat in judgment.*

There was the sound of a gong being struck somewhere off toward the main part of the Temple. The Daughters rose smoothly from their stools around the table in unison; Mikayla scrambled awkwardly from hers a beat afterward, but managed to push her stool under the table at the same time as the rest of the girls.

The Eldest Daughter smiled kindly at her. "It is time for the ritual of the Second Hour of Darkness, Younger Sister," she said, "but you need not attend it tonight. You will have time to become more familiar with the rituals before you are expected to take part in them. You may go to bed now."

"Thank you, Eldest Sister," Mikayla said with sincere gratitude. The Daughters fell into line behind the Eldest Daughter and passed beyond the curtain, beginning to chant softly as they went through the antechamber.

Mikayla went to her room, changed into a night robe she found in the clothing chest. The night robe was almost as heavy as the daytime clothing, but given the cold air surrounding her, Mikayla was glad of it. She climbed into bed and pulled the sphere out from under her clothing. Fiolon's face appeared in it almost immediately.

"Mika, are you all right?"

"Yes, I'm fine," Mikayla assured him. "You'd love this place; they're teaching me to sing. So far we've studied seven musical services, and those are just the everyday ones. They probably have a lot of special ones for holidays and festivals."

"I was watching when that Timon tried to kiss you," Fiolon said grimly, "but when the priest took you away I couldn't see you anymore."

"You didn't see their library, then?" Mikayla asked. "That's a shame; they have more books and scrolls than the Citadel and the Archimage put together. You don't need to worry about Timon; he won't get near me again. They've put me in with the Daughters of the Goddess, so I'll be so well chaperoned that even Haramis couldn't complain. And how is Haramis?"

Fiolon shrugged and spread his hands helplessly. "About the same. When are you coming back?"

"Seventy days from now. That's when the new body will be ready."

Fiolon looked at her in surprise and delight. "They can do it, and they agreed?"

"Yes," Mikayla said, smiling. "Finally I'm doing something right. It's a wonderful feeling—especially after two years of living with Haramis!"

Fiolon looked concerned. "What do they want in exchange for the body?"

"What I'm doing now," Mikayla assured him. "They just want me to be one of the Daughters of the Goddess for a while."

"That doesn't sound too dangerous," Fiolon said. "But if anything goes wrong, summon a lammergeier and get out of there, all right?"

"I will," Mikayla said reassuringly. "But I don't think anything is going to go wrong. The people here all seem very nice—except for Timon, and he has been ordered to leave me alone."

"Do you think he'll obey that order?" Fiolon asked anxiously.

"Don't worry about that," Mikayla said. "I'm sure he will. The Husband of the Goddess is a kind man, but he's not someone you disobey."

"Be careful, Mika."

"I will be. Don't worry." Mikayla yawned. "I'm going to sleep. It's been a long day. Give my love to Uzun. Good night, Fio."

"Good night, Mika. Sleep well."

Mikayla stuffed the sphere back into the front of her night robe. "I'll probably chant in my sleep," she muttered as she lay down and pulled the blanket over her.

The chiming of a bell in the main room woke Mikayla shortly before dawn. She hastily got up, washed, and dressed in one of the heavy white robes, making certain that the sphere and its ribbon were hidden. Then she went into the main room. The other Daughters were there already, and Mikayla was glad to see that they were dressed as she was.

*I guess I picked the right outfit,* she thought with some satisfaction. *So far, so good.*

The Eldest Daughter walked over to her and whispered in her ear. "We do not speak until after the ritual of the First Hour. Follow us to the chapel and take your place with us, but do not sing until I give you permission."

Mikayla nodded silently and fell in at the end of the line as the Daughters went through the curtain. Their place in the chapel turned out to be a bench off to one side of the dais where she had first seen the Husband of the Goddess. There was a curtain between their bench and the rest of the room so that they could not be seen by the congregation. Remembering the way Timon had looked at her the day before, Mikayla was just as glad of that.

The Husband of the Goddess entered from the other side of the room, robed in black and wearing the gold mask. The Eldest Daughter picked up her mask from a shelf under the bench, put it on, and went to join him. They started the chant, and the Daughters and the congregation joined in. Mikayla clamped her jaws together to keep herself from singing along.

*Hail to you, O Meret,*
*Lady of Eternity, Queen of Gods,*
*Many-Named, Holy of Form,*
*Lady of Secret Rites in Thy Temple.*
*Noble of Spirit Thou presidest in Derorguila,*
*Thou art rich in grain in Labornok.*
*Lady of memory in the Court of Justice,*
*Hidden spirit of the caverns,*
*Holy in the caves of ice,*
*The Sacred Peak is thy body,*
*The River Noku thy blood . . .*

The chanting went on for about half an hour, and Mikayla soon realized that she didn't remember even half the words. And when the chant started to repeat and the Daughters changed from melody to the descant in a different language, Mikayla was completely lost. They hadn't even begun to teach her this part.

*By the Flower,* she thought, *I have a great deal to learn before I can even begin to function as one of the Daughters. I only hope I can do it.* One side effect of her insecurity, however, was that she was not going into trance as she had the day before. She wasn't sure whether that was good or bad. It was certainly an uncomfortable feeling, sitting there and trying to hear and remember all the words and the tones that went with them. Slipping back into trance would have made all her nervousness go away, but then she might forget and start singing, and then they'd be angry with her. She definitely didn't want that to happen.

Finally they reached a point that Mikayla recognized as the end of the Dawn ritual. She tensed in her position on the end of the bench, getting ready to move when the other Daughters did. But the only person who moved was the Eldest Daughter, who came back behind the curtain and sat down on the far end of the bench from Mikayla. Mikayla peeked at her along the line of bodies and noticed that she wasn't even taking her mask off. The Daughters all sat still with their eyes cast down to their laps, where their hands were clasped. Mikayla imitated their position and waited for something to happen.

After a period of silence that seemed endless to Mikayla, the Eldest Daughter got up again and rejoined the Husband of the Goddess on the dais. Another round of chanting began, and after a few moments Mikayla recognized it as the ritual for the First Hour after Sunrise.

*Oh,* she realized. *There's so little time between the two rituals that everyone just stays here.* She tried to remember how long the First Hour ritual took. *I think it's a bit shorter than the Dawn ritual, but that may be wishful thinking. I just hope that we get breakfast when this is over. I'm starving.*

Finally the ritual came to an end, the Eldest Daughter returned to the bench and replaced her mask, and then led the Daughters back to their quarters. To Mikayla's relief, there was breakfast on the table. It was bread and fruit, with water to drink, but at least there was plenty of food, and her new Sisters kept passing it to her, so she got enough to eat.

After breakfast everyone remained at the table for a discussion of the day's schedule. "He Who Causes to Live wishes to speak to our new Sister this morning," the Eldest Daughter announced. "You two"—she indicated the two girls sitting next to Mikayla—"will accompany her to his workroom after the Third Hour." Both girls nodded, and Mikayla followed their example.

She assumed that by "after the third hour" the priestess meant after the relevant ritual, and by now Mikayla was figuring out her place in the scheme of things. *All I have to do is keep my mouth shut and follow my Sisters, and I should stay out of trouble—probably for the first time in my life. And I think I can actually do this. It's a very strange feeling not to have anyone scolding me or disapproving of me. I think I like it.*

"Until the third hour, we will work on the Dawn Chant again," the Eldest Daughter announced. The girls all moved to their places on the bench by the fire and started the chant again. This time they all sang it together, section by section, and Mikayla could feel it sinking into her mind.

*I'll learn all of this yet,* she thought with satisfaction. *I'm not stupid and hopeless after all.*

The workroom of He Who Causes to Live was one of the most fascinating places that Mikayla had ever seen. One entire wall was covered with bins containing more types of wood than she had ever known existed. Another wall had a board with all sorts of tools hooked to it. Briefly Mikayla regretted being stuck with the Daughters; being apprenticed to this man looked like a very interesting job.

He Who Causes to Live was a comparatively young man compared with the Husband of the Goddess; he was only in early middle age. But Mikayla noted as he set a stool for her next to his workbench that he had the hands of someone who had been working with them for a long time. The other two Daughters sat side by side on a bench near the door of the workroom, where they could watch Mikayla but not hear the conversation as long as Mikayla and He Who Causes to Live kept their voices low.

"I understand I'm to make a new body for an effective spirit," the man began. "What does the body need to be able to do?"

Mikayla concentrated, wanting to be sure that she didn't leave anything out—especially something important. "It needs sight, hearing, speech, and the ability to move, including the ability to climb and descend stairs. It has to be able to tolerate extreme cold, such as the temperatures in an ice cave or on the back of a lammergeier flying above the mountains. And it needs to be able to tell when something is about to damage it."

"Sounds like it almost needs to be human," the man remarked, scribbling notes on a scrap of parchment. "What about the ability to eat and drink?"

"If that's what it needs to maintain the body, it will need them. But it hasn't eaten or drunk in nearly two hundreds now." Mikayla smiled briefly. "And he hasn't been complaining about the lack of food."

"I hear he's been a harp?" the man asked, apparently not quite ready to believe this.

"Yes, that is true," Mikayla replied calmly.

"Incredible," He Who Causes to Live murmured. "What about sex?"

"He's male."

"No, I mean does he need to function sexually?"

Mikayla stared at him for a moment in shock, and then visualized Haramis's probable reaction to that. "I don't think that would be a very good idea," she choked out. "The Lady wouldn't like it, and besides, everyone else he ever knew has been dead for a long time."

"Very well." He Who Causes to Live made another note. "Now, what is this body supposed to look like?"

"Oh dear." Mikayla chewed on her bottom lip. "I don't know what he looked like; he was turned into a harp long before I was born. He was a Nyssomu, if that's any help."

"It will do for a start," the man said. "I can begin work with what you've given me." He handed her a piece of parchment and a burned stick. "But it would be helpful if, sometime in the next few days, you could draw me a sketch of what he's supposed to look like, particularly the head and face. Faces are important."

"I'll do my best," Mikayla said. *Maybe Fiolon will be able to get a description from Uzun.*

"One more thing I need," said He Who Causes to Live, lowering his voice even further. "I need his true name."

"Uzun," Mikayla whispered.

He Who Causes to Live stood, and Mikayla followed his example. "Thank you, Daughter of the Goddess," he said formally. "I shall begin work at once."

"Thank you," Mikayla said, smiling shyly at him before turning to follow the other two Daughters back to their quarters.

• • •

The rest of the day alternated between attendance at the rituals and studying the chants for them. Luncheon was after the ritual of the Hour of the Sun at Zenith, and dinner was after the Hour When the Sun Embraces the Peak. Apparently servants came in to clean while the Daughters were at rituals, for although Mikayla didn't see any servants, the dirty dishes disappeared, the floors were swept, the fire in the main room was kept burning, and the washbasin in her room was emptied and the pitcher filled with fresh water.

There was a break after the ritual of the Ninth Hour when the Daughters went to a bathing chamber, a room with thick woven carpets covering the floor, with a small hot spring in the center of it, where they bathed and washed their hair. Mikayla carefully concealed her sphere inside the clean robe she had brought with her and put it back on when she dressed again.

But it was a long day, and by the end of dinner Mikayla was having difficulty sitting up straight. She envied the other Daughters their seemingly effortless perfect posture.

When the Eldest Daughter excused her from the Second Hour of Darkness ritual, Mikayla could have wept in relief. Instead she thanked her gravely and retired to her room. She wanted nothing more than to crawl into bed and sleep, but the parchment that He Who Causes to Live had given her earlier was propped up next to the washbasin. She put on her night robe, pulled out her sphere, and bespoke Fiolon.

"You look awful!" he exclaimed.

"I'm all right," Mikayla said wearily, "just very tired. Fio, I need to know what Uzun's body is supposed to look like; the man who is making it wants a drawing, especially of the face. Can you get a description from Uzun?"

"I can do better than that," Fiolon said enthusiastically. "I found something interesting in the mirror today. Did you know that it keeps images it has displayed?"

"No, I didn't know," Mikayla said. "How does that help?"

Fiolon was donning heavy clothing and pulling on his boots. "Orogastus used it to spy on the princesses, remember? And Uzun was with Haramis for part of her journey."

"Oh!" Mikayla exclaimed. "Do you mean that the mirror has a picture of Uzun?"

"Several of them," Fiolon assured her.

"That should help," Mikayla said, watching the walls flash by as Fiolon ran down the stairs. "I wish you were here, though; you draw so much better than I do."

Fiolon cut across the storeroom into the ice caves and entered the room with the mirror. It took him only a few seconds to call up the image he wanted.

In the mirror Uzun stood in front of Haramis. He was short; his chin was at the same height as her waist. His head was round and his eyes were a dark yellow color, almost amber. He had a wide mouth, with small sharp teeth, and an extremely short nose, but his upright ears, their points sticking out through his silky pale hair, were long enough to make up for the shortness of his nose. As Mikayla watched the image the ears swiveled back and forth, obviously trying to locate some sound only Uzun could hear.

Mikayla giggled. "He was cute," she said, reaching for the parchment and the charcoal stick. "Now if I can just get this on parchment . . ."

"Link with me," Fiolon said, "and I'll draw it for you."

"Can you?" Mikayla asked.



"I think so," Fiolon said, "and it's worth a try. Just sit back against the wall, hold the stick and the parchment, close your eyes, and relax."

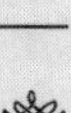

Mikayla did as he said. She was so tired it was easy to relax; she was almost falling asleep. But she jerked suddenly awake when her hand started to move.

"Stop fighting me," Fiolon said. "Your hand is going to move; it's the only way to draw. Just relax and let me move it for you."

"I'm sorry," Mikayla apologized. "I was just startled, that's all. Try it again." She sagged back against the wall, closed her eyes, and ignored what her body was doing. She was about three parts asleep when Fiolon's voice pulled her out of it.

"Mika, wake up!" She blinked and looked down at the parchment in her lap. It contained a very good likeness of Master Uzun as seen in the magic mirror. "How does it look?"

"Perfect." Mikayla swallowed a yawn. "Thank you, Fio; I never could have done anywhere near so good a job."

"You're welcome, Mika. Now put that someplace safe and go to bed. Good night."

"G'night," Mikayla said sleepily. She shoved the sphere back under her robe, put the parchment inside her clothing chest, got into bed, and fell asleep as soon as she lay down.

# 17

*Seventy days went by much faster than Mikayla had* expected. She was so busy studying that she didn't even notice when her fifteenth birthday passed. By the time Uzun's new body was ready, she knew all the daily chants in both languages, and nearly all of the festival ones. For the last thirty days she had been allowed to take part in all of the daily rituals, including the Second Hour of Darkness. This meant that she couldn't bespeak Fiolon, since now she was never alone, but she reasoned, when she thought of it at all, that he could see her in the mirror if he wanted to.

But finally the body was ready, and the Husband of the Goddess Meret summoned her to the library. "You have studied hard and have served the Goddess faithfully," he told her. "We are pleased with your progress." The Eldest Daughter of the Goddess Meret, who had accompanied Mikayla, nodded agreement.

"Thank you, my Father," Mikayla replied respectfully.

He handed her a scroll. "This contains the instructions for bringing the body to life and placing the effective spirit into it.

The body has been packed." He indicated a bundle on the bench just inside the door. "Do you have a way to transport it?"

Mikayla cast out with her mind, quickly locating the nearest lammergeier. "Yes, Father."

"Are you ready to leave now?"

"Yes, my Father. Thank you for all you have done for me. And thank you also, Eldest Sister."

"Remember that you are to return in the spring," the priestess reminded her.

"I remember," Mikayla assured them. "And I keep my promises."

"Good," the priest remarked. "We expect that of our Daughters."

Together the three of them walked through the main Temple into the hall of columns. Mikayla carried the package with Uzun's body, which was more awkward and bulky than it was heavy.

"Holy Meret!" the Daughter gasped, seeing the shape perched by the outer pillars. "Where did that come from?"

"The lammergeier?" Mikayla asked. "I called it, Eldest Sister. It has come to take me home." 

"Go with our blessings," the priest said, laying his hand briefly on Mikayla's head, "but remember that this is also your home."

"I shall remember," Mikayla said. "I'll be back in a few months anyway." She smiled up at him. "You'll barely have time to miss me." She put Uzun's body carefully onto the bird's back and climbed up behind it, holding it in place with her body and carefully clutching the scroll in one hand. "Be well," she said.

"Fare well," the Husband and Daughter replied in unison, "and return to us at the appointed time."

The lammergeier dropped her on the Tower balcony less than an hour later. Mikayla thanked it and dragged Uzun's body indoors as the bird launched itself skyward again.

"Fiolon?" she called. "Where are you?" There was no answer, so Mikayla dragged the body down the stairs to the study, hoping that He Who Causes to Live had packed it securely. Of course, she was pretty sure he had; he was definitely a man who took pride in his work.

"Who's there?" the harp asked sharply as she dragged the package into the study.

"It's Mikayla, Uzun," she replied, "and I've brought your new body with me." She set the body flat on the floor and carefully put the scroll on a shelf behind a pile of books so that it wouldn't roll off.

"Thanks be to the Lords of the Air that you are safe!" Uzun exclaimed.

"Why wouldn't I be safe?" Mikayla asked. "I've spent the past seventy days shut up with the Temple virgins, and the most strenuous thing I've been doing is singing." She stretched, noticing that quite a few of her muscles had stiffened up during the ride home. She also noticed that her feet were cold.

Looking down, she saw that she was still wearing the sandals and robe of a Daughter of the Goddess Meret. "Please excuse me, Uzun," she said. "I need to take a hot bath and put some warmer clothes on. I'd forgotten how cold it is on the back of a lammergeier."

"Of course, Princess," Uzun said. "Go and thaw out. It's good to have you back."

"It's great to have you back," Fiolon's voice came from the doorway, "but you had better thaw out quickly—and change out of those clothes. Haramis is on her way home."

Mikayla looked at him in horror. "By lammergeier?"

"No, by fronial, but she'll be here within the hour."

Mikayla fled the room. Behind her she could hear Fiolon start to explain to Uzun why it had taken him so long to notice Haramis's approach, but Mikayla knew it was more urgent for her to be properly dressed, with nothing to indicate that she had ever left the Tower, before Haramis arrived.

Mikayla took the quickest bath of her life, hid her clothing from the Temple under the bottom of her mattress, and changed into one of the light tunics Haramis had had made for her. It was noticeably shorter than she remembered it; apparently she had grown a bit taller while she was at the Temple. She hoped that Haramis would be too tired to notice such details.

When she returned to the study, Uzun and Fiolon were still discussing Haramis's imminent return.

"Yes," Fiolon agreed, "I should have been keeping a closer watch on her. But she was making a good recovery, and I discovered the system the Vanished Ones used for musical notation about two weeks ago. You were as excited about it as I was, Uzun," he pointed out, "so surely you can understand how I failed to notice that she had started the journey home."

Mikayla tried and failed to stifle a giggle. "I can understand it perfectly," she said.

"We have failed her," Uzun said mournfully. "We should never have allowed ourselves to be distracted from her welfare."

"Is there anything wrong with her?" Mikayla asked.

"Mika, she's had a brainstorm!" Fiolon reproved her.

"I know that," Mikayla pointed out. "She had it before I left, remember? But if my parents let her travel, she must be much better, and I doubt if they sent her without an escort. So unless you saw her buried under a rock slide or some similar disaster, I don't see what the problem is."

"We should have known she was coming," Uzun repeated stubbornly.

Mikayla ignored him. "How many folk are in her party, Fiolon?"

"Three," Fiolon replied. "She's in a litter slung between two fronials, and there are two women with her—both human," he added.

"They would tolerate the cold better," Mikayla said absently. "I'll tell Enya to have rooms made ready." She tugged on the bellpull to summon the housekeeper.

"There is one problem," Fiolon said. "How are they going to get across the chasm?"

"Oh dear," Mikayla said. "You're right. She left by lammergeier, so that silver pipe she uses to extend the bridge is probably somewhere in her room. And this is not a good time to tear her room apart looking for it. Maybe there's another way to extend the bridge. Enya might know."

Enya, arriving at that point, did indeed know. "There's a device in the gatehouse. Get one of the Vispi to show you." She reckoned on her fingers. "The Lady, you, Lord Fiolon, and two more humans—that's five for dinner." She looked without favor at the large package in the middle of the floor. "I don't know what that is, but I suggest that you get it out of here before dinnertime. And speaking of time, Princess"—she fixed Mikayla with a stern look—"where have you been the past few months? I'm sure the Lady will want to know."

"I was at the Temple of Meret, on the far side of—"

"Silence!" Enya cut her off, her fingers making the gesture the Nyssomu used to ward off great evil. "Do not speak that name again; it is a Dark place."

"Most caves carved into a mountain side are dark," Mikayla

said calmly. "And I certainly don't expect you to lie to the Lady. Tell her anything that you think an elderly woman too ill to ride even a fronial should know."

Enya frowned, and Mikayla was suddenly sure that Haramis wasn't going to hear about her absence from any of the servants. "I'm sure you've kept the Lady's room ready against the day of her return," Mikayla continued, "but we'll be needing rooms for the two women with her."

"How do you know there are only two?" Enya asked suspiciously.

"By scrying," Mikayla replied.

"Hmmph." The Oddling woman left to go about her duties.

Mikayla looked at Fiolon and sighed. "I wasn't trying to take credit for your work, Fio. . . ."

Fiolon shook his head. "No matter. The less said about any recent events, the better. Let's wait until we see what sort of condition Haramis is in."

"That's the most sensible thing you've said all evening," Uzun said sharply. "And if the thing Enya was telling you to get out of the way before dinnertime is my new body, I suggest that you do so. The Lady is likely to be shocked enough to find Fiolon here without adding any more surprises."

Mikayla grinned. "I can just imagine her reaction to coming in to find us in the middle of the ritual to put you into a new body. Besides, I haven't had time to read all the instructions for the ritual yet, and it's probably very long and complicated."

"What shall we do with it?" Fiolon regarded the package dubiously. "It's awfully large."

"It's not heavy," Mikayla assured him. "A lot of it is packing material to protect the body from damage. He Who Causes to Live spent seventy days making it, so you can believe that he packed it very carefully before he handed it over to me to be brought here on the back of a lammergeier. We could probably throw it off the balcony without harming it."

"I don't think I want to try that," Fiolon said.

"I know I don't," Mikayla agreed, "but if you take one end and I take the other, we can take it downstairs on our way to extend the bridge for Haramis and her party." She bent and grabbed one end of the box. After a second Fiolon picked up the other, and they maneuvered it into the hall and started down the stairs.

"Where are we going to put it?" Fiolon asked.

"I think we'd best put it with the devices of the Vanished Ones, and if we can hide it behind a few other boxes, so much the better." Mikayla frowned. "I'm not sure how Haramis is going to take the idea of giving Uzun a new body, so it's much better if she can't find it."

"But surely she couldn't be so selfish as to wish him confined to that harp forever!" Fiolon protested.

"Have you ever known Haramis to be unselfish?"

"In the old ballads—"

"No, not when she was a girl. Now, since you've met her."

Fiolon was silent for the rest of the trip down the stairs, and when they reached the storage area he led the way to the darkest corner and stacked enough boxes and barrels in front of the body so that it wasn't visible from any angle.

"Very good," Mikayla said, surveying his work approvingly. "You've even left undisturbed dust on the tops of the barrels."

"Let's go find the device that extends the bridge," Fiolon said. "The Lady should be here anytime now."

Mikayla followed him in silence to the gatehouse. Obviously Fiolon didn't want to admit that Haramis, Crown Princess and Archimage, heroine of so many of his favorite ballads, was less than perfect.

*And as long as he doesn't insist on behaving as if she were,* she thought, *I'm not going to make him admit out loud that she isn't.*

# 18

*The device that controlled the bridge was obvious as* soon as one looked for it. It was mounted on the wall at about shoulder height. Mikayla pressed it, and she and Fiolon went out on the plaza to watch for Haramis's arrival. The sun was dropping fast, and the evening breeze was springing up, but the solar cell that made up the plaza was still warm underfoot. Mikayla realized that she didn't feel cold, even in her light indoor robe and house slippers. Fiolon, who had grabbed a short cloak on his way through the storage room, looked at her in surprise. "Aren't you freezing?" he asked.

"No." Mikayla shook her head. "I just realized that I seem to have adapted to colder temperatures during my time at the Temple. It's quite cold there, but after a while I stopped noticing. I was cold when I got off the lammergeier, but we were a good deal higher than this. I'm warm enough here. Perhaps the heat from the solar cell is enough for me."

Fiolon shaded his eyes and looked toward the approach to the bridge. "There they are," he said.

Mikayla watched as the fronials approached the bridge and stepped onto it without so much as a quiver. "Those are the Archimage's fronials, all right," she remarked. "You couldn't get an ordinary fronial on that bridge without blindfolding it and coaxing it every step of the way." She giggled softly. "That guardswoman on the first fronial looks more nervous than it does."

"There," Fiolon said with satisfaction. "They're all safely across. I'll go retract the bridge."

Mikayla smiled, perfectly able to understand his desire not to greet the Archimage at the moment. "I'll go welcome her home," she said, crossing the plaza toward the party.

The guard on the first fronial had dismounted, as had the woman bringing up the rear. "Princess Mikayla," the guard greeted her.

Mikayla quickly racked her brain for the proper name. "Guardswoman Nella," she said. "Be welcome to the Lady's Tower. The servants will be out to take the fronials in a minute." She nodded to the other woman, whom she recognized as one of the Queen's ladies who had some skill in herb lore. "Lady Bevis, be welcome. How is the Lady?" She looked anxiously at Haramis, who seemed asleep.

"Well enough," Lady Bevis assured her, "but it has been a long trip. She should be put to bed as soon as possible. Where is her room?"

Mikayla indicated the Tower looming above them. "About two thirds of the way up, I'm afraid." Both Nella and Lady Bevis looked appalled.

Haramis woke and looked around, frowning as she tried to figure out where she was now. It had been a long, tiring, and confusing trip, and all she wanted was to be home in her own bed. She looked up at the Tower. "Good," she said. "We're home." Then she looked around and frowned. Something was different. "What happened to the plaza? It should be white."

"The snow melted, Lady," Mikayla said respectfully.

"Oh." Haramis was confused. The snow had never melted on the plaza in all the time she had been there. Probably the child had done something to it. She glared at Mikayla. "Are you planning to keep us standing here all night?" she snapped. From what she remembered of that wretched brat, she probably was.

"No, Lady," the girl said. "We were trying to think how best to get you to your room. There are rather a lot of stairs to climb," she added in apologetic tones.

*She seems to have learned some manners at long last,* Haramis thought with satisfaction. *I must remember to thank Uzun.*

"So call some of my servants!" she snapped.

Mikayla smiled faintly. "Yes, Lady," she murmured, bowing her head briefly. Three lammergeiers swooped down to the plaza. One landed, but the other two hovered while Mikayla unhooked the litter from the rear fronial and passed the carrying straps to one of the great birds. Nella hesitantly followed her example with the front end of the litter, looking up at the bird with some awe. Obviously she had never been this close to one before.

The fronials just stood there, as if this were an everyday occurrence. Haramis wondered a bit at that. Certainly she had put time and effort into training each generation of fronials, but she had not realized that she had trained them quite this well.

The birds flapped their great wings in unison, carrying her smoothly toward the balcony. A few seconds later the third bird, with Mikayla on its back, swept past her to set the girl on the balcony. By the time the birds gently lowered the litter, one of Haramis's Vispi servants was there to take an end of it. Mikayla took the other, and between them they carried it carefully to Haramis's bedchamber, where Enya was waiting to put Haramis to bed.

Haramis stifled a sigh of relief when she was finally settled in. *At last I'm home. I don't have to move anymore; I don't have to spend any more time being jolted over mountain paths between two fronials. I'm home.* "Where's Uzun?" she asked. "Why hasn't he come up to see me?"

Mikayla, who had been assisting Enya, looked uncomfortable. "He's in the study, Lady," she said. Haramis noticed that the girl seemed to be worried about something.

"Doesn't he know I'm back?"

"Yes, Lady," Mikayla assured her, "and I know that he's looking forward to seeing you when you are able to go downstairs."

"Why doesn't he drag his lazy body up here?" Haramis demanded fretfully. *Doesn't he realize how ill I've been?*

Enya muttered something about dinner and fled from the room, casting an anxious look at Haramis as she did so.

*What's the matter with her?* Haramis wondered. *Why is everyone acting so strange?*

"Lady," Mikayla said hesitantly, "have you forgotten that you turned Master Uzun into a harp? He can't climb stairs; he can't even move on his own."

*By the Flower,* Haramis thought, *I had forgotten that. But I'm not going to admit it and have them all treat me as if I were an idiot.* "Well, have the servants bring him up here, then!" she snapped.

"Right now, Lady?"

"Yes, now!"

"As you wish, Lady." Mikayla curtsied and left the room.

*Can't I get anything done here without an argument?* Haramis wondered irritably.

Her question was answered sometime later when she heard voices in the hall. Enya had brought her a light supper, and Lady Bevis was sitting with her while she ate. Her bedchamber door was open, so the comments coming from the hall were clearly audible.

"I still don't think this is a good idea." The voice was that of a young man. Haramis didn't recognize it.

"It is the Archimage's specific order," Mikayla said, in tones that suggested that she agreed with the first speaker.

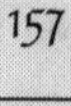

"We got it up the stairs without its hitting anything." That was the guard the King had sent with Haramis—what was her name? Oh yes, Nella, or something like that. "Why should there be a problem?"

"Harps are very delicate instruments," the young man said. "Master Uzun hasn't been moved from his place in the study for many years. I am afraid that subjecting him to the change in temperature and humidity involved in moving him to the Lady's bedchamber may damage him."

"I don't care if it does." *That voice must be Uzun's,* Haramis realized; it had the sound of harp strings. It was followed by a sudden thud.

"Careful!" three voices snapped in unison: two human and one harp.

Nella's voice said, "I'm sorry; nobody warned me that it talked."

"And you're already out of tune, Uzun," the young man remarked. "I told you it was too cold in the hallways."

"You can retune me when we get to the Lady's room," Uzun said calmly.

By now, even Haramis could tell he was out of tune. *That clumsy guard must have dropped him.*

"My place is with the Lady," Uzun continued, "no matter what happens." Haramis had a vague memory—or was it a dream?—of being in the mountains with Uzun when he was still a Nyssomu and seeing him freeze, almost to the point of death.

Three weary-looking humans dragged the harp into the room. "Here he is, Lady," Mikayla said. "Where do you want him?"

Haramis turned her head to the right. "Next to the head of my bed," she replied.

"But that's right next to the heating grille," the young man protested. "Excessive heat could crack the frame."

"He's been near the fire for years!" Mikayla protested.

"Near it, not directly in front of it!"

"Enough!" Haramis snapped. "I'm tired of listening to your bickering. Put him there, tune him, and leave us!"

"Yes, Lady." Mikayla sighed. Carefully they set the harp in place.

The young man pulled a tuning key out of his belt and carefully began to retune the strings. Haramis frowned, trying to place him. He looked familiar, but she didn't remember him as being one of her servants; in fact, she didn't think she had human servants. But Mikayla was ordering him around as if he were one. Had Mikayla acquired more servants while Haramis had been away?

*How long have I been away? I'll ask Uzun when we're alone.*

It seemed to take forever, but finally Uzun was back in tune. "Leave us, all of you," Haramis commanded.

Nella bowed and left the room quickly; she had been hovering by the door looking as if she wished to be elsewhere the entire time. Lady Bevis picked up Haramis's empty tray, curtsied, and withdrew gracefully. Mikayla paused to pat the frame of the harp briefly, then started to follow Lady Bevis, but paused in the doorway, obviously waiting for the young man. He ran a hand down Uzun's forepillar, frowned in concern, and whispered, "I'm sorry, Uzun." Then he joined Mikayla in the doorway and they left together.

"Who is he?" Haramis asked Uzun irritably. "Has that girl been hiring more servants while I've been gone? How long have I been gone anyway? And has she made any progress at all in her lessons?"

"My heart rejoices in your safe return, Lady," Master Uzun replied. "I feared I might never see you again—not that I can see you in this form—but I feared never to hear your voice again."

"I'm glad to see you, too, oldest of my friends," Haramis said, momentarily disarmed. "But tell me, what *has* been going on in my absence?"

"Not much," Uzun replied. "I have been tutoring the Princess Mikayla in magic, and she has made good progress. She has now read every book in your library, and is quite proficient in scrying. I had her practice by checking to see how you were doing every few days."

"So that's how she knew to be there to extend the bridge," Haramis mused. "And can she call the lammergeiers as well?"

"Yes, I'm fairly certain that she can."

"She seems to have outgrown that case of the sulks she developed after Fiolon left. . . ." Haramis's voice trailed off as she suddenly realized who the young man was. "That was Fiolon, wasn't it?" she demanded. "What is he doing back here?"

"You may remember," Uzun said hesitantly, "that right before you took ill, Lord Fiolon inadvertently caused it to snow at the Citadel."

"Yes, I do remember that." It was all coming back to Haramis now. "They were bonded together, and Mikayla was playing with weather magic—and by now, I suppose they're permanently bonded! How could you let this happen?" she demanded furiously.

"Mikayla is still a virgin," Uzun said firmly, "and I'm fairly sure that Fiolon is as well. Their bond is emotional, not physical, and had been well established for about five years before your ill-advised attempt to sever it."

Haramis gasped. No one had dared speak to her so in almost two hundreds.

"The bond was reestablished within ten hours," Uzun continued, "but from the descriptions both children gave of the pain involved it was clear that it did not involve the lower centers at all. I don't think you could have severed it permanently without their full cooperation then, and now I'm quite sure you can't. You've been gone over a year and a half, and I've been training both of them."

"You've been training that boy?" Haramis exclaimed in horror. "Have you lost your mind? Do you want another Orogastus running loose?"

"Lord Fiolon is nothing at all like Orogastus," Uzun said firmly. "And a child, which is what he was then, with a little knowledge of weather magic and no control over it is very dangerous. He needed to be trained, for the safety of everyone around him, and for the sake of the land."

"And so you took it upon yourself to train him, in my home, without my consent."

"Is this not my home as well?" Uzun said quietly. "And you were in no condition to give your consent; at first you did not even remember that either Fiolon or Mikayla existed. I did as I thought best, for them, and for the land. And now he is trained, and nothing can change what is."

"Perhaps you are right," Haramis said grudgingly. "But he can't stay here. It isn't proper. He should not have been living here unchaperoned with the Princess Mikayla all this time."

"It's not as if it were generally known," Uzun pointed out. "I'll bet no one at the Citadel even missed him. And now that you're here, they're not unchaperoned."

"He's a distraction to her studies," Haramis said firmly. "He leaves tomorrow, and this time I'll summon a lammergeier and send him back to Var!"

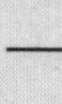

"You can summon the lammergeiers again?" Uzun said. "That is good news. When you were first ill, they could not bespeak you at all, and we were quite concerned about that."

"We?" Haramis asked. She wasn't sure she could summon a lammergeier now, but she wasn't going to admit it.

"Fiolon, Mikayla, and I," Uzun replied. "We didn't see any need to tell the servants just how ill you were."

Since Haramis couldn't really remember exactly how ill she had been, she was just as glad to hear that her servants had not been gossiping about her health. She suddenly realized that she was very tired. "I'm going to sleep now, Uzun. Good night."

"Good night, Lady," she heard him reply as she fell asleep. "Pleasant dreams."

The next morning Haramis summoned Mikayla and Fiolon and announced her intention of sending Fiolon away at once.

"But, Lady," Mikayla protested. "I need him to help me transfer Master Uzun to his new body. The spells are too complex for one person, and the process is long and complicated."

"New body?" Haramis asked.

Mikayla looked at Uzun. "You didn't tell her?"

"What body I'm in isn't important as long as I'm with her," Uzun said quietly.

Fiolon ran his hands over the harp's frame. "You won't last

more than half a year in this form if you stay here in this room," he said in a tone of professional appraisal.

"I'm sure I'll be up and about soon," Haramis said, "and we'll be able to move him back to the study."

"All that does is buy him more time," Fiolon said firmly.

"And it's very upsetting for him to be blind and immobile," Mikayla said. "He found it particularly distressing when you were ill at the Citadel and he couldn't even scry to see how you were. He had to depend on us to do it for him, and he couldn't even see what we saw—all he knew was what we could describe for him. He was really miserable."

"It wasn't that bad," Uzun said.

"Stop trying to spare her feelings," Mikayla snapped. "That wasn't what you were saying last year."

*Uzun would always try to spare my feelings,* Haramis remembered. *He always used to talk about dying in my service as his highest goal in life.*

"Where did you get a new body?" she asked. "And what is it like?"

"It's Nyssomu in form, made of painted wood, with articulated joints," Mikayla replied. "He Who Causes to Live at the Temple of Meret made it. It looks as much like Uzun's old body as we could manage."

Haramis felt her head beginning to ache. "I've never heard of the Temple of Meret. What is it?"

"It's on the north side of Mount Gidris, opposite where you found your Talisman," Fiolon said helpfully.

"Meret is a sort of Labornoki earth goddess," Mikayla said. "Mount Gidris is considered to be part of her body, and the River Noku is her blood, with which she nourishes the land."

"They use blood magic?" Haramis asked sharply.

"Only symbolically," Mikayla assured her.

"I still don't like it," Haramis said. "You are not to do anything with this until I have had a chance to study it. And you don't need Fiolon; if I determine that this idea has merit, I shall do the ritual myself."

Both young people looked appalled.

"But you don't know the ritual!" Mikayla protested. "It took me months to learn even the simple daily rituals of the Goddess Meret."

"I'm really concerned about the structural integrity of the harp," Fiolon added.

"It need not concern *you,*" Haramis informed him coldly. "You are going to Var, today. Go and pack whatever you can carry on a lammergeier." Fiolon didn't move; he and Mikayla both stared at Haramis in astonishment. "Go!" Haramis repeated.

Fiolon looked at Mikayla, shrugged, and left the room.

"You can't send him to Var!" Mikayla protested. "He hasn't been there since he was a small child. His home is here in Ruwenda."

"Where he keeps sniffing around you as if you were in heat!" Haramis snapped. "I intend to send him as far away as possible; I won't have him distracting you further from your studies."

"I learn better when he and I study together," Mikayla pointed out. "And we are *not* being unchaste, and your accusations are idiotic! Did Uzun not explain that to you—or did you not understand him?" Clearly the girl was furious, but Haramis couldn't imagine why.

"He is obviously a bad influence on you," Haramis said coldly. "Your manners become atrocious as soon as he becomes the subject of conversation."

"I happen to care about him," Mikayla said. "We have been best friends ever since we were small children. We were planning to marry, until you came along and spoiled that, but you can't expect my feelings for him to change just because *you* say I can't marry him."

"I expect your feelings for him to change when he's far enough away from you," Haramis informed her. "That's why I'm sending him to Var—obviously the Citadel isn't far enough away."

"How are you going to get him to Var?" Mikayla asked.

"She can summon a lammergeier," Uzun said. "She told me so last night."

"She was mistaken, Uzun," Mikayla said gently. "They still can't reach her; I asked them this morning."

"Then you will summon one for me," Haramis told her. "If *you* can talk to them."

"I can talk to them," Mikayla said. "Who do you think had them carry you up here yesterday? But what makes you think I'll help you send Fiolon away?"

"You seem to be forgetting, girl, that this is my home," Haramis pointed out.

"Isn't it also Uzun's home?" Mikayla asked. "He invited Fiolon to stay here."

"Yes, he told me that he wished to train Fiolon for a time,"

Haramis said, "but I believe that training is finished now, is it not, Uzun?"

"He's not an inadvertent danger to himself and others anymore," Uzun admitted, sounding reluctant.

Fiolon returned, carrying a small backpack and dressed for cold weather. "I'm ready to go to Var," he announced.

"She can't send you," Mikayla told him smugly. Haramis wished that she were strong enough to smack the girl. "She still can't talk to the lammergeiers."

"You can," Fiolon pointed out.

"Why should I?"

"Because I'm asking you," he said gently. "Don't be so worried, Mika; I'll be fine. I'm still the king's nephew, whatever else I may be." He drew her aside, held her gently with his hands on her shoulders, and spoke quietly to her for several minutes. Haramis strained unsuccessfully to hear what he was saying, and she couldn't see Mikayla's reaction because the girl's back was toward her. Fiolon's face gave nothing away until his last words. Apparently Mikayla had agreed to summon a lammergeier for him, for he smiled at her.

Haramis felt a stab of envy; she couldn't recall that anyone had ever looked at her like that. There was so much love and acceptance in his face that Haramis was astonished. *How can he care so much for that sulky, stubborn, little brat?*

Fiolon bent and kissed Mikayla lightly on the forehead. "You're not losing me, you know," he said. "You'll still see me in your mirror."

*Whatever does he mean by that?* Haramis wondered.

Mikayla clung to him, shaking, and buried her face in his shoulder. Fiolon wrapped his arms around her and held her until she composed herself. Then he released her and bowed to Haramis. "I thank you for your hospitality, Lady," he said politely.

"I wish you a safe journey," Haramis responded automatically.

Mikayla didn't turn or speak as she left the room with Fiolon, but a few minutes later Haramis heard the rush of wings as a lammergeier landed on the balcony, followed shortly by the sounds of the bird's departure.

Mikayla did not return to Haramis's room. When Haramis asked where she was, Enya informed her that Mikayla had locked herself into her bedchamber and was not answering anyone who came to her door.

Haramis sighed. "She's probably sulking again. Just leave her alone until she surfaces. No doubt she'll come out when she gets hungry." *I swear by the Flower, the fronials are easier to train.*

# 19

*Mikayla watched as the great bird carried Fiolon away* to the south. She could understand his not wanting to stay at the Tower now that Haramis was back. In the mood Haramis was in, Mikayla didn't want to be there either. That was the only reason she had agreed to summon a lammergeier to take Fiolon to Var—she certainly wasn't doing it as a favor to Haramis.

She went to her room and locked herself in, then sat on her bed and pulled out her sphere from under her tunic. She called up Fiolon's image in it, but did not try to speak to him. She didn't wish to distract him while he was flying.

She watched as the bird flew over the Thorny Hell, the Blackmire, and the Greenmire, crossed over the western half of the Tassaleyo Forest, and finally picked up the track of the Great Mutar River, which ran through Var to the Southern Sea. Fiolon directed the bird to bring him down on the west side of the river, about a league south of the border between Ruwenda and Var.

*He didn't need me to summon the lammergeier at all,* Mikayla realized. *He can bespeak them as well as I can.*

That was her last coherent thought for some time. As Fiolon slid from the bird's back and his feet touched the ground of Var, the world shifted around him and, through their link, around Mikayla as well. She fell backward on her bed like a rag doll as Fiolon sank to the ground. Both of them were helpless in the face of the sensations overwhelming Fiolon and, through him, Mikayla.

It was as if the entire country of Var had reached out and seized Fiolon, as if the land were trying to take over his body. The rivers, most notably the Great Mutar, were replacing his blood, and the winds blowing in from the Southern Sea were becoming his breath, filling his lungs and spreading throughout his body. The day that their boat had capsized at the junction of the Golobar and Lower Mutar rivers was nothing compared with this.

In spite of the fact that it was early winter, there was vegetation everywhere. It was not the wild growth of the great swamps of Ruwenda, but orderly, cultivated winter crops, not just in a band surrounding the Great Mutar, but spread out all over the country. The cultivated area occupied most of the land from the Tassaleyo Forest, which covered the border between Var and Ruwenda, almost all the way to the sea.

Nothing had ever prepared Fiolon for the sea. More water than he had ever known existed splashed ashore all along the coast of Var. He felt as though part of his body was lying on the beach, being splashed by every incoming wave, at the same time that part of him held the Great Mutar River and part of him was the cultivated fields.

Yet another part of him held the cities, small ones such as existed in Ruwenda, and the capital and main port city of Mutavari. He remembered, a very faint, dim memory from early childhood, living in Mutavari, but he didn't remember it as being so large or as having so many people. Ships were tied up all along the wharves that stretched out along both sides of the river, and people from all over the known world dashed back and forth, loading and unloading cargoes, running errands, making business deals. . . . Fortunately, he wasn't linked with all of those people; being linked with the land was more than enough to try to cope with. But he could still feel minds in contact with his, even if they weren't those of the people he saw. . . .

"Mika?" His thought was faint, but Mikayla caught it easily. Whatever was happening to him was not enough to destroy their bond, even if both of them did feel as if their heads were about to split open and their bodies were much too small.

"I'm here, Fio."

"Do you hear them?"

"The voices? Yes." Mikayla could hear wave after wave of something halfway between voices and thoughts. "They're not human—"

Both of them realized it at the same time. "—they're folk!"

What would normally have been a dialogue between the two of them was now one chain of thought, with neither of them sure who was contributing which idea. Not that it mattered; in many ways it had never mattered to them who thought of what.

"Not Nyssomu . . . nor Vispi . . . definitely not Skritek . . . but one of them is rather savage . . . one of them? Yes, that's right; there are two distinct groups . . . in Var, that would make them the Glismak—they'd be the savage ones . . . and the Wyvilo."

"But why can we hear them?" That thought was Fiolon's.

"I can hear them because you can," came Mikayla's reply. "As to why you can hear them—Fio, has Var ever had an Archimage?"

"Not that I ever heard of." Fiolon's head was spinning and the river and the sea still seemed to wash through him at regular intervals, but his mind was becoming a bit clearer. "Granted, I haven't been in Var since I was a small child, and I don't know its history as well as I do yours, but I've never heard of Var's having an Archimage."

"I think it has one now."

"What?"

"You. Fio, you're the Archimage. Think—or at least try to think. Haramis and Uzun have spent the past three years trying to teach me how to be an Archimage, and you've learned everything I have and then some. So you know *how* to be Archimage. And if Var has been sitting there, waiting, until someone with the right knowledge and skills came along . . ."

"Waiting to reach out and grab the first suitable candidate . . ." Fiolon could feel the land in every part of his body. "It certainly grabbed me," he thought, "but how do I control it? I've been lying here for who knows how long, and I can sense the land, but I can't move my body, or even feel it properly."

"Try music." Mikayla's thought swept through him, faintly amused. "That's always been your favorite way of bringing order out of chaos."

"Music." Fiolon breathed in deeply and exhaled slowly, struggling for control. The winds became a chorus of fipple-flutes of varying sizes and pitches. But now they were together and the sounds they made harmonized. The waves hitting the shore became the dominant beat, and the flow of the river the weak beat, as the pulse of the land settled into a smooth rhythm. Fiolon could feel his heart pumping in time to it, and the blood flowed easily through his veins as the river ran to the sea. The sounds of the Glismak and the Wyvilo faded into counterpoint in the background, to be examined more carefully later. Fiolon opened his eyes and slowly and carefully sat up. His body was stiff and sore, so presumably he had been lying there for quite some time, but the lammergeier still stood over him, keeping watch.

"White Lord?" The bird's thoughts came to him as clearly as Mikayla's ever had. "Do you wish to continue your journey?"

Fiolon blinked up at the bird. "Can you take me to Mutavari?"



"Of course, White Lord."

The bird stretched out a wing and assisted Fiolon to climb onto its back, and they flew onward, south to the sea, and to the court of Var.

Mikayla opened her eyes and tried to sit up. When that failed, she rolled over, falling off the edge of the bed and landing on her hands and knees on the floor. *I wonder if that's what Haramis meant when she spoke of "land sense." I'll have to ask her.*

Mikayla dragged herself to her feet and hobbled around her room, holding on to the furniture, until her legs were willing to support her again. *How long have I been lying here?* she wondered. *Maybe I should get something to eat; I'm dreadfully hungry.*

But her curiosity about what had happened to Fiolon was stronger than her hunger. She checked her appearance in the mirror, thinking that there was no point in annoying Haramis before she even opened her mouth. There was nothing she could do about the pale, tired, circles-under-the-eyes look on her face, but she brushed her hair and straightened her tunic before heading for Haramis's room.

Haramis's door was open about halfway, but Haramis was sleeping, with Lady Bevis dozing in a chair at her bedside. Mikayla looked for Uzun, but the spot at the head of Haramis's bed where she had last seen him was empty. *Oh, no!* she thought in dismay. *Fiolon* told *her it was too hot for him there!*

Mikayla turned and ran for the sitting room. Uzun was back in his place in the corner by the fireplace, but the fire had been allowed to die down to a very low level. "Uzun!" she gasped, dropping to the hearth and trying to blow more life into the flames. "Talk to me!" she pleaded. "What happened to you?"

"Fiolon was right." Mikayla felt tears fill her eyes. The harp's strings were badly out of tune and his voice was creaky. Mikayla lit the lamps in the room with a word of command, although the effort made her sag limply onto the hearth. But even lying there she could see the damage to the harp's finish and, more ominously, several cracks in the wood of his frame. "It was too hot in the Lady's room," Uzun continued, "and the hallways were too cold, and now the temperature in here isn't right. . . ." His voice trailed off.

Pure fury gave Mikayla the strength to rise to her feet and pull repeatedly at the bellpull to summon Enya.

It seemed forever before the housekeeper appeared, clad in her nightclothes and yawning. "So you're done sulking, are you?" She regarded Mikayla with disfavor. "The Lady said you could eat whenever you chose to leave your room, but do you have any idea what time it is?"

"I don't care what time it is!" Mikayla snapped furiously, gesturing at the harp. "Just look at that fire! Are you deliberately trying to destroy Master Uzun? Surely after all these years, you know the level the fire is supposed to be kept at."

"By the Flower!" Enya looked in dismay from the fire to the harp, then closed her eyes briefly to bespeak the other servants. "There will be more wood here in a few minutes, Princess," she said quickly. "I am terribly sorry; we let the fire go out when Haramis had Master Uzun moved upstairs, since no one was using this room, and she had him moved back only this evening, and we . . ." Her voice trailed off.

*You forgot,* Mikayla finished the sentence in her head. There was no point in berating the housekeeper further, however; the point had obviously been made. But Mikayla resolved to check on Uzun's condition at frequent intervals just the same. "Master Uzun is back here now, and I shall be continuing to use this room," she said quietly, "so I would appreciate it if the temperature could be maintained at its customary level."

"Yes, Princess," Enya said quickly. "I'll make sure of it. And

I'll go bring up a tray for you. You must be hungry; you haven't eaten in days."

"Thank you, Enya." Mikayla made herself smile at the housekeeper, despite her lingering annoyance at the way Uzun had been mistreated. "That's very kind of you. I'm afraid that I was working and lost track of the time."

As soon as Enya was out of earshot, Uzun asked, "Working? Locked in your room for over two days? Just what were you doing?"

"Over two days?" Mikayla asked. "No wonder I'm so hungry. I hope they'll feed Fiolon when he gets to Mutavari."

"You were linked with Fiolon again." It wasn't a question, so it didn't matter that Uzun couldn't see Mikayla nod her head. "What happened to him?"

"It was really strange, Uzun," Mikayla began, then stopped speaking as one of the Vispi men came in with an armload of wood and began to fix the fire. He was still working on the fire when Enya arrived with a tray containing a large bowl of adop soup and half a loaf of bread. She admonished Mikayla to eat slowly so that she wouldn't make herself ill. Mikayla began to nibble on the end of the loaf, waiting for the servants to leave so that she could talk freely to Uzun.

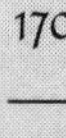

When they were alone again, she told him what had happened. "Do you think that Fiolon really *is* Archimage of Var?" she finished.

"It certainly sounds like it," the harp replied. "But I wouldn't tell Lady Haramis about it."

"I wasn't planning to," Mikayla assured him, "but I don't think she'll get suspicious if I ask her what it was like when she became Archimage, do you?"

"Not suspicious of Fiolon, at any rate," Uzun said dryly. He sighed in satisfaction. "I do feel better now that the fire has been built up, Princess. Thank you for that."

"They should have done it without my having to order it," Mikayla said, pressing her lips together in annoyance. "If they actually managed to forget that you are a sentient being who needs regular care, I'll make certain that *that* doesn't happen again! I'll stop in and see you as much as I can, Uzun."

"If you're not knocked out for days at a time again," the harp pointed out.

"I shouldn't be," Mikayla said cheerfully. "An experience that intense has to be a once-in-a-lifetime occurrence."

. . .

She went to talk to Haramis the next morning. Encouraging her to reminisce about her youth wasn't at all difficult, and the descriptions made Mikayla even more certain that her theory of what had happened to Fiolon was correct.

But when she ventured a very general question about what it felt like to have land sense, Haramis glared at her. "Have you developed land sense for Ruwenda?" she asked sharply.

"No, Lady!" Mikayla gasped in horror, shaking her head vigorously. *By the Flower,* she realized with sudden dismay, *she's lost the land sense! But I certainly don't have it, and Fiolon doesn't—not for Ruwenda. So who does? Does anyone?* She cast her mind outward, trying to sense the land. Faint images came back; the land was still ill, and there was still nothing Mikayla could do about it. "I only wondered, that's all. You said something about it once."

Haramis looked at her in disdain. "It is not something which need concern *you* yet. Go to the library and continue your studies there."

"Yes, Lady." Mikayla curtsied and left the room. She had read every book in Haramis's library long since, but she knew that the servants would tell Haramis if she disobeyed, so she went to the library and spent the rest of the afternoon holding an open book and thinking. Her thoughts were not happy ones.

# 20

“*By the Lords of the Air, Uzun, stop telling me not to* upset Lady Haramis!” Mikayla glared at the harp. She had come to him for sympathy after another of her arguments with Haramis, but Uzun wasn’t cooperating. Haramis had allegedly resumed training Mikayla, but this training largely consisted of having Mikayla sit at her bedside for long hours while Haramis told her the same things over and over and over again. Mikayla spent a lot of time fighting a losing battle not to scream with frustration.

“I don’t understand why you’re not upset with her,” she snarled at Uzun. “Just look at what she did to you! First she turns you into a harp; then, when we get a new body for you—and you don’t know what I had to promise to get that!—she forbids us to transfer you; and to top it all off, she has you dragged up to her room where she’s keeping it hot enough to cause permanent damage to the harp—after Fiolon warned her that it would! In your place I’d be furious with her!”

Uzun sighed. “I don’t have to be angry with her, Mikayla;

you're angry enough for both of us. Try to remember that she's been ill. She didn't intend to harm me, and she doesn't intend to hurt you."

"That would be a much more convincing argument if she had showed any more consideration for us before she became ill than she does now," Mikayla pointed out.

"Just please don't yell at her." Uzun sighed again. "It hurts her feelings, and that's bad for her recovery."

"Why should I care about her feelings?" Mikayla demanded furiously. "She doesn't care about *mine*!" Haramis had recovered from her illness just enough to be thoroughly unpleasant to be around, and Mikayla was finding the strain intolerable.

"Nobody cares about my feelings; I'm just a pawn. I'm not a person; I'm just a thing: Archimage-in-Training. Choose semi-suitable child—it doesn't matter if she's a round peg, cut off the round parts and shove her in a square hole! Never mind what she wants, never mind how much you're hurting her, never mind the damage you're doing, never mind what she would have been if you hadn't interfered. Haramis doesn't care. Nobody cares! All anybody ever cares about is Haramis and what she wants!" Mikayla paused to blow her nose.

"And whatever happens to Haramis, everybody blames me! If she gets a headache, it's my fault. If she gets dizzy, or forgets to eat lunch, it's my fault. If she fell down the stairs and I was at the other end of the Tower, somebody would blame it on me! I'm not a sorceress; I'm a scapegoat.

"She says that she's training me, she says that she's trying to teach me to be the very best Archimage I can be—but, believe me, the day she realizes that I'm better than she is at *anything,* she'll go through the roof of the Tower! She doesn't want another Archimage; she wants a slave, to learn only what she wants me to learn and only up to the point she wants me to learn it.

"The one thing I can't ever, ever do is surpass her. I think if I did, she really would kill me. It's a good thing that she conveniently managed to forget that I can talk to the lammergeiers as soon as Fiolon left!"

"You should be ashamed of yourself, talking about the Lady Haramis like that," Uzun said sternly.

"Why should I be ashamed of *myself*? I never asked to come here. I'm doing my best, but I never seem to do anything right, and everybody hates me, and everybody blames everything that goes wrong on me. I wish I were dead!" She burst into tears, but continued to speak through her sobs. "And anytime *I* get unhappy, everybody just says 'Oh, don't upset Lady Haramis.' Well, if Lady Haramis doesn't want to be upset, maybe she should have chosen somebody else for her successor!

"I know she's part of my family, sort of, and I'm supposed to love her; I know she's my mistress and I ought to serve her faithfully"—by now Mikayla was sobbing so hard that her words were coming out in short semi-intelligible bursts—". . . but I don't even *like* her . . . and I don't like myself . . . and I don't like my life. I hate it here; I'd rather live with a band of Skritek."

She scrambled to her feet and headed for the door. "I'm going out for a walk."

"Isn't that dangerous?" Uzun protested. "Where are you going, and when will you be back? It's not that long until dark."

"I'm going wherever I want to go, and I'll be back when I'm damn good and ready—probably when the three moons rise together in the west!"

*And it might be that long after all,* Mikayla thought uncomfortably several hours later. She was cold and completely lost in the dark. *I could die out here. Storming out of the Tower with no supplies, no lantern, and clothes that really aren't warm enough to wear outside after dark was not the most intelligent decision I ever made. I ought to control my temper better, I guess. If I live though this, I suppose I'll really have to make more of an effort. . . .*

She trudged steadily onward, not knowing where she was going, but knowing that if she stopped, she would freeze to death all too quickly. *And now that dying is a real possibility,* she thought wryly, *I'm not so sure that I want to die after all. But I'm still not sure that I want to go back to the Tower and be Haramis's good little girl. I wish I had somewhere else to go. For that matter, I wish I could see where I'm going—I would have to pull a stupid stunt like this on an overcast night.*

It was then that her inability to see where she was putting her feet finally caught up with her. Whatever she stepped on—she was never sure; it happened so fast—slid under her feet, or maybe she slid, but she was slipping, falling past the edge of something, dropping terrifyingly fast. Then she hit the ground, or more accurately, the water. Running water.

*Funny, I didn't think there was any unfrozen water anywhere near here. I wonder where I am. Not that it makes much difference now; I'll be unconscious in minutes and dead soon after.* Still she thrashed about, trying to keep her head out of the water enough to keep breathing. Suddenly something lifted her bodily out of the water by the back of her tunic (her cloak had been lost when she fell) and flew through the air with her.

It was excruciatingly painful. Mikayla was soaked to the skin, and whatever was holding her was flying quickly. Icy-cold air stung her face and body, the wind slapped her wet hair into her face like a whip, and when a thick strand of her hair blew into her mouth, she discovered that the water on it had frozen solid. Claws poked through her tunic and scratched her back. She still couldn't see anything in the dark night and was too miserable to care whether whatever carried her could see, or to wonder whether it was trying to rescue her or simply wanted her for a snack.

They flew upward and it got even colder. It seemed that they flew forever, and then apparently they passed over a ridge and began to descend again. The air seemed much warmer suddenly, and Mikayla remembered that the Vispi lived in valleys warmed by hot springs and consorted with the lammergeiers. But lammergeiers were diurnal; a lammergeier shouldn't even be awake at this hour, much less be able to see anything.

Whatever it was, however, apparently it could see. Mikayla felt the change in air pressure and flow as the wings above her swept back and inward as they entered some sort of tunnel or narrow cave.

The claws released her, and she fell, again into water. But this water was boiling hot. *It not only wants a snack, it wants it cooked!* she thought, screaming in pain. She clutched at the stone side of the pool she was in, trying to drag herself out, but her muscles weren't responding. All she could do was keep her head above the water and breathe in painful gasps. Tears ran down her face; she didn't think anything in her life had ever hurt so much.

It seemed forever before she noticed that the water wasn't really boiling; it was just warm enough to be thawing her out, which was obviously necessary, however much it hurt. The pain began to lessen, she started to relax, and then she heard the voice in her head.

". . . and they call *me* a birdbrain!" it was saying. "What were you doing out alone at night, anyway?"

"Running away," Mikayla said crossly. "And now I suppose you'll drag me straight back." There was a dim light coming from a tunnel off to the left of the pool and she could see the pale shape of her rescuer. "You are a lammergeier, aren't you?"

"Of a sort," it replied, leaning in for a closer look at her. She saw then that what she had taken for color caused by reflected light off the snow outside wasn't; the bird really was white. Completely white. And his eyes . . . . "Call me Red-Eye," it said with a sigh. "Everyone else does."

"It *is* unusual coloring," Mikayla said as politely as she could. "And you may call me Mika." *Never give out your true name to strangers—and this is definitely strange.*

"I may or may not return you to whatever you were running from," the bird continued. "Since I ran away from my creators, I have a certain sympathy for runaways."

"Creators?" Mikayla asked. "You mean you weren't simply born like this?"

"Have you ever seen a creature born without its normal coloring?"

"I've read about it," Mikayla said. "It happens naturally sometimes in both animals and people. It's called albino."

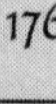

"Well, in my case, it was not natural," Red-Eye snapped. "They made me this way, and they tried to control me, to make me do their bidding, to spy for them, to fetch and carry things at night—that's why I look like this; they wanted a lammergeier that could function at night."

"Who are 'they'?" Mikayla asked, fascinated. Changing a living creature out of its natural form before it was even born was a level of magic she had not previously encountered.

"The Priests of the Time of Darkness," Red-Eye replied. "They live on one of the other mountain peaks."

"Which one? And where are we now? I got rather lost when I ran off, after it got dark."

The bird had been holding its head cocked to one side, listening carefully to her speech. "You're from Ruwenda, aren't you?"

"Yes," Mikayla replied. "How can you tell?"

"By the way you speak," it replied. "I found you on the peak you call Mount Brom, and we are now on the one you call Mount Rotolo. As for where the Priests of the Time of Darkness live, if you are fortunate, you will never find out." His tone was grim enough to keep Mikayla from voicing her suspicion that they lived on Mount Gidris—after all, it was the only one of the three main peaks the bird hadn't named. Something about Mount Gidris had frightened Enya, too.

Mikayla dragged herself reluctantly out of the pool. By now the water temperature felt comfortable, but the skin on her hands was shriveling up in a definite sign that she'd been in the water too long.

"There's a pile of furs back there," Red-Eye said, flicking a wing tip toward the light down the tunnel. "Hang up your clothes to dry, then curl up in the furs and get some sleep. I'm going out to hunt. I'll be back around dawn, but please remember that I sleep during the daytime. Tomorrow night we'll discuss what's to be done with you."

Mikayla had no fault to find with that plan; she was as tired as she had ever been in her life. "Thank you," she said, "and good hunting."

Life with Red-Eye quickly settled into a comfortable pattern. Mikayla sensed that the bird was lonely, and it seemed glad to have her company. For the first few days she was content to rest in the cave and to eat whatever it caught on its hunting trips, though she suspected that it was flying great distances to bring back such delicacies as togar, a bird that she knew perfectly well lived in the swamps. Various types of vart seemed to be a staple of its diet, and the small rodents were perfectly acceptable food to Mikayla, who had never been a fussy eater.

Red-Eye, after declaring that her clothes were hopeless as protection from the cold, taught her how to control her body temperature by magic. It knew quite a bit of magic that Mikayla hadn't encountered before. She wondered where it had learned, but she remembered the bitterness with which it had spoken of its creators and refrained from asking.

Once she had learned to control her body temperature, Red-Eye started taking her out at night with it. She learned how to sense the way the wind curled through the mountains and wrapped itself around the peaks and to tell how thick a cloud layer was from either the top or the bottom without having to fly through it. Her night vision, which had always been good for a human, improved still further. *Of course,* she thought, *the fact that I don't see daylight these days probably helps.* Like Red-Eye, she had become nocturnal; now she slept all day.

One evening she was wakened by the jingling of the sphere against her chest. She sat up yawning, and pulled it out to dangle in front of her face. She could see Fiolon quite clearly in it; the sphere seemed to glow with its own light, but she knew that it was only the lamps in the room with Fiolon that provided the illumination. "What's the matter, Fio?" she asked sleepily.

"What's the matter?" Fiolon repeated in irritation. "You storm out of the Tower at twilight and don't return, leaving Guardswoman Nella and two search parties of Vispi to spend a week looking for your body, you don't even contact *me,* and when I bespeak you, you yawn and ask what's wrong!"

"Sorry, Fio," Mikayla apologized sleepily. "I'm just waking up. And I forgot that you couldn't just ask the mirror to find me anymore."

"Oh, Uzun tried that first," Fiolon snapped.

"He did?" Mikayla asked. "How? Did Haramis relent about his new body?"

"No, Haramis is still about the same."

"She's not worried about me, then?" Mikayla grinned. "I didn't think she would be."

Fiolon sighed. "Let's not discuss Haramis, all right?"

"By all means," Mikayla agreed. "I'm sorry if Uzun is worried; I never meant to worry him—I just couldn't stand it there! Is he all right? He was damaged by being dragged about, just the way you said he would be."

"I can understand your desire to leave," Fiolon said. "But he was dreadfully worried about you; he was afraid you were dead. As for his condition, the damage is pretty much stabilized. And I'm sending a harp builder back with Guardswoman Nella to see how much can be fixed."

"Nella's with you?" Mikayla asked. "Where are you?"

"I'm in Let."

"Let?" Mikayla was surprised. "The last thing I knew, you were going to Mutavari."

"I did," Fiolon replied. "And when my uncle the King found out that I could deal with the Wyvilo, he sent me to Let to trade with them. The lumber I'm getting is helping his shipbuilding no end, so he's thrilled with me. He's talking about giving me a dukedom."

"Sounds a lot better than being locked in a Tower in the middle of nowhere," Mikayla commented.

"Parts of the job are rather tricky," Fiolon pointed out. "I couldn't do it properly without the land sense. Trees have to be cut very selectively; you can't just chop down everything in one area, or you'll get erosion, which damages both the land and the water. I'm rather enjoying it, actually," he admitted. "I'm admitting to some magical ability, but not telling anyone how much I really have. I don't want to announce that I'm an Archimage and be regarded with superstitious awe. The senses and skills I have are to be used for the good of the land and its folk, but apparently I don't have to cut myself off from all human contact to use them."

*Then why does Haramis do it—and expect me to follow her example?* Mikayla wondered. *If being the Archimage just means having land sense and using it for the good of the land and its folk, that's not so bad. . . .*

"Anyway"—Fiolon was still speaking—"Uzun swore Nella to secrecy and told her how to use the mirror. She asked it to locate you, but all it showed was blackness—which, incidentally, is all I'm seeing in this sphere. I can hear you just fine, but I can't see you."

"It's dark in here, Fiolon," Mikayla said calmly. "You couldn't see me if you were sitting right here."

"That might have been the problem, then," Fiolon said absentmindedly, "because when he told her to have it locate me, it worked just fine. So he sent her to find me, to ask me to find you."



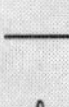

"Poor Uzun." Mikayla sighed. "If he had his new body, he could probably scry for himself, and he could certainly use the mirror."

"Would his new body be able to stand the cold down there?" Fiolon asked. "A Nyssomu can't."

"We stored his body down there, Fio, remember?" Mikayla reminded him. "And I specified tolerance for extreme cold when I told them what I needed for the body."

"I didn't know that," Fiolon said thoughtfully. "I thought we could store it down there only because of the way it was packed."

"No." Mikayla shook her head. "It should be fine down there even unpacked. In the meantime I hope your harp builder is good at repairs—you haven't seen the damage, have you?"

"Nella gave me a good description."

"Did she tell you that the finish is crazed over most of the wood and the frame has cracks in three places?"

"She said two places, and she said the finish looked funny."

"Well, I suppose that's a reasonable description, especially from a guard. To her, 'crazed' probably means someone not right in the head, not small cracks all over wood finish. Anyway, please give her my apologies, and my thanks for her efforts on my behalf —or Uzun's behalf."

"You still haven't said where you are, Mika."

"In a cave, someplace on Mount Rotolo."

"That doesn't narrow it down much," Fiolon protested.

"Just tell Uzun that I'm safe and well," Mikayla said. "Believe me, Fiolon, Haramis doesn't really want me there. The woman hates me; I swear it. She didn't like me much to begin with, and now she's old and sick and unable to use her magic, and I'm young and healthy and able to use it—although she keeps forgetting that. She doesn't even remember that I can bespeak the lammergeiers. Her idea of 'training' me is to make me sit by her bed and listen to stories as if I were a small child."

"That doesn't sound all that bad," Fiolon said. "Useless, perhaps, but not intolerable."

"She tells the same stories every single day, Fio. Day after day after day after day after—"

"I'll grant intolerable."

"I knew you'd understand." Mikayla sighed. "I was turning into a monster there; I just had to get away. It wasn't just her I hated; I hated myself as well. Now I'm someplace where I don't hate myself, and I'm going to stay here for a while—maybe even until I have to go back to the Temple."

"The Temple?"

"You remember the Temple, Fio. I have to stay a virgin, and I have to go there every spring for the next seven years. That was the price for Uzun's body."

"But Uzun doesn't have his body," Fiolon protested.

"That's not their fault," Mikayla pointed out. "They kept their word, and I shall keep mine. What Haramis does," she added bitterly, "is quite beyond our control."

"True," Fiolon agreed. "I'll send Nella and the harp builder back by lammergeier tomorrow, with a message to Uzun that you are well. What he tells Haramis is his decision."

"Thank you, Fio. Give Uzun my love, and tell him I'm sorry that my behavior gave him cause for worry."

"I shall. Take care of yourself, Mika, and bespeak me from time to time."

"I will. Don't worry about me."

Fiolon muttered something she didn't quite catch as the sphere went dark.

"What was that?" Red-Eye's thoughts whispered in her head.

"My cousin," Mikayla explained. "He was worried about me. He's right, I should have contacted him."

"You communicate with that little ball?" The bird cocked its head to one side, looking at the sphere Mikayla still held in front of her.

"Yes," Mikayla replied, tucking it back into her tunic. "We found them—he has one just like it—in some ruins on the Golobar River a few years ago. I suspect that we could bespeak each other without them, but they're a convenient focus."

"He can bespeak the lammergeiers?" Red-Eye asked. "I did hear him say that, didn't I? How does he do that?"

Mikayla shrugged. "He just does. It's not all that hard; I can hear you, and I'll bet most of the Vispi can, too, if you call to them. In his case, I think the fact that he's Archimage of Var probably has something to do with it."

"So Var has an Archimage," Red-Eye said. "That's interesting. It's too bad that Labornok doesn't."

"Doesn't it?" Mikayla asked. "I thought the Archimage of Ruwenda was also Archimage of Labornok. After all, the two Kingdoms have been joined since she became Archimage."

The bird's eyes narrowed in what passed for a frown and it lowered its head until its eyes were level with hers. Mikayla had been around it long enough to realize that this was a sign of avian displeasure.

"The Archimage has never paid any heed to her responsibility for Labornok," it said, "and lately she has been ignoring Ruwenda as well. This is bad, for both lands and for their folk."

"She's been ill," Mikayla said. "It's not completely her fault—Ruwenda, that is. As for Labornok, she's probably never forgiven them for killing her parents."

"The welfare of the land is more important than the personal feelings of the Archimage," Red-Eye said sternly.

Mikayla decided this was not a good time to tell him she was supposed to be the next Archimage. *Besides,* she thought, *Haramis may be wrong about me. If I didn't get the land sense when she lost it, perhaps someone else has it. The land may have chosen a new Archimage already.*

# 21

*Time with Red-Eye slipped past in a calm even series of* nights, punctuated by occasional talks with Fiolon. Shortly after midwinter, when there was too much rain for the logging to continue, Fiolon went back to the King's court at Mutavari. Mikayla even stayed awake long enough one morning to see something of the city through Fiolon's eyes as he walked through it, showing it to her.

One evening in the spring she awoke before Red-Eye, who had flown farther than usual the night before. The nights were getting shorter now, and there was still some daylight outside of the cave, but when Mikayla pulled out her sphere and idly began to scry Mutavari, she saw that it was already dark there. Of course, she thought, it's farther east than here; it gets dark sooner there.

She focused on the palace, preparing to bespeak Fiolon. He was in his room, so she looked to be sure he was alone. Since she was scrying with her sphere, instead of using it to link directly with him, she could see him and his surroundings. He wasn't alone. There was a woman in his bed, a young woman only a few years older than Mikayla, and much prettier. She had a figure, which Mikayla didn't yet, and long dark hair and sapphire-blue eyes. Mikayla hated her on sight. The fact that her dress was carelessly tossed on the clothing chest at the foot of the bed did not make Mikayla feel any better about the situation.

Very cautiously, Mikayla linked with Fiolon, so softly that he was not at first aware of her. Of course, most of his attention was on the woman in his bed. But apparently he had just walked in and found her there; he was still fully dressed, and Mikayla sensed that he was almost as surprised as she was. "What are you doing here?" he was asking the woman.

"I came to congratulate you, my Lord Duke," the woman replied in seductive tones.

"You could have done that perfectly well in the Great Hall when the King made the announcement," Fiolon pointed out, striving for calm. Mikayla could feel his emotions, but she wasn't accustomed to these: a mixture of nervousness and excitement. Fiolon had always been the calm one.

"In the Great Hall?" The woman, whoever she was, laughed. "Your elevation in rank should be celebrated, and we certainly couldn't celebrate it properly there." She flowed out of bed and across the room—like a swamp worm, Mikayla thought viciously—twined her arms about Fiolon's neck, and kissed him full on the lips. Mikayla felt a jolt run through her and realized that her link to Fiolon was leaving her wide-open to everything he felt. And he was feeling very strange. It didn't feel at all the way Mikayla had felt when Timon had tried to kiss her; this felt sort of warm, and dizzying, like some sort of magic, as energy flowed between their bodies. It reminded Mikayla of the way the chant had taken hold of her, that first day at the Temple of Meret. Fiolon's thoughts were shutting down, just the way hers had; his shields were completely down, and the woman was pulling energy from him like a Skritek drowning its prey.

"Fiolon!" Mikayla bespoke him urgently. "Wake up! Fight it!"

"Mika?" Fiolon lifted his head and looked around the room in a dazed fashion.

"Think, Fiolon! What are you doing?"

"Mika?" the woman said inquiringly, wriggling against Fiolon and trying to pull him closer to her—which Mikayla would have sworn was physically impossible. Fiolon felt fever hot through their link, and Mikayla felt very strange herself. When Fiolon pushed the woman forcibly away from him, a part of Mikayla ached along with him.

"My betrothed," Fiolon snapped, grabbing a cloak from a peg near the door. "I'm leaving, and I suggest you dress and do likewise. If I find you in here again, you will regret it." His tone was grim enough to make the woman look frightened.

"I didn't realize you were betrothed," she said nervously. "Why do you never speak of her?"

"Doubtless because idle gossip has never been one of my preferred pastimes," Fiolon said crushingly, turning on his heel and stalking from the room.

He went outside and made his way to a deserted stretch of beach. The fishermen whose boats were dragged up on the sand had doubtless all gone home for supper, Mikayla thought.

Fiolon pulled out his sphere. His face looked drawn and troubled. "Mika?" he asked. "Are you all right?"

"I think so," Mikayla replied shakily. "What was that? Who was she?"

"Nobody important," Fiolon replied. "Just one of the court ladies with even less sense than morals."



"It felt as though she was trying to use magic on you," Mikayla said uneasily.

Fiolon shook his head. "No. That wasn't magic. Just sex. For most of the women at court, it's their only asset."

"Is that why you said we were betrothed? So that she'd leave you alone?"

Fiolon sighed. "It might help—she'll gossip about it, of course; they all do. Not that my being betrothed would stop some of them. There are several of them that my being *married* wouldn't stop."

"But what if they find out we're not really betrothed?"

"I'll talk to the King and make sure he doesn't deny it," Fiolon said. "There isn't enough travel between here and the Citadel for anyone to ask your parents about it, and they don't know what you're doing these days anyway."

"But they know that I'm supposed to be Archimage. . . ." Suddenly Mikayla realized something. "You're an Archimage, and nobody seems to expect you to be celibate. Does this mean I don't have to be?" She felt hopeful for a moment; maybe she and Fiolon could marry after all. . . . "Oh, that's right; they don't know you're an Archimage, do they?"

"No," Fiolon said, "but I don't think it makes much difference.

They do think I'm a powerful magician. And I've watched other magicians at court—several of them don't seem to feel the slightest need to be celibate." He frowned. "I'll have to do some research on this," he said.

"While you're doing that," Mikayla said, "see if you can find out why I haven't become physically mature yet. My sisters all were by the time they were my age. I'd forgotten that I should be, but what just happened did bring it back to mind."

"I'll see what I can find out," Fiolon promised her. "I seem to be aging more slowly than normal, too, so it may be because we use magic."

"If you're not fully mature either," Mikayla asked, "why was she trying to compromise you?"

"Oh, that's simple," Fiolon explained. "My uncle the King just made me Duke of Let. He announced it at court today."

"I see." Mikayla understood perfectly. She may not have paid concentrated attention to court politics as a child, but she would have had to be blind and deaf not to have figured out the way things worked in a court by the time she was nine or ten, let alone twelve. Fiolon was now a prime catch; he would be a target for every ambitious maiden in the Kingdom. No wonder he wanted to pretend to be betrothed!

Well, that was fine with her. If it weren't for her promise to the Temple of Meret—and the fact that Haramis would undoubtedly have a fit and do something dreadful to them, Mikayla would have been willing to fly to Var and marry Fiolon that very night.

She could hear feathers rustling nearby; Red-Eye was waking up. "I have to go now, Fiolon," she said. "It's time to go hunting. Will you be all right now?"

Fiolon grimaced. "I have to go back to the palace and change for the formal banquet to celebrate my new rank. I just hope I can keep my room clear of unwanted company."

"How about an illusion?" Mikayla suggested. "Giant lingats spinning sticky webs all over the bed—or night carolers swooping through to snag their wings in the hair of anyone who troubles you?"

"Definitely an idea," Fiolon said, beginning to smile thoughtfully.

"Oh, my Lord Duke," Mikayla added in teasing tones, "don't take this the wrong way, but—congratulations!"

Fiolon threw back his head and laughed aloud, startling several seabirds. "Thank you, Princess," he said with a courtly bow. "Good hunting."

"Good luck avoiding the hunters," Mikayla replied. "Be well, Fio."

"Be well, Mika."

Mikayla continued to fly with Red-Eye, and Fiolon returned to Let as soon as he possibly could. But the incident had reminded Mikayla of her promise to return to the Temple of Meret at the appointed time. So, she watched the moons and waited for the time to come.

"Red-Eye," she said as they were preparing to fly out one beautiful spring night, "I've enjoyed being with you more than I can tell you, but tomorrow I have to be someplace else. Can you take me to Mount Gidris at dawn?"

"Mount Gidris?"

*Funny,* she thought, *it sounds upset, almost frightened. Oh yes, its creators live there, don't they?*

"You don't have to stay there long," she said reassuringly. "Just swoop in before dawn and drop me off near the Temple of Meret. It's on the northern side—"

"I know where it is," the bird said grimly. "What business have you there?"

"A promise to fulfill," she replied.

"Tell me," it said. "What is your promise?"

"To remain a virgin, and to spend a month there each spring for seven years, as one of the Daughters of the Goddess Meret."

Red-Eye dropped its head and looked fiercely at her. "And what do you get in return for this?"

"They made a body for a friend of mine, whose spirit is trapped in a harp. They have kept their promise, and I must keep mine."

"Does your cousin know about this?" Red-Eye asked. It had made a point of being awake and listening whenever she spoke to Fiolon. The idea of a male Archimage seemed to fascinate it. "Does he approve?"

"He doesn't own me," Mikayla pointed out. "And yes, he knows."

The bird made a sound of disgust. "And does he know anything about this Temple?"

"Not much," Mikayla said. "When I was first being trained, I talked to him every night while the other Daughters were at the ritual for the Second Hour of Darkness. But once I learned enough to join them in all the rituals, I didn't have much chance to bespeak him anymore."

"Because you speak to him aloud," Red-Eye said.

"It's certainly easier that way. And there isn't much privacy in the Temple," Mikayla admitted. "I had to be careful to keep them from finding the sphere."

Red-Eye looked at her. "If you go in there dressed as you are now, they'll spot it at once."

Mikayla looked down at herself in dismay. Ever since she had learned to control her body temperature, she had paid little attention to her clothing. She had made a point of washing her tunic at intervals, but now it was badly faded, and either it had shrunk or she had grown again. And the neckline was nowhere near high enough to cover the sphere's ribbon, which was still, after everything it had been through, the same bright green it had been the day she had found it. "You're right," she said. She looked up into the reddish eyes looking down at her. "Could you keep it for me, please?" she asked it. "Just for a month."

Red-Eye dropped its head again.

*It's really upset,* Mikayla thought. *Why?*

"I shall keep your sphere safe," it said, "and I shall take you to the Temple before dawn and fetch you from there again a month hence. But I want a promise from you in return."

"What?" Mikayla asked. "What can I do for you that you can't do for yourself?"

"Every night, when you go to your bed after the ritual of the Second Hour of Darkness, you are to bespeak me. No matter what happens; no matter how tired you are. Every single night. You can do this silently; no one there will know what you are doing. Do I have your promise?"

"You do."

"Every night?"

"Every night."

"Good. And if your cousin who can hear the lammergeiers should use the sphere to bespeak you, I will tell him where and how you are."

Mikayla reached out impulsively and hugged as much of the great bird as she could reach. "Thank you, Red-Eye. You are a prince among lammergeiers."

"Come then." Red-Eye extended a wing. "Let us fly."

• • •

Shortly before dawn, Mikayla stood again on the path near the Temple on Mount Gidris and watched Red-Eye fly away, her sphere wrapped securely around one leg. "Fly well, Red-Eye," she whispered. Then she went down the path to the Temple, setting a glamour to keep herself unseen until she could get to her room, wash, and change into the proper clothing for the dawn ritual.

The Eldest Daughter looked approvingly at her when she joined her sisters in the procession to the chapel, but, as usual, no one spoke until after breakfast. By then, Mikayla had slipped back into the rhythm of the rituals and was beginning to feel that she had never left.

"You remembered your promise, Sister," the Eldest Daughter said. "The Goddess is pleased."

"Thank you, Eldest Sister," Mikayla said. *It's good to be back here,* she thought. *It's nice to be approved of, and human company can be pleasant on occasion—depending on the humans, of course.*

As she had promised, she bespoke Red-Eye every night, even though she had nothing to tell him. Every day was like every other day in the Temple, and after a few days she felt as if she had never left. The only change in the routine was the Spring Festival, which celebrated the annual rising of the River Noku as the snow began to melt.

The Youngest Daughter of the Goddess represented the Goddess in the procession, and spent most of the day being carried about by the young men of the Temple on a richly carved high-backed wooden throne, while the other Daughters, dressed in green robes, walked on either side of the throne carrying fans that prevented most of the congregation from seeing whether there was anyone sitting there at all. They had all had to learn more chants for the Festival, but by now Mikayla found the Temple chants easy enough to learn.

She dutifully reported this to Red-Eye, along with her opinion that this was a truly boring ritual. The lammergeier seemed amused.

Then the Husband of the Goddess Meret came to the Daughters' room one afternoon. Mikayla was startled to see him there, but the others showed no surprise. Nervousness, and a certain subdued excitement, but no surprise.

"Why is he here?" Mikayla whispered to the girl next to her.

The girl looked at her in surprise. "It's the Choosing," she whispered back. "He chooses the Youngest Daughter for next year."

"Oh." Mikayla stood silently, following the example of the other girls. She remembered her first night there, last fall, when she had realized that one of the Daughters was called "Youngest" whether she was or not. She had no idea, however, how this "Youngest" had been chosen. *I guess I'm about to find out.*

The priest was robed in black, as usual, and wore his golden mask. The Eldest Daughter put her mask on as well; apparently she had brought it from its place in the chapel for this purpose. She went and fetched a small chest out of her room and set it on the small altar at one side of the room. Mikayla had noticed the altar, of course, when she had first arrived in the Temple, but she had never seen it used before.

The Eldest Daughter removed a golden headdress from the box. Mikayla stared at it in awe. It was the most incredible thing she had ever seen. It seemed to be of pure gold, judging from the effort it took for the Eldest Daughter to lift it out of the box. The headdress was made in the form of a lammergeier, shaped so that the bird's neck would rest on the top of the wearer's forehead with its neck arched and the bird's head facing straight ahead. The spine of the bird would lie along the top of the wearer's head, with the tail feathers sticking out behind, and the wings, which were so perfectly crafted that each individual feather was incised into the gold and the pin feathers looked capable of motion, swept downward so that they would lie along each side of the wearer's head. *It must be heavy,* Mikayla thought, watching as the Eldest Daughter and the Husband of the Goddess held it between them as they stood before the altar.

The Daughters went to sit in their places on the long bench in front of the fireplace, and Mikayla hastily joined them. If anyone had noticed her staring, they ignored it, but Mikayla felt gauche and unsure of herself for the first time since she had finished learning the chants.

The priest began a new chant, one Mikayla hadn't heard before. "Give praise to the Peak of the South," he intoned.

"Kiss the ground before her *hemsut,*" the Eldest Daughter replied.

"Praise to Meret, the Powerful One."

"Praise to Meret, the Hidden One."

"Praise to Meret, the Lofty One."

"Praise to Meret, the Mother of the Land."

"Praise to Meret, the Source of the River."
"Praise to Meret, the Source of the Sea."
"Praised be Meret in Her Boundlessness."
"Praised be Meret in Her Hiddenness."
"Praised be Meret in Her Darkness."
"Praised be Meret in Her Choice."

Together the Husband and the Eldest Daughter walked along the line of maidens sitting still and silent on the bench. They held the headdress over each girl in turn. Mikayla watched out of the corner of her eye, wondering what the point of all this was, since nothing seemed to be happening. Then they came to her, and as they held the headdress over her head, it seemed to slip from their grasp.

Although it had been only a few inches above her head, it felt to Mikayla as if the headdress had been dropped from a great height. She braced her neck against its weight and clasped her hands together tightly in her lap. For an instant she had the curious feeling that the headdress was moving, like the bird it represented, adjusting itself in a more comfortable position on her head—more comfortable for it, at any rate. Mikayla did not think she would ever consider it comfortable.

"Praised be Meret in Her Choice." The other Daughters joined with the Eldest Daughter and the Husband of the Goddess to repeat the chant as they helped Mikayla to her feet and drew her to stand in front of the altar. Mikayla stood there quietly, wondering what was expected of her. Apparently nothing was, for no one gave any indication that she was failing in anything she was supposed to do.

The Daughters began to line up in the order in which they usually progressed to the chapel, and Mikayla realized that it was time for the ritual of the Hour When the Sun Embraces the Sacred Peak. Before she could move to her accustomed place at the end of the line, however, the Husband and the Eldest Daughter pulled her between them.

When they arrived in the chapel, the Daughters sat on their bench, each girl sitting one place down from her usual spot, leaving two spaces at the end where the Eldest Daughter sat. The Eldest Daughter and the Husband of the Goddess, who were still holding Mikayla between them, took her onto the dais in full view of the congregation. Mikayla, who hadn't had that many people staring at her since she dropped a knife at a state dinner when she was ten, felt frozen with self-consciousness. *Don't worry,* she told herself firmly, *the Husband and the Eldest Daughter don't want you to make mistakes, and they'll make certain that you don't.*

Fortunately no one seemed to expect her to speak, which was a good thing because Mikayla wasn't sure that she could talk with all that weight on her head. The Husband and the Eldest Daughter of the Goddess did all the talking—or chanting—as they presented Mikayla to the congregation as the Chosen One, the Beloved Youngest Daughter of the Goddess. Then the Eldest Daughter led Mikayla back behind the curtain and indicated the seat next to hers. The girl in the next place down, who had been the Youngest Daughter for the previous year, held the box for the headdress in her lap. The Eldest Daughter removed the headdress and replaced it in the box, which the Daughter then tucked under the bench. Mikayla suppressed a sigh of relief as the weight was removed from her head.

The Eldest Daughter returned to the dais, and the ritual proceeded normally from that point on.

After the ritual, when the Daughters returned to their room for supper, the other Daughters congratulated Mikayla on having been granted the favor of the Goddess. When they sat down for supper, Mikayla was placed between the Eldest Daughter and the previous Youngest Daughter, and she realized that this represented a permanent change in the ranking order—*at least until next year when they choose someone else,* she thought.

The ritual of the Second Hour of Darkness was back to normal as well, aside from Mikayla's new place in line. But still, she was unusually tired when she went to bed—so tired that she almost fell asleep before she could bespeak Red-Eye.

She fought sleep as she cast her thoughts toward Mount Rotolo. "Red-Eye."

"Mika." The bird's reply was immediate, as usual. Mikayla suspected that it knew her schedule as well as she did. "Another quiet day, I trust."

"Not quite," Mikayla thought back. "I've been Chosen."

"Youngest Daughter for next year?" There was a trace of anxiety in the bird's thoughts.

"Yes," Mika thought back. "And that headdress is almost as heavy as you are, and I am sooo tired. . . ."

"Mika!" The thought was sharp. "Did anyone say anything about a jubilee?"

"No," Mika thought sleepily. "What's a jubilee?"

"Are you sure?" Red-Eye was insistent.

"Yes, positive. I've never heard the word in my life." That stirred a thought, even through her sleepiness. "There was one word in the ritual I hadn't heard before."

"What was it?" the bird demanded.

"I'm thinking." Mikayla ran backward through the day in her mind. " 'Kiss the ground before her *hemsut*'—the Eldest Daughter said it. What's a *hemsut*?"

"Oh that." Red-Eye sounded relieved. "It's nothing you need to worry about, it's just a special word for a female spirit. She was talking about the Goddess, wasn't she?"

"Yes," Mikayla thought sleepily. "It was part of a long chant of praise of the Goddess."

"That's all right, then. Go to sleep, Mika."

That was a suggestion Mikayla had no trouble in following.

The next morning after the ritual of the First Hour, the Eldest Daughter put the headdress back on Mikayla and drew her along toward the back of the Temple, along a route in which the floor got higher and the ceiling lower with each room.

"Where are we going?" Mikayla whispered softly, anxious enough to ignore the custom of not speaking until after breakfast.

"You are to be presented to the Goddess," the Eldest Daughter whispered back. "Be silent."

Mikayla had to close her throat against a gasp of surprise when they reached their final destination. The part of her that lived in the Temple realized that she was in the Holy of Holies, the Sanctuary where the Goddess lived, where only the highest of the priesthood ever went. The part of her that had explored Orogastus's Tower with Fiolon recognized this as the room she had seen in the magic mirror.

The Husband of the Goddess was there, as was another man both robed and veiled in black. Mikayla was fairly certain she had never seen him before. The two men opened the shrine, a cabinet set against the solid rock wall, and reverently lifted out the wooden statue of the Goddess.

Mikayla kept a close eye on the Eldest Daughter so that she could guess what she was supposed to do. Together they undressed the statue and laid it on the table. The man in the black veil anointed the statue with some sort of oil that smelled very strange to Mikayla—it didn't even remind her of anything she had ever smelled before. While he did that, the Husband of the Goddess stood at Her head swinging a thurible that gave off a thick cloud of incense.

When the anointing was done, the women dressed the statue in fresh clothing from a clothing chest at one side of the room, while the men produced food and wine from another chest and placed it on a small table next to the shrine. Then the men lifted the statue to a standing position in front of the shrine, and the Eldest Daughter pushed Mikayla gently to indicate that she should kneel before the statue.

Mikayla knelt and looked up at the statue's face. Even though she knew that it was only painted wood, she could have sworn that the eyes actually saw her, measured her, and judged her while the Husband and the Eldest Daughter asked the Goddess to bless her Chosen Youngest Daughter. Mikayla was glad when the ritual was over and the Eldest Daughter led her back to the chapel to replace the headdress in its box before they took it back to the Daughters' room and joined their Sisters for breakfast.

The rest of Mikayla's month at the Temple was divided between chanting the daily rituals and learning the part of the Youngest Daughter for next year's Spring Festival. It was a pleasant, tranquil life, and she was almost sorry when her month was up and it was time for her to return to the world outside, especially since she suspected that it was her duty to return to the Tower and see how Haramis and Uzun fared.

But it was time for her to leave. Red-Eye fetched her just after dark, after the ritual of the Hour When the Sun Embraces the Sacred Peak, and took her straight to Haramis's Tower. "Did Fiolon tell you to bring me here?" Mikayla asked it.

"Yes," the bird replied. "He says you are needed here."

"Oh dear." Mikayla sighed, slipping from the bird's back onto the balcony. Red-Eye held out a claw so that she could disentangle her sphere from it. She replaced the sphere around her neck and hugged the great bird. "Fly well, Red-Eye, and good hunting."

"Be well, Mika," the bird said as it took off into the night.

Mikayla crept quietly indoors and made it to the sanctuary of her room unseen. She had missed supper at the Temple, but she didn't feel inclined to roam about searching for food. She would rather go hungry than have to face anyone in the Tower that night.

# 22

*Mikayla woke suddenly. She knew at once that it was* about two hours before dawn, and despite the heating in the Tower her room was cold from the autumn chill. Something was very wrong; she could feel it. She tried to narrow it down, to move from feeling generalized uneasiness, verging on terror, to focus and determine exactly *what* was wrong.

Then her bed was being shaken violently from side to side, but her room was still completely dark. She called out, "Who's there?" but no one answered, and she felt silly. If anyone had been in her room, she would have known.

After what seemed like several long minutes, but was probably actually less than a minute, the shaking stopped. Mikayla sat up in bed, called up a light, and took stock of her surroundings. The pillow, which she had shoved away in her sleep, had fallen onto the floor, but the room appeared otherwise intact. *It was an earthquake,* Mikayla thought. That was what had wakened her, the sense that a major earthquake was about to occur.

But there couldn't be an earthquake, especially here. There must be some other answer. Was this some magic Haramis was working without her? Was Haramis recovered enough to work magic?

It had been half a year since Mikayla had left the Temple of Meret and returned to the Tower. Guardswoman Nella and Lady Bevis had returned to the Citadel about a month after Mikayla's return, saying that the Lady was recovered enough not to need them, but still Mikayla hadn't noticed any sign that Haramis was recovering her magical abilities.

By now Haramis was able to dress and feed herself, if a bit sloppily, and she could walk well enough to go down to her study and spend hours sitting talking to Uzun. Uzun was still a harp, although Fiolon had kept his promise and had the harp repaired while Haramis was still confined to her bed.

Mikayla wished she could just lie down again and go back to sleep, but she suspected that she was going to be needed very shortly. So she got up, put on her robe and slippers, and went to find out what was going on.

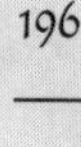

Haramis was not in the workroom, nor in her study, where Mikayla found Uzun leaning against the wall. She hurried to restore him to his normal upright position. "What happened, Uzun?"

"That was an earthquake, Princess, and, I fear, an ill omen as well." The harp, in a minor key, sounded foreboding. "I am glad that you are here."

"An earthquake?" Mikayla was incredulous. "We're sitting on top of a league of solid rock! How can we have an earthquake here?"

"We shouldn't," Uzun replied. "Where is the Lady?"

"I don't know," Mikayla said. "I was looking for her when I came in here. I thought she must be working some spell, but she's not in the workroom. And surely she can't have slept through this—nobody could have!"

As if to prove her point, Enya came hurrying in. "There you are, Princess," she said. "Are you all right? Is Master Uzun?"

Mikayla nodded. "Except for the fact that I don't particularly care for being awakened two hours before dawn, I'm fine. Have you seen the Lady?"

Enya frowned. "No, I haven't, and she's usually the first one stirring whenever anything strange happens."

"Maybe we should go find her," Mikayla said hesitantly. "I'm not sure I want to disturb her if she's still asleep, but—"

Enya shook her head positively. "She would never have slept through this. We'd better go see if she's all right."

Enya softly opened the door to Haramis's bedroom, then stopped with an exclamation of dismay. Mikayla, looking over her shoulder, could see Haramis lying on the floor near her bed, clearly visible in the light spilling in from the hallway. Together they hurried to the Archimage's side. Her eyes were open, and she seemed to recognize them, but when she tried to talk, her speech was so slurred as to be unintelligible.

Enya drew in her breath sharply and made a sign against evil.

Mikayla forced down the feelings of terror and panic welling up inside her. *It's another brainstorm,* she realized. *It has to be—why else would the very land shake so? What do I do now? I don't know how to take care of her when she's like this! But nobody else around here does either, I'll bet. What if she dies? Is this my fault? I haven't done anything to annoy her in months! And even if sometimes I wish she were dead, I don't really mean it!*

Mikayla looked from Enya to Haramis and decided at least to try to be practical. Enya didn't seem ready to be much help yet; she still seemed to regard what she was seeing as an evil spell.

"Let's get her back into bed," Mikayla suggested. "She can't be comfortable on the floor like that."

It was fortunate that Haramis was not a large woman, for she was almost completely deadweight as they lifted her and dragged her into her bed. She didn't seem to be able to control her arm and leg on the left side or, for that matter, to move them at all. This made Mikayla all the more certain that this was the same thing that had happened to Haramis before, at the Citadel. *And I wish she were there now,* she thought. *There, at least, they knew how to take care of her.*

Once Haramis was safely tucked into bed, Enya's wits seemed to start functioning again. "There is an old Healer woman who attends the servants," she said. "Perhaps we should summon her. The Lady's hands and feet are very cold; I will make her some hot tea and put hot bricks at her feet. That at least could do no harm."

When the tea was brought Haramis could not sit up to drink, so Enya held her upright and spooned a little of the hot brew into the Lady's mouth. Mikayla, who didn't want to have anything to do with nursing someone who was so sick she couldn't move, was happy to accept Enya's suggestion that while she was feeding the Lady, Mikayla should go at once to the servants' hall and ask the Oddling woman who cared for the servants when they were ill or injured to come at once.

"Her name is Kimbri," Enya told Mikayla. "The Archimage has always been so hearty and healthy that she has never needed a Healer before—not when she was here at any rate, and there are no human Healers here."

Mikayla ran down to the kitchens, grateful for an excuse to be out of the room. One of the women there making bread told her that Kimbri had gone down to the house of the gardener's wife, whose child was due in a few days. All of the rest of the servants seemed to be clustered in the kitchen, comparing notes on how the earthquake had wakened them. Mikayla sent the Vispi man who worked in the stables to find the Healer, but the way he looked at her reminded her that she wasn't dressed. She dashed back to her room and threw on the first clothes that came to hand before returning to the hall to watch for the Healer.

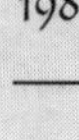

Before very long the Oddling woman appeared. She was a deceptively frail-looking Vispi with graying hair done up in a coil over her forehead. Mikayla told her what had happened, trying not to sound as upset as she felt.

The Oddling said peacefully, "Aye, she is not young. I am not at all surprised that she has begun to suffer the ills of age. My own grand-dame was so stricken when she was ninety. Don't be frightened, little Lady. It is not likely that the Lady will die if she is living yet. Those who are struck down like this usually die at once; and if not, they may live for a long time. It is quite likely that the Lady might go on living for a good many years."

"I certainly hope so," Mikayla said. "If anything happened to her, I'd be Archimage. And I'm nowhere near ready for that yet." She followed Kimbri upstairs to the Archimage's room, and Kimbri bent over the old woman's limp body and felt for her pulse.

"There is nothing more we can do," she told Mikayla. "She will live and grow stronger or she will not; that is all anyone can do, now."

"But what causes it?"

"No one knows. Maybe the Ancients knew, but we have so little of their wisdom."

"But—isn't there anything we can do?" Mikayla demanded.

"This happened to her before, at the Citadel, and they treated it with swamp-worm venom."

"Do you know how much they used, how it was administered, and where to get some?" Kimbri asked gently.

Mikayla shook her head.

"Then all we can do is to be patient," Kimbri said, adding sympathetically, "although that is sometimes the hardest thing of all. And try to keep her spirits up as much as you can."

Mikayla thought that might be the most difficult thing to do. She knew well that Haramis did not suffer either fools or weakness gladly—if at all. She had a feeling that a sick Haramis was going to be a very unpleasant person to be around—especially when she recovered enough to start complaining about her condition.

Mikayla was determined that Haramis would recover. It never occurred to her to think that if Haramis died, she might then be freed; she knew now that that would never happen. She was becoming resigned to being Archimage. *But, please, not yet,* she thought. *Not for a long time yet.*

She sighed as she went downstairs to tackle her next task: breaking the news to Uzun.

The harp sobbed like a child, but with a breathy twanging sound.

"I love her so much," Uzun said at last. "If it were not for her and her magic I would long ago have gone to join my ancestors in whatever afterworld there may be. For her alone I was willing to stay. Should the Lady be gone, my long life will be but a weariness."

Mikayla, although she felt frightened herself, tried to comfort the ancient magician.

"Don't worry, Uzun; she'll be better soon."

"Will she? She is far older than I; and all my family and friends are many years gone. If anything should happen to her, I would be all alone in the world."

Mikayla felt like saying, "No you won't, Uzun; I'm still here, and if anything should happen to her, I'll need your counsel more than she ever did." But she knew that her relationship with Uzun was very different from his with Haramis, so she held her tongue.

And, as if she didn't already have enough to worry about, Mikayla remembered that Haramis had once said that when the previous Archimage died, her Tower had crumbled immediately into dust—which was why Haramis had come to live in this one, built by Orogastus. Mikayla hoped this would not happen to Haramis's Tower.

She felt younger than ever. She felt as if she would like to break down and cry; but in Uzun's sorrow, how could she expect him to care about her troubles? She patted the forepillar of the harp, glad that Fiolon had kept his promise to have it repaired, and said awkwardly, "Don't cry, Uzun. Some people do get better, so Kimbri says. And Haramis got better before. I know she would hate to see you so unhappy; so you must be strong for her when she needs you.

"Sometimes," she added artfully, remembering something else the Healer had said, "cheerful company can make all the difference between who lives and who dies. So you must be strong, and you must not cry when she needs you. Her mind must be at rest, and this would only make her more unhappy."

Uzun sniffled with a liquid sound of strings. "You are right; I will try to be cheerful for her."

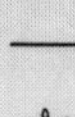

"Good," Mikayla said. She wondered what would happen to Uzun if Haramis did die while he was still in the harp, bespelled with her blood. Would he crumble to dust, as the old Archimage's Tower and possessions had? She did not, however, feel that this was a question she could ask Uzun, and obviously she couldn't ask Haramis at present.

For the next several days it seemed that Haramis grew neither better nor worse. The nursing was done by the Oddlings, and Mikayla had very little to do, except to try to cheer Uzun, who had stopped weeping, but evidently held out no very great hopes for the recovery of the Archimage. For that matter, neither did Mikayla, even though the Healer had said that every day a person so stricken did not die, the chances were better for her eventual recovery of all her faculties.

Although she tried to block it out, Mikayla could feel the land nearly all the time now. It definitely was not the land sense of an Archimage; she knew what Fiolon had with Var, and what she felt was nothing like that strong. She felt as though she could hear voices crying in the wind, but couldn't make out the words, or as if there were shadows in every corner that vanished when she tried to look at them. The land was not happy, and neither was Mikayla.

. . .

It was about ten days later, and Mikayla had taken Kimbri's place sitting beside Haramis in the old woman's bedroom, for this morning, Kimbri had felt she must go and visit her own neglected family and see to her other patients.

Mikayla felt nervous and very much alone. She had nearly fallen asleep in her chair from boredom when she suddenly saw that Haramis's eyes were completely open, and that the old woman was watching her.

Mikayla started a little, and said softly, "My Lady Haramis, are you awake?"

The old woman's voice sounded slurred and indistinct—and cross. "Yes, of course I'm awake; what's the matter with you? And where is Enya? What are you doing here?"

Mikayla wished desperately that Kimbri or Enya—or anybody except herself were there. But Haramis's tone was so sharp that she could do nothing but try to answer.

Since she wasn't sure if Haramis even remembered her or knew who she was—after all, she hadn't the last time—she tried to avoid any details. "You have been very ill, Lady. Shall I go and call Enya for you?"

"No. Not yet," Haramis said. "How long has it been? Why is Uzun not with me?"

Mikayla had no idea whether she should say anything to Haramis about how long she had been unconscious. But Haramis was looking at her expectantly, so Mikayla said, "About ten days, I think, Lady. We were all very frightened for you."

"And where is Uzun? Why is he not at my side? If he is concerned for me, why does he not haul his useless old carcass up the stairs to see me? Or is it too far for the old fellow to walk?"

Mikayla paused, not quite knowing how to answer; but after the first moment of confusion, the old Archimage's mind seemed comparatively clear.

"Oh, yes," she said. "It had slipped my mind for a moment; Uzun cannot walk now, of course. Perhaps later, if I cannot go down the stairs, someone can manage to drag him up to visit me —but not up those circular stairs. Even when he could still walk he had trouble on that staircase. I cannot imagine why Orogastus ever had the thing built. He always did prefer style to function and other practical considerations."

She closed her eyes, and seemed to sleep for a moment. Then she said, "And of course you cannot carry him. Well, I suppose my need for his counsel must overcome my need for repose." She tried to sit up and, after gasping for a moment and struggling, said, "Help me to sit upright." She sounded very surprised. "I find I cannot sit by myself."

Mikayla put her arms round the old woman, pulling her to a sitting position, and said, "Shall I run down the stairs and tell Uzun that you are asking for him? He will be very glad to hear that you are awake. He has been dreadfully concerned about you, of course; we all have."

"Now, what good would that do, when he could not come up and join me?" Haramis asked testily. "Why upset the old fellow without cause? Is Kimbri here?"

"She has gone to see if the gardener's wife is ready to have her child. As soon as she comes back I will have her come to you."

"Don't bother," Haramis said. "It is not for nothing that I was made Archimage." Then, without raising her voice, she said, as if speaking to someone in the same room, "Kimbri, come here; I need you."

In a short while, Kimbri came running up the stairs. Mikayla met her at the door, and asked softly, "Did you hear the Lady call you?"

"No," Kimbri whispered back. "I checked on the gardener's wife, and she is doing well, so I decided to look in on the Lady. Did she call me?"

Mikayla nodded. Kimbri said softly, "It seems quite likely that her natural faculties would return before her magical ones. Try not to worry about it." She continued on into Haramis's room. When she saw the Archimage sitting upright, she said, "It is good indeed to see you looking so much better, Lady." As she started to examine Haramis Mikayla took the opportunity to slip out of the room to tell Uzun the good news.

She ran down the stairs to the study and found the huge harp apparently dozing. They had never decided whether Uzun really slept or not, but since Haramis had been ill, Uzun had seemed to be asleep on several occasions when Mikayla tried to talk to him.

"Wake up, Uzun," she cried. "The Archimage is awake, and she asked at once for you."

If it was possible for a wooden harp to look self-satisfied, she would have sworn that Uzun looked smug. "You say she has asked for me? I might have guessed that would be her first act when she wakened," he said. "Can you take me to her?"

"No." Mikayla sighed. "Haramis doesn't think we can get you up all those stairs. And even if *she* doesn't remember what happened to you last time we dragged you up to her room, I do! But I can run messages back and forth for you."

"I suppose that will have to do." Uzun sighed.

"Unless you have an ambition to become a pile of kindling wood, it will indeed have to do," Mikayla said firmly.

# 23

*Somehow it did not greatly surprise Mikayla that* Haramis suddenly forgot her previous opposition to giving Uzun a new body.

The first hint of this change of heart came the next week, when Kimbri came to check on the Archimage again. “How are you feeling today, Lady?” she asked respectfully.

“Not well,” said Haramis. She sounded tired, and very old. “Certainly not well enough to teach Mikayla all the things she must learn before she becomes Archimage. At least, not at this moment, but I feel she should not wait any longer to learn them.” She leaned back and closed her eyes; or rather, Mikayla thought, let them fall shut. After a while she said, without opening her eyes, “I think what you should learn first, Mikayla, is to keep in touch with the whole of this realm with your Sight, through what I have already taught you of the use of the scrying bowl. Go then, and fetch it.”

Mikayla went and fetched the silver bowl, filling it to the rim with pure water as she had been taught. She did not feel that this would be a good time to remind Haramis that she had taught Mikayla to scry the entire realm some years ago. She strongly suspected that Haramis didn't remember how long Mikayla had been living in her Tower. *I suppose it's a good sign that she remembers me at all,* Mikayla thought, *and I certainly don't want to upset her. After all, Kimbri said that she should be kept calm—and that's difficult at the best of times.*

When she returned, Haramis asked her, "What would you like most to see in this Kingdom?"

Mikayla stopped to consider that for a moment. It was the first time Haramis had ever consulted her about her preferences. What should it be, then? The Skriteks? Definitely not. The city ruins toward which she and Fiolon had been seeking on that first day when they had met with the Archimage? After a moment she said cautiously, "I would like to see how my cousin Fiolon fares."

Rather weakly, Haramis moved her right hand. "Look, then, into the water."

Mikayla looked into the bowl, remembering the instructions of the Archimage on other occasions. She did remember how to use the bowl, even though she always used the sphere around her neck when she was scrying for herself. After a moment the reflections of the windows in Haramis's room swirled on the surface of the bowl and formed into a tiny picture of Fiolon, cloaked and booted for riding, on a gray fronial. Behind him, a smaller fronial trotted, heavily piled with luggage.

Mikayla recognized his surroundings; he was nearby and headed to this Tower. *Why is he coming here?* she wondered. *Haramis sends him away every time she sees him.*

Haramis said sharply, "Well, child, what do you see?"

Mikayla bit her lip. *She's obviously not well if she looks at me and sees a child,* she thought, *and telling her that Fiolon is coming here may anger her. But she's bound to find out he's here when he arrives—the servants won't lie to her, not about this.* "Fiolon is coming here, Lady," she said, "with two fronials. He's within half a league of the chasm at the edge of the plaza."

"Those must be the fronials and the baggage I left with his parents on the day I called the lammergeiers to rescue you from the Skriteks," Haramis said promptly. "No doubt Fiolon is bound here, returning them to me."

Mikayla stared at her openmouthed, then forced herself to close her mouth. Obviously Haramis was once again not living in the present, but at least now Mikayla was getting some idea of *when* Haramis thought she was. *At least she's not angry that Fiolon is coming here. And she said "his parents"—perhaps she thinks he's one of my brothers.*

"Look in the top drawer of the table by my bedside, Mikayla," Haramis instructed her. "It contains the little silver blowpipe I use to summon the bridge. By the time you reach the bottom of the Tower, he will be here, so go at once."

Mikayla didn't think he would be here quite that soon, but she was glad enough to obey the Archimage—and to get out of the room. She took up the little pipe, and hurried down the long stairs to the entrance that let her out on the edge of the plaza on the south side of the Tower. She was glad to see that the solar cell was clear; she suspected that Orogastus's "magic mirror" might be needed very soon. *Fiolon would not be coming here without a very good reason.*

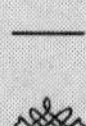

As she stood on the plaza waiting for Fiolon's arrival, she had plenty of time to consider the state of Haramis's mind. Sometimes, she knew from the Healer, old people who suffered this illness lost much of their memory, or could not use their powers of speech or reason. This would be likely to make Haramis very angry—if she even realized what was happening at all.

Mikayla quailed to think of Haramis's situation. She had obviously lost at least part of her reason and did not seem to know it. She still thought Mikayla was an untrained child; the Lord of the Air alone knew what she thought of Fiolon. . . .

The whole land was without its mother and guide. Well, after a fashion . . .

Mikayla stood on the plaza, thinking unhappy thoughts until Fiolon came into sight. She blew a note on the pipe, as she had seen Haramis do the first time she had sent Fiolon away, so many years ago—years, apparently, that Haramis did not remember.

The bridge extended itself smoothly over the great chasm, almost at the precise moment Fiolon and his fronials drew up before it. Mikayla found it hard to wait while Fiolon and his fronials crossed the bridge, but as soon as he was there, she ran forward to hug him, practically dragging him off his fronial in the process.

"Oh, Fiolon, I'm so glad to see you. It seemed too good to be true when I saw you were on your way here!"

"You knew?" Fiolon said, hugging her back and continuing to hold her. "That explains why you were here to meet me. Are you ready to be Archimage yet? I can tell that something is seriously wrong with Haramis, is it not?"

"Yes," Mikayla said, "you're right. You will find her very much changed, I fear, and not for the better. She has been very ill, and for a few days we feared she would die."

Fiolon sighed. "Another brainstorm?" he asked. Mikayla nodded. "And you aren't anywhere near ready to take her place, I suppose. That would explain the mess."

Although this was what Mikayla had herself been thinking for some time, she was not flattered that this should have been Fiolon's first thought. She said rather snappishly, "I know perfectly well that I'm not ready; Haramis has been saying nothing else for the last few days and so has Uzun. Anyone would think I was only six years old. Why don't you go up and see her, and then you can all agree on how hopeless I am!"

She stomped off into the stables to press the button that retracted the bridge and to tell the groom to take care of the fronials, but when she turned, she found Fiolon right on her heels.

"I'm sorry, Mika," he said, putting an arm around her shoulder. "It must be wretched for you, having her like this."



"Just wait until you see her," Mikayla said with a certain grim satisfaction.

"And I didn't mean that you couldn't take over as Archimage," Fiolon continued. "In fact, I think you should."

Mikayla stared at him in horror. "But that could kill her!"

"Perhaps she would rather die than continue what this is doing to the land," Fiolon said gently. "The damage is spilling over into Var. I feel it; that is why I came here."

"I knew you must have a very good reason for coming," Mikayla said, "knowing the way Haramis sends you away every time she sees you. But she may not exactly remember who you are at the moment—she seems to think you're one of my brothers."

"I shall not disillusion her, then," Fiolon said, "and I promise not to tell her that I'm Archimage of Var—she'd probably have a fit. I assume you never told her."

"Of course not," Mikayla said. "Uzun knows, but he won't tell her."

"All right, then," Fiolon said. "Let's go see how bad it is." He patted her gently on the back and gestured for her to proceed.

The young people toiled up the stairs and into the room of the old woman. "Here is Fiolon come to see you, Lady Haramis," Mikayla said formally.

"Come in, child," Haramis said, weakly extending her right hand toward Fiolon.

*It's the same as it was last time,* Mikayla suddenly realized. *She can use her right side, but not her left. I wonder why that is.*

Fiolon bent over Haramis's hand and kissed the back of it in a courtly fashion. "Lady," he replied.

*He's certainly developing polished court manners,* Mikayla thought resentfully. *Of course,* he *gets to spend time at court; I'm the one who's spending her entire life trapped in the mountains.*

She stood in the doorway and glowered while Fiolon made vague social conversation, suitable for an elderly lady who couldn't be expected to know much, if anything, about what was going on in the world. It would have been ridiculous if it hadn't been so pathetic, Mikayla thought as she listened to Fiolon assure the Archimage that his parents were in excellent health. Obviously Haramis had only the vaguest idea of who he was, or she would have remembered that his mother had died in childbirth and that no one had ever known who his father was. *Well, maybe his father* is *in excellent health; there's certainly no proof to the contrary.*

Haramis tired quickly. Telling Mikayla to have the housekeeper make up a room for her brother, she dismissed them both.

Mikayla, who had already asked Enya to have a room prepared for Fiolon, dragged him off to her room for a private conference. The two of them dropped into the chairs on either side of the small table next to the fireplace and looked at each other in dismay. Then Mikayla groaned, dropping her head onto her forearms on the table. "She's really not all here." She sighed.

"You're right about that, I'm afraid," Fiolon agreed. "When did I become your brother?"

"No doubt when Haramis decided that's what she wanted you to be." Mikayla straightened up, scowling. "Some days I really hate her. She decides what she wants reality to be, and then she expects everyone to agree with her. And everyone does! If she said the sky were green, Uzun and all the servants would assure her that it had never been any other color.

"She keeps telling long repetitive stories of her girlhood. The first three or four times they were sort of interesting, but after the twentieth, no!"

"She forgets what she's said?" Fiolon asked.

Mikayla nodded. "She's like that first music box we had back at the Citadel when we were children, remember? It played the same tune every time you put it on the same side. With her you get the exact same speech at intervals. I haven't figured out yet just what corresponds to the sides on the music box, but it does seem to be an analogous phenomenon. Once I hear the first few words, I can tell you the rest of the speech, word for word, inflection for inflection—and I'm so sick of it I could scream!

"Remember the tower at the Citadel where we used to play? We could spend hours there and nobody would bother us. Here, if I'm out of her sight for half an hour, she sends Enya to find me. She doesn't want me to have any time to myself, she doesn't want me to be where she doesn't know where I am, she doesn't even want me to be able to think for myself . . . it really bothers me.

"It's as if she's trying to wipe out my personality and replace it with her own—almost as if she were trying to possess me, as if she's trying to spread her soul over two bodies, hers and mine, without any regard for what happens to my soul." She shuddered and looked anxiously at him. "I do have a soul of my own, don't I, Fio?"

"Of course you do," Fiolon assured her. "You're probably just upset because she's ill. Have you been getting enough sleep? And have you been eating, or is the household so upset that you're not getting proper meals again?"

"I take some fruit or something if I'm hungry," Mikayla said. "As for sleep, I almost wish I weren't—I get nightmares and then I wake up and I'm trapped here!"

"You're not exactly trapped here," Fiolon pointed out. "You never promised to stay."

Mikayla looked at him incredulously. "Of course I'm trapped here—I have been for years. I didn't choose to be Archimage—she kidnapped me from my home, brought me here, and has been 'teaching' me for years, without ever once asking what I wanted."

"Yes," Fiolon agreed, "she brought you here without your consent—but that was years ago. You could have gone home anytime you chose ever since you learned to talk to the lammergeiers—and before that, if you were willing to take a fronial through all the snow. By now, being here is your choice, even if you haven't made it consciously. Think about it, and choose. What are you going to do?"

"Oh, I have a choice," Mikayla said sarcastically. "For the Lords' sakes, Fio, don't you start this. You're supposed to be my friend—I really need a friend, and you're the closest thing I've got to one. Don't you take her side, too, please don't. I can't stand it; I just can't live like this. This isn't what I wanted."

"What did you want?" Fiolon asked quietly.

"I don't know anymore," Mikayla sobbed. "I get so confused here. But it can't have been this or I wouldn't be so miserable." She tried to think clearly about it. "I wanted what everybody wants, I guess: a nice husband—preferably you—a few children, a comfortable home someplace, a garden, friends. . . ."

"You have Uzun," Fiolon pointed out.

"I'd prefer friends who are a little more ambulatory." Mikayla sighed. "I mean Uzun's very nice, but you have to be *really* fond of music to appreciate him as he ought to be appreciated. . . . You were always my best friend, and you know as well as I do that the first thing Haramis wanted when she got us here was to send you away. She wants me to be alone and totally dependent on her, and it's not fair!"

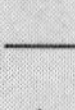

"But, Mika, you can summon a lammergeier, can't you? Even at night, Red-Eye would fly across two mountain peaks at your first call."

"That's true."

"Then it's not that you don't have any choice," Fio pointed out. "You can summon a lammergeier, fly to anyplace you want, and never come back. So if you're still here after all this time, I'd say you have made a choice. I'm really sorry that you're unhappy, but you must have some reason for staying here."

Mikayla frowned. "This is going to sound crazy, but I think the land wants me."

"It doesn't sound crazy at all," Fiolon said promptly. "I think it does, too."

Mikayla looked slightly sick. "Since she took ill this time, I keep thinking that I hear it crying—the land, or the winds, or something. I really feel awful, but there doesn't seem to be anything I can do about it. I don't have the land sense—not the way you do. The problem is that I don't think Haramis has it either."

Fio shrugged. "I don't know. It's not something that you can tell about someone else." He touched his fingertips to the spot on his tunic where his sphere was. "If you had it, of course, I could tell, but with her, I can't."

Mikayla's fingers went to the lump at her chest, carefully hidden under at least two layers of clothes at all times, the sphere that was twin to Fiolon's. She always wore it next to her skin; it was the one thing she had kept from the time before her life with Haramis, the singing spheres that she and Fiolon had found on their last trip into the Mire. "Are we linked that strongly?" she asked. "I keep thinking that I can feel your presence, and hear your voice in the chiming noise it makes, but I thought it must be my imagination."

Fiolon smiled at her. "Mika, the one thing you never did have much of was imagination." He shook his sphere gently, making it ring. Mikayla felt hers vibrate with it. "It is said that scrying is notoriously unreliable, especially for humans, but using this as a link, we can scry each other very clearly. I've been following your lessons for years, even some of those chants at the Temple of Meret."

Mikayla groaned, remembering a lot of those lessons. "And you do them a lot better than I do, too. When you landed in Var and got the land sense, you could cope with it. I spent two days sick in bed just from being linked with you."

"I think you'd do a lot better if you'd relax and stop fighting the whole situation."

"No doubt."

"I wonder if there's anything in the library about the effects of having both an Archimage and a trained successor."

"Trained?" Mikayla said. "Me? Everybody agrees that I'm not trained yet."

"But you've had more training than I had when I became Archimage of Var," Fiolon pointed out.

"You're right," Mikayla said. "Do you suppose that means that I wasn't supposed to be trained in the first place? Could that be why Haramis keeps getting brainstorms—because there *are* two of us?"

"Look in the library," Fiolon suggested.

"There's nothing in the main library," Mikayla pointed out. "I've read every book in it at least once. But if we do some more exploring in the ice caves, we may find more of Orogastus's stuff, something that we overlooked before."

"Good idea," Fiolon said. "According to some of the old stories, he was a lot more interested in varied uses of power than Haramis ever was."

"I believe that," Mikayla said. "And there may be something in

the library at the Temple of Meret, though what excuse I could come up for wanting that information I can't imagine!"

She looked speculatively at Fiolon. "But how do things go for you? Are you still having trouble with the women at court?"

Fiolon frowned. "I don't pay much attention. None of the girls in Var is really seriously interested in me, in spite of the dukedom, especially since I spend most of my time there. There are all sorts of stupid stories about my father's being a demon or something, and there's certainly no doubt that I'm a bastard."

"You mean there aren't girls who find that glamorous and romantic?" Mikayla teased.

Fiolon groaned. "I won't deny that there are girls at court who are that stupid, Mika, but you know perfectly well that I've never found stupidity attractive. At least you have a brain—even if you don't seem to be using it much at the moment."

Unfortunately this reminded Mikayla of her original complaint. "Oh, I don't have a brain, Fio," she said with acid sweetness. "Haramis has two: hers and mine. As far as she's concerned, I'm a cross between her property and a part of her body.

"Look at the way she treats Uzun. He was a person once; he was her friend and her teacher . . . and what is he now? Her harp. He can't move on his own, and she can pick him up and cart him around anyplace she wants, subject, of course, to the difficulty of moving a harp that large.

"He's a thing, I'm a thing, her servants are things, and you're a nuisance—to her, that is, when she remembers who you are. I certainly think of you as a person; it's as if you're the only real person here. I'm not even sure that I'm a person or that I'll ever be a person again. And you know that as soon as she remembers who you are and why you're here, she'll send you away again."

"You don't know what's been happening in Var," Fiolon said. "I'm not leaving this time just because she tells me to. I'm not twelve years old anymore."

# 24

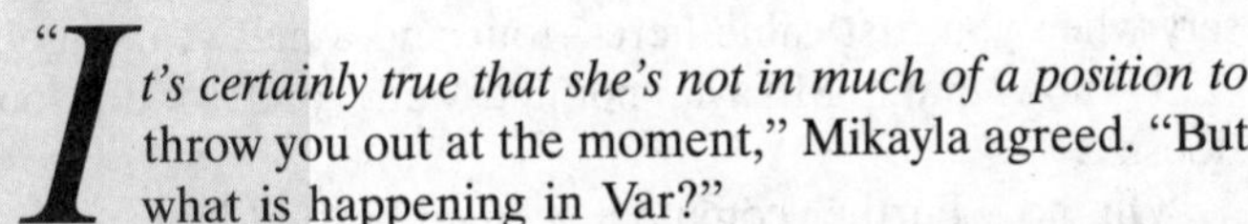

"*It's certainly true that she's not in much of a position to* throw you out at the moment," Mikayla agreed. "But what is happening in Var?"

"Something is coming down the Great Mutar River and killing all the fish," Fiolon said. "And that's only what is immediately obvious. I was at Let when it started, overseeing the timber shipments, and there's a wrongness in the water. I sent a message to my uncle the King that I was going to investigate, and then I went to the Citadel. I passed through Lake Wum on the way, and every fish in the lake is dead—and so are some of the folk who were on or near it when whatever it was happened."

"Wyvilo?" Mikayla asked.

"Mostly Wyvilo, but some humans died as well, and many more were made very ill."

Mikayla gasped. "How is that possible?"

Fiolon looked unhappy. "I don't know. Ruwenda isn't my land, so, while I can feel that there is something seriously wrong, I can't feel exactly what it is or how to fix it."

"Couldn't you feel it while you were in Var?"

Fiolon shook his head. "The problem isn't in Var—that is, Var isn't part of it. All I could feel in Var is something horrible coming out of Ruwenda, down the river. And I'll tell you one thing," he added, "it would be much worse if the prevailing winds blew from Ruwenda to Var instead of the other way. At least I was spared the wrongness in the air until I crossed the border. From the Citadel I traveled by fronial so that I could go through the Mazy Mire and see how things were there." He looked her straight in the eyes. "Mikayla, your land is *very* sick."

"Haramis's land," Mikayla reminded him. "Not mine."

"By the Flower, Mika, it's your home!" Fiolon looked appalled. "Don't you care about it at all?"

"What good would it do me to care?" Mikayla shrugged, trying to hide the hurt she felt. "Do you actually think Haramis would let me do anything about it? Do you know why I was waiting for your arrival?"

She didn't wait for him to answer the question; he looked confused by it in any case. "The reason that I was standing on the plaza waiting for you is that Haramis, now that she's ill, has decided she needs to speed up my training. She's teaching me to water-scry."

"What do you mean?" Fiolon asked. "She taught you to water-scry when you first came here—four and a half years ago!"

"I know that," Mikayla pointed out, "and so do you. She doesn't."

"Oh, no." Further comment seemed beyond him.

"I'm pretty sure that she doesn't have the land sense anymore," Mikayla added, remembering, "and I don't think she's had it since her first brainstorm. When you got the land sense for Var, and I asked her a general question about what it felt like to have land sense, she asked me quite sharply if *I* had it for Ruwenda."

"But if she doesn't have it," Fiolon asked, "who does?"

"I don't know"—Mikayla sighed—"and neither does Uzun—I asked him about it then. We think that if someone else had it, we'd know by now, so it must be in abeyance somehow. I know I don't have it."

"Well, even if you don't have the land sense, we've got to do something about this mess!"

"We can try." Mikayla sighed. "Can you make a list of what needs to be fixed?"

Fiolon made a face and shook his head. "My perceptions of Ruwenda aren't that detailed."

"Detailed!" Mikayla snapped her fingers and bounced to her feet. "Come on," she said impatiently, heading out of the room.

"Where are we going?" Fiolon asked.

"The mirror. If you want detail, that's definitely the place to get it."

"You need more clothes if you're going down there," Fiolon pointed out.

"No I don't," Mikayla said blithely. "Red-Eye taught me to control my body temperature last year. You can get warmer clothes for yourself while I get parchment and ink, and I'll meet you down there."

By the time Fiolon arrived in the ice cave that held the mirror, Mikayla was sitting cross-legged on the icy floor, directly in front of the mirror, scribbling furiously. "I've found what's killing your fish, Fiolon," she said. "It's some sort of tiny little plant that produces a powerful poison when the conditions are right—which fortunately isn't often. When Haramis had this last brainstorm, we had some really bad earthquakes—"

She broke off and spoke to the mirror. "Mirror, display earthquakes during the last two months."

"Working," the mirror replied. A map of Ruwenda appeared with an overlay of pale blue lines across it. For several seconds it just sat there, then one spot after another sprouted a bright blue dot with jagged lines running out from the dot in various directions, but always strongest along the light blue lines.

"The one here," Mikayla said, reaching up to lay a fingertip on a spot at the northwest edge of the Thorny Hell, "was the first one. It happened before dawn the morning we found Haramis on the floor in her room. Then they spread through most of the northern portion of the Goldenmire." She twisted her upper body to look at Fiolon. "Is that the route you took here?"

Fiolon nodded silently, with a wary look at the mirror.

"Were there still tremors in the area then?" Mikayla asked.

He nodded again.

"How often and how strong?"

Fiolon looked at the mirror again, and Mikayla suddenly realized what his problem was. "It's all right, Fiolon, you can talk without changing the pictures. It responds only to requests that start with its name."

"Its name?" Fiolon asked.

"Its use-name; if it has a true name, I don't know it," Mikayla explained. "Mirror, show abnormal water levels in the Mazy Mire."

"Working." The picture changed, becoming a black-and-white map of the Mazy Mire with varying unusual shades of brown and blue covering most of the white.

"The blue is where the water is higher than it should be," Mikayla explained. "The darker the blue, the deeper the water. The brown is where the *land* is higher than it should be, and gets darker as the land gets higher."

Fiolon shivered, looking ill. "No wonder the land felt wrong."

"True," Mikayla agreed. "You were probably lucky to make it here without getting lost."

"I did get lost," Fiolon admitted. "Several times. I just used my sphere to track yours whenever I couldn't recognize where I was. That way I knew we'd at least end up in the same place, wherever you might be. It's not as if you're always here, you know," he pointed out. "There was your little half-year side trip to Red-Eye's cave on Mount Rotolo, to say nothing of the time you spend at the Temple of Meret."

"Which is a month every spring, and can be predicted," Mikayla pointed out. "But I think we're going to have to leave here to fix as much of this as we can. Lake Wum alone is going to take a lot of work."

Fiolon groaned. "Let's eat dinner first, shall we?"

Mikayla chuckled. "By all means. You must be starved." She rose to her feet, gathered up her writing materials, and spoke to the mirror. "Mirror, thank you. Recharge."

"Hiatus for recharge," the mirror replied, going dark.

Mikayla led the way back to the Tower, controlling the lamps in the hallway with whispered commands.

"Do you talk to everything around here?" Fiolon asked.

"Most of the *things,* yes," Mikayla said. "The people, not much. Enya's pretty busy, the other servants ignore me, and as for Haramis . . ." She sighed and did not finish the sentence.

As they passed the kitchen Enya popped out. "There you are, Princess," she said. "You are to go to the Lady's room at once; she's been asking for you for the past two hours."

Mikayla made a "what did I tell you?" face at Fiolon and assured Enya she would go see the Lady immediately.

"She's ordered dinner served in her room," Enya added.

Mikayla nodded and continued up the stairs, waiting until she was out of Enya's hearing before mumbling, "Oh, joy," in her most sarcastic tones.

"Mika, show some respect," Fiolon reproved her. "She can't be that bad."

"If we both weren't needed to repair the damage to the land," Mikayla said, "I'd let you stay here in my place and see for yourself. As it is, we'd better transfer Uzun to his new body, and leave *him* to sit with her and listen to her stories."

"Will she let us do that?" Fiolon asked. "Last time she wouldn't allow it."

"This time," Mikayla replied firmly, "I'm not planning to ask her permission. If Uzun agrees to the transfer, I'll do it, even if I have to do it alone." She looked questioningly at Fiolon.

"If you do it," he said, "I'll help. Any ritual from the Temple of Meret probably needs as many people as possible."

"Thanks." Mikayla smiled at him, then composed her face to blankness as they entered Haramis's room.

"Where have you been, girl?" Haramis demanded.

"Downstairs," Mikayla replied quietly.



"Didn't it occur to you that I might want you?"

"I'm sorry if you needed me and I was not here," Mikayla said politely, avoiding the question Haramis had actually asked. Fortunately Enya came in then with dinner, so Mikayla was spared the rest of the harangue, at least for the moment.

Haramis spent most of dinner complaining about how much she missed Uzun and why couldn't she be carried down to the study so that she could visit him, since he couldn't visit her. Mikayla was relieved to note that Haramis apparently had some trace of memory that prevented her from demanding that Uzun be brought to her room again. *Even if she doesn't remember why,* she thought, *at least Haramis doesn't consider dragging the harp up here to be an option. Thank the Lords of the Air; I couldn't stand it if he were damaged again.*

"Perhaps in a few days, Lady," she said, "we can arrange for you to see him. In the meantime you need to rest and recover your strength, so we shall bid you good night." She stood up, and sent the dirty dishes down to the kitchen with an unobtrusive wave of her hand. Fiolon bowed to Haramis and followed Mikayla from the room.

"Do you feel up to fetching the body now," Mikayla whispered to him once they were alone in the hall, "or are you too tired?"

"I can help you carry it up," Fiolon replied, "but we should probably wait until morning to start the ritual."

"Agreed," Mikayla said, "but I think we need to have the body at the same temperature as the harp for the transfer, so if we leave it next to Uzun tonight, it should be ready by morning."

"Sounds reasonable," Fiolon agreed. "Let's go get it."

"There's just one thing we need to do first," Mikayla said, pulling Fiolon into the study as they passed it. "Uzun," she said, "it's Mikayla and Fiolon."

"Lord Fiolon," the harp said. "This is a pleasant surprise! What brings you here?"

"Troubles with the land, I'm afraid," Fiolon replied.

"I feared that would happen when the Lady took ill." Uzun sighed. "I wish I could go to her; I am certain she misses me."

"At least this time she remembers that you're a harp," Mikayla said, "so she's not as ill as she was that time at the Citadel. And she seems to realize that dragging you up to her room again will damage you. But you are correct; she did spend dinner complaining about how much she misses you."

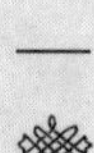

"If only there were something I could do about it." Uzun's strings positively jangled with frustration.

"Maybe there is," Mikayla said. "Remember the body I got for you at the Temple of Meret?"

"I thought Haramis had destroyed it," Uzun said.

Mikayla looked at Fiolon. "It's still where we left it," he said. "I checked on my way to the ice caves, and the wrappings look intact."

Mikayla walked over to the bookshelf and tilted several books forward. The scroll from the Temple was still behind them, right where she had put it when she first brought it home. "We will bring the body up here and unwrap it, Uzun," she said, "and make certain that it has not been damaged. If it is not damaged, are you willing to take the risk of attempting to transfer to it?"

"How is the transfer done?" Uzun asked.

Mikayla unrolled the beginning of the scroll and scanned it hastily. "I have the instructions for the ritual here," she said. "The process appears to be similar to the one Haramis used to put you into the harp."

"Then I want to try it," Uzun said. "Just remember your promise to me, in case anything goes wrong."

"If anything goes badly wrong, I'll set your spirit free," Mikayla said. "I promise." She placed the scroll back in its hiding place. "Come, Fiolon, let's go get the body."

It took most of an hour to carry the body upstairs and unwrap it. Fortunately, by that time all the servants had gone to bed, so there was no one to interrupt them.

"This is a true work of art," Fiolon said, admiring the painted wooden body as he bent each of its joints in turn to be certain that they were all functional. "It looks just like you, Master Uzun —at least it looks just like the pictures the mirror showed me of you and Haramis." He looked at Mikayla across the body. "It seems to be in fine shape to me." He yawned and apologized.

"Why don't you go to bed now, Fiolon?" Mikayla suggested. "I'll sleep here tonight to make sure that nothing is disturbed. And I want to read through the ritual before I sleep, anyway."

"That's fine with me," Fiolon said. "Good night."

"Sleep well," Mikayla replied. "I'll be locking the door when you leave, so call me with your sphere before you come down in the morning."

"All right." Fiolon headed toward the room assigned to him, and Mikayla locked the door, added another log to the fire, retrieved the scroll, and sat down to read it. She read the chants silently, but the directions out loud so that Uzun would know what to expect.

When she had finished, she turned to him. "Do you still want to do this?" she asked formally. "You can refuse, you know."

"I've wanted to do this for years," Uzun pointed out. "I'm not going to back out now."

"You do realize that you won't be aware of most of the ritual, don't you?" Mikayla pointed out. "Once we've begun the first step, removing the bone from the harp, you won't know anything more until we've finished successfully."

"What time is it now?" Uzun asked.

Mikayla could feel it, but she moved to the window and checked the position of the stars in the night sky anyway. "About two hours before midnight," she replied.

"Then, since the first step involves soaking the skull fragment from midnight until dawn in a bowl of tears, you might as well start now," Uzun said. "Otherwise you'll have to wait until tomorrow night, and you'll lose an entire day. And," he added tartly, "you may not have that day to lose. I know that you and

Fiolon will have to go out into the land as soon as I am free to look after Haramis."

"You are truly wise, Uzun," Mikayla said. "I'll start setting up now then. Do you think that Haramis's scrying bowl from the workroom would be appropriate for the tears?"

"Yes, I think it would be most appropriate," Uzun replied.

Mikayla visualized the bowl in the workroom where she had left it, and then visualized it in her hands. The bowl landed in her outstretched hands with a soft puff of displaced air. Mikayla looked at the scroll again to double-check the first instruction. "Soak the skull fragment from midnight until dawn in a silver bowl, with the bone covered completely by the tears of a maiden who mourns the person's death."

Mikayla bent her face over the bowl and thought of Uzun, of all his kindness to her, of his unwavering friendship and loyalty, of his courage in the face of damage and of Haramis's illnesses. She thought of how she would feel if this ritual failed and he were gone from her life for ever. Her tears fell freely, filling the bowl.

She didn't know how long she cried; it seemed that all the pain of the land flowed through her, in addition to all the pain she had ever felt in her life, and the pain she felt for Uzun. She cried until her body seemed desiccated, as if not another tear remained in her. Her face and eyes were dry now, so dry that she had to blink several times to get her eyes to focus.

She looked at the bowl in her hands. It was filled almost to the brim. She set it aside and checked the time. It was almost midnight.

"The bowl of tears is ready, Uzun," she said. "Are you?"

"Yes." The harp strings quivered a little, but Mikayla didn't blame Uzun for that. If she had strings, she knew that they would be quivering more than just that little bit.

She climbed onto a chair so that she could reach the top of the harp's forepillar easily. Carefully, using the ends of her fingernails, she lifted out the fragment of bone that was all that was left of Uzun's original body. She carried it to the bowl and watched the night sky. At the instant of midnight, she immersed the skull fragment in her tears, and the bowl was filled precisely to the brim.

# 25

*Mikayla dozed fitfully on the sofa by the fire until* shortly before dawn. Then she used her sphere to wake Fiolon.

"Mika, it's not even dawn yet," he complained, "and I've been traveling for weeks. Can't we wait until later to start?"

"I'm sorry, Fio," Mikayla said sympathetically, "but Uzun insisted on starting last night. I'm going to need you within the hour. And on your way down," she added, "please tell Enya that we will be working in the study with Uzun all day and don't wish to be disturbed for *anything*—including Haramis."

"What about meals?" Fiolon protested.

"Bring a tray of food, enough to last us all day," Mikayla said. "We don't want to be interrupted to be asked if we're ready for lunch when we're in the middle of the ritual."

"All right." Fiolon sighed. "I'll be there soon."

Mikayla went to the window to watch for dawn. As soon as the first gleam of sun was visible, she lifted the skull fragment out of the bowl and set it on a cloth beside the body. Then she picked up a small box that had been in the package with the body, and began to lay out the supplies in it: a jar of ointment, a white robe with embroidered symbols, only some of which Mikayla recognized from her time at the Temple, a black chisel made of some very sharp stone, and a long thin knife made of the same material.

By the time everything was ready, Fiolon had arrived. Mikayla let him in and had him set the tray of food on the table. She was much too nervous to eat. Oddly enough, Fiolon, who could usually eat anytime there was food available, seemed to share her feelings. Ignoring the food, he asked, "What do we do now?"

Mikayla handed him the scroll. "Read the first spell while I anoint the body."

"Soak the skull in virgin's tears?" Fiolon said in surprise, looking at the scroll.

"That part's done," Mikayla said. "Start where it says 'I have plowed the sky. . . .' "

She took the ointment and began to rub it carefully over every part of the body while Fiolon read. Her hands tingled, but she couldn't be sure whether this was due to power running through them or to something in the ointment. It felt very strange.

Fiolon was reading the spell, but his voice sounded different, as if some power were speaking through him. "I have plowed the sky, I have harvested the horizon, I have traveled the Land to its far boundaries, I have taken possession of my spirit, because I am one who retains my magic. I see with my eyes, I hear with my ears, I speak with my mouth, I reach with my arms, I grasp with my hands, I run with my legs."

Mikayla finished anointing the body, dressed it in the robe provided, and propped it up into a sitting position in a chair. Already she was getting a sense of it as real, rather than a simple statue.

She picked up the skull fragment and carefully coated both sides of it with the ointment, nodding to Fiolon to read the next section.

"I have kept in my body those things which I had in the past; now I use them to appear in glory."

Mikayla set the skull fragment carefully back on the cloth, picked up the sharp knife, climbed on the chair, and scraped out a bit of the inside of the hole in the forepillar of the harp. She stirred the material, a combination of wood and Haramis's dried blood, into the bowl of tears. Then she took the point of the knife and jabbed her fingertip. Holding her hand over the bowl, she squeezed exactly seven drops of her own blood into it, then made her finger stop bleeding and the wound close up. She remembered Uzun teaching her and Fiolon how to do simple healing spells during one of their late-night sessions her first year at the Tower, and thought how fitting it was that this knowledge should be used to help Uzun in turn. She handed the knife to Fiolon, who followed her example, then took up the scroll again.

Mikayla stirred the liquid together so that her tears and everyone's blood were completely mingled together. Then she lifted the bowl and poured its contents into the hole left in the top of the body's head, which ran through the head and neck and down to where the heart should be. The liquid looked strange, *like fire would look, if it could be liquid,* Mikayla thought. Heat seemed to radiate from it, and Mikayla half expected it to start steaming, like water boiling over a fire.

The liquid filled the channel completely as Fiolon read the next spell. "Hail to Thee who endures in power, Lady of all hidden things. Behold, all wrong is washed away from my heart, and my heart is born anew, born of the blood of those that love me. May I live on it as Thou livest on it; be gracious unto me, and grant me life."

Mikayla picked up the skull fragment, holding it carefully—the ointment had made it a bit slippery and her hands were trembling. This was the most important part of the ritual; the joining of the old body with the new one. There weren't even words for it; this part she had to feel in her heart.

The bone was so warm in her hands that it threatened to burn them, but Mikayla forced herself to ignore the pain. Power seemed to run through her entire body; she felt both hot and cold at the same time.

She placed the bit of skull carefully into place, praying without words that this magic would work and that Uzun would live again. The bone seemed to spread slightly under her fingers, or perhaps the wood closed in on it, as the two pieces fused together. Holding her breath, she looked at the face. Uzun's eyes looked back at her, and there was intelligence behind them. Mikayla let out her breath in a sigh of relief, and turned to pick up the sharp stone chisel.

She ran it gently between the lips of the body as Fiolon read the spell for opening the mouth. "I have arisen from the egg which is hidden, my mouth has been given to me that I may speak with it in the presence of the Goddess. My mouth is opened by Meret and what was on my mouth has been loosened by her Chosen One. My mouth is opened, my mouth is split open by the fingertip of the Land. I am one with the great winds of the sky, and I speak with my true voice."

Mikayla set down the chisel with a trembling hand, Fiolon rolled up the scroll, concentrating on it as if he didn't dare to look up.

"Is that it?" Master Uzun inquired. "Are you quite done?"

Both of them looked at him and collapsed to sit on the floor, limp with reaction and relief. "It worked," Fiolon whispered, his voice somewhere between awe and exhaustion.

Uzun stood up and began to move about the room, testing his new body. His movements were jerky at first, but quickly smoothed out with a little practice, as if he were working out the stiffness of a body that had just wakened in the morning.

He looked from Mikayla to Fiolon, then picked up the tray of food and set it on the floor between them. "Eat!" he commanded. "You both look ready to fall over, and there is still the Land to be dealt with."

An hour later both Mikayla and Fiolon had eaten and were feeling considerably more human. "Now," Uzun said firmly, "we go talk to the Lady Haramis. The land has no time to waste."

"This should be interesting," Mikayla murmured softly as they followed Uzun up the stairs to Haramis's room.

Fiolon was still admiring the new body, watching the way it moved. "That is the most incredible workmanship I have ever seen," he marveled. "And they just gave it to you?"

"In return for my remaining a virgin and spending a month each spring in their Temple for the next seven years," Mikayla reminded him. "And this coming spring I'm to represent the Goddess in the Spring Festival."

"How did you get picked for that?"

"There's a ritual where the Goddess chooses which of her Daughters will do it," Mikayla replied briefly, just as they reached Haramis's room and had to drop that line of conversation.

Haramis looked confused to see them. *No wonder,* Mikayla thought. *She doesn't remember Fiolon much, and last time she saw Uzun, he was a harp.*

"Uzun?" Haramis said in bewilderment. "I must have been dreaming—I thought I turned you into a harp. . . ."

Uzun took her hand between his. Mikayla almost felt sorry for Haramis; it must have been a shock to discover that his hands were made of wood. "You did, Lady," he said, "but that was long ago. Now I have a new body, and I can see and move again." He drew up a stool and sat at the head of her bed, still holding her hand.

"I fear that I bring ill news, Lady," he said softly. "There is great sickness in the land."

Haramis frowned, and tried, unsuccessfully, to sit up. "I felt earthquakes," she said. "What else?"

"The shape of the earth and water in the Goldenmire has changed," Mikayla said, "and there is some sort of poison in Lake Wum that kills fish and folk—even humans."

"Alas," said Haramis, "that I have come to this. I have no power to protect or heal my land."

"Then you will have to allow them to do it," Uzun said firmly.

Haramis looked at him as if he had taken leave of his senses. "Uzun, they're children!"



"They are less than two years younger than you were when you became Archimage," Uzun pointed out, "and both you and I have been training them. Perhaps neither one could accomplish the task alone, but together I believe that they can repair at least the worst of the damage. I shall advise them, with your consent, Lady." Uzun did not sound as if he were asking for Haramis's permission.

Haramis was clearly too tired and weak to protest. "Very well, Uzun, do as you wish. You always did," she added querulously.

"Thank you, Lady." Uzun bent to kiss her hand, then dragged Mikayla and Fiolon out of the room and back to the study, where he tugged the bellpull and ordered Enya to bring dinner for Mikayla and Fiolon.

Enya looked at him in astonishment, then turned to Mikayla. "Who is this, Princess—another of your odd friends?"

*Of course she doesn't recognize him,* Mikayla realized. *None of the servants has ever seen him as anything except a harp!* "This is Master Uzun, Enya," she said firmly, "and it is the Lady's will that you continue to obey his requests."

"Master Uzun." Enya looked dubious but prepared to go along with this. "And do you require food as well, Master Uzun?"

Uzun looked at Mikayla, who shook her head slightly. "No," he replied. "This body does not require food."

Enya left the room, shaking her head in disbelief. "This household gets stranger every day," she muttered.

"Now," Uzun said briskly, "what needs to be done with the land?"

"The Goldenmire is greatly changed," Mikayla said, "but it is sparsely peopled. Any harm that was going to happen there has already happened. We can't bring the dead back to life, and the living are already adjusting to the way the Mire is now."

"I agree," Fiolon said. "I traveled through there on my way here, and I don't think we need do anything to it. The real problem is Lake Wum."

"The mirror says that if the fish are all dead, then the fish-death will be dead as well," Mikayla said.

"Fish-death?" Uzun asked.

"It's some sort of tiny plant that produces poison," Fiolon explained.

"So we need to put fish back into Lake Wum," Mikayla said. "Master Uzun, have you any suggestions as to where we should get more fish?"

"Was there much damage near the Bonorar River?" Uzun asked.

"No." Mikayla shook her head. "The Dylex region is far enough to the east of us that it was spared most of the disturbances caused by the Archimage's illness."

"And the Bonorar flows into Lake Wum anyway," Fiolon said. "So if the fish are upriver and we move them down to the lake, that should start to build up the fisheries again."

Enya came in with dinner then, and everyone fell silent while Mikayla and Fiolon ate. Even Uzun seemed lost in his own thoughts.

"We can fly there," Fiolon continued, sending his empty dishes back to the kitchen, "check to be certain that the lake water is clean again, and then take a few fishing nets upstream and bring some fish to the lake."

"That probably would be better than trying to teleport living creatures," Mikayla agreed, sending her dishes to the kitchen with a flick of her hand.

"But there's one problem you are both overlooking," Uzun said unhappily. "What will the folk think—especially the Skritek and the Glismak—if you are seen flying about on lammergeiers and doing the Lady's work? What will they think of the Lady?"

"Probably the truth," Mikayla said.

"I can handle the Glismak," Fiolon said at the same time.

"Do we really want the folk of the Land to know how sick the Archimage is?" Uzun asked quietly.

"It probably would be better if they didn't guess," Mikayla said after a few minutes' thought. "Faith can be a powerful force, regardless of the reality behind it."

"Especially if it means we don't have to cope with a Skritek uprising," Fiolon added wryly.

Mikayla shuddered. "You're right about that," she agreed. "So we'd better do this by night and make sure we're not seen."

"But the lammergeiers can't fly at night," Fiolon protested, "and it would take months of travel by fronial, especially if we're trying to stay hidden."

"Red-Eye flies at night," Mikayla pointed out.

"You're right," Fiolon said. "And he's certainly large enough to carry both of us. But would he be willing?"

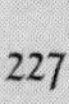

"I'll just have to ask him," Mikayla said. "After all, we don't have half a year to do this; I have to be back at the Temple of Meret in less than two months." 

Red-Eye agreed to help its friend Mikayla, with a touch of smugness that there was something it could do that an ordinary lammergeier couldn't. It arrived shortly after darkness the next night and landed them near Tass Town, at the southern end of Lake Wum, just before dawn.

While it spent the day asleep in a tree in the darkest part of the Greenmire it could find, Mikayla and Fiolon, dressed in waterproofed boots, loose pants tucked into their boots, and oiled leather hooded jackets, suitable for grubbing through the swamp, wandered about the edge of the lake, checking on the condition of the water as well as that of the vegetation surrounding the lake. They found that the mirror had been right; the lake was clean of fish-death and had enough small plants growing again to support fish. So that night they borrowed several fishing nets from a dock in Tass Town, flew up the Bonorar as far as the Dylex, and brought back several nets full of fish of various sizes.

Red-Eye's flying skills were incredible, Mikayla noted. It managed to drag the nets of fish the length of the river without ever pulling them out of the water, catching the nets on rocks or tree roots, or doing anything that would harm the fish. About an hour before dawn they reached Lake Wum and deposited the fish in the center of the lake, hoping that this would give them a chance to multiply before the local fishermen discovered them. Red-Eye dropped Mikayla and Fiolon off in Tass Town so that they could return the nets and went back to its temporary roost in the Greenmire.

The three of them spent the next several weeks flying about the land, checking for damage that needed to be put right. But they quickly discovered that the Land seemed to be healing itself.

"I wonder if the Land's health is tied to Haramis's," Mikayla said to Fiolon one evening as they waited for Red-Eye to wake and come for them.

Fiolon, who had been using his sphere to bespeak Uzun every morning, nodded thoughtfully. "I think it may well be," he said. "Master Uzun says that Haramis is recovering well."

"I'm glad," Mikayla said. "By the time I get back from the Temple, she may be feeling more charitable toward me."

"Do you have to go back there?" Mikayla looked up and saw that Red-Eye had landed silently behind her.

"You know I do, Red-Eye," she said. "I promised. And this is the year I have to represent the Goddess in the Spring Festival."

Red-Eye sighed. "Just remember your promise to bespeak me every night," he said. "When must you go?"

"Tonight," Mikayla said. "I'll need to be there before dawn."

"I'll stop off at the Tower and report to Master Uzun if Red-Eye doesn't mind taking me there," Fiolon said. "Uzun can decide how much to tell the Lady. Then I'll have to go back to Mutavari and report to the King. After that, I'll probably be back in Let for the summer and fall."

"Then we had better fly," Red-Eye said, extending a wing.

# 26

*After all the excitement and crises of the last months,* Mikayla found it very pleasant to be back at the Temple of Meret. As she had promised, she bespoke Red-Eye every night, even though she had nothing to tell him. It was virtually no different from the previous year.

She took the Youngest Daughter's part in the Spring Festival, representing the Goddess in the procession, and spent most of the day being carried about by the young men of the Temple on a richly carved high-backed wooden throne while the other Daughters, dressed in green robes, walked on either side of the throne carrying fans that prevented most of the congregation from seeing whether she was sitting there at all. She didn't even have to sing the chants for the Festival that she had learned the previous year.

She dutifully reported this to Red-Eye, along with her opinion that the ritual was even more boring for the Youngest Daughter. "I could be replaced with a fan, and no one would know the difference."

"I'm glad to hear that," Red-Eye said. "Perhaps that will discourage you from volunteering to do it again."

"We don't volunteer," Mikayla reminded him. "The Goddess chooses whomever She wants. But I'm glad to be done with it."

When the Husband of the Goddess Meret came to the Daughters' room for the Choosing, and someone else was chosen as the Youngest Daughter for next year, Mikayla was happy to move down one place in the order.

She spent the rest of the month enjoying the peace and quiet and the orderly life imposed by the rituals. At the end of the month, Red-Eye came for her again and took her back to the Tower.

Having Uzun for company had improved Haramis's temper considerably. The harp that had formerly been his body still functioned perfectly well as a harp, and Haramis had recovered enough to walk down the stairs to the study each morning. She spent her days on the couch, listening to Uzun play and sing his old ballads to her, and then climbed back up the stairs to her own bed at night. She seemed perfectly happy to live her life in this fashion and didn't seem to care about anything else.

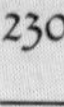

She bid Mikayla welcome, refrained from asking where she had been, and said nothing about further training for her. Now that she had her old friend Uzun back, she seemed quite indifferent to Mikayla's actions, or indeed, to her whereabouts.

Mikayla took advantage of this disinterest to spend her afternoons in the ice caves studying the mirror and some of the other devices left there. Now that she and the mirror understood each other—and now that she had learned to read well enough to recognize warning labels on old containers—she was able to poke through the storeroom without having to worry about setting anything on fire or blowing the Tower up. She spoke to Fiolon in the evenings, using her sphere, which Red-Eye had returned to her when he brought her back from the Temple, keeping Fiolon apprised of anything interesting that she found. Fiolon, in turn, told her of life at court in Var, and of the logging operations he was still running when he wasn't in court. He seemed to find the court in Mutavari rather boring, for he was most often in Let, his own dukedom.

"It seems strange," he told her, laughing, "to be assigned a portion of the Land and told that I'm responsible for it. The King doesn't know that I'm responsible for his entire Kingdom."

"That's probably just as well," Mikayla pointed out. "In a Kingdom without a tradition of having an Archimage, he might regard you as a threat to his crown."

"Really, Mika"—Fiolon laughed—"be serious. We're only seventeen years old."

"I am serious," Mikayla said. "I've been reading the history of Labornok, and they have executed *children* for high treason. We're not children, even if we are growing more slowly than normal."

"At least we are growing," Fiolon said. "I never did get a chance to tell you, but I found out why a sorcerer grows so slowly. It's just because we live so much longer than normal people, that's all—it doesn't mean that we'll be children forever. Even as young as we started, we should be physically mature by the time we're thirty at the latest."

"That's a relief," Mikayla admitted. "The thought of looking like a child of twelve for the next two hundreds wasn't appealing."

Mikayla frequently slipped out at night to go flying with Red-Eye, until it seemed to her that she knew the land by night better than she did by day. But she enjoyed its company, and it seemed to enjoy hers.

Life was good that year, until one morning in the early spring, when Mikayla woke suddenly before dawn, moments before an earthquake hit.

"Oh, no, not again!" she groaned, rolling out of bed and running for Haramis's room. Uzun arrived right behind her, with Enya only a few minutes behind him. Mikayla left them to put Haramis back to bed and send for Kimbri—not that she thought there was much the Healer could do—while she went to the ice caves and had the mirror show her where damage was occurring in the land.

Mikayla knew that Haramis would have used the sand table for this task, but Mikayla didn't share Haramis's prejudice against technology. The mirror would show her what was happening in the land without her having to expend the energy required to sense the land's condition through the sand table. All she needed to do the repair work—aside from a *lot* of her own energy—was a clear visualization of what she was doing, and that could be done more easily with the mirror as well. This meant that nearly all of

Mikayla's energy could be devoted to the work that actually needed to be done. She spent the rest of the day damping down earthquakes and aftershocks, diverting flooding rivers away from populated areas, and hoping that this time the conditions wouldn't be right for fish-death to return.

Several hours after dark, when she was feeling cold and tired, having exhausted her usual ability to control such physical failings, Fiolon came in, bundled up in warm clothing and carrying a mug of hot ladu-juice.

"Red-Eye fetched me," he explained. "Drink this, go eat something, and go to bed. I'll take the next watch."

"Thank you," Mikayla said, rubbing her cold hands together until she had enough feeling in them to hold the mug. "Watch the spot where the Nothar River runs into the Upper Mutar—it's been threatening to flood for the last four hours. And we're still getting aftershocks from the earthquake, all over the place."

"I'll take care of it," Fiolon said. "You eat and get some sleep."

Mikayla just nodded as she staggered toward her room.

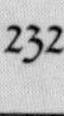

She relieved Fiolon shortly after dawn, and for the next few days they took turns so that one of them was always watching and ready to fix any damage. After a few days, the worst was over and the aftershocks had subsided enough so that they couldn't be felt by anyone who didn't have land sense. Uzun volunteered to watch the mirror while they both got some badly needed rest.

"I'm so glad that they made him strong enough to withstand these temperatures," Mikayla remarked to Fiolon as they went up the tunnel back to the Tower. "In his natural form he would have frozen to death there."

"It certainly helps," Fiolon agreed. "How many more years do you have to go back to the Temple to finish paying for this?"

Mikayla counted on her fingers. "I've done two, so that leaves five more. I'll be twenty-one my last year there."

"How long before you have to go back there this year?"

Mikayla groaned. "Two weeks. I'd really better get some rest."

"I'll stay here while you're gone," Fiolon volunteered. "Uzun may need some help. He's a decent enough magician, but land magic's a bit different."

So Mikayla went back to the Temple of Meret for the third year. It was peaceful enough, and it gave her much-needed respite from holding Ruwenda together and watching Haramis make an even slower recovery than she had before. But when the Choosing came, Mikayla was dismayed to be chosen again.

"That's twice in three years," she complained when she told Red-Eye. "You'd think the Goddess could spread it out a bit more—after all, there are five of us."

"Did they say anything about a jubilee?" the bird asked anxiously.

"Yes," Mikayla admitted. "There was some brief reference to it during the presentation to the congregation. You wouldn't believe how heavy that wretched headdress is—it's given me an awful headache. What's a jubilee?"

"I'll tell you when I fetch you at the end of the month," Red-Eye said.

"Fine," Mikayla said. "At least after the presentation to the Goddess tomorrow morning I don't have to wear the headdress again, and the ritual isn't until next year."

Red-Eye fetched her at the end of her month of service. Instead of taking her back to the Tower, it took her to its cave on Mount Rotolo. But when it tried to explain the concept of the Goddess's Jubilee, she didn't believe it.

"You're crazy, Red-Eye," she said. "They aren't going to kill me; I still owe them three more years of service *after* next year."

"But that's what the Jubilee is," Red-Eye insisted. "Every two hundreds the Goddess needs a new heart to renew her life and rule for the next two hundreds. And it's the Youngest Daughter of the Goddess that they sacrifice."

"If they haven't done it for two hundreds," Mikayla pointed out, "you can't possibly know about it."

"But I do," it insisted. "The Priests of the Time of Darkness—the ones who made me—are the ones who perform the sacrifice. They are part of the priesthood of the Goddess Meret."

"How could I have spent three years in Her Temple and never met them?" Mikayla asked skeptically.

"You've spent three months there," the bird replied, "not three years, and you've spent it all shut up with the Temple virgins, which doesn't let you see much of what goes on in the Temple as a whole. The Priests of the Time of Darkness are nocturnal. Your rituals run from Dawn to the Second Hour of Darkness. The rest of the night is theirs. The only time they come out in the daytime is for the sacrifice."

"If you say so," Mikayla said politely, privately thinking that the bird was paranoid about its creators, even if they did belong to the Temple. "I think you'd better take me back to the Tower, Red-Eye. Last I heard, Haramis wasn't well at all. I'm probably needed there."

Haramis was indeed still very unwell, unable even to rise from her bed. Uzun spent all his time with her, and Fiolon left for Var shortly after Mikayla's return, saying that he had to see to things in Let.

Mikayla spent most of the next year being bored and feeling useless, so when the time came for her to return to the Temple, she was ready to go. But to her amazement, Red-Eye flatly refused to take her.

"I told you they'll kill you if you go there," it said, almost hysterically. "You can't go!"

"I promised I would," Mikayla said. "If you won't take me, I'll just have to wait until morning and ask one of the other lammergeiers."

"I'll tell your cousin," Red-Eye declared. "He'll stop you."

"He's in Var," Mikayla pointed out. "And he knows that keeping my promises is important to me. He won't try to stop me."

# 27

*Haramis sat bolt upright in bed and stared at Uzun in* horror. "Mikayla is doing *what*?"

"She's going to be sacrificed to Meret," Uzun said wretchedly. "That was the bargain she made in exchange for my new body. But she didn't know what she was agreeing to," he added urgently. "We have to stop her!"

"When and where is this taking place?" Haramis asked, feeling sick. *I knew the girl was unhappy here, I knew she didn't like me, but I had no idea . . .*

"The day after tomorrow, at dawn," Uzun replied grimly. "At Meret's Temple on Mount Gidris."

"Why Mikayla?" Haramis asked. Uzun sighed, and she said hastily, "I know you said it was in exchange for your body, but why would they want to sacrifice Mikayla, rather than someone else? What makes her special to them?"

"She's a royal virgin," Uzun said bitterly. "I'll bet they were thrilled when she fell into their hands. I should never have complained about being a harp," he added miserably.

"She's hardly the only royal virgin in existence," Haramis pointed out. "Her youngest brother is probably still one—what is he now, sixteen? And Fiolon is royal and presumably still a virgin."

"They're male," Uzun said. "Mikayla's the virgin daughter of a King."

"So what?" Haramis said without thinking. "So am I." Then she realized what she had said, and repeated it with a different inflection. "So am I. If all they want is the virgin daughter of a king . . ." Her voice trailed off as she thought.

"No, you could not take her place," Uzun snapped. "You don't look anything like Mikayla."

"A simple glamour," Haramis said. "She and I are nearly the same size; all we'd have to do is change clothes."

"Haramis," Uzun said through clenched wooden teeth. "You can't cast a simple glamour. You can't even talk to the lammergeiers anymore. You can't even scry! You have been ill, and you do not yet have your powers back."

Haramis just looked at him, feeling the pieces of her life slip into a pattern. "I'm sorry, old friend," she said softly. "I can take her place, and I must. I owe it to her, and I owe it to the land. I have had," she continued dispassionately, "at least two major brainstorms in the last five years, and the Flower only knows"—her fingers went to the bit of Trillium embedded in amber in the Talisman about her neck—"how many minor ones. I haven't been able to talk to the lammergeiers since the first one, and with each successive attack, I lose more of my abilities. I have virtually no magic left, and my physical body is failing. Since it's over two hundreds old, that shouldn't be too surprising. And every time that I get sick, so does the land. Look what happened last time—the damage was so bad that Fiolon came running up here all the way from Var! If the inhabitants of Var are noticing our troubles, I am not doing my job."

"Fiolon was the only one who noticed," Uzun said, "and he and Mikayla were able to fix the damage. Besides, that was the time before last, not last time. Nothing dreadful happened last time."

"Mikayla ran away again." Haramis shot a sharp look at Uzun. "What do you mean 'Fiolon was the only one who noticed'—why should he be the only one?"

Uzun sighed. "Fiolon is the Archimage of Var."

"What?" Haramis gaped at him. Whatever she had been expecting to hear, she told herself, it wasn't this. "You mean that he's still linked with Mikayla, and—"

"No." The reply was definite. "Oh, he's probably still linked with Mikayla—and thank the Flower for that, because that's the way we're getting most of our information; they still talk to each other every night."

"How?" Haramis asked.

"They found a pair of spheres in the old ruins on the Golobar right before you brought them here. The first time you sent Fiolon away, they discovered they could use them to scry each other—in fact, Mikayla uses hers to scry everything, unless you're watching her. When Mikayla's at the Temple and can't hide the sphere from the priests, she has her favorite lammergeier keep it for her, and then she and Fiolon both communicate through the bird."

"So they've been in constant communication for the past five years?" Haramis asked. "Even when I sent Fiolon back to Var?"

"Exactly," Uzun said. "You may remember that Mikayla made a bit of a fuss over that. . . ."



"She locked herself in her room for two days," Haramis said, remembering. "And she was awfully quiet for a long while after she came out."

"She locked herself in her room and linked with Fiolon," Uzun said. "She told me about it later. It seems that she'd been sharing all of her lessons with him—and you had taught her quite a bit by then, probably more than you realize. You still held the power and the land sense for Ruwenda, but nobody did for Var, and the second Fiolon set foot on the ground there he got its land sense."

"And Mikayla, of course, got the backlash." Haramis didn't need that part explained to her. "No wonder she suddenly got interested in what it meant to have land sense and be Archimage. I thought she was finally becoming resigned to her fate. But she was just gathering information for Fiolon, wasn't she?"

"To her mind, yes," Uzun said. "But she's not stupid, and she couldn't pass on to him what she hadn't learned herself."

"A male Archimage." Haramis shook her head in wonder. "Are you absolutely sure, Uzun?"

"Yes," Uzun replied. "But if you doubt my perceptions, question him yourself." He crossed to the bellpull and gave it a savage tug.

"Is he here, then?" Haramis asked. "I hadn't realized that we had guests."

"He is here as *my* guest," Uzun said. "I don't know what you have against him, Haramis, other than the fact that he's male, but *I* like him."

Enya arrived while Haramis was still trying to think of a reply to that. Uzun asked her to find Fiolon and send him to Haramis's room. Haramis didn't protest, but Enya did.

"But, Master Uzun, he's probably back in that cave; that's where he was headed—"

"So send one of the Vispi for him," Uzun snapped. "The Lady wants to see him, and surely you don't expect *her* to go down there after him!"

"No, Master Uzun." Enya curtsied her way out of the room. "I'll have him fetched at once, Lady."

Of course, when it involved sending someone below the Tower and along the tunnel to the ice cave, and then having the person you wanted make the return journey, "at once" was a long time. Uzun spent the time trying to convince Haramis that she couldn't possibly take Mikayla's place, but he wasn't making any headway when Fiolon joined them.

"White Lady." Fiolon bowed formally to Haramis, then smiled at Uzun. "Master Uzun. How may I serve you?"

Haramis studied the young man. He didn't look at all like the young men she had known when she was a girl. He had the ageless, serene quality of a great Adept—or of an Archimage. She tried to remember how old he would be by now. *Let's see, he's the same age as Mikayla, which would make him—eighteen? Yes, eighteen. Uzun must be at least partially correct,* she realized. *This is definitely not your normal eighteen-year-old.*

"You can help me talk some sense into the Lady," Uzun snapped. "She has the crazy idea that she can take Mikayla's place!"

Fiolon looked at Haramis for several minutes, and then looked sadly at the Oddling. "I'm sorry, Uzun," he said soberly, "but she's right. It is possible, and I fear that it would be best for the land."

"The land!" Uzun practically screamed. "Is that all you Archimages care about?"

"The land and its folk," Fiolon said gently. "I'm sorry, Uzun; I know you don't want to lose her. Neither do I. But I don't want to lose Mikayla, either."

"Of course I don't want to lose Mikayla!" Uzun protested. "But it's my fault she's in this mess—*I* should be the one to be sacrificed in her place. Haramis can barely walk, and she certainly can't cast a glamour that will make them think she's Mikayla. Besides, Mikayla is descended from the royal family of Labornok; Haramis isn't."

"The two lands have been joined since Princess Anigel married Prince Antar," Fiolon reminded him. "You should remember that; you wrote half the ballads about it."

"Are you saying that I'm Archimage of Labornok, as well as of Ruwenda?" Haramis asked curiously.

Fiolon stared at her. "Aren't you?"

Haramis shrugged. "I never thought of it."

Fiolon frowned in concentration and began to pace the room. "That might explain why the cult of Meret still flourishes in Labornok," he said. "If you don't have the land sense for Labornok, maybe someone else does—or nobody does." He turned to look at her. "Lady, have you ever been in Labornok?"

"No." Haramis shook her head. "This Tower is as close as I've ever been to the border, and we're well on the Ruwendan side here. Movis is about halfway down Mount Rotolo, and even the ice cave where I found my Talisman was on this side of Mount Gidris. So, no, I've never set foot in Labornok, or even flown over it."

"That may be the problem then," Fiolon said. "But it's not our most urgent problem right now. Did Uzun tell you about the sacrifice?"

"Just that it's to take place the day after tomorrow at dawn."

Fiolon nodded. "I've been watching in the mirror. It's a very useful device; I've been able to map out the entire Temple by using it." He grinned briefly. "And I'm probably the only man alive, except for their priest—the one they call the Husband of the Goddess Meret—to have seen the rooms they keep the Temple virgins in. Since the mirror will show me any part of the Temple on request, I can use it to keep track of Mikayla when I'm here, instead of having to scry her personally or bespeak her lammergeier."

He sighed. "But now the news is not good. She's to fast all day tomorrow and keep vigil alone in the outer cavern tomorrow night. I suspect that the purpose of that is to make her too weak to put up much of a struggle when she discovers what's going on, but while she's alone Red-Eye and I can go in, grab her, and get out without being seen."

"Red-Eye?" Haramis asked.

"It's a lammergeier," Fiolon explained.

"Lammergeiers are diurnal," Haramis pointed out. "They sleep at night, and they can't see very well in the dark."

"Red-Eye is an exception," Fiolon said. "It's an albino—totally white, with no pigment in his eyes."

"Albinos have pink eyes," Haramis pointed out.

"So does Red-Eye," Fiolon said; "it just refuses to admit it. It says that 'Pink-Eye' is a ridiculous name. And it has been a good friend to Mikayla, so I'm willing to humor it in this. It has excellent night vision and it's nearly invisible against snow."

"So you go in on this Red-Eye," Haramis said, "grab Mikayla, which should be easy enough for you—"

"No," Fiolon said. "It won't be easy. She's not going to come willingly. She says that she gave her word that she'd do this ritual, and she keeps her word."

"What about her promise to be Archimage?" Haramis demanded crossly.

Fiolon gave an odd crooked smile. "When did she ever promise that?"



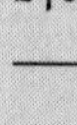

"When she came here, of course," Haramis said, and then thought about it. "I guess she never did actually promise to be Archimage."

"You didn't ask for her promise," Fiolon pointed out. "I was there, remember. You told her she was to be Archimage after you, and when she asked if she was to be given a choice, you said no. You said that the matter was too important to be left to the whims of a child."

Haramis sighed. "You're right, that is what I said. I should have spent less time talking and more time listening—I daresay Uzun knows her better than I do. Well, no matter now. Can Red-Eye carry me as well as you?"

"Yes," Fiolon said. "But you don't absolutely *have* to take her place. I can just pull her out."

"And have Labornok attack Ruwenda for the second time in as many hundreds," Haramis said, "with magic, yet—and no one in Ruwenda properly trained to repel it."

"I guess you have a point there," Fiolon said unhappily. "The priests of Meret are pretty ruthless, more than Mikayla realizes. I've seen them more than she has—and under different circumstances. They keep the Daughters of the Goddess very sheltered, so she doesn't see much when she's there, and I don't believe that she's ever watched them in the mirror since the first day she found them.

"They know that Mikayla belongs here at the Tower," he continued. "They know she's supposed to be Archimage, so this is the first place they'd look for her. And she'd be no help fighting them off; in fact, I'd have to lock her up to keep her from summoning a lammergeier and going back to them."

"But she can't go back to them if they're not there," Haramis said.

"What do you mean?" Fiolon asked.

"Mikayla doesn't know she's to be killed; is that right?" Haramis said.

"Red-Eye tried to tell her, and I've tried to tell her," Fiolon said unhappily, "but she won't believe us. She says that she was chosen as the Youngest Daughter of the Goddess two years ago and survived just fine, thank you, and besides she owes them three more years of service after this one, so why should they kill her now? She doesn't understand that for the Jubilee Festival, it's different. They'll cut her heart out of her living body, to give the Goddess a fresh heart and another two hundreds of life."

"Is that what they do, then," Haramis asked, "put her on the altar and cut out her heart?"

"With their ritual black obsidian knife. And then they give her body to the river, which is the Goddess's blood," Fiolon said. "I observed a session where the priests were planning the ritual, choosing who was to officiate, and so forth. I got a lot of details from listening to that, and then I had the mirror show me the chamber where they do the sacrifice. The sacrificial altar is right over the point where the river comes out of the rock, on the west side of the Temple."

"You've seen it then," Haramis said. "What is the altar made of?"

"Living rock," Fiolon said. "That whole chapel is carved out of —oh, I see. Yes, it's definitely part of the land. It's not something artificial brought in. If you can use the land on the Labornoki side of the mountains, you can use the chapel, altar and all."

"Use?" Uzun asked.

"An Archimage draws power from contact with her land," Fiolon explained.

*He really does understand this,* Haramis realized. *Uzun must be correct, but it still doesn't feel right to have a male Archimage.*

"Actually," Fiolon continued, "an Archimage can use any land somewhat; I found when I was working with Mikayla that I could tap into Ruwenda just a little bit." He looked sideways at Haramis. "I would have asked your permission, Lady, but you were so sick then. . . ." His voice trailed off.

"The important thing is that the land be well," Haramis said. "Who heals it is not a major consideration." *And I should have realized that years ago,* she thought. "To get back to our current plan," she continued. "Tomorrow night, Fiolon, you and I will fly to where Mikayla is keeping vigil. Since we do not wish to spend the entire night in argument, I would suggest that we take along some means of rendering her swiftly and silently unconscious."

Fiolon nodded. "There's a liquid in a bottle in the cellar that will do that," he said. "It's one of the things Orogastus collected. But I have a great advantage over him," he said, smiling impishly and suddenly looking close to his actual age. "*I* can read the directions."

"You can?" Haramis was startled. "How did you learn the language of the Vanished Ones?"

"The mirror," Fiolon said. "Orogastus's 'magic mirror' is, among other things, a teaching device."

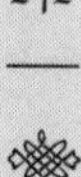

"I knew it was a machine," Haramis said, remembering. "I realized that the first time I saw it. There Orogastus stood, invoking all sorts of nonexistent Dark Powers, and there was this old machine, barely in working order."

Fiolon laughed. "Too bad Orogastus didn't realize that. He built this Tower right on top of the machine's power supply." He noticed Haramis's blank look and explained. "It's powered by sunlight, and there was a solar cell built on top of it to collect the sunlight and store it in batteries." Haramis wondered what "solar cell" and "batteries" were, but didn't interrupt to ask. Judging from the context, they must be some sort of energy collection and storage devices. Fiolon continued. "Orogastus didn't know what that black flat surface was for, but it was there, and clear, so he put his Tower on it. And then he let snow cover what the building didn't, so the machine couldn't recharge the batteries effectively. This meant that he couldn't use it much. Mikayla found it when you were ill at the Citadel, and she figured out what and where a solar cell was, which was pretty intelligent of her—though she's always been good with mechanical things—and so we cleared the plaza, which exposed the solar cell, and then the mirror started working just fine. We used it to see how you were doing, and to learn the language of the Vanished Ones. That's how Mikayla found the Temple of Meret in the first place."

"The mirror would have shown her where it was," Haramis remembered. "It showed my sisters' locations when Orogastus showed it to me."

"Yes," Fiolon said. "She had it display human workers of magic until she found someone who could make Uzun a body. Then she left me here to keep Uzun company while she went there to learn the technique."

"I should never have let her go!" Uzun burst out.

"You couldn't have stopped her," Fiolon reminded him gently. "I don't think I could have at that point, either. She was so angry at life that she needed a battle she could fight. Finding you a proper body was her battle—her way of striking back at the fate that had stuck her here."

"So you can render her unconscious," Haramis said, dragging the discussion back on track. "I can then change clothes with her, and you can bring her back here. Keeping her here long enough for the sacrifice to take place is your problem. As for me, the fact that Mikayla supposedly has been fasting and has spent all night sitting in the cold should account for any weakness or difficulty in walking on my part. But, Fiolon, as Uzun reminds me, I can't even manage a simple glamour anymore. Can you cast one on me before you leave me?"

Fiolon nodded. "I can cast a glamour that will make you look like her as long as you are alive and your body is intact. But when they take out your heart, it's likely to collapse."

"Good." Haramis smiled grimly. "I hope I'm still able to see their faces at that point. Try to tamper with my chosen successor, will they? I think not."

"I'll put a pain-block spell on you, too," Fiolon said. "I should be able to link it with the land there, so it should hold unless you're floating in midair or something equally unlikely."

"That should take care of things, then," Haramis said. "I'll rest until it's time to go—around midnight tomorrow, I should think. I'll have Enya bring me some soup and bread about two hours before that; there's no reason for *me* to fast. That should ensure that I have the strength to do what I must."

"But, Haramis . . ." Uzun protested.

"I'm sorry, Uzun," Haramis said firmly, "but I have to do this. Fiolon, you and Mikayla will take care of Uzun when I'm gone, won't you?"

"Yes, Lady, of course we will"—Fiolon forced a smile—"when he's not taking care of us."

"Good." Haramis sank back against her pillows, suddenly feeling very tired indeed. "I'd like to rest now."

"Certainly, Lady." Fiolon bowed and left the room, pulling Uzun with him.

Haramis heard the Oddling's voice as he was dragged down the hall. "Does she think I *want* to live with her gone?"

*My poor old friend,* Haramis thought sleepily, *what have I done to you? What have I done to all of us?*

# 28

*Haramis spent the next day resting and eating. Shortly* before she and Fiolon were due to leave, Enya came to her room with a long white robe, high-necked and long-sleeved. "Lord Fiolon told me to bring this to you, Lady," she said. "He says Mikayla left it in her room last time she was home."

Haramis didn't recognize the garment. She guessed that it must be one Mikayla had worn home from the Temple of Meret. With any luck it would be identical to what she would be wearing now, and changing clothes with her might not have to involve stripping to bare skin on a cold mountainside. "Thank you, Enya," she said. "Help me to put it on, please."

As Enya complied Haramis surveyed the little Nyssomu woman. It hardly seemed fair, after all her years of faithful service, to leave her without so much as a word. "Enya," she said, "I'm going out tonight."

Enya sniffed. "Tell me something I don't know. Master Uzun's been moping about all day, talking about how you're going to Certain Death."

Haramis smiled faintly. "Melodramatic, as always, but, I'm afraid, substantially correct. It is very probable that I won't be coming back alive."

"Oh, Lady," Enya gasped. "And here I was thinking he was exaggerating, as he usually does."

"Fiolon is going with me, and he should be bringing Mikayla back with him," Haramis said. "When I die, one—or possibly both—of them should become Archimage of Ruwenda." She paused. "I think. Do you know, Enya, I suddenly find I'm not so certain of any of the things I used to be sure of."

"Don't worry about it, Lady," Enya said briskly. "The land will take care of things. It always does, if you let it."

"Yes," Haramis said. "I've finally decided to stop fighting it. I've made rather a mess of things, but I think it's not too late to set them right. At least I hope it's not." She took a deep breath. "I want to thank you, Enya, for your service to me. You have been a faithful servant and a good friend." She hesitated. "I don't know if you will wish to stay here with Mikayla or not. But whatever you choose, you have my blessing." She laid her hand on Enya's head and felt warmth briefly pulse through her fingers. *I guess I haven't lost quite* all *my powers,* she thought. *I'm glad of that.*

She added boots, mittens, and a warm cloak to her outfit and went to find Uzun. He was moping in front of the fire in the study, where he had spent so many years as a harp. "Old friend," she began, and then her voice choked up on her. "Oh, Uzun," she said, tears streaming uncontrollably down her cheeks, "I'm going to miss you. And I most humbly ask your pardon for everything I ever did to hurt you."

"You never hurt me, Princess," Uzun replied quickly. Haramis knew he lied, for she could recall numerous instances of her thoughtless or selfish behavior harming both Uzun and others around her. But Uzun would probably rather die than admit she wasn't perfect. "And don't worry about me." The wooden Oddling sniffed. He was actually crying, Haramis noticed. What an incredible piece of craft this body was. "I'll stay here long enough to compose a ballad about your bravery and sacrifice, and then I'll be along after you. Mikayla promised long ago to set me free when you were gone."

Haramis hugged him. "Do whatever you think best," she said. "Fare well, oldest and dearest of my friends."

"Fare well, Princess." Uzun turned back to the fire and buried his face in his hands.

Haramis went slowly up the stairs to the balcony where the lammergeiers landed. Fiolon was already there, holding one of the special sleep sacks that Haramis used to send Nyssomu messengers to the lowlands. "I thought it might be best to put Mikayla in this for the trip home," he explained.

"Good idea," Haramis agreed.

"Yessss," a voice came out of the darkness above them. Haramis looked up in surprise. Fiolon was right, she realized. Against a white background, such as either snow or her Tower, the great bird was invisible, except for its eyes.

"You're Red-Eye," she said. The bird dipped its head briefly in acknowledgment. "Thank you for your help in this matter," Haramis said.

She couldn't hear the bird's reply herself, but Fiolon repeated it for her. "I'm glad to help," the bird had said. "Mikayla is a friend." It hopped down to the balcony floor and extended a wing. The gesture was as clear as the words "Let's go" could possibly have been.

Fiolon helped Haramis climb onto the bird's back, then scrambled up behind her. The lammergeier beat his wings and lifted smoothly into the night sky.

It seemed no time at all to Haramis before they were dropping toward the ground again. Then the great bird banked to the left and flew into an enormous cave. The pillars at the entrance, which Haramis thought at first were giant icicles, were more than far apart enough for Red-Eye to fly between. Just inside them Haramis saw a small figure seated cross-legged on a fur rug. Mikayla looked up at them. "Red-Eye, what are you doing here? I'm supposed to be keeping vigil alone!"

Haramis couldn't hear what Red-Eye said to Mikayla, but she was willing to bet it was some version of "you cannot do this."

"We've been through this before," Mikayla said with the weary patience of someone who had been through this many times before. "I gave my word."

"But you didn't know what you were promising." Fiolon slid off the bird's back and extended a hand to help Haramis.

"Nobody ever really knows what they're promising on the important things in life," Mikayla said impatiently. "My parents married a week after they met—do you think they knew what they were promising in their wedding vows?"

"I think it certain that they knew more of what they were promising than you did," Haramis said, sliding down to stand on the fur rug. Her knees gave out almost at once, and she wound up kneeling, face-to-face with the girl she had tried to train as her successor. Fiolon faded back into the shadows and began slowly to edge around behind Mikayla.

"Lady Haramis," Mikayla said in surprise. "You should be home in bed. Did Fiolon drag you all the way out here in the middle of the night to help him argue with me?"

"No," Haramis said quietly. "I came to take your place."

Mikayla stared at her incredulously. "You can't," she said. "This isn't your affair. You didn't promise anything."

"Maybe not in words," Haramis said. "But when I took Uzun from his friends and isolated him in my Tower, I made myself responsible for the consequences. When I took you and Fiolon from your home and family, I took on responsibilities for both of you as well. I cannot allow you to lay down your life—especially at such a young age—to mend things I should not have done in the first place." Mikayla stared at her, too shocked by the Archimage's words to comment. Haramis went on. "I do not know if the land sense of Ruwenda will come to you when I die. I thought you were intended to be my successor, but"—she smiled sadly—"lately I've discovered I have been wrong about a number of things. If you are meant to be Archimage, it will come to you. If not"—she shrugged—"I don't know what will happen. My only hope is that, whatever happens, you will live and be happy."

Fiolon, who by this time had moved behind Mikayla, suddenly leaned forward and held a cloth soaked in liquid over her mouth and nose. Mikayla struggled briefly, then went limp. Fiolon laid her body down gently and hastily stripped off all her clothes but the underrobe. As Haramis had suspected, it was identical to the one she wore.

"Lady." Fiolon helped Haramis change her cloak, boots, and mittens for the ones Mikayla had been wearing.

As he bent to pick up Mikayla's unconscious body, Haramis said, "Wait!"

As Fiolon looked inquiringly at her Haramis pulled her Talisman, which she had worn constantly since the day she found it two hundreds ago, from around her neck. Slipping it over Mikayla's head, she said formally, "I give my Talisman, the Three-Winged Circle, to my kinswoman Mikayla." She sat back. "Fiolon, you can take her home now. Take good care of her for me."

Fiolon lifted Mikayla's body, placed it carefully in the sleep sack, and fastened it to Red-Eye's body. Then he turned back to Haramis. "I'll set the spells now," he said. "First, the glamour."

Haramis couldn't feel a thing, but the bird cocked its head appraisingly and nodded.

"Thanks," Fiolon said briefly. Haramis wondered if the bird had made some comment to Fiolon that she was unable to hear. "Now, the pain-block," Fiolon continued. He took off his mittens, murmured a few words, too softly for Haramis to catch them, touched his hands together briefly over her head, and passed them down beside the sides of her body. He finished on his knees in front of her, placing his bare hands flat on the floor on either side of the rug. "I think that's anchored to the land," he said. "How do you feel?"

"Just fine," Haramis said. It was true. Every ache and sore joint she had had suddenly vanished. She had not felt this good in over a hundred. "Thank you, Fiolon. Go now, with my blessing." She placed her hand on his bowed head.

"Thank you, Lady," Fiolon said. "I only hope that when my time comes I will be as brave and as wise as you."

Haramis didn't know what to reply to that. She didn't think she was being particularly brave, and she certainly didn't feel wise. "Fare well, Fiolon," she said finally. "Now go, before someone sees you."

Fiolon climbed on Red-Eye's back behind the sleep sack, and the bird inclined its head silently to Haramis before taking off through the columns and into the night sky. It vanished from sight at once.

Haramis sat in Mikayla's place, keeping the vigil. For the remaining hours of darkness she sat there, quietly remembering her life: her parents and sisters, her teachers and friends—especially Uzun; the time when she was newly made Archimage and was still trying to figure out what it entailed; the finding of her Talisman. . . .

*I found my Talisman on this same mountain peak,* she thought, *on the other side of it.* She remembered how unstable the ice caves there had been. *I wonder if the land on this side is unstable as well.* She reached out with her mind, trying to touch the land around her. She thought she could sense the land a little bit, very faintly, and she thought that perhaps she sensed a flaw in it somewhere above where she was sitting. *I think it's above the Temple,* she realized. *Good. I may be able to use that—assuming that this isn't all just wishful thinking on my part.*

They came for her just before dawn, four young maidens in light blue-gray robes, singing a hymn. They had to help her to her feet, for her body was stiff from sitting in one position for so many hours. There were also several young men, carrying the poles that supported an ornate chair—*almost a throne,* Haramis thought. One of the young men gave her the nastiest smile she had ever seen on a human face. *In fact,* she thought, *I've seen Skritek with kinder expressions. I wonder what Mikayla did to this one. Surely nothing that would justify his gloating over her death like this.*

She ignored him; she ignored everyone. Since she didn't know who any of these people were, this seemed the safest course. It wouldn't do to have them discover that she was not Mikayla too soon. Fortunately, no one seemed to expect her to speak. Still singing, they carried her back into the Temple.

At a curtained arch deep inside, the men with the chair stopped, and the women led her across a carpet-covered floor into a bathing chamber. They bathed her, wove her hair in an intricate arrangement of braids, and anointed her skin all over with some sort of oil. Haramis noticed that the women were all careful to wash the oil off their hands when they were done. *There must be some sort of drug in it,* she thought. *Something to make me more tractable, perhaps? Or maybe something to increase pain—this sort of sacrifice does get a good deal of its power from the pain and fear of the victim. I expect to be a sad disappointment to them.*

The women put a clean robe and a set of ornate golden armbands on her and led her outside again. There, the men waited with the chair to carry her to the other side of the Temple, where the sacrificial chamber was located.

Haramis looked at the chamber with interest, paying no attention to the two priests, robed in black with their faces covered with masks, who were advancing to greet her. As Fiolon had told her, the chamber was carved from living rock. A crude statue of the Goddess seemed to grow out of the far wall, with a stone altar at the level of her waist, stained with old blood. A stream, which Haramis knew was the beginning of the River Noku, came out from under the altar and flowed freely through the room. It was bridged with a few planks of dark wood near the entrance to the chamber, but in front of the altar it was uncovered, and there was, Haramis noted, plenty of room to drop a body into it. The current was swift and the water was undoubtedly extremely cold.

The priests spoke to her, but Haramis did not recognize the language they used and did not bother to attempt a reply. They exchanged quick glances, then reached up to help her down from the chair, being careful to grasp her by the armbands rather than touch her bare skin. Haramis wondered if they were simply being careful to avoid the oil or if it was forbidden to touch the sacrifice directly. *Or maybe both,* she thought. Then her bare foot touched the ground. Haramis gasped and her knees buckled under her. She barely felt one of the priests grasp her around the waist and hold her up. *By the Flower, Fiolon was right,* she realized as the land sense of Labornok flowed into her at full strength. *I should have come here long ago. Has it been waiting for me all this time?*

"Princess." The priest spoke in an urgent undertone, muffled by the black mask he wore. "Pull yourself together! Do you wish to be a disgrace to the high honor to which you have been called?"

Haramis looked at him blankly for a moment before the sense of his words sank in. Then she drew a deep breath and stiffened her knees. "I'm all right now," she said softly. "You can let go of me."

The priest released her waist, but both men kept a firm grip on her armbands as they led her to the altar and turned her to face the people. The entire population of the Temple seemed to be there, Haramis thought, and only a few of them looked sad for Mikayla. The predominant expression was that of a Skritek on the hunt. *I don't think I'll mourn their deaths overmuch.*

"Behold the Chosen One," the priest intoned.

"Hail!" the crowd replied.

"Beloved Youngest Daughter of the Goddess," chanted the second priest.

"Hail!"

"Who gives her heart to her Mother."

"Hail!"

"Who gives her life for her Mother."

"Hail!"

"Who dies that her Mother might live."

"Hail!"

Haramis was helped onto the altar and positioned so that her feet were toward the back of it and she lay looking up at the Goddess's face—such as it was, Haramis thought. The carving was crude indeed, and the face was more a suggestion than a clear image. The main function of the statue of the Goddess seemed to be to hold up the ceiling of the chamber. Haramis could sense that almost the entire weight of the room ran through that section of the wall. The people were behind her now, so she could no longer see them, which was just fine with her.

One priest had left her side, while the other still kept a restraining hand on her armband, but now the first priest came up to the right side of the altar, holding the obsidian dagger of which Fiolon had spoken. *He must have gone back toward the entrance and crossed over the bridge,* Haramis thought, followed by, *It's strange how the mind dwells on trivialities in the face of approaching death.*

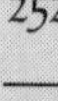

Something was obviously bothering the priests. The priest on her left still had a firm grip on Haramis's arm as if he expected her to try to struggle or attempt to flee. The priest on her right took hold of her armband with one hand and raised the dagger with the other, but held that position while the two of them exchanged what Haramis assumed were worried looks. *It's a good thing for them that they're wearing masks,* she thought, almost amused. *Otherwise the congregation would be suspecting by now that something is very wrong indeed.*

"What's the matter with you?" the priest with the dagger hissed. "Don't you realize that you are about to die?"

Haramis blinked at him. "Of course I do."

"Then why aren't you afraid?" asked the other priest.

"Why should I be?" Haramis countered. *It is my time to die, and I die for the land. That is as it should be—why should I be afraid? Of course,* she thought with some amusement, *I'm much older than they realize; they think they have a terrified child.* She thought of Mikayla in her place and repressed a shudder. *I'm glad they don't have her.*

"What do we do now?" the priest on her right whispered.

"Proceed with the sacrifice," the priest on her left replied. "What else can we do? Where is it written that the sacrifice must be frightened?"

"But the energy isn't right!"

"I know, but we can hardly explain that to the people—who *are* waiting for us to proceed," the man muttered behind his mask. He reached out with his left hand and pulled a slab of stone slightly larger than his hand out of the breast of the statue of the Goddess. He set the slab on the altar beside Haramis. Haramis could see now that there was a cavity in the statue. There was something small and shriveled up inside it, presumably the heart of the last sacrifice. "Go ahead," the priest whispered to the priest with the dagger. "The pain should make up for the lack of fear." He added warningly in a low tone, "It had better."

*That's what you think,* Haramis thought. *Bless you, Fiolon, I think we've managed to sabotage this sacrifice quite thoroughly.*

The priest slashed at her with the dagger, slitting her robe down the front to her waist. When he raised the dagger Haramis saw blood on the tip of it, but she didn't feel a thing. Both priests looked down at her calm face, and Haramis felt as if she could see their anxious expressions through their masks. She smiled serenely up at them. By now, both of *them* seemed to be feeling all the terror any vengeful Goddess could possibly wish.

The man with the dagger gulped visibly as he slit open her chest, broke apart several ribs (Haramis could hear them snap) and cut her heart free. Haramis didn't feel any pain, although as she started to lose large quantities of blood she began to feel light-headed.

But, as Fiolon had predicted, when her body was no longer intact, the glamour faded out. The pain-block, being powered by the living rock under her back, stayed in place. The priest on her left, who had turned away to remove the old heart from the statue, gasped in horror when he turned back in time to see Mikayla's face become that of an old woman. The priest who was holding her heart aloft to show the people that the sacrifice had been carried out looked down at her and nearly dropped the heart. "Holy Meret!" he whispered. "Who are you?"

"What is your name?" the other priest demanded urgently.

*Does he really think I'm fool enough to tell them?* Haramis wondered, feeling ironically amused. *Without my name, they have no hope of salvaging this ritual—do they think I don't know that?*

"Your goddess is false," Haramis told him calmly, forcing herself to remain conscious for a few more seconds. "I am the land, and I never die." She reached out with her mind and tugged at the flaw she had perceived earlier. She felt it give, and knew her work was finished.

She slipped easily out of her body then, and watched, hovering above it as her heart turned to dust and trickled through the fingers of the horrified priest. Her body also turned to dust, and above it, the statue of the Goddess began to do likewise. Haramis saw a bright light above her, and she rose toward it, passing through the stone ceiling collapsing on top of her as if it weren't there. She was flying through the sky toward the light, and the Lords of the Air, in the form of great lammergeiers, accompanied her. Her life was over, and the work that had been given to her was complete.

# 29

*Mikayla started to come to as they removed her from* the sleep sack on the balcony. Red-Eye looked down at her and looked at Fiolon. "I'll let you handle the explanations," it said, quickly taking flight.

"Coward," Fiolon said softly. "It must have had some experience with Mika's temper." He bent and picked up Mikayla's limp body and carried her down to the study, where he put her on a sofa near the fire.

Uzun hovered over her anxiously. "Is she all right?"

"She'll be fine," Fiolon said. "In a few minutes she'll doubtless be wide-awake and yelling at us."

"And the Lady?"

"All was well with her when I left."

Uzun bowed his head in silence.

It took Mikayla only a few minutes to wake up completely and take in her surroundings. "Fiolon, you idiot! Take me back before they miss me!"

"They won't miss you," Fiolon said. "Haramis took your place, remember?"

"Right." Mikayla looked at him in disgust. "Haramis can really fool them into thinking she's the Youngest Daughter of the Goddess. She doesn't even know the rituals. And she hasn't been able to cast a glamour on herself since her last brainstorm—or was it the one before that?"

"Two before that," Fiolon said. "I put the glamour on her." He added, for Uzun's benefit, "And a pain-block spell. She won't feel a thing—I tied that one into the land, and the altar is carved out of living rock. The glamour will probably go when they cut her heart out—"

"When they *what*!" Mikayla practically screamed. "Oh, by the Flower, Fiolon; it's just symbolic! I did the ritual two years ago, and you will notice that I'm still alive and well."

"This is a jubilee year," Fiolon said. "For a jubilee, it's *not* symbolic."

Mikayla sat up abruptly. "We'll go down to the mirror and watch it," she snapped, "then you'll see!" She looked startled and pressed her hand to the front of her tunic, then started dragging at the chain around her neck. "What's this?" She pulled it over her head and held it in front of her, staring at the silver wand with its circle and three wings. "I've never seen it before."

"It's the Three-Winged Circle," Uzun said in a mournful voice. "Haramis's Talisman, her part of the Great Scepter of Power."

Mikayla frowned at it. "For some reason, it reminds me of the Queen's crown."

"The Three-Headed Monster," Uzun said. "That was Anigel's part."

"What happened to Kadiya's?" Mikayla asked curiously, twisting the Talisman back and forth on the end of its chain.

"She took it with her into the swamps, and no one has seen her or it since."

"So we can't use this for the Scepter of Power," Mikayla said, diverted temporarily from her other concerns. "What is it good for and why do I have it?"

Fiolon groaned. "You have it because Haramis gave it to you. It's true magic—not one of the toys of the Vanished Ones—so be careful with it. Uzun, can you teach her how to use it?"

The Oddling shook his head. "No. I don't know how. Only Haramis ever used it, and I wasn't with her then."

Mikayla stared at both of them in exasperation. "Do you mean to tell me that, after all the years Haramis spent teaching me things that anyone could figure out for herself, she suddenly dumped this on me without a word of warning and with no training in how to use it?" She frowned. "How powerful is it?"

"You can kill people with it." Fiolon and Uzun spoke in chorus.

"Ugh." Mikayla held it out carefully at arm's length. "In that case, I'm going to put it away. I'm not stupid enough to do random experiments with things that can kill people." She stood up. "I'll be back in a few minutes," she said, "and then we can go watch the ritual at the Temple."

As she left the room she heard Fiolon saying to Uzun, "You don't have to watch this."

Uzun's reply drifted down the hall after her. "If I don't watch, how can I write a proper ballad about her heroism? No. I missed too much of her Quest; I'll watch this to the bitter end."

Mikayla led the way to the cave with the mirror. "Mirror, View Princess Haramis of Ruwenda," she commanded.

"Scanning," the mirror replied. Then it showed Haramis being helped out of the carrying chair by the two priests, showed her knees giving way, and the priests holding her up.

"What's wrong with her?" Uzun gasped.

Fiolon studied the picture carefully. "She's barefoot," he noted. "Mikayla, is this the first time you would have set foot to the ground since we left you?"

"They'd use the chair to bring me from the mountain to the bathing room, and then from the bathing room to the main Temple. I don't know why she's out of the chair in this chamber; normally the Youngest Daughter never leaves her chair—all day."

"What's the floor in the bathing room made of? Is it bare rock?"

"Of course not," Mikayla said indignantly. "Just because the Temple is hidden in a cave doesn't mean the whole thing is a cave. The bathing room has carpets on the floor."

"So this would be the first time she actually touched the land of Labornok," Fiolon persisted.

"Hasn't she ever been there before?" Mikayla asked. "She's been Archimage for nearly two hundreds!"

"Mikayla, will you answer the question?"

"You mean is this the first time she would have set bare foot to bare ground? Yes, probably it is. Why?"

"She's all right, Uzun," Fiolon said reassuringly. "She's just getting the land sense for Labornok, which can only help."

"Just getting it?" Mikayla said. "Now? What kind of Archimage ignores half her land? And why is she getting land sense for Labornok when she hasn't felt it for Ruwenda in years?"

"Mikayla, will you please be quiet!" Fiolon snapped.

Mikayla shut her mouth. This wasn't the way Fiolon usually spoke to her. *What's wrong?* she wondered. *Why is he so angry?*

"She's back on her feet," Uzun commented, "walking bravely to her doom."

*He sounds like a ballad, all right,* Mikayla thought. *But "walking bravely to her doom" is ridiculous.* She didn't, however, say anything aloud. She still didn't know why the ritual was being changed; normally they didn't spend much time in the chamber they were in. *Maybe I should just be quiet. If I'm right, they'll see it soon enough, and they can go get Haramis, and I can give her Talisman back to her. If I'm wrong . . .* She shuddered. *I hope I'm not wrong.*

As the ritual continued it became only too clear that Mikayla was wrong and that everyone who had tried to warn her had been right. Mikayla watched in horror and disbelief as the priest cut Haramis's heart from her body. *How can she look so calm while they're doing that?* Then the heart was a handful of dust, slipping through the priest's fingers, the body turned to dust, and the entire room began dissolving. The roof fell in with a resounding crash, and the echoes reverberated throughout the mountain. The last thing they saw before the mirror went dark was a great wall of snow crashing toward them.

Mikayla collapsed to the floor, hands over her face. Dimly she heard the mirror say, "Subject no longer exists. No living people in that location."

Then she felt it. It started with the feeling that she was sinking into the rock beneath her, becoming a part of Mount Brom. Then Mount Gidris became part of her body as well. She felt the avalanche on the north face, and broke it up into smaller pieces so that it would do a minimum of damage. Then she felt Mount Rotolo, with its hot springs and hidden valleys. Briefly she was aware of Red-Eye, sleeping in its cave. From the mountain chain her awareness expanded in both directions, north along the River Noku and across Labornok to the Northern Sea, and south along the River Nothar, across the Thorny Hell, the Dylex, the Goldenmire, past the Citadel and the Great Causeway, the Blackmire and the Greenmire, past Lake Wum and the Tass Falls, along the Great Mutar River to the border of Var, where an image of Fiolon stood guard.

"Fio?" she said aloud.

"I'm right here, Mika." Strong arms picked her up and carried her out of the cave. Behind her she heard the sound of the door sliding closed, followed by Uzun's wooden footsteps, but she could also hear rivers rushing to their respective seas and insects chirping in the Mires.

Fiolon set her down briefly at the entrance to the cave so that he and Uzun could both lean on the great door to close it. Then he picked her up again. Mikayla considered protesting, saying that she could walk, but the jumble of images in her mind overrode anything else.

*If Haramis felt like this, no wonder the priests had to hold her up,* she thought. *This is much worse than it was when Fiolon got the land sense for Var. Of course, it is at least twice as much territory and I'm getting it firsthand—at least I think I am. . . .* "Fio? Can you sense the land?"

His reply cut briefly through the babble in her head. "Just Var. Are you getting Ruwenda?"

"Yes, and Labornok."

"Don't bother trying to talk," Fiolon advised her. "Just relax and let it sort itself out."

*Sort itself out? Oh, I hope it will!* She lay limp in his arms as he carried her into the kitchen, propped her on a stool by the fire, and asked Uzun to hold her. She was barely aware that he and Uzun had switched places until she saw Fiolon's face in front of her, holding a mug. "Drink this." He helped her to hold it steady, until she had drunk it all. It was hot adop soup and it made her feel a bit more like Mikayla and a bit less like every inch of ground in two kingdoms.

"Better?" he asked. She nodded carefully. Her body still didn't seem to be quite all hers.

"Good. Now eat this." He handed her a strip of dried meat. She chewed it with considerable effort, but by the time she was done, she was herself again. All the clutter in her mind was gone; in fact, when she tried carefully to reach for it, it wasn't there.

"Fio," she said in horror, "I've lost the land sense."

"No, you haven't," he quickly reassured her. "It's just turned off for a bit. Hot food and meat will do that. Getting the land sense for two kingdoms at once would be a lot for anyone to handle, especially someone who's been fasting for over a day and has just seen her kinswoman die."

"Haramis." Mikayla shook her head, wishing she could deny what she had seen. "Uzun." She turned her head to look up at the Oddling. "I am so sorry."

"No, Lady," Uzun said. "It was my fault. I should never have asked for a new body."

"Considering that it was Haramis who turned you into a harp so that you needed a new body so that you could take care of her when she was ill," Fiolon remarked, "it seems to me that the blame could be spread all around. Besides, it's pointless. Done is done, and it wasn't really *anyone's* fault."

"And Haramis had lost her magic," Mikayla pointed out. "It wasn't coming back, was it?"

Uzun sighed. "I don't think so; and at the end, neither did she. I think that's part of why she insisted on doing this."

"Did she mean to destroy the Temple the way she did?" Mikayla asked.

"I think so," Fiolon said. "When we were planning this, she said something about your not being able to go back there if it wasn't there. I asked her what she meant, but then the discussion got sidetracked and she never did answer me." He paused. "But I think she did intend to destroy it; you know how she felt about blood sacrifice—especially unwilling sacrifice. That's what really ruined their ritual, you know," he said thoughtfully. "They wanted an unwilling sacrifice, young, terrified, and in pain. What they got was an Adept who was ready and willing to die."

"That would change the energy involved quite a bit," Mikayla admitted.

"Remember those priests," Uzun said. "They were more afraid than she was! This is going to make a great ballad." His face suddenly quivered and he started to cry. "Excuse me," he sobbed as he hurried from the room and clattered up the stairs.

Mikayla stood up a bit unsteadily and stretched. "I think I can walk as far as my room now, Fiolon. All I want to do at the moment is to sleep for a week. I feel so numb and empty I don't think I could do anything else if I tried."

"Sleep is probably the best thing for you," Fiolon said. "It's much easier to absorb land sense if you're not trying to do anything else at the same time."

"I believe that," Mikayla said fervently. Then she thought of something else. "Fiolon, on the chance that Haramis didn't deliberately destroy the Temple, I think that when either of us dies, we should be sure to do it outdoors. Binah and Haramis were rather hard on buildings."

Fiolon chuckled. "You may have a point," he agreed. He had to carry her to her room; she fell asleep before they reached her door.

A few weeks later Uzun sang his ballad for them. It was a stirring epic, full of praise for Haramis's wisdom and bravery, Fiolon's cleverness, Mikayla's loyal friendship, and Red-Eye's flying skills. When he had finished it, Uzun looked at them uneasily. "What do you think?"

Mikayla, blinking away her tears, said, "It's beautiful, Uzun. Haramis would have loved it."

"You'll have to teach it to me," Fiolon said. "Some of that chording is truly original."

Uzun hesitated. "I'll sing it for the mirror," he said, "and it can teach it to you."

"That's a good idea," Mikayla said. "That way the mirror will always have it, just the way you sang it, even hundreds after you're gone."

"Speaking of going," Uzun said, "do you remember what you promised me, Mikayla, the day you found the spell Haramis used to put me into the harp?" He looked at the harp, which he had been using to accompany himself.

*No!* a voice inside Mikayla's head protested. *I don't want to lose him, too!* But she reminded herself sternly that she had resolved not to be selfish, as Haramis had been, with the lives of those around her. "Yes," she said, as steadily as she could. "I remember. I promised to release you when you asked." She gulped. "Are you asking now?"

Uzun nodded. "Tomorrow before dawn would be best, I think. That will give me time to teach my ballad to the mirror."

Mikayla bowed her head to hide her tears. "Tomorrow, then."

"Thank you," Uzun said quietly. "Good night."

After he left the room, Fiolon turned to Mikayla. "Did he just ask you to kill him?"

"In a way," Mikayla said. "Technically I suppose he's been dead since Haramis put him into the harp. But he wanted my word that I'd release him when she was gone."

"Do you really have to do this?" Fiolon protested. "I'll miss him."

Mikayla's eyes filled with tears. "I'll miss him, too," she said. "But, yes, I do have to do this. I promised. I gave him my word."

Fiolon sighed. "In that case, I'll help you. What do we have to do?"

The next morning at dawn, Mikayla and Fiolon stood on the stone roof of the tower. They had burned Uzun's wooden body in a bonfire on the roof, and the fire had just finished burning out. They stood on either side of the ashes that remained, facing the rising sun. As the dawn wind came up it swept the ashes from the roof, scattering them in the air.

Mikayla held a small box of bone dust, all that was left of Uzun's original skull. She poured half of the contents into her hand, then handed the box to Fiolon, who poured the rest into his hand. Together they lifted their hands and blew gently, sending the bone dust into the morning wind, streaming toward the sun.

"Now he is one with the Lords of the Air," Mikayla said softly.

Together they went down to the study, where Fiolon took up the harp and played an old song, the first of Master Uzun's compositions that he had learned. "It seems strange to think that this is just a harp now," he said. "I suppose it will always seem a little bit like Uzun to me."

"Then we'll always have a little bit of him with us," Mikayla said. *Assuming that there is an us.* She forced herself to ask the question she had been dreading to have answered. "What will you do now, Fiolon? Will you have to return to Var?"

"I'll have to go there from time to time," Fiolon replied, "just as you'll have to travel about your lands. But I thought, if you have no objection, that we could make this our primary home. We'll have to get more books, of course," he added teasingly, "by now even I've read everything in the library."

Mikayla laughed in relief. He wasn't going to leave her; she wasn't going to have to be alone the way Haramis had been. "I have, too," she agreed. "Years ago. So we'll get more books. What else do we need?"

"Children," Fiolon replied. "I know it's early to think of that, but in five or ten years you should be old enough to bear children —if you don't dislike the idea?"

Mikayla shook her head. "I think I'd like to have children of my own, when the time is right. Of our own, I mean," she hastily added.

"We can raise our children with a knowledge of magic and respect for the land, and have enough of them that the land will have plenty of choices for our successors."

"Does this mean that Haramis was mistaken when she said magicians have to be celibate?" Mikayla asked.

"Only if they make magic their entire life, if they're seeking Ultimate Power," Fiolon intoned solemnly. "If magic is just a tool we use in our work, we have only to stay reasonably healthy." He grinned. "And with two of us, we can help each other out. We've always been a good team." He grew serious again. "Mikayla, I've loved you since we were seven years old, and we're of age now and don't need anyone's permission. Will you marry me?"

Mikayla flung both arms around him and hugged him tight. "With all my heart," she replied.

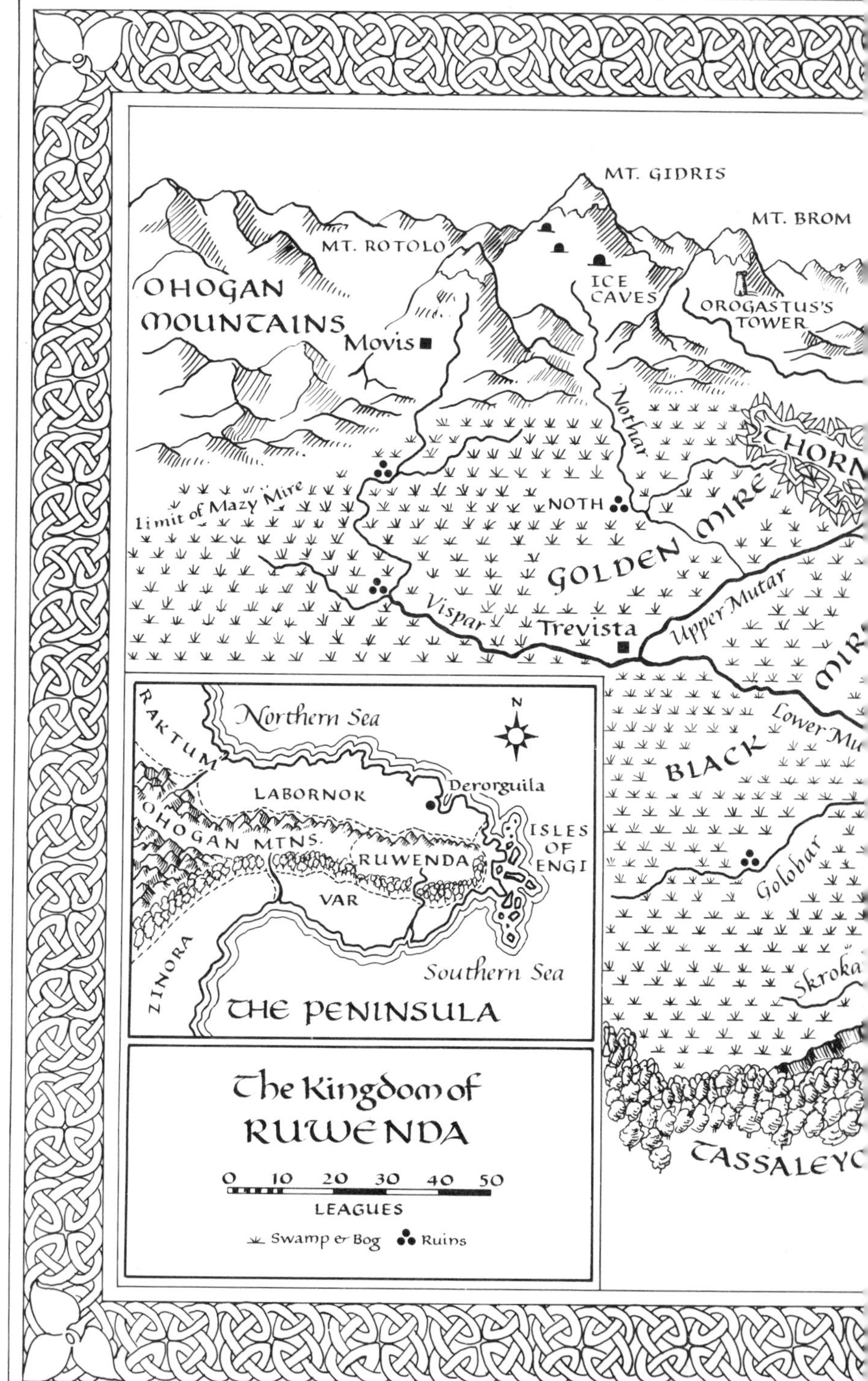

MT. GIDRIS
MT. BROM
MT. ROTOLO
OHOGAN MOUNTAINS
Movis
ICE CAVES
OROGASTUS'S TOWER
Nothar
THORN
Limit of Mazy Mire
NOTH
GOLDEN MIRE
Vispar
Trevista
Upper Mutar
BLACK MIRE
Lower Mu
Golobar
Skroka
TASSALEYO
Northern Sea
N
RAKTUM
Derorguila
LABORNOK
OHOGAN MTNS.
ISLES OF ENGI
RUWENDA
VAR
ZINORA
Southern Sea
THE PENINSULA
The Kingdom of RUWENDA
0 10 20 30 40 50
LEAGUES
Swamp & Bog
Ruins